NO MORE MASQUERADE

SECRETS OF STONE: BOOK TWO

ANGEL PAYNE & VICTORIA BLUE

NO MORE MASQUERADE

SECRETS OF STONE: BOOK TWO

ANGEL PAYNE & VICTORIA BLUE

WATERHOUSE PRESS

*To my amazing family, especially the
man who puts up with all the takeout,
late nights, and pointless tears.
Thomas, you are my rock...forever.*

*They say a friend is someone who sees all of you
and loves you, anyway. Victoria Blue, you're the Key
to my Peele, the Schmidt to my Jenko, the Thelma to
my Louise—and I hope we never stop driving over
cliffs together. I love you so much. Now go
throw my jacket into the river.*

*During the creation of this book, so many amazing
events happened to make me so grateful for the
support pillars on this crazy writing journey of
mine. You all know what blessings you are, in your
own amazing ways...*

*Jenna Jacob, Carrie Ann Ryan, Shayla Black,
Kennedy Layne, Shannon Hunt, Desiree Holt,
and Shayla Fereshetian. Thank you,
my wonderful goddess friends!*

—Angel

My dearest David and Kadin are the two most amazing men a girl could ever dream of knowing, and I have them both in my life to love and love me back. That in itself makes me the luckiest girl in the world. But I've been given another gift we named Ivy. Lately she has shown me what bravery, strength, love, compassion, empathy, heartache, and fortitude look and feel like. She reminds us all what our purpose is every day, and when we step out of line, she quickly tugs our leashes and we snap back into place. So for our sweetest girl, I marvel that this book was completed on time and even makes sense in a lot of places.

With that in mind, I must thank the four most amazing women in my life, starting with the gift I was given as my writing partner, appropriately named—Angel. Putting up with late nights from hospital rooms and lots of tears this time around, thank you from the bottom of my heart for the encouragement and the belief in my ability. I love you truly.

And my dear friends, Elisa, Anna, and Kim. I can't imagine my life without the three of you. I don't know how I would get through a day without checking in with you, or hearing your kindness, or goofiness or love and support. I would be lost in a really cruel world without you.

xoxoxo

—Victoria

CHAPTER ONE

Claire

The world was exploding.

It was my usual reaction when getting swarmed by the paparazzi and their flashbulbs. It probably wouldn't ever change. I wasn't sure I wanted it to. Did anyone ever get used to this?

Eight months after I'd publicly become Killian Stone's girlfriend, the shutterbugs still enjoyed tracking me down when photo ops were thin up north in LA. Their latest opportunity—and a Fellini-like horror straight from my nightmares—occurred on a Saturday morning when I got home with groceries in my arms, a sloppy ponytail on my head, and my rattiest beach shorts paired with a faded Queen T-shirt. The tee was a classic, Mercury not Lambert, so I could get away with the rip in the right sleeve.

"Good morning, Claire. You look great, girlfriend. Give us a smile? Just one?"

"Guys," I protested, "aren't the Oscars in a few weeks? There has to be someone in Hollywood being fitted or waxed or plucked—or whatever they do to get ready for that stuff. You have to know where all the salons are, right?"

"*Pffft*. They all hire private stylists now. We're not getting anything before the red carpet these days."

"It's a beautiful Saturday morning," I persisted, "and we're only going to have this Indian summer for a few more days. Take the day off. Go to the beach. I give you permission."

They chuckled. Then kept clicking away.

"Speaking of you and the permissions you grant... You've captivated Stone longer than any woman before. Will there be a ring on that left hand soon, Claire?"

My gut clenched. It wasn't as though I hadn't been asked the question before. I was sure Killian had been asked twice as many times. But he wasn't getting down on one knee until a lot more of mine were answered. Until he exposed those shadows I could still see in the depths of his gaze...

"Answer's the same, Hal." I shrugged. "No comment. Can you make yourself useful and shut my car door, please?"

"Need it locked?"

"It'll do that by itself."

Of course it did. The winter white Audi A8 did everything on its own except yell at idiot drivers and levitate over traffic jams. After Killian had given it to me, I'd told him my name wasn't Captain Picard and refused to drive the thing for a month. But then he'd driven me in it for a long weekend in Santa Barbara. And had shown me how it detected every Starbucks within a five-mile radius. And had given me a couple of hours in its back seat, parked in a eucalyptus grove overlooking Goleta Beach, that still made parts of me tremble with desire...

Now I needed a cold shower.

I settled for a glass of ice water, retrieved after putting away the groceries and enjoyed on my favorite chair in the house, an old leather recliner I'd had since college. The chair joined the Napa-style décor in my rented Mission Hills bungalow, where I'd lived since graduating. I didn't care that planes flew overhead at all hours of the day and night. The neighborhood was my favorite part of the city and the chair my favorite part of the house. It was like a friend who knew all my warts and still loved me. It was just what I needed right now. A reminder of closeness on its most basic level.

Exactly what I was missing with Killian now.

I sighed. This feeling sucked. He'd given me so much already, and I didn't mean the material things. While being his queen was sometimes like walking through a luxury-living magazine, all of it was simply background to the magnificence of him. His power, grace, sensuality, intensity...all of it enthralling me more with every minute we spent together, even if it was over the miles and especially if it was face-to-face. With every consuming kiss, every sinful look, and every tingling touch, I gave the man more of my heart.

It scared me.

Too good to be true.

How many times were those words more right than wrong?

The doorbell couldn't have butted in with better timing.

I gratefully left my insecurities behind in the chair, despite the discomfort of what I faced. I liked Hal and his buddies, but having to shoo them off like magazine salesmen wasn't fun.

My door didn't have a peephole, but I slid back the small peek-a-boo door set into the heavy wood, checking it really was Hal and not somebody selling money-saving solar panels.

I blinked in surprise. No Hal. A small woman stood on the porch, neatly groomed and shyly smiling. I tried to make out the logo on her T-shirt, but the sun blasted me in the eye, bouncing off the neighbor's clay-tile roof from across the street.

"Can I...help you?"

She nodded quickly. "Hi. I'm Christina. From Mystic Maids?"

"Well, *I'm* mystified." I laughed, unable to help myself. She'd pitched it over the plate, but I was still down in the count. I hadn't hired a cleaning service. She glanced at her paperwork, clearly certain she was at the right address.

We stood there trying to figure each other out...and then it hit me.

Killian.

"Dear Lord." I unlocked and then opened the door. "Please come in. Christina, right?" I looked back over my shoulder while the young woman followed me in.

"Do you mind if I put my lunch in your refrigerator?" She was so adorable. It was going to kill me to tell her she wouldn't be here long enough to eat the meal.

"Listen, Christina...I didn't actually hire you. While I'm sure you do a great job, and I appreciate you coming all the way over here..." I grimaced as her eyebrows met in confusion. "Please, if you can sit tight while I make a quick phone call to my over-the-top boyfriend, we'll get this straightened out."

On cue, Justin Timberlake's "Sexy Back" blasted from my phone. Heat crawled across my face. Christina giggled. Again, endearing to the power of ten. Damn it, she was growing on me by the minute.

"Speak of the devil." I gave her a commiserating wink. "Excuse me for one sec."

I picked up the call after walking into the front sitting room.

"Good morning, fairy queen. How's my girl today?"

God, he was so perfect.

And frustrating.

"Good morning to you too. I was just about to call you." I caught Christina starting to move things in the kitchen, dusting into the corners. *Better talk fast, girlfriend.*

"Oh, yeah?" His voice descended to a growl that would tempt a nun. "Were you dreaming about me again? Wait while I close my office door and you can tell me all about it."

"Why are you in the office on a Saturday?"

"And you're not working today?"

"Not...right at the moment."

"The door's closed. Better idea. Let me video call you. Then you can act out your dream for me. Go to the bedroom. I'll wait."

I swore I could hear his eyebrows waggling across the line. It made my blood dance in delicious ways. A lot of things mesmerized me about the man, but his lighthearted side neared the top of the list. He showed it to so few, and it made me kind of swoony to think I was the leader of that privileged crowd. I liked that position. A lot.

Where the hell was I?

Frustrating. Him. Same sentence.

"We have to switch to serious for a minute."

"Okay, but only a minute."

"This girl showed up at my house this morning. From Mystic Maids?"

"Hmm. Good. She's right on time. They came recommended for their thoroughness and punctuality."

"So you not only hired a service but researched the whole thing."

"Yes and yes."

"Damn it, Kil."

"What? The new acquisition has been a boatload of

extra work for your team. And with the unexpected damage control from Father's episode, added to your propensity for perfection...you've been working too fucking hard."

"Said the pot to the kettle?"

"The last thing you need to be worrying about is keeping the house clean."

"How is Josiah doing, by the way?"

"They released him yesterday. Simple heartburn, as everyone knows thanks to you. Don't change the subject."

"It's my subject, buddy. You're in the hot seat here, not me."

"You're not Cinderella, for chrissake. In spite of the wicked stepsister and the questionable stepmother, the mice on your hearth don't get to gawk at your cleavage if I don't." There was a beat before he got the humor of his own line and started snickering.

"Stop it," I snapped. "You're violating our agreement, and I'm peeved."

"We didn't have an agreement. We had a talk. I'm not violating a damn—"

"I don't need you to keep doing stuff like this for me! I'm sending her home."

"Don't. You. Dare."

Shit. Now I'd pissed him off. Big-time. And damn...was it hot.

"Really? Or what? What are you going to do, Chicago? Hmmm. That's right. You're all the way in Chicago. Oh, boo."

Why the hell was I goading him? *You know damn well why. He soaks your panties when he's in prowling panther mode, that's why.*

"I could be there by this afternoon, Miss Montgomery.

Then I doubt you'd have such a pert little attitude."

Miss Montgomery. Shit. When he called me that...using that dark, dangerous tone...

"I'm perfectly capable of cleaning my own house, Killian. This is ridiculous."

"But I don't want you to." The line rustled. I imagined him straightening in his Odin's throne chair at the office, leaning over his big desk, the long fingers of his free hand pushing at the wood as his face hardened with command. "That should be enough of a reason. Do you understand?"

More heat suffused my face. My eyes slid shut, letting the heat of his imperative tone wreak all kinds of chaos on my bloodstream. I had no idea what to do with him when he got like this. While it was infuriating as hell, he elevated caveman to a new level of sexy. If he commanded me to jam my hand down my shorts and touch myself while he spoke I would've complied, even with Christina in the next room.

"Claire?"

"What?" I retorted.

"If you send her away, I will be very disappointed."

"Tell me." Only half my breathy emphasis was feigned. "How disappointed?"

"Don't push me," he grunted without embellishment. "Goddamnit, why do you make this shit so hard? I like doing things for you. It's important to me. And I won't be questioned over every single decision I make."

I stared out of the window, feeling pulled by an undertow and then slammed by a ten-foot breaker. After eight months, he could still do this to me. I seethed at him. Burned for him. Hated him. Wanted him.

Loved him.

"Claire? Are we done here?"

I fumed for another long moment. "Fine. Yes. We're done here. Jerk."

"I love you, baby."

"I love you too, jerk."

His chuckle filled my ear before I disconnected.

I showed Christina where I kept my vacuum and whatever else she needed to clean the place but drew the line at her doing my laundry. I'd wash my own damn underwear, thank you very much.

After packing my laptop, some files, and a bottle of water into my beach bag, I headed out. Before leaving, I demonstrated the alarm-setting procedure for Christina. Apparently, she'd be stopping by on a weekly basis from now on.

The second I was settled in with my towel, chair, and laptop at the beach, my phone rang for the fifth time. I already knew who it was. Persistence should have been the man's middle name, not Jamison—especially when he knew I was unhappy with him.

"Yes, dearest?"

"Why are you letting my calls go to voicemail?"

"I was driving to the beach. Sorry, I almost waited for the shoulder carriage but figured you'd cancel the order when learning about the four studs that came with it."

"I was worried about you." He ignored my sarcasm in favor of a gentle tone. It was likely the closest thing I'd get to an apology right now.

"It was less than ten miles."

"Most fatal accidents occur close to home. And your driving scares the hell out of me. You know that."

"So I'm supposed to make it worse—and break the law—

by picking up your call?"

"I'll just get you a driver too. Two birds, one stone. You can get more work done instead of stressing about the commute, and I won't have to worry when you don't—"

"Kil!" I couldn't help laughing. The alternative reaction wasn't pretty. "I swear, you're going to drive me to drink."

"Fairy."

"What?"

"Don't be mad about the housekeeper."

"I'm not. Anymore."

"You deserve to be taken care of."

"I'm over it, okay?" I sighed, my own version of a not-apology. "You're actually very sweet, Mr. Stone—if overbearing and presumptuous."

He cleared his throat with purpose, making my pulse race—and the rest of my body prepare for the tone that came next. Silken seduction. "You fell in love with me this way."

"And I still love you."

"That's damn good." He let a long beat stretch by. Another. "Because there's a little more coming."

I could hear him breathing in measured lengths, likely bracing for my tirade. Just listening to the sound made me take pause, halting everything—yes, even the rant.

A wince grabbed my face. What was my problem? The man adored me. He was doing his best to spoil me, and I was acting like an ungrateful shrew, all because of my unfounded fears about the what-ifs. I needed to live more in the moment.

I needed to be a better girlfriend.

"Th-There's more?" I finally croaked.

As he laughed into the phone, I pictured him running his fingers through his gorgeous dark hair, which was probably a little too long at the moment. Translation—completely perfect. "Hold on," he finally stammered back. "Are you really not going to yell?"

"I guess not. Do you want me to?"

"No!" He chuckled again. "That's completely fine. Shit, San Diego. You certainly keep me on my toes."

And what amazing toes he had. Yes, I'd treated myself to a full inspection one night at his place while we'd binged on *Shark Tank* and Chinese takeout. Conclusion—God had even crafted the man's feet to perfection.

"Soooo," I prompted, "back to my 'more.'"

"What about it?"

"Don't make me pop up into your play and then refuse to catch the ball, mister." I huffed. "Come on. Tell me what it is."

"Nope. I want to surprise you when you get here next weekend. Can you wait that long?"

"Probably not." *Good girlfriend, remember?* "But I will. I know you'll make it worth it."

One of his pleasure-filled growls resonated over the line. "You're sexy when you're amenable." He continued the sound, keeping me baited. "So be even more so and let me send the jet for you this time."

I huffed again, but there was a real smile behind it. Gee, my fabulously gorgeous boyfriend wanted to send his private jet to pick me up and then fly me to him for a weekend in his gazillion-dollar penthouse on the Lake Michigan shore. I think I could be okay with that.

But just this once.

"Yes, Mr. Stone. I would love that." A silence went by. Not one of our comfortable pauses either. "And Kil..."

"Yeah?"

"I need to...apologize to you. About earlier."

This shit never came easy for me, and the man knew it. His voice became softened with understanding. "It's okay."

"No, it's not. I let my I-am-woman-hear-me-roar run a little too wild over the tundra. The housekeeper is great, and I was ungrateful. I hope I can make it up to you?"

I tried to finish off with playful and sexy, hoping he caught on to my hint. Who was I kidding? The man made innuendoes off my boring media spreadsheets.

"Hmmm. Maybe a little more begging is in order—on your knees in particular, in something small, black, and scandalous. Maybe you can...coax out my forgiveness."

Hell. He'd gone from sultry to throaty, melting my panties by corresponding degrees right here on the beach. What his words alone were capable of doing to me... Yeah, I had every right to be scared. If he truly knew what kind of putty I became in his thrall...

God, I was in such danger. And I wasn't sure I ever wanted to be safe again.

"So, tell me where you are." He purposely jumped onto a more innocent track. "What beach did you head to?"

"Torrey Pines," I supplied. "I usually don't come here since it's a little farther from home, but since Christina is taking care of the chores, I had some extra time." I paused, sensing him smiling through the phone line. He warmed my skin more than the sun itself. "I wish you were with me, though. You could rub lotion on my hard-to-reach spots."

His groan was low and telling. "Oh, I know all about your little...hard spots."

So much for innocent. I was certain the man had secretly taken euphemism courses at MIT. I was about to laugh off his tease but realized I didn't want to. Today's events—facing the paparazzi, our tiff on the phone, doubting my capability to be the compliant partner he needed—made the distance between us feel like galaxies instead of miles.

And the shadow that fell across every star in those galaxies? The secrets he was still keeping from me. The double meanings in conversations I would sometimes overhear. The distance that sneaked into his eyes when he spoke about himself sometimes, as if looking at in from an outsider's viewpoint...

How could I feel so close to him yet so far?

I fell back on the easy stuff. The lust. After covering my legs with a towel, I pushed them together and then slid one foot up the opposite leg. The friction on every tissue between my legs was enticing, exquisite...

And just like him.

A dark, unattainable pleasure.

"Claire?"

"Yes," I rasped. "I'm here. Sorry."

"Why are you apologizing? What's wrong?"

"Nothing." Everything. Oh, hell. Maybe I really wasn't cut out for this role...this being Killian Stone's damn girlfriend. I second-guessed every other thought in my head and comment from my mouth because when I didn't, I flew off the handle and pushed all his buttons anyway. He said he loved me this way. Even called me adorable and exciting and claimed he liked living life *on his toes*. I loved him more for it but wondered if the toe talk came from how far in the deep end we both were with this thing. And what would happen if we both drowned. And if I needed to check for a life preserver before it was too late.

"Well, that's bullshit if I heard any," he muttered.

"I just miss you." My voice was sloppy and thick with emotion. "I know it's only been six days. I'm just...sad." And lonely. And pathetic. Was being in love supposed to make you sound so morose?

"Only six days?" He repeated it like I'd told him the earth was really a square. "You mean the one hundred and forty-four hours of sheer hell we've just endured? Because I wasn't counting or anything."

I let a watery laugh spill out before waving my hand, actually thinking I could dismiss my gloom like a pesky fly. Sure. That was going to be effective. "Go back to work, Chicago. Forget all this. I'm just being a dumb girl. I'll be okay by tonight, and—"

"No."

"No...what?"

"I'm not forgetting about it." He expelled a hard breath. "We've been apart too long."

"But it's only been a week."

"And it's been too long."

I really felt silly now. "Killian, come on. I just need to chill out, and—"

"No. You need me near you, just like I need you near me. You need me pulling you off your feet and kissing you until you're dizzy from it. You need my hands tearing off your clothes and then all over your naked skin...every fucking inch of it...until my fingers find their way inside you and spread you, getting you ready for my cock. Why don't you tell me what you need after that, baby?"

"You." Thank God for my sunglasses and sun hat. I pulled the brim lower, hiding the way I panted for every breath and shut my eyes, fantasizing all the images he painted. "Inside me, Killian. With me."

"Yeah, my sweet fairy. That's exactly right. And that's exactly what I want. I'm so hard, so hot, so miserable. I need to be near you, holding you, a part of you—reminding you who you belong to, where you belong. With me. Nowhere else." His breaths were just as rough and fast as mine. "Does that sound about right?"

Damn him. How I love him.

"Why can't it be next weekend already?" It was a needy, desperate whisper, and I didn't care. "I wish I were wrapped in your arms..."

"Done."

"Huh?"

"You heard me. Go home and pack. Bring your work clothes and files with you because you're working from the headquarters office this week. And you'll spend every night in my bed, damn it."

"All week?" I should have been miffed. Instead, my heart sang.

"I'm sending a driver and the plane. I'll text you the details. Don't bother arguing." The line went rough, as if he'd adjusted his grip on the handset again. His voice had thickened with pure command. "I need you. Not just with my body. With—" He grunted as if trying to talk himself into saying something. My heart tripped over at least ten beats. "I'm done with this bullshit, Claire. Two weeks is too damn long. By tonight, we'll be together."

"I love you." I sounded loopy and lovesick, even to my own ears. It didn't matter. Nothing did, except the idea of getting to see him for more than forty-eight consecutive hours.

"I'll see you soon. Now go get packed."

I threw all my stuff back into my striped beach bag and headed for the car. A quick dusting of baby powder made sure the sand stayed at the beach, and I'd be ready to hop right into traveling clothes. As I drove home, the songs on the radio sounded happier, the breeze seemed lighter, and even the traffic seemed more agreeable.

Killian Stone made everything in my world better.

So, was it such a horrible thing that he preferred to keep some things in his world private?

I turned the question over in my mind during the flight.

How bad could the damn secret be, anyway? Wasn't there a good chance I already knew all the major issues his family had thanks to the research I'd helped pull during Trey's sex scandal last year as a member of the PR cleanup team? It wasn't like Andrea, my boss, had allowed that file to grow cold, either. Killian's brother was already showing signs of pulling the black fleece out of the closet again. He'd frequented a few clubs that had been his bad-boy candy stores, showed up late to meetings, jetted to Miami for long weekends. Oh, yeah, he was back on everyone's radar.

I actually smiled while enjoying a sip of the champagne the flight attendant had opened before takeoff.

Trey's addiction to fun was extra stress for everyone, but after all that, how huge a bomb could Killian have to drop? And was it possible I'd created that bomb in my mind, bracing myself for an explosion that was never to come, just because I couldn't trust in the good of what we had?

I had to stop constantly pushing back. Had to trust that Killian would open the door and let me see the secrets of his tower when the time was right. I'd fallen this hard for him without the invitation. I could certainly wait a little longer.

Until then, I vowed to be less his adversary and more his girlfriend. Be more gracious about the extravagances, even if I didn't need them.

I had to stop being tempted to run again.

Because one day, he'd refuse to give chase.

Then I would truly know what devastation was. If being apart two weeks at a time was doing this to me, not having Killian at all was...

Unthinkable.

I directed my thoughts to another path. A viable action plan.

Maybe it was time *I* chased *him* a little.

Maybe it was time to rethink a permanent move to Chicago.

I had a week to look at things with new eyes...and perhaps at the end of it, to surprise my Prince Charming with a sparkling surprise of his own. Finally, I could hit him with something he'd never see coming.

★ ★ ★ ★

Around eight o'clock CST that night, I deplaned the Stone Global private jet at Midway Field.

The world's most stunning man waited for me on the tarmac next to the Stone Global town car, the wind kicking at his thick dark hair and his long leather trench.

With each step I took down the stairs, my heart leaped one notch higher in my throat. Hoping this feeling never went away, no matter how long we were together, I scurried into the strong haven of his arms, burying my face in his neck while he pressed every inch of my body against his.

I was home.

I was his.

While I never wanted the embrace to end, I finally pulled away enough to kiss him, grabbing his neck to keep him close. When we dragged apart, the night became day again with the brilliance of his smile.

"Hi there, San Diego."

My grin couldn't be contained. *San Diego? Maybe not for much longer, Mr. Stone.*

"Hi there, Chicago."

"How was the flight?"

"Unbearable without you." I giggled as he rolled his eyes but sighed when he moved in for a deeper kiss. His tongue rolled against mine, tasting like a little Scotch and a lot of lust. We'd be lucky to make it to the penthouse if this kept up. "Thank you for this," I murmured. "You spoil me rotten, and I promise I'll start to love it more."

He brushed away the hair that had escaped my wool cap, his gaze raking my face with intensity. "That sounds really nice, fairy—because you haven't seen anything yet."

I was happy to know his surprise hadn't slipped his mind. It sure as hell hadn't escaped mine. I grabbed his hand with an expectant grin, but the man returned an evil smile before ushering me into the car. He didn't say a word as the driver loaded my bags into the trunk. Still nothing as we pulled away from the airport.

"We probably should feed you first." His statement was all business, but his gaze was pure mischief. "Did you eat on the plane? Before you left?"

"Aggghhh." I whacked his chest, but that only fed his

mirth. I straightened, folded my arms, and drawled, "You want to know what I did do on the plane?"

Inside a second, his stare turned to sensual velvet. "Does it involve you sprawled on the bed with your fingers in your panties?"

I smacked him again but let my hand linger on his coat. The mix of the night wind, his cosmopolitan cologne, and that thick leather...*wow*. "I don't use the bed unless you're in it with me. You know that."

He curved his palm over mine, making me stay close. "I'll be good. For now. Tell me."

"I worked on new affirmations. I'm going to be better about accepting surprises from you."

A rare, soft smile lifted his lips. It was the look he didn't use very often, reserved for occasions like visits to the no-kill animal shelter he championed and Sunday dinners with his mom. "I really like the sound of that."

"Me too." Since he had his animal rescue eyes on, I put on my best matching stare, along with a corresponding pout. "So...?"

"So?" He slid the smile back into a smirk. "What?"

"Damn it," I groaned. He chuckled. "Are you going to make me beg? I'm not above it, Mr. Stone."

That ended the smirk. His face took on a thousand angles of lusty possibility, concentrated most fiercely in the sensual sweeps of his lips. As he tugged me against his chest, he let them part in heated promise before quietly ordering, "Yeah. I do want to hear you beg."

I didn't need another cue. While pressing closer and lifting my face, I whispered, "Please don't make me wait any longer. I'll do anything you want."

His panther's growl took greater force in his throat. "Anything? Hmmm. You may regret that promise, fairy."

"Try me," I challenged.

"You know I would've told you anyhow, right?

"But making a deal with the devil is so much more fun."

As he laughed, he readjusted our positions, setting me back by a bit—and clearly trying to wrestle his crotch to a less conspicuous swell. I bit my lip hard, gazing at that bulge. It was just as difficult for me to hold back from grabbing a good feel.

"Okay...here goes." He actually seemed a little nervous, and that made my heart pound again. "You know how you've been moaning about your passport gathering dust?"

"Ummm...yeah?" I didn't hide the questioning lilt to it.

"Does three weeks sound like ample time to do some dusting?"

Forget the pounding. My pulse took off at a gallop. "Wh-What do you mean?"

"I mean three weeks. You and me. Your birthday is coming up, and I thought we could celebrate with a splash. Italy and France, maybe Spain if we have time. Rome? Venice? Marseilles? Paris? What sounds good?" His gaze narrowed when I could do nothing with mine but gawk. "We leave in ten days, so I can have the travel girls tweak the arrangements. I know you've also lusted after Tuscany. It's harder to get to, but we could work in a small side trip if you—" He halted, staring at me with a hint of panic. I could count on one hand how many times I'd seen that look on his face. It stunned me just as much as what he'd said. "Claire?" He tapped a nervous thumb on his thigh. "For God's sake, say something."

I swallowed, forcing myself to comply. "I...it's...well... whoa. Three weeks. Wow."

"Which means what in English?"

I felt like an ass. Shock had me going for the nonstop stammer, and it all seemed to be the wrong damn thing.

"I'm sorry. No, wait—I mean, I'm not sorry, not about—oh, hell. Did Andrea really agree to this? How pissed was she when you—?"

"You're worried about Andrea?" He looked as furious as a wildcat stuck in a barrel over Niagara Falls—with my words as the rushing water.

"I'm ruining this," I muttered. "Again." When Killian's jaw clenched so hard his chin nearly formed a V, I dropped my head and fell into silence, knowing if I said anything else it would emerge in a tearful blubber.

Killian yanked me close again. "I have Andrea handled, baby. She's Barney compared to the T-Rexes I've taken on in my life."

I giggled at the image of my boss's elegant face poking out of a purple Barney costume. But what the hell did he mean by T-Rexes? And wasn't I not supposed to care anymore, anyway?

That handled my resistance to the tears. Perfect. Now I was slinging the waterworks at him too. And, oh, how he loved that. Not.

I pushed away, burying my face in my hands. "Please. I need a redo, okay? I'll get this right, I promise."

Killian growled. Hard. Right before clutching the back of my neck and forcing my face into the command of his mouth-mashing kiss. A whine tore up my throat, thick and needy. I clawed at his arm, making it my anchor during my ride into blissful surrender.

"You're getting it right already." His voice was as coarse as the steel in his stare. "Understood?"

I started bawling harder.

Would he ever stop being amazing? Ever?

"Oh, baby." He rubbed my cheek with a big thumb. "Don't cry. I just wanted to make you happy. We don't have to go. I can just have the girls cancel and—"

"Don't. You. Dare." Though my order spurred him to more laughter, I added, "I'm crying because I'm happy. And..."

"And what?"

"And because of my own stupidity." I returned his caress, pressing a hand to the magnificent, high plane of his cheek. "You are amazing. And perfect. I'm just not used to all of it...to your generosity, to you filling all my dreams like this. I'm not used to trusting it, to trusting any kind of happiness, so I don't. Instead, I turn on the soundtrack of suspicion, unwilling to believe that this is really happening."

He blinked hard. For a moment, the clarity in his gaze was replaced by dark-gray clouds, as if only half his thoughts were still here and half had jumped to the moon. "I know." His words were so full of commiseration, I felt it to the marrow of my bones.

I pressed my hand a little tighter to his skin. "You do know, don't you?" When he reacted simply by kissing me softly, I went on, "I love the surprise. I really do. Thank you, Mr. Stone. Now I just need to pinch myself to assure I'm not dreaming."

"Hey." He threw a mock glower. "If there's any pinching going on around here, I'll be the one doing it." After a quick kiss to my nose, he grinned again, obviously pleased with himself for blowing my mind. "Now, no more crying, Miss Montgomery. Let's get you some food."

"Okay." I giggled and sniffed. "That sounds really good. Maybe a big salad—and an even bigger glass of wine."

"Fuck." He rolled his eyes. "No way. You're getting a burger. And some goddamn fries. And then the wine." He finished the look by letting his stare darken back to sensual velvet. "And then me."

As usual, the man knew exactly what it took to make my world perfect.

And for once, I chose to believe that it wouldn't all disappear tomorrow.

CHAPTER TWO

Killian

Magic. It wasn't a word I tossed around in my usual vernacular. My world, professional and personal, had always been about logistics and realisms. Yes, even on vacation. Even in a city like Venice, Italy.

This time, it was different. Perhaps even magical.

I'd been here a handful of times already, always for business and never enjoying the city beyond a few cordial dinners with colleagues—if enjoying was the right word. It wasn't easy to see the allure of a city that was literally sinking into its own lagoon. Of course I knew the history of the place, that turning it into a swamp had actually saved its ass from enemies back in the day.

But that was the other Killian. The one who hadn't yet grasped what magic could be.

Through Claire's eyes, I rediscovered...everything. Eating lunch on Torcello had sparked a conversation about her passion for Guido Daniele and his whimsical handimal art. A trip to Murano had turned into an afternoon of seeking out Christmas ornaments for everyone in the SGC home office. At the top of the St. Mark's Campanile, I'd seen the world from the clouds...literally.

The best part of each experience? Ah, God, her kisses.

Yes. There was always one, a little longer than the rest, that was announced by such a stunning fire in her golden eyes I forgot all the photographers who were determined to document every second of our adventures. Their lenses clicked nearly as often as Claire's, though *her* shutterbug tendencies were easier to tolerate. Having a legitimate excuse for ogling her ass certainly didn't hurt the cause. It was even easy to dismiss the scowls she flashed when I kept insisting we could return as many times as she wanted. Ultimately, we both knew her skepticism was no match for my resolve. Perhaps it was why she took healthy payback in the form of a we're-in-love selfie to commemorate each of our adventures.

Hell. The woman had me taking fucking selfies.

All too soon, it was the night before we were to depart Venice for Rome. Special arrangements for the evening were nonnegotiable. I'd learned there was going to be a one-night charity gala performance of *La Bohème* at the Teatro La Fenice, so it seemed fated that we attend. As a nod to her independence, I had the travel team leave the arrangements on the itinerary, knowing she'd want the advance notice for packing an appropriate gown and shoes. I simply made sure they left other details *off* the program, such as the fact that the ticket purchase included every seat in the box and that her gown would probably need some embellishments...like a pair of Tiffany Aria earrings, just in time for her birthday.

The selection of the jewelry wasn't just appropriate. It was perfect. I took advantage of a lull in the music to study how the earrings enhanced her beauty, already a mind-blower of regality by how she'd styled her hair into a high twist, and found myself unable to look away. In the dim light of the back row of our box, she was damn near a secret treasure for my eyes alone.

The serene lift of her lips. The gorgeous slope of her neck. The perfect angles of her cheeks. Even the curves of her eyelashes and the sweeps of her eyebrows. No matter where I looked, I found my senses clobbered by her fairy queen scepter...while the woman didn't show a drop of perspiration for it.

She ruled me. Possessed me. Terrified me.

And I loved her completely.

The music soared again. I watched her chest rise as she gave in to the emotion of the scene, her eyes closing when the soprano hit a high, emotional note. All the moisture left my mouth as hers parted a little, deeply tempting me to lean over and consume her body the same way the music roared through her soul.

When she opened her eyes, she turned her head and lifted her gaze to mine. I don't know if she sensed my ongoing scrutiny or just wanted to share the force of the music with me. It didn't matter. I delved my stare into hers, drowning in the dark amber depths that took my breath away just as they had the first night we'd sipped wine together in my office. Christ, I'd never get tired of seeing her like this, her eyes huge and luminous, brimming with all the intensity of her soul, now tangling around the helpless prisoner of mine. Did the woman know how funny she sounded when pegging me as the conquering overlord? Did she know how my heart literally lay at her feet? How one well-placed kick from her would send it sliding into the shadows?

It was why she could never know the truth now. Why my secret would remain that, no matter what measures it took. She was in love with Killian Stone, not Killian Klarke—simplifying my own choice between the two for the first time in my life.

As of tonight, Killian Klarke was dead.

The fires of her eyes made it even simpler to burn the remaining shreds of him in my mind.

She pulled me back—not that I'd gone very far—with a gorgeous little tilt at the ends of her lips. I dipped closer toward her, letting my stare roam every inch of her face. She averted her gaze, all but broadcasting her blush despite the darkness we were in. Still, I needed to test for myself. Or maybe I just wanted an excuse to touch her.

Gently, I cupped her cheek. Sure enough, her skin permeated mine with warmth.

"It's all so beautiful," she whispered to me.

I threaded my fingers back, using the tips to play with the wisps that had escaped her hairdo. "Yes. It is."

She pursed her lips in chastisement. "You're not even watching."

"Of course I am. Very avidly." I lifted my other hand to her collarbone, running a knuckle along it to the place where the black lace of her sleeve barely hugged her shoulder. The same lace formed a thin, sheer edge to the gown's barely legal neckline, drawing my attention exactly where it had dipped the first time I'd set eyes on her in the sparkly floor-length thing. It sure as hell had solidified my insistence that we sit in the back of the box instead of the front. I was going to gawk my fill of her tonight, no matter where the relocation took my thoughts...and quite possibly my actions.

My imagination started taking off with the possibilities.

"Really?" she returned. "You've barely been paying attention. Do you even know what's happening in the story right now?"

"Spoiler alert. Somebody dies."

Her eyes widened. She raised fingers over her lips to stifle her giggle. I tugged at them, quickly pressing my mouth down in their place. "You're awful," she rasped when I pulled up. "And morbid."

"We're at the opera, baby. Somebody always dies." I ran my hand to the middle of hers, stroking her palm with my thumb while I absorbed the perfect sight of her all over again.

"That's no reason to joke about death." She spread her fingers around, along the back of my hand, in order to return it to her face. "That asshole doesn't have a sense of humor. And I'll be damned if he decides to come for you even one day too early."

Her words were bold, but her tone was raspy. When her fingers trembled too, I lifted her face toward mine. "Death doesn't want me, Claire. I'm a bigger jerk than he is."

Her lips twitched. "And likely a hell of a lot more gorgeous." She kissed my fingertips. "You'd steal his game with the girls."

"Nah. I'd be too busy with the re-org of hell. He'd have to fall in line. No more late-night parties down at the seventh ring."

The soft laughter I expected didn't materialize. Instead, her features tightened. "Don't die on me, Killian." She slid a hand beneath my shirt, gripping urgent fingers to my nape. "Just...don't."

Once more, her syntax was snippy, but her voice was desperate, as if she saw a greater truth to which I was blind. Or was it simply that she sensed the decision I'd just made...to never tell her about the real origins of my identity? That as of tonight, part of me really was dead?

Or could it be that the woman really loved me as completely as I loved her?

The magnitude of the realization consumed my mind—

and points deeper—like the music soaring to the building's rafters. It ached. And pierced.

She loves me.

And flew. And pulsed.

She loves...Killian Stone.

For the first time in my life, there was nobody I was more grateful to be. No more regrets about what—or who—could've been. No wild wonderings about how happy I'd be if I were just the son of the Keystone estate's groundskeeper. Killian Stone at last knew who he was. The man Claire Montgomery gazed at with such longing and need. The man who'd ensure she wanted for nothing else for the rest of her life, that she was happy, fulfilled, and spoiled rotten. The man who'd absorb the force of her love and return it to her tenfold with every passing day.

The music softened, again a perfect complement to the atmosphere of my soul. While the knowledge of her love was crashing cymbals, the acceptance of it was a peaceful harp, flowing into the kiss I skimmed across her lips. Sometimes, especially *this* time, it felt good to simply taste her...savor her...

"Dying isn't an option," I whispered. "Unless I'm slaying a dragon for you, baby."

Claire curled a hand into my tuxedo lapel. "Not even then. Promise me."

Her entreaty was so soft and exigent I couldn't help kissing her again. Our lips met with more urgency, seeking the assurance of each other...the perfect click of our souls. It didn't take long. I barely held back a moan as her passion reached to mine, giving it wings like the music flying from below. Splendor. Harmony. My sublime aria. My queen Claire.

"I'd promise you the cosmos if it kept you in my arms

forever."

A shiver visibly claimed her. She worried me for a moment, but when I pulled her face up, my stare was filled with the adoring smile on her lips...and the sparkling tears on her cheeks.

Yet again, I couldn't move. Below us, a tenor sang of heartache. Above us, reflections scudded like clouds. Between us, there were only inches of tangled breath, barely banked fire—

And unstoppable magic.

She initiated the kiss that turned our embers into a full blaze, yanking my bow tie out of its knot to do so. As our mouths crashed, she burrowed her hands under my jacket, scraping them against my shirt until she finally had the damn thing pulled free from my pants.

It took her less than a second to slide her touch directly to my skin. Her fingers were already like fire, forcing me to tear my mouth from hers in order to breathe without groaning. Even then, I worked to regulate myself from sounding like a grizzly tempted to hump the hottest she-bear in the forest.

Who the fuck was I kidding? I was beyond tempted. And I was in Italy, for fuck's sake. If any of the *signori* in this place found themselves alone in a box with a woman like this, with her golden eyes burning at them with every fuck-me-please sign in the book, they'd do exactly what I did. Surged out of my seat and onto the floor in front of her, planting my knees hard. Jammed both hands beneath the black layers of her skirt—how many *were* there, for chrissake?—until I found her scanty lace panties.

And tore them apart in two ruthless rips.

I absorbed her gasp with my mouth, sucking on her lips

as I yanked her ass to the edge of her seat. She wrapped a hand around my neck again, using the leverage to bury her head against my chest—a well-timed move since her next gasp was higher and sharper than the first. Could have had something to do with how I slicked both thumbs to the hot flesh between her legs, teasing on both sides of the quivering little ridge that popped up for me.

The music swelled, building toward the climax of a chorus.

I trailed my thumbs back the way they'd just come...except inward, over her clit.

Her tiny scream vibrated through me as she threatened to tear open my back with her nails. The sweet pain spurred my own ferocity, driving my hands around her buttocks in order to pull her tight against me, wrapping her hips around mine.

I worked my mouth into the warm grotto of her ear. "Baby, you're wet." When she returned my rasp with a feverish nod, I nipped at the skin around the sparkling diamond triad embedded in her lobe.

Not the vision for helping your self-control, asshole.

"And, baby, you're trembling."

Her head bobbed up and down again as she scratched me harder, betraying how completely on board she was with the whole let's-hump-in-the-woods idea. Problem was, this wasn't the woods. And while it *was* Venice, home to some of the world's most famous debauchery, subterfuge sounded like a damn erotic idea tonight.

"And you're hot. So damn hot, Claire. Your cunt is already burning my fingers."

I didn't get a nod for that one. Instead, she worked those eager, deft hands into the scant space between our bodies, opening my fly with frantic tugs. Despite her efforts to make the action quiet, the slide of my zipper coincided with another respite in the music, causing discernible stirrings in the booths to either side of us. I even heard a man's knowing chuckle— not that I cared anymore. The second she reached inside my briefs, palmed my balls, and then ran her hand up the length of my shaft, enough heat blasted through me to burn this building down for the fourth time in its history.

I muffled my groan by biting her neck and gripping her hips harder—not exactly a wise move, since it compressed her fingers tighter around my cock. Her hand was situated so close to the crown, squeezing the small surge of white heat that told us both how goddamn ready I was to be inside her.

"Shit. Claire!"

"Mmmm-hmmm." Her sigh spread warmth over my neck and then into my ear as she worked me with passion, rolling her sweet little fingers all over my erection, spreading my cream everywhere. My dick was damn near as wet as her pussy now... but not quite. My testing finger in her channel came back as soaked as one of the sidewalks outside on this high-tide night.

"*Ti voglio. Ho bisogno di te,*" she whispered. *I want you. I need you.*

Burying another groan in her neck, I pushed up into her again. "And I need this," I grated. "I need to fuck you, Claire. Right here. Right now."

Damn. Dante may have been a celebrated son of this country, but his inferno officially had nothing on my bloodstream right now. The sexy sneak of a woman. So this was her end game in picking up the fast-learn language courses after I'd told her about the trip. How I'd chuckled like the indulgent boyfriend as she'd regaled me with her increasing fluency in ordering wine and asking about bathroom locations—when in secret, she'd taught herself how to turn my dick into a pillar of agony from the impact of her words alone.

Would she ever stop amazing me?

Did I ever want her to?

Her whispered nastiness curled into me, twisting through my extremities until I again pushed past the cloud of her skirting and then hitched her legs up to the armrests of her chair. She was fully spread for me now, her pussy hot and open.

And very, very ready for my cock.

The delectable O of her mouth confirmed that, along with the high sigh that erupted from it—thankfully drowned by the new surge of music through the theater. But even the opera wouldn't be a decent veil for what I planned to do to her next, so I yanked her yet closer, crushing our mouths back together as I did.

My bare cock slid against her soaked sex.

We clung to each other like lovers in a storm.

I paused the action, letting us both modulate our breathing. *Right. Winner of an idea, Kil.* With our lips fused, our bodies pulsing, and our heartbeats meshing, we'd jumped on a speeding train together—and the brakes had just burned out.

I angled my hips and pressed my crest through her folds once. One push more was all I needed to slide deep inside her hot, wet sheath.

She shuddered from head to toe, seized my nape before she twisted her hand into my hair. Bit at my lips as waves of heat rushed through her, betraying her mounting struggle to stay silent. The same surges turned into convulsions around my cock, drawing on me, tempting my body's ultimate bliss, boiling in the depths of my balls. In lieu of desperate screams, she poured her passion into clinging to me. Whimpering against my lips. Wrapping her pussy tighter around me.

Tighter...

I rolled my hips forward, seating myself harder into her. My thighs burned. My ass clenched. My mind narrowed to the excruciating tunnel of heat that joined us, obsessed with filling it, conquering it, branding myself into it. The woman would never want or think of anyone there except Killian Stone, ever again. The resolve settled things for me too. I'd never want to be anyone else again, either.

Deeper. I had to get deeper.

As I shifted my hold to her ass, impaling her body onto mine by another inch, a mesmerizing sound burst from her. I'd never heard it before. The cry was strained yet melodic, twining so perfectly on the air with the plaintive aria from the stage that stifling her felt like an awful crime to my body *and* spirit. Our forced silence was a sudden irony. Even if I could speak, my throat was strangled by intense desire and grateful amazement. My body supplied no air except what it took to fill her, consume her, enflame her...

Free her.

Her whole body clenched as the first wave of her orgasm hit. She ripped her lips from mine and then bit my neck so hard, I was damn certain I'd have a mark—and fuck would it be worth it. The next moment alone served as my affirmation, giving me an image I swore to burn on my memory forever. She rocked her head back, neck arched, the nimbus of her hair glowing in the light that filtered to the back of our box. As she did, the music burst into a crescendo, drums pounding, strings flowing, a hundred voices at full volume.

We transcended erotic, careening into ethereal. This

moment was all that mattered, a vortex drawing us to deeper and darker waters, especially as I leaned to suck her neck and surrendered to the pull of her body on mine.

Like fingers racing up a harp, my release roared up my cock. When it detonated, I bit into her shoulder with the same force she'd used on me. But I still had no sound to partner with it. I was lost to her. Annihilated by her. While the character Mimi died in the scene below, I willingly gave over to the sweet suicide of emptying myself into her. But unlike Mimi's, my death led to a rebirth. The renewal made possible only by giving myself to this woman. Completely. Perfectly. Endlessly. Every fatality more devastating—and transforming—than the last.

She bucked in my arms, drawing out the constrictions of her flesh on mine, squeezing every last drop from my very willing cock. If she demanded more than that, I'd find a way to give it with just as much passion.

Slowly, as if timing ourselves with the orchestra yet again, our breaths evened. Still, she didn't move. Neither did I. We let the music spiral through us with foreheads touching, lips brushing, breaths twining...and hearts singing.

As the show ended, the building shook with applause. Loud *bravos* and other praises punched into the air. With my hands still hidden by the froth of her skirt, I was able to zip up in privacy while guiding Claire's legs back into their proper locations.

Finally, I glanced over my shoulder. "Hmmm. Look, baby. A standing ovation. Want to join them?"

She gave my shoulder a playful whack. "Why don't you do the honors for both of us? Make sure to bellow that it was the best opera I've ever been to."

I chuckled and then leaned in for another long kiss. "Me too."

She didn't let me get very far in pulling away. Well, her stare didn't. Accompanied by the soft tilt to her kiss-roughened lips, the bronze lights in her eyes consumed me. I yearned for a lifetime of staring back into them.

Yet again, my resolve was sustained. Making the decision to kill off Killian Klarke was one of the best of my life.

Choosing that exact moment to reflect on the fact wasn't.

"Kil?" The glow in her gaze dimmed. The intensity of her question was joined by the new press of her fingers against my jaw. I forced down deep breaths, despite knowing it was just the beginning of her little curiosity spurt. She'd been edging closer to that inquisition more often during the trip—making it harder to order her to stop.

At least in this instance, I had an alternative. It was wickedly easy to grasp the back of her neck and yank her to me for another passionate kiss. Dirty move? Undoubtedly. But I could argue that she'd tried to take advantage of the postcoital glow first.

"Stay here," I directed. "The crush will make it impossible to leave for a while. I'll grab a towel from the bar so you can clean up. After that, what about a final cruise on the Grand Canal?"

I expected an eager grin in response. Instead, her face tightened a little—and around her mouth more than that. I didn't like causing that expression, as if she were peering into a shop window at a dress she couldn't have. Damn it, I abhorred the idea of her wanting for anything—but in this case, I knew exactly what she was after. The secret hallway in my castle. Yeah, the one with the chamber at the end—containing the cursed spinning wheel. One touch of the needle on that fucker and the entire kingdom went to ruin.

Why didn't she understand that by now? I'd explained, with as much patient force as I'd been able to, that some things belonged in the past, and pulling the scabs on them would only cause a giant pool of blood. Or worse.

Much worse.

So why the *hell* did she keep pushing at that door? Why did she look at me like that, though I'd given her every other dress in the whole damn shop? Showed her things I'd never exposed to anyone else. My surly moods when ideas woke me at two a.m. The ogre faces I made when I worked at the free weights in the home gym. Every geeked-out part of my stamp collection. She'd been for beers with the guys from the polo team and to Sunday brunches with Father and Mother. She was intimately familiar with every corner of my life now.

Except the end of the damn hallway.

I accepted the clean towel from the bartender with a frustrated snap. After a muttered *grazie*, I turned back toward the box with hard steps—and new determination. It was time to screw a more level head back onto my shoulders. I was Killian fucking Stone. I had this shit under control, and that included all the useless anxiety over Claire's I-need-to-read-your-mind-now stares.

"She'll put it away," I muttered beneath my breath before flashing a fake smile at a couple who recognized me. The towel seemed to throw them from any further socializing, making it possible to move on at a faster pace. "She'll have to, goddamnit. She'll leave it alone—eventually."

And if she didn't, I'd put on the fucking ogre face for this as well. I hoped it wouldn't come to that. I hoped that for once, she'd accept that the matter was closed for discussion, and she'd find a new dress to be fascinated with. Maybe even a new trinket.

Like the one in the velvet box I'd tucked inside my jacket.

Correction—the box now burning a damn hole of anticipation in my jacket.

It was just a matter of the right timing. Maybe beneath the stars on the Grand Canal tonight. I sure as fuck hoped so.

★ ★ ★ ★

The stars decided to cooperate. So, it seemed, did the whole city. The restaurants along the Grand Canal were filled with lively laughter and music, throwing a kaleidoscope of color across the waters. The gondoliers, seemingly inspired by the influx of opera fans for the benefit, broke out into spontaneous songs that ranged from the classical music we'd just heard to operatic versions of the latest pop hits.

The boat traffic on the canal started to resemble Lake Shore Drive during Fleet Week, so I asked the gondolier to steer us toward a quieter channel. Claire nestled next to me, pulling the thick blanket close along with her jacket, giving me the chance to curl a hand around her head and twirl the loose strands of her hair. Her face, illuminated by the moon and the softer glow from the buildings we floated past, was truly that of a fairy queen.

My fairy queen.

Her gaze crinkled a little. She pushed up to align our gazes more. "Kil." It wasn't a full question, though the dip in her tone implied as much.

"Hmmm?"

"What are you thinking?"

"I'm wondering if the fairies are wondering where their queen disappeared to yet."

Her lips tightened.

Shit. Not now.

"I'm serious."

"So am I."

She pulled one hand up under her chin. With the other, she scraped at my new stubble with her fingertips. "That day you came and found me...at my dad's wedding..."

"One of the best days of my life," I murmured.

"You said you wanted to share everything with me."

I lifted my head. Yes, with the purpose of gaining higher ground in the conversation. Yes, without a drop of guilt about the tactic. "And I have."

Since I meant every fucking word of it, I saw no barriers to her acceptance of it. But her mouth tensed again. She pressed her fingers a little harder. I was damn sure it wasn't the only push she intended now.

"Let me in, Kil. All the way. Please."

A phone rang.

Thank fuck.

She recognized the ring along with me. My personal cell. It had been turned off during the opera, but I'd activated the volume when we'd left the theater in case there was news from home. Father had been discharged from the hospital before we'd departed the States and was recovering well, but I appreciated Mother's updates.

Claire gave me a puzzled look when I raised the device and Trey's number appeared. "Isn't he still in New York with the acquisitions team?"

I nodded. "It's four o'clock in the afternoon there. Maybe they've come across some big meat."

She rolled her eyes. I'd made no secret about my professional hard-on for SGC's need to diversify into the alternative-energy field. It seemed a good project to dip Trey's toes back into the big pool of Stone Global, and for the last few months, he and his team had traveled across the country to interview companies willing to partner up. So far, his toes had been doing a pretty decent job.

Inside the next minute, I wondered if the fucker could even feel his toes.

"Kil? Kil? You—you there, man? Ohhh, Kil-lian..."

My brother's drunken sing-song of an ending was couched by two, maybe three, female giggles. There was a distinct *smack* before one of them shrieked a little.

Hell.

I shoved to a full sitting position, pinching the bridge of my nose while I looked down at Claire's hand, now wrapped anxiously around my elbow. Her left hand—still bare.

Hell.

"Where are you?" My demand had no inflection, an effect I hadn't even worked for. Though rage tore through me, Trey wasn't worth the effort of expressing it.

"What the fuh kinda queshion is that? I'm in New York, dorkwad. And I'm celebratin'." When his pause stretched into an uncomfortable silence, he blurted, "Okay, don't you wanna know why?"

I forced in a deep breath. "Sorry. I was too busy chasing the wagon."

"The wagon?"

"The one you just tumbled off?"

He huffed. Several times. I began to wonder if I'd have to start dealing with drunk tears from my goddamn big brother. It wasn't Trey's MO, but I didn't know what to expect from the idiot anymore.

"Shit. You're really something, Kil, you know that?" He twisted the huff into a growl. "I go and land fucking Sunbreak Technologies, and all you can do is count my cocktails?"

I raised my head. "Sunbreak." Well, damn. I wondered why the buildings on either side of the canal hadn't transformed into a rock and a hard place. What was I supposed to do now? Tell the bastard he could go ahead and polish those bottles off and then fuck every woman in the room because he'd secured a deal with the biggest fish we'd been pursuing in the alternative-energies pond? But raking him over the coals for the bender made *me* worse than a bastard. "That's—well, that's awesome. Good job."

"Shank you," he drawled. "Shank you verah much." His snicker trickled out. "'Shank you.' Oh, fuck. Now that's funny."

I took a turn at rolling my eyes. "Yeah. All right. Just do me one favor, okay?"

"Whaz dat?"

"Make sure the celebration doesn't involve your naked ass in the tabloids tomorrow."

"Huh?" There was a glugging sound, like a bottle being tipped. "Whaz wrong with my ass?"

"It's not my favorite subject for conversation, for one thing. And certainly not the sight I want associated with you before getting ink from Sunbreak on this deal."

Trey snarled again. "Goddamnit! There is *nothing* wrong with my ass."

Claire tightened her hold. I glanced to her. Sure enough,

Trey's tirade had brimmed over the confines of the phone. Wonderful.

"Brother, you're very drunk."

"And, brother, you're a piece of work. You know that?" The bottle sloshed again. "'Brother.' *Ha.* Oh, now that's even funnier, isn't it? What a joke we are, Killian. What a joke *you* are."

"I'm hanging up now, Trey."

"Of course you are, Mr. Stone. Why not? The mask still fits perfectly, doesn't it?"

"Good night, brother."

A fitting wrap-up would've been another line of praise for the Sunbreak deal, but it'd been quashed in that beautiful wave of "love" Trey kept up from his end.

That must be a new record for you, asshole. Less than five minutes to turn my mind from pondering all the ways I love Claire to the single way you can destroy my life. Bravo, Trey. Maybe you'll get a present from one of those girls to help celebrate landing Sunbreak. Like a nice thriving case of Hep C.

I slipped the phone back into my pocket before leaning back and letting Claire press herself against me again. Tension must have been rolling off me in waves, but she pushed through it, gently massaging my neck. While I welcomed her touch, it would be hours until my stress fell away again. And the ring in my pocket? It wasn't going anywhere either. The dream of slipping it onto Claire's finger was gone, at least for tonight.

What the fuck had I been thinking? Exterminating Killian Klarke...it was as useless as killing my own shadow. It was why Trey returned to his old shit with such confidence, knowing there wasn't a damn thing I could do about it—especially if all Josiah's mates learned I didn't have a real drop of the man's blood in my veins. It would crumble the Stone Global empire.

It would wipe out the lie Claire believed right now.

And what will she do then, do you think? Not only when she learns that the man of her dreams is a damn good hoax—but has knowingly continued that sham month after month?

I shut the thoughts down.

I was still one move ahead in my chess match with fate—for now. If Trey collapsed SGC with a wild move like unmasking me, Josiah would pull the asshole's inheritance faster than it took to twist open a new bottle of Stoli. For now, both Trey and I got what we wanted. I made up excuses for him in the press releases, and he let me keep the woman who wrote them.

Fair trade. For now.

But it was clear I needed a long-term game plan. About five minutes ago.

CHAPTER THREE

C l a i r e

The view inside our suite in Rome was as breathtaking as that just beyond the floor-to-ceiling panes. My stunning, god-like boyfriend lay sprawled out on the king-size bed in nothing but the plush hotel robe, while his ebony hair glistened with drops of water fresh from the shower we'd shared. My fingers tingled, wanting to run through the thick strands. I'd never been this sexually insatiable in my life. He was turning me into a wanton, lustful, sexed-up plaything, and neither of us were complaining.

We had been eating, shopping, and sexing our way across Europe, enjoying every single minute of each other's company—until last night. We had done the unthinkable—but unforgettable—during the opera, awakening my whole body with a naughty but satisfied buzz before we'd even stepped into the private gondola afterward. With the moon high, the breeze crisp, and the this-is-better-than-a-novel factor running high, I honestly thought Killian was preparing to propose.

The call from Trey had stabbed that vibe right in the gut. There were times—and that had definitely been one of them—when I longed to chuck Killian's cell into the drink and never look back.

Such a mature thought, Claire. Really.

I wasn't about to apologize for the sentiment. The damn thing rang at all the wrong times. But I'd be lying if I claimed no relief at its interruption just then. Saved by the bell, indeed. All right, it wasn't like I never wanted him on one knee, even in a wobbly gondola, with a ring in his hand and those words on his lips. I loved him. Helplessly. One-hundred-percently. And I wanted to spend the rest of my life with him. But not until we got a few more things out on the table. He clearly wasn't willing to spill those things yet. Until he did, we wouldn't be moving forward or down the aisle.

So yes, when his phone had rung, I had been ready to replace Trey's ringtone with the "Hallelujah" chorus. Kil hadn't shared my jubilance. Though Trey was on the brink of landing one of Stone Global's biggest deals ever, he still wasn't Kil's favorite person to be chatting up over the transatlantic airwaves. He'd tensed up during the exchange with his brother, even more than usual—which only added to the confusion gathering in the corners of my mind. The few words I'd overheard were fodder for even more bewilderment. The innuendoes in Trey's voice had been so thick and had stirred such tension in Killian afterward that a single conclusion thudded in the pit of my stomach from it all.

Something is not on the level with these two.

The niggling didn't stop, continuing to twist my gut—worsened by the realization that my boyfriend, for all his resemblance to a god, harbored the very mortal stupidity that he couldn't trust me with a shred of it. So even though I was working on being a better girlfriend, and my self-esteem issues and worthiness for him along with it, there was still some big piece of the life puzzle I was missing with him.

The shittiest thing? I sensed it was big.

As in monumental.

By the time we'd reached Rome, I felt my neurosis was fully justified. What the hell was going on with him? And how hard could I keep pushing to figure it out? He'd really started to push back, even when I applied the pressure tactics that I knew to work, so maybe it was time to research new ones.

Despite all the uncertainties, I was positive of one point.

Something had to give, or our relationship wouldn't make it past Paris.

Of course, I knew all about the stresses of Killian's life. The last thing I wanted to do was add to them. But I also yearned for our real relationship to start, for the "we" to become "us," for our life to be a partnership. It was the only way we could progress into the future and survive. If he didn't see it the same way, I needed to know—soon. Because God help me, the man possessed more of my heart with every passing day.

I must have momentarily joined him in the far-off gazing contest because before I knew it, he was waving his hand in front of my eyes. "Huh?" I blurted.

The corners of his mouth quirked. "Earth to Claire," he murmured.

"Sorry."

"Why?" He cocked his head and grinned, sending the typical wave of fluttery awareness through every drop of my blood as he did. "Where were you, baby?"

I gave a shallow laugh, trying to think of something that would sound plausible. Pushing him again so soon wouldn't be wise. Correction. It would be lunacy. "Just daydreaming about everything we've seen and done," I finally said. "It's been so wonderful."

His smile grew. "I'm glad you approve, Miss Montgomery."

"You know you're making all of my dreams come true, don't you?" I sighed as he sat up. That robe was starting to loosen in all the right ways.

He scooted over and stretched out his arms, capturing me around the waist—and setting my blood fully ablaze by resting his face against my stomach. I hummed in pleasure, weaving my fingers through his midnight hair, savoring this moment of complete connection between us. We had nothing but our imaginations to fill the hours of this magical night, not a bad thing when the streets of Rome lay at our feet.

I bent forward, tenderly kissing the top of his head, wondering how much further he'd let my lips progress down his breathtaking body.

A distant buzzing interrupted my progress.

He growled. I groaned.

"Not mine," I defended. "I left my ringer on in case Dad tried calling."

Killian grunted, rose, and crossed to the nightstand.

"Stone." Clipped, in control, and still damn sexy. That was my guy. At least until ten seconds later, as the caller completed their news. "He what?"

I spun around as his roar made the chandelier rock. I tried catching his eye, but he dropped his head and pinched his nose with two fingers.

"Goddamnit, Mason...if this is one of your stupid jokes..." He lifted his head, letting it settle back on his shoulders, now rigid with tension. "Yeah. I wouldn't joke about it, either. Right. Okay. Fuck. Give me ten minutes. I'll have to find my computer and link up. I'll call to the main line."

He ended the call, gritted out something else involving his favorite profanities, and then threw his phone across the room. It bounced off the wall and—miraculously—landed on the thick carpet in one piece. The moment, while jarring, allowed me a second for quick deduction. There was only one Mason in the world who could boil Kil's blood like this with a phone call. He was a legal genius, meaning he handled all the key cases for the family and the corporation. That conclusion led easily to the next.

All the key cases lately had contained one common name. Trey.

While my mind raced, my posture remained still. I knew better than to move or say anything. This Killian was not the one to be messed with. Period.

"Fuck." He stabbed at the keys on his laptop after slamming it onto the desk.

I continued staring, still silently balanced between asking questions and yearning to reassure him everything would be okay. The assurance would ring as meaningless as it was. So I hung back, waiting for him to offer more information at his own pace. Long before I'd even kissed the man, I'd learned it was the best approach when he hit pissed-off beast mode.

"Trey." His snarl of explanation didn't interrupt his long fingers on the keys by one beat.

"Never could've guessed." I tried for gentle and supportive with the reply.

"He's going to kill me, Claire—but not before being the ruin of the company I've worked my entire life to make stronger."

His stabs at the laptop intensified.

I retrieved his cell phone from where it had landed as he continued abusing his machine. I approached carefully and set his phone on the desk beside his computer. Before I could pull away, he grabbed my hand. In one powerful sweep, I was sitting on his lap.

"You're a godsend," he murmured. "You know that, right?"

I wrapped my arms around him and rubbed his back, hoping to calm him. "You want to tell me what happened?"

He didn't reply right away. Dipping his face to my upper chest, he nuzzled me with rough masculine jabs, inhaling hard against my skin. After a long minute, he pulled back, his face set once more into angles so commanding, they could've been the new face of the thousand-dollar bill.

"Do you mean what was the asshole arrested for this time?"

The announcement shouldn't have startled me, but it did. "Again?" I retorted.

He nodded with open weariness "This time, the charges aren't going to be so easy to cover up. A fancy tuxedo and some well-placed press releases don't make drug-possession charges disappear."

"Damn it."

"Looks like the DA is going for intent to sell on top of the possession charge due to the quantity he had in his Lambo. Fortunately, he was driving back into town from his trip to New York, so we can keep this thing at home. If he'd gotten caught in New York, he'd be floating down Shit Creek in a barrel, ready to tumble over Niagara Falls."

I glanced to the bottle of Tuscan red that the hotel had sent up as a Benvenuti a Roma gift. "Why does he insist on inviting disaster back in? On tormenting you like this?"

While the tension in his body ratcheted higher, Killian fell into inexplicable silence. No. Wrong. There was an explanation. He simply wasn't sharing it. Again.

I slipped off his lap. He dropped his head into his hands.

"So what's the plan?" I swallowed in an effort to keep the anger from the words. "Who do you need to call in to speak to?" I lowered to a chair across from him and snapped open my own computer. "Or is this a we kind of thing?"

Still no anger—though my edge of challenge clearly registered with him. Shadows answered me from the depths of his gaze, seeming like a mix of remorse and rage, before he answered, "Mason contacted Andrea in San Diego. I know Kate's been doing a great job of running point on your duties during the trip, but this isn't a spill on aisle three. It's a Hazmat effort and will take a full team."

I didn't miss the curt efficiency of his tone, either. "I completely agree." I added a diplomatic nod, garnering me a softer glance from across the table.

"Britta's rounding everyone up for a video conference call," he went on. "We'll discuss strategy for the shit storm. The press is starting to sniff. I want them bored and moving on about five minutes ago. We're too close to laying down ink with Sunbreak." He released another harsh breath while leaning back. "Of course, that's easier said than done."

"Why?" I asked it straight to the fury clamping anew around his jaw.

"Mason's pretty sure he's out of favors to call in on Trey's behalf. He's not certain if posting bail is even an option with these charges."

I sucked in a rough breath of my own. "Okay. Let's cross that bridge if we're forced—"

The whump of Kil's fist against the table cut me off. "Just once, I'd like to get through a day without worrying about stepping in the shit that idiot's cooking up on the side," he uttered. A bitter laugh escaped him. "Lance was the smartest one of the family, wasn't he? Got away and found his real dreams."

My stomach lurched as the wheels in my head spun faster. No wonder Killian had gotten creative with the profanity. If Trey was really given a body-cavity search and an orange jumpsuit, the press would declare a very messy field day for the Stones.

But the rage of Killian's declaration hadn't distracted me from the wistful look in his eyes when he'd mentioned Lance. There was something deeper there, much deeper—a something we needed to touch on at another time, when I wasn't struggling to organize the thousand thoughts in my brain.

"Let's not get too far ahead of this thing," I stated. "There's a lot going on in the news right now—and if we're lucky, the fascination factor for Trey has fizzled to closing tidbits instead of opening teasers." I reached for his hand again. "Can I get you a bottle of water before we start?" I nodded toward the wine. "Maybe something stronger?"

Killian grunted. "A hemlock martini?"

I rolled my eyes before rising and grabbing two waters from the small refrigerator. I had to face that we might be getting on an airplane after the call, cutting our trip to an ugly end. Putting our life on hold—because of another selfish stunt from Trey. As the minutes passed, I felt less and less charitable about the idea of helping him out of another PR bind. How the hell did Killian find it in his heart to save the douche over and over again?

"Don't you get tired of it?" After he took his own turn to stare in confusion, I clarified, "Of him? Of saving someone who clearly is his own worst enemy? If I didn't know better, Kil, I'd almost think he was blackmailing you."

His eyes flashed dark heat. "Don't be ridiculous," he snapped. His voice surpassed challenging, going straight for an acid of anger.

"Excuse me?" I managed to return.

"Don't say things like that, damn it—not when you have no fucking idea what you're talking about."

"Whoa." I recoiled. "Hold on, Chicago. I'm the one from the land of the nutty ones, remember?"

"Sorry." He tried to make the words count, but they were just a fraction above lip service. "Crazy just took a giant shit on our parade."

"I realize that. But I'm just trying to make things better. Trey may be driving you to an early grave, though doing it by blackmail seems harsh even for him. Let's just get this ordeal over with and see about salvaging the rest of the day...if we can."

"I love you." Damn. From menacing CEO to lost boy in the blink of an eye. I'd be concerned if he still didn't look like such a hunk about it. "I love you so much, Miss Montgomery."

"Don't I know it." I motioned toward my screen with my chin, clipping my headset on. "Okay. The line's ringing."

He winked over his screen, making my heart bounce against my tummy like a quarter on a trampoline. All was forgiven. Life was too short to get upset over each and every thing. But inside, I still reeled—more than a little. His anger had been brutal. Though likely the fallout from his tension, I still hoped to God he didn't plan on unleashing it again anytime soon. And the look that accompanied it? I wasn't even going to go there. Not now. Not ever again.

"Mr. Stone?"

I smiled when seeing Britta's face on the screen. "He's here, and so am I, Britta."

"Claire." The instant enthusiasm in her voice warmed my heart.

"How are you?"

"How are you? Is Europe wonderful? And romantic? Are you having fun?"

I exchanged a meaningful glance with Kil. He slid a finger to his temple, regarding me with eyes that had gone as dark as the moisture in his hair. "Oh, yes. Lots and lots of fun," he inserted with growly, sexy emphasis.

Britta made a choking sound. "Well, I didn't want to enjoy that coffee anyway."

I gasped. "Did you spill?"

"Near miss. Thank goodness, because I'm wearing that new cardigan today."

"The pale-blue one we looked at before I left?" I grinned as Killian rolled his eyes. They sparkled with alluring light now, conveying how pleased he was that Britta approved of his choice of mates. "That brings out your eyes so well," I added.

She smiled sheepishly before getting back to her task. "Why don't I connect you to the call now?"

"Thanks, Britta," Killian said.

He finished that with another wink—this one more sensual than the first. I reached for his hand. It was funny that Britta spoke of connection...when the only bond that truly mattered to me belonged to the man with his fingers meshed to mine.

All too soon, our moment was over. The line came alive with the sounds of a busy conference room, Killian instinctively pulled his hand back, sat taller in his chair, and cleared his throat to signal he was calling our meeting to order.

"Thanks for being on the call, everyone. I'll keep this as brief as possible, as Miss Montgomery and I are still hopeful of salvaging our holiday, despite my brother's newest escapade. For the record, I'm disgusted that Trey's taken this path once more, infringing on Stone Global's reputation as well as everyone's personal time."

"Well, you know what they say. Our time is your time, Mr. Stone."

My stress quotient officially leapt to Killian's level. Though he almost snickered out loud at Margaux's sneering tone, every inch of my stomach clenched.

"I appreciate the support, Margaux," he responded, "because I believe managing this crisis will require the ingenuity and expertise of us all." His conclusion was cut with dark sarcasm. "Everyone strap yourselves back in and hold on for another PR blitz centered around the one and only Trey Stone."

"Have no worries. This is what we do, Mr. Stone." Andrea's voice rang out, clear and confident. "I certainly hope you two lovebirds are having as much fun as Mr. Montgomery and I did while we were in Europe on our honeymoon a few months ago."

Killian slanted a quick smirk. "I can definitively state that fun is being had by all."

I flung one of the hotel's pens at him.

"Outstanding," Andrea submitted. "You can be most confident we can handle this from here, and you needn't cut your vacation short. As we speak, I believe Mason is working another one of his magical tricks."

Killian leaned forward. "Oh?"

"We believe Trey won't even remember the color of the paint inside the holding cell, he will have been there for such a short time. And, Claire darling, you just keep enjoying yourself. We're bearing up. We have a few interns who can handle the demographics until you get back, and as stated, we probably will have this wrapped up in a nice little package and put away and long forgotten by then." There was a pause and a rustle. I could practically see the woman straightening and smoothing her skirt, two moves short of a full-on preen. "You kids run along, have fun, and let us handle the hard stuff, okay?"

All the butterflies Kil had been sending to my stomach withered, died, and plummeted into a moldy heap at its pit. Even then, my mouth dropped open in disbelief. Killian only had to glance at me once before settling to his elbows and taking back the reins on the exchange.

"Your confidence is appreciated, Andrea, as always." Andrea. Not Mrs. Montgomery. I wanted to hug him. He knew the little ways to soothe me.

Like nails on my personal chalkboard, Margaux crooned, "That is why we get paid the big dollars."

"Let's check back in, say, in four hours?" Killian spoke as if Margaux hadn't. "I'd like to see a detailed preliminary strategy report at that time."

"Of course," Andrea replied. Tension trickled under her voice. Margaux had colored way outside the lines, and Mommy Dearest was well aware of it.

"Good." Killian returned to being cool, crisp, and utterly jumpable—especially because the bathrobe didn't seem fond of properly containing his rippled body. I certainly wasn't complaining. "Prepare all the usuals," he directed further. "You understand what I expect to see at this stage. You can email me directly, Andrea. I don't need the whole team involved in that communication. Does anyone have any other concerns at this point in time?"

Disjointed murmurings of "No, Mr. Stone" filtered over the line. I smiled a little, picking out Michael's, Talia's, and Chad's voices. Even in their subdued states, I could tell they all wavered between cringing and laughing at Margaux and Andrea. Their dilemma wasn't helped when Margaux leaned in to insert her last chiming dig.

"Mother's right. You two run along and have fun while we work out this mess for you. You can count on us to handle everything...like we always do."

Andrea quickly took over, covering for Margaux's insolence by chatting up Killian about the best places for gelato near the Coliseum, but we could still hear Margaux in the background. "Well, let's go, little people. Some of us have to work around here. We aren't all sleeping with the client."

"Mr. Stone." Andrea sounded terser than I'd ever heard her. Oh, forget that—she was pissed, earning her at least one tiny cookie in my commiseration jar. "Don't you spend another thought on this. The report will be in your mail in four hours, though I'm cautiously optimistic we can handle this one faster than that. There's a lot going on in the news cycle right now. We'll just have to see who bites when the news hits. No matter what, we will do our best to minimize the damage. You can count on us."

"I'm quite sure I can," Killian answered over steepled fingers.

"I'll be in touch soon."

I closed the conference-call software on my screen and tore the headset from my ears. Before it skidded across the desk, I was on my feet.

"Claire—"

I whirled on Kil, fully aware I looked like a petulant thirteen-year-old back-daggered by her campus nemesis. "I hate her."

"I know."

"It's not mature. It's not nice. And I don't care. I hate her with every fiber of my being." Lovely. Juuuust lovely. Tears burned my eyes and welled over. They were the worst damn kind too. Angry tears, the big, fat kind that branded skin as they rolled down, and making me more disgusted for crying them in the first place—especially because she didn't deserve them.

So I cried more.

I turned toward the window, looking out on the sunset over the centuries-old city, congratulating the dark-red sky for perfectly matching my spirit. Before I knew it, Killian wrapped his big strong arms around me from behind and then followed the embrace with the warm nearness of his body—and simply remained like that. Standing there with his lips pressed into my hair, not saying anything dumb like "She didn't mean what she said" or "Don't let her get to you." Why? Because he was the best man on the planet and just knew me. He simply knew that I needed to have my moment and move on.

After a few minutes, I took a deep breath and turned into his chest for a proper hug. When I had the courage to look up into those bottomless black eyes of his, he smiled.

"Better?"

"Yes, but you know that."

His eyes narrowed, twinging with his secret, strange sadness. "I don't have all the answers all the time."

"You did now. And handled her perfectly." I popped on

tiptoe and kissed his strong-as-Zeus nose. "Thank you."

"Well, she is a righteous bitch. There is no denying it. It'll be fucking refreshing when she moves on to a new conquest."

I cocked my head. "Maybe you could set her up with Trey?" We both laughed as I stepped away and headed into the dressing room. Suddenly I was starving. "I think we need pasta and sex, and maybe not in that order."

"I like the way you're thinking, San Diego, but I need to make one more phone call before we head out." He swept up his phone in a decisive motion. "I'm pulling the trigger. Having Trey removed from the Board of Directors of Stone Global as soon as possible. I think with all of these legal proceedings it will be just cause, but I need to have Mason advise me of the bylaws and then the process."

I paused in the archway separating the two parts of the suite. Blinked at him slowly. "Wow."

"It's not a sudden decision, fairy." He spoke it softly into the quiet pause I'd left—and I thoroughly believed him. Somewhere in my gut, I knew Kil had been wrestling with this move for months, perhaps going to battle with some of his board members over it. There was that secret logic at work again. Killian had given Trey more second chances than every miscreant playboy in Hollywood and New York combined, though it seemed only God knew why.

"I know," I finally replied.

He jerked out a nod. "But it also has to be done exactly right. Trey has spent his life taking advantage of loopholes, so he'll find a way to worm back in if he can. It's time to play some tough ball with the dickhead."

As he issued those decisive finishing words, I watched him leave a quick voicemail for Mason, explaining he was sending over an urgent email. Before he was done with the voicemail, he started tapping out the written version of his intent.

During those minutes, a strange combination of awe and discomfort dug at me. He looked so passionate about every stab at the keyboard...while typing the words that would oust his own brother from the company their father had toiled to build up. It made me squirm, wrapping my arms around the new twists in the center of my belly. This ruthless side of Killian— the man I loved, who had just held me so patiently in his arms, nurturing me—was, to be equally brutal, disturbing. I knew all about business is business, but it was such a contradiction to every other side of him, even the boardroom commander from the SGC offices, that I was temporarily stunned.

When I found my voice again, I murmured, "Maybe...this isn't the time or place to go to extremes."

He didn't break a second of pace on the typing. "You think I want this to be the time or place? He's forced my hand. End of story."

I shifted from one foot to the other. "I'm just having trouble understanding. You've had the patience of Job about all this, but all of a sudden—"

"Claire." He actually stopped. Swung around to impale my gaze with his. "You don't know what you're talking about. There are some things you should just stay out of and let me handle, okay?"

Pain stabbed my stomach again, just as it had during the conference call with the team. "Wow, baby. That's a first. I could've closed my eyes and sworn Margaux had just morphed into a man. Thanks for the wholly horrific trip into weird."

I turned on my heel and went back in the dressing room. This time, I closed the door and locked it. The hot, heavy, terrible tears rolled out again—only now, I endured them on the floor, in the middle of a ridiculously large closet, in a hotel room in Rome.

Alone.

CHAPTER FOUR

Killian

Search for the upside.

It was one of my mother's favorite things to say to me when I turned, in her words, into moody Killian. Usually, the term earned her nothing more than a pout and stomp off toward my room in response.

This time, the label probably fit.

Damn it.

Which meant that finding the upside wasn't an option. It was a necessity. My gut torqued on the grim acceptance. I had to make things right with Claire again...somehow. Things in Rome had gone from cracked to crumbling inside an hour, a situation I could only partially blame on the disaster known as my brother. But Trey had been using his leverage on me for years as the diving board into his lake of licentiousness. Wasn't I used to his fuckery by now? Why did it grate on me so deeply this time?

The answer came as easily as a gaze across our suite at the Hôtel Fouquet—and the woman standing out on the terrace, watching twilight take over the avenues converging on the Eiffel Tower. She was dressed for our Seine dinner cruise in a wine-colored dress with a fitted bodice over a sparkled belt and a skirt of layered flowing fabric that had a graceful life of its own with every move she made. Though the skirt ended just below the knee, it might as well have been a mini for all the ideas it gave me. Or maybe those came from simply gazing at her from behind, my vision feasting on the swan's swoop of her neck and the perfect angles of her face, now in profile to me. I clenched my fists, fighting the urge to join her out there—but if I did, we'd never make it out of the door in time to board the boat. Within five minutes, her neck would be laid waste beneath my lips as her body undulated on the bed, spreading at my command. And she'd love every second. I'd make damn sure of that.

Anything not to lose her.

A fact Trey had clearly—and gleefully—figured out.

Every new threat he made to expose me was as good as the bastard grabbing my head and submersing it in an icy vat of fear. He knew it with wicked clarity and was using it to fly as close to the edge of the envelope as possible. I should have known the clown would abandon his new commitment to responsibility as soon as a better opportunity came up—like getting away with everything just short of murder and knowing I wouldn't do a damn thing about it.

To a point.

I didn't give a shit if Trey drowned in his own muck, but he sure as hell wouldn't take SGC into the mire with him. The Stone name, and all it meant to me in its newest sense, sealed the determination behind my vow. I had no doubt the board would vote behind me in the matter.

So why the hell did I still feel so unsettled?

"Pull yourself together, fucker." I muttered it while securing my tie and slipping into my suit jacket. The dictate was well-founded. Life was better than it had ever been. I was in Paris with the woman of my dreams, who heard my rustling and glanced over her shoulder with the most gorgeous smile hinting at her lips. While the ugliness of what had happened in Rome still marked both of us, the allure of making happier memories in Paris was difficult to resist.

"Well," she murmured, walking back inside on strappy silver heels that only encouraged the erotic fantasies the dress had started, "don't you clean up well?"

"Complete illusion," I returned. "Because there's not a damn clean thing about what I want to do to you when I see you in that dress."

She slid a finger down the middle of my tie. "Mr. Stone... flattery will get you everywhere."

She tangled the fingers of her other hand around my nape, filtering them into my hair to pull me down for a kiss. It was the most time she'd allowed me to spend on her mouth since our fight in Rome, and I wasn't about to waste the opportunity. When she let me slip my tongue between her lips, I groaned with her sweet taste, an ambrosia of strawberries and champagne.

Was this possibly the beginning of her forgiveness? Fuck, I prayed so.

After we dragged apart, I kept my lips hovering less than inch over hers in order to return her words with a husky whisper. "I sure hope so, Miss Montgomery. Absolutely... everywhere."

★ ★ ★ ★

A fine mist had fallen over the city during the course of the cruise. Claire gazed past the boat's front window to where the spotlights on Notre Dame blended with the condensation, turning the night into a sparkling palette of amber and silver.

"It's so beautiful." Her stare didn't depart from the soaring towers and flying buttresses of the city's icon, but I didn't veer my gaze from her. In fascination—and disconcertment—I watched her lips linger on the rim of her wineglass. They remained somber even after she'd savored and swallowed, leading me to reach for her fingers as she lowered the glass. Gently, I curled my fingers under hers. She'd painted her nails lavender, a lighter shade than usual for her...and a contrast to the slashes of dark bronze in her eyes.

Was that a good thing or a bad thing?

"Yes," I responded to her comment. "It's breathtaking."

That coaxed some movement from at least the edges of her lips. "You're not even looking."

"Of course I am." I wrapped my whole hand around hers. "At the only thing that matters." Even that didn't pull her smile to her eyes, so I pressed, "Though doing so isn't answering a very important question I have."

"What question would that be?"

"Why are you so sad?"

She turned that dark-umber gaze to me briefly before tilting her head back toward the heights of the cathedral. "I was just imagining a Quasimodo lingering up there."

"The pissed-off and murderous version or the about-to-jump-off-the-bell-tower version?"

Even the bait of my sarcasm didn't brighten her. "Maybe a bit of both," she answered, her voice edged in wistfulness.

Her sympathy for the fictional bell ringer moved me. But admitting it was strangely disturbing, especially when it funneled into my next words. "Which version do *you* like better?"

I didn't want to cop to my desperation at knowing her answer. Or was it the answer that mattered at all, when I'd challenged her to confront the idea of a man having duality like that in the first place?

"Neither," she finally replied. "Because neither was truly him. Quasimodo's anger and loneliness were how the world saw him—and, subsequently, how he saw himself. Esméralda's kindness, her ability to look beyond his face, opened up his vision of himself. With her, he was no longer a deformed ogre. He became a prince."

"I know the feeling."

I didn't need to say more. In her parted lips and softened gaze, I saw her understanding—at least to the level she could. The woman would never completely know what she'd done, how fully she'd pulled me from my own lonely bell tower and into the light of her love, but I yearned to spend forever trying to tell her. To show her my gratitude each and every day of our lives...

And this was the moment to begin that journey.

I reached for the ring box in my pocket.

But I was stopped by her hand, reaching and gripping me tight. Her face tensed in exactly the same way.

Hell. No.

"Killian—"

I exhaled hard. "*What?*"

She squeezed my fingers tighter. "Come on. *I love you.* This isn't the Spanish Inquisition."

"No." I drawled it with the cheer of a caretaker. "It's the new and improved French version."

Tension radiated through both sides of her jaw. "Don't

you see that—?"

"This is completely unnecessary?"

Did I spit it as a smokescreen? Every syllable. But the woman's tenacity, one of the things most alluring about her from the moment we'd met, seemed to be turning against me more and more lately.

Or maybe you've just turned into a paranoid ass who snaps at her for the simplest questions. Yeah, maybe that's it.

The fucking rub? I couldn't seem turn the shit off. Yes, me. Killian Stone. The Enigma of the Magnificent Mile, famous for my ability to focus on a goal with no emotions except those that brought the business to the table and the opposition to their knees. Fate surely laughed now, stabbing its middle finger at me for actually thinking I could enjoy my life for once.

"Really?" she flung at my bark. "So you think that it's unnecessary to be real and open and honest with each other, even if that means going to the top of the bell tower and sharing the ugly stuff?" She didn't relent on her grip. "Killian, why won't you just let me—?"

"What?" It snarled out of me, and I was actually glad—because I was desperate. Better that she see the rage instead of the terror. Anything but the terror. "Let you do what, Claire? Be my Esméralda now? Save my ass from the dark ogre inside?" Nothing like a shit ton of truth to lend some backbone to a derisive chew-out—or the impressive lurch to one's feet after it. "Haven't you gotten it yet? Things don't work that way. Not with me."

Her gaze, as wet and glowing as the wine in her glass, threatened to unravel me with its intensity. "Of course," she rasped. "How could I have forgotten?" A mirthless laugh spilled from her wobbling lips. "It's much easier up in the tower, isn't it? When you sit there, all the presents get to come from you. All the surprises get to be yours. All the goodies get to rain down from you. 'Wow, look,' everyone in the kingdom says. 'What a beautiful, benevolent king. We adore him.' And it's all fine and good, right—until somebody tries to come share the place with you? God forbid anyone tries to crack those ramparts...when it's the one thing you need the most."

I took another step back. "I think, by this point in my life, I'm fully aware of my needs, Miss Montgomery."

She reacted like I'd speared her with daggers of ice. Not a surprise, since I'd wielded them as such—and abhorred myself for it. But in the end, my purpose had been accomplished. From the way Claire folded her napkin, laid it across her half-eaten lobster tail, and averted her gaze back out of the window, I knew our conversation had sped to its bitter end.

Beyond surface courtesies, we didn't say anything else to each other during the rest of the cruise. The limousine ride back to the hotel was an equal balancing act between cordial and miserable, ended when we pulled up in front of the hotel and Claire exited the car, slammed the door, and then walked inside without looking back.

Congratulations, asshole. You're probably the first man in history to murder the romance of a Seine dinner cruise.

I wore the honor like a disgruntled teenager, stomping into the suite in her wake and silently peeling off my jacket. Claire unhooked her shoes and then walked barefoot out onto the terrace—again without looking at me.

I followed, at least until reaching the doorway. Damn. Even now, with tension clouding things between us, the sight of her yanked my cock to attention. The breeze tossed the silky hem of her dress and the burnished ends of her hair, tempting me to reach out and play with both.

She turned her head to peer down the street as the hourly light show on the Eiffel Tower started. In her eyes, I watched the light and dark dance together, fascinated by how her beauty accommodated both. It was a reflection of her soul's strength and her heart's capacity. Was I underestimating her? Should I just bring her in, sit her down, and tell her?

Tell her what? That the man she fell in love with isn't who he says he is at all? That despite what the records say, he's not really a Stone and was only turned into one because of the family's archaic ideals about an heir to the dynasty? That all he is, is a stud horse with a glorified saddle?

I could practically write the script for the rest of that scene now. Oh, she'd smile in all the right ways, tell me that it just didn't matter, spew the politically correct nonsense—but for how long? How many weeks, even months would it take for the masquerade to eat at her spirit, so dedicated to authenticity that even the damn paparazzi didn't know what to do with her sometimes? How long would it take for me to hate the compromise I'd be forcing on her? This wasn't like requesting she sleep on a different side of the bed or change her brand of coffee creamer. This was asking her to bend her moral compass and help in the perpetuation of a lie in the name of the Stone empire.

A church clock somewhere in the streets below gonged out the arrival of midnight. At the same time, the wind kicked up, making her shiver a little.

"Come inside," I bade softly. "You're going to catch a chill, fairy."

I meant every drop of the protectiveness in my tone. I hated the thought of her getting sick. I'd caught a bad cold after Christmas, and she'd stayed for an extra couple of days in Chicago to nurse the shit out of me—then had gone home and promptly come down with it herself. I'd flown out to her place to repeat the treatment in reverse.

"I think, by this point, I'm fully aware of what my health can withstand, Mr. Stone."

I had that one coming.

And accepted the blow in silence.

With equal quiet, I walked out and draped my jacket over her shoulders. Though she still had her pashmina wrapped in place, the long scarf was a thin thing designed for fashion instead of warmth, and it took all of two seconds for her to wriggle a little deeper into my covering. A fast glance of her gratitude, though clearly given reluctantly, followed. I wasn't about to push for more. Again not saying anything, I leaned against the rail and stared out over the famous city.

Down the avenue, glittering lights still engulfed the Eiffel. The show would only last for a few more minutes, the last one for the night. The lights of the city complemented the sight, a mix of modern and classic illumination that served up a magical representation of the city's well-deserved nickname.

I meshed my fingers together. It was the only way to avoid reaching out to haul her into my arms. We should have been savoring this sight entwined around each other, not standing like strangers on a wet terrace, as good as miles away from each other.

"Kil...I'm not the enemy."

"I know."

"No. I'm not sure you do."

"Professes the person who's not my enemy."

I rose fully and turned, deliberate about the challenge

of it. I wasn't sure what to expect from her, though her silent amber gaze wasn't a shock. But the fingers she raised to my face, silently running along my jawline as the magic of that stare intensified? *One perfect shock, coming right up.*

My own hand lifted, as if drawn by the magnetic field of hers. When our fingers meshed, my whole body felt like the tower up the street, a thousand blinking strobes. Did she know what she did to me? Could she feel this too, how she ignited even the darkest parts of me? Did she see how my life had lights before but possessed *light* now—and how terrified I was of the dark currently?

Decision made. I wasn't going to lose her. If that meant some unconventional warfare, then so be it.

"Do you remember, after we first met, when you asked me to let go?" she finally whispered. "You begged me—hell, ordered me—to trust you enough to stop running. When I finally listened, you made me the happiest woman in the world."

I scowled. She was moving toward a point, and I was fairly certain I wouldn't enjoy it. But her touch and her voice were a goddamn hypnosis, turning me into her fool whether I liked it or not. "What does that have to do with—?"

"I stopped running, Killian. Now you have to stop hiding."

I managed to glower harder. "Baby, *why* do you keep thinking that I'm—?"

"I've overheard things, all right?" She rushed on, reacting to my raised eyebrows. "*Not* intentionally. But Trey hasn't been the most subtle bastard about any of this. He's taunting you like a wild dog off his leash and peeing all over the furniture while he's at it." She let her hands slip down to my shoulders. "It's because he's confident you're not going to yank back the restraint. Why?"

Of all the women in the world to fall in love with, I had to pick one with perceptive powers that bordered on supernatural.

"Fuck," I muttered.

"Tell me," she entreated.

"*Fuck.*"

"Killian. Damn it!"

I jerked away and wasn't gentle about it. My motions were lurching testaments to the shit that churned in my gut before exploding out to the ends of my limbs. If this were a movie, it'd be the part where the murderer watched his alibi unraveling with all the evidence pointing to him.

No. *No.*

This isn't going down like that.

I wheeled around and stalked back inside, hearing the frantic pace of Claire's pursuit, first on the terrace and then the carpet, kept up from behind. I halted her by spinning back around with one arm extended like some ridiculous sorcerer. Lame as the comparison was, I got the point across. She froze in place, only her chest moving, pulling in desperate breaths.

"Damn it." It snarled from me, slow and seething. "I am Killian. Fucking. Stone!"

For half a second, her mouth opened. A little. Didn't mean anything. I'd seen the woman preface some fireballs of rage with less preparation. I should've known she wasn't going to make this easy. Should've realized that with the soft squirm of her shoulders and the pleading moisture in her eyes, she'd unravel me worse than any raging comeback.

"And I'm the woman who desperately loves him."

I grunted. Dropped my arm as my hand twisted into a fist—and wondered why it hadn't morphed into the paw of an ogre. "Then do that," I finally flung. "Love me, Claire. Stop trying to break me!"

Her mouth fell open again. A lot wider this time. "*Break* you? Is...is that what you really think I'm trying to do here?"

I firmed my jaw. "You want the one-word yes or the extended essay answer?"

Her own hands flew to her hips. "You know what? Screw you. This isn't some game show, Killian. I'm not going for the win and the designer dining room set for a prize just because I crack you open in some way."

"Damn good to know." I didn't relent my gaze. "Because you're well past the crack."

She actually stepped back. The *good* news about her insightfulness? It had also allowed her to see hundreds of places in my life where no other person, let alone a *woman*, had been before. With that recognition softening her features, she replied, "I know. And I'm grateful, Kil...but—"

"But it isn't enough." The pain of my own words backlashed on me. "Is it?" I hated the rough grate that my voice turned into. "When will it be enough, Claire? Or will it ever be?"

"Stop it. You're making me the enemy again."

"Right. Of course I am." Bitterness lent me new strength. There was enough left over to spread my arms across the back of the couch, one of my favorite power stances. Over-the-top analogy? The longer this dragged out, the more I thought not. Was this a lovers' tiff anymore—or a battle of control? The thought of the latter should have encouraged me. I never lost such skirmishes. Had fate picked tonight to pop my cherry on that too?

"I'm not fighting against you, Kil! I'm fighting *for* us."

"And I'm not?"

"I didn't say—"

"So your holy war is fine, but mine isn't?"

"If we're on the same side, it shouldn't matter." She busted past my sorcerer's lock, approaching the couch with her elbows angled back, that sexy skirt swirling and anguish flashing in her eyes. "I've given you everything I am. Every corner of my thoughts, every secret of my heart, every drop of my love. I will follow you into any damn battle, Killian. I will defend you against any enemy that life hurls at you." Her arms flung out, fingers spread and upturned. "I. Am. Yours!"

It wasn't just her offering. It was her plea. I knew it, saw it, heard it...but was paralyzed by it. I'd been dumped into an emotional wilderness to which I'd never journeyed before, without a fucking compass. Fear was a monster in my blood and desperation a blaze in my gut. Fear was *not* part of Killian Stone's vernacular. Desperation sure as hell wasn't. They had never been a choice in the survival guide from the first day I'd walked through Keystone Manor's front door. Mentally, I tore them to shreds now.

"You don't think I know that?" I finally got out. "And damn it, I'm yours too—"

"Are you?" Her head fell to one side. Her lips trembled again. "*Are you?*"

I couldn't conquer the fear this time. It was a damn demon, trailing fire from its claws as it dominated my guts, my chest, my limbs. Survival instinct took over. *Attack or be decimated.* And losing was not a damn option.

"What the hell do you want from me, Claire? *What?* My fucking soul?"

She straightened her head. During the trip, a glare ignited every inch of her face. "Let's at least start with the honesty of it,

Kil. How about that for once?"

More of my gut tore apart. The sound of my name on her lips, spat like a necessity instead of whispered in adoration...it raged my instincts into a giant wildfire, fed by kindling of a raw, defensive rage.

"Fine. You want honesty?" I grabbed my jacket. Dug into the pocket for the velvet box I'd been hauling across Europe with us. A dozen times, I'd almost dropped to my knee with it. No kneeling now. With my glower on her, unblinking and unrelenting, I let the thing tumble from my fingers to where it landed, crazily enough, upright on the cushion between us. "How's that for fucking honesty?"

Her lips parted. Her stare didn't leave the box. "Wh-What...is that?"

"I want to marry you. That's what that is. Honest enough? Real enough? Is *that* what you wanted, Miss Montgomery?"

Moments in life sometimes came with their own presets of expectation. I'd learned long ago not to rely on those damn buttons—or at least thought I had. The presets were definitely blown to shit, and reality's revision was a disaster of epic proportion. After Claire backed away from the couch like I'd tossed a snake down instead of a custom velvet box from Harry Winston, her chest vibrated on harsh breaths. I moved back myself, possibly wondering if I should've simply killed a guy on the terrace. The stare she finally lifted at me, glistening with pain and tears, was another stab of confirmation of that.

"Really?" she shouted. "That's the way you want to do this? That's the way you *did*?"

Dinner was nothing but bile in my stomach. How had everything gone from the bliss we'd known in Italy to this fucking fiasco?

Pretty easily, asshole...when you refuse to be completely real with the woman you love.

I was on the brink of spearing a mental middle finger at the voice when my cell rang.

The Celtic-sounding chime identified the caller as Britta. Back home, it was still late afternoon—but it was Sunday. A number of conclusions came to mind as explanation. None of them were good and all of them led back to one name.

Trey.

"What the hell has he done now?" I spat into the device. When I could hear Britta's labored sigh but nothing else, I insisted, "Goddamnit, Britta, out with it!"

"Killian."

Her soft utterance made me sink onto the couch's arm. It wasn't uncommon for her to use my first name but never in this somber, careful tone.

"What?" It spilled from the new pit of dread in my gut.

"You need to come home. Now."

"Why?"

"Keystone Manor's on fire."

CHAPTER FIVE

Claire

Keystone's burning.

The words played in my head on a continuous loop. Every time they hit my frontal lobe, a new meaning settled in with them, ranging from the surreal to the stunned.

I held Killian's hand as we sat facing forward on the SGC jet, strapped in like ordinary passengers on a plane heading home from any other vacation. But as much as I wished it so, we weren't. Though we flew high over the clouds, I had a feeling the bigger storm was only beginning.

Every time I tried to relax about the premonition, all I had to do was look at Kil for a fresh shot of stress. He fixed his gaze everywhere and nowhere, his eyes glazed, his mouth a taut line. I was sure I'd be able to look out in the sky and find his awareness...and my gut clenched while I wondered if I'd ever connect with him again.

So I held on tighter. Meshed my fingers with his and gripped with every emotion I had, forcing myself to let it be enough for now. Afraid to let go. Half-sure that if I did, I wouldn't be able to find him again.

I hated this feeling. Really, truly hated it.

We'd packed our bags with the help of the staff at the Fouquet, assured that if we'd left anything behind—and I was certain we had—they would send it to us in Chicago. I'd been in robot mode ever since, simply going through the motions but more concerned about Killian than ever before.

"Keystone's on fire."

He mumbled the words for the hundredth time, pushing them to the brink of a question even as the proof glared at him from the news feed on his smart pad. The images were surreal. The beautiful manor I'd been to so many times, enjoying brunch on the veranda and even Thanksgiving in the grand dining room...now a scorched ruin. The kitchen wing was completely gone too, though it looked like they'd saved some of the outer buildings and the pool house.

"Keystone."

His voice shook now, nearly like a child seeking comfort. His fingers twined tighter between mine.

"Killian?"

He swung his head but didn't say a word. His eyes were red and weary but no longer distant. He searched my face incessantly, seeking...what? Forgiveness? Comfort? He had both from me already, and I desperately tried to communicate that in my stare. My heart was breaking for him. He seemed scared and lost, and no matter what I said to reassure him, I knew I wasn't reaching him.

Maybe going for the innocuous was best. "How long do you think the trip back will take us?"

He shrugged, still not saying a word.

Okay. Strike innocuous.

With a decisive sigh, I pulled the armrest up between us up and patted my lap. He just stared at me, still clearly confused. I tugged on his shoulder, guiding his head down into my lap. "Come here, Mr. Stone."

Though the positioning was awkward, he unclicked his seat belt and shifted his weight to the side in order to lie more fully against me. I was shocked but heartened by his compliance, though I knew if I suggested we lie down, he would have said no. I gladly took this opportunity for the gift it was, stroking my fingers through his thick, dark hair, letting my nails scratch his scalp. The second my fingers made contact, his eyes grew heavy as midnight and then drifted shut. He loved this more than anything when he couldn't relax—and now more than ever, it helped me too.

After a few wordless minutes, his breathing finally evened out. His neck relaxed and his head lolled, heavy in my lap. I knew he was sleeping when he began to twitch every now and then, probably having dreams of what we were returning to. We hadn't been able to get clear answers about exactly what had happened at Keystone, but the pictures definitely showed the worst of the damage around the kitchen and staff quarters. I prayed, once again, that the staff Kil had so much affection for had all gotten out safely. Though I hadn't heard him asking Britta about any of them, I knew some of the stress he carried was directly related to their welfare. Sometimes, he could be an obstinate ass—but he was always an ass who cared about the entire world.

The flight attendant came by, bearing a thick navy-blue blanket for him. After I helped her cover Killian with it, she returned with a glass of chardonnay, placing it within reach for me. I mouthed a silent *thank you,* thinking that sometimes it was damn nice to be surrounded by staff who knew one's habits and likes, before reaching for the glass and taking a huge gulp. *Ohhh, yes.* Wine beneath one hand, my man beneath the other. For the moment—and a lot more after that—I had everything

I needed.

I let my head flop back, seizing the chance for some reflection. The trip really hadn't gone the way either of us had planned—a thought that immediately tempted me to laugh. *Understatement of the year, anyone?* Hell...that disaster of a marriage proposal. My mirth dissolved as I fought to banish that moment from memory, while accepting it would be burned there for the rest of my life. And yes...I had seen the scorch marks in the back of Killian's gaze too. I wasn't sure how we were going to put the pieces back together after all of it—and that part scared me to death.

I tilted my head to gaze down at his face, a rare sight in its utter peace. He captivated my heart with this glimpse into how he must have looked as a boy. Perfect. Beautiful.

My heart couldn't beat without him.

As awful as things had been in Paris, I needed him in order to exist. It remained the truth of my being. But we had some major renovations to make, and I wasn't convinced we had the equipment in our toolbox to make it happen. We'd both been out of our comfort zones. *Way* out. I'd witnessed parts of him that hadn't been comfortable to take in, adding significant tears to my European travel journal.

Or was *I* the lost one? Were all relationships like this?

I missed home. I missed the gang—even Chad's one-liners—and I couldn't think about Dad without tearing up. And I didn't just miss Talia. I needed her. A trip to Espresso Mio and a nice long girl talk were in order to get some solid advice about what was going on, despite the caution I always had to take due to the complicated state of being with a man like Killian.

Normal itself was no longer part of my world. Not in a

relationship with someone like Killian Stone.

But I desperately needed normal. I couldn't help but think my mind was swiftly drowning, and I needed a life preserver thrown out—soon.

An invisible force tugged my head up. When I raised my gaze, it was met by a pair of stunning onyx eyes.

For a blissful instant, all was normal again.

"Hey." His voice was deep and husky from sleep.

"Hey, you." I smiled because he still took my breath away. Oh, yeah. Definitely...still.

"How long was I out?" His lashes rested on his cheeks as he closed his eyes, looking like little fans.

"Long enough for my heart to stop a few times at how gorgeous you are. Then to do something about it by drooling all over you. Then there was the cleanup..."

A smile crept across his lips. "You're good for my ego, Miss Montgomery."

I leaned closer and kissed his proud forehead. "I'm good for a lot of your things, Mr. Stone."

He smiled wider but kept his eyes closed. "Indeed you are."

I couldn't resist scraping my fingers through his hair again. "Do you want to rest longer? I don't mind at all."

He shifted. "I need to get back online. Emails haven't been checked. And maybe they have more news about the fire."

"Hmmm." I didn't hide my disappointment. "Back to reality."

"Afraid so." He stood and stretched and then extended a hand as I unclicked to do the same. But as I rose, I didn't stop. I pressed myself fully to him, stretching on my tiptoes to get a deep kiss in on his full lips.

"No," I whispered. "Not quite yet." I pulled back, waiting for his full attention. He gave it, though with a quizzical edge. That was okay. I had an explanation. "Killian...listen to me. We're going to get through all of this, all right?"

The curiosity hovered on his lips, and his eyes glittered at me with a smile. He gently brushed the hair from my forehead. "Yes, ma'am."

"Damn straight, yes, ma'am." I returned his gesture and pressed my fingers with deeper emphasis. "I love you so much. I can't live without you. That's all I know. So no matter what— we're going to get through this."

He wrapped me in the best Killian hug I'd felt in what seemed like weeks. Warm and perfect without being too tight, molding his body fully against mine but not in a sexual way. It was as if he silently proclaimed he would become a part of me if he could. And God, how I felt the same...and told him so with all my might.

When he finally pulled back, it was only by inches. His eyes were shadowed and hooded—and sensual. They immediately dropped to my lips as his own opened, blatant with hunger— and seduction.

So much for not sexual. Not that I was complaining.

He tugged me closer again. Slowly. Our hips locked, his erection fitting to the crux of my thighs. There was no way to miss his message now. His burgeoning length pushed at me, growing bigger by the second. "I need to get inside you, Claire."

"Yes." *Oh, yes.* We needed to connect on this level. Badly.

Without another word, he turned, keeping one of my hands locked in his. We walked toward the bedroom, reminding me of a time not so long ago when we'd walked down this hall for the first time. Just like then, my nerves zinged, my heart thrummed, and everything below my navel grew wet and tight with desire.

Before we even cleared the bulkhead, I started unbuttoning my blouse. Killian watched as he turned and walked backward into the small bedroom, eyes growing wider with each freed button. A smile teased my lips. He mirrored the look, turning him into a gorgeous, playful devil.

He sat on the edge of the bed and pulled me between his legs. "I'm going to watch you," he dictated in a low growl. "Bare yourself to me, fairy queen."

As his words curled smoke through my limbs, I tugged my shirt from my jeans and finished the buttons. The fabric slipped from my shoulders and fell to the floor.

"Fuck." Killian released a long breath. "So beautiful."

"Only because I'm looking at the man I adore."

One side of his mouth curled a little higher. Damn. Could the man get any hotter?

"Now the jeans," he commanded.

Ohhhh, yes. Much hotter. His eyes were as black as the sky outside. We left the drapes open. Why not? It was me, him, and the constellations at thirty-five thousand feet.

I slid my palms down my stomach to the button fly of my jeans. One by one, I flicked them open while watching Killian wet his bottom lip with a slow slide of his tongue. My body temperature rose. Higher. Higher.

I spread open the two flaps of denim. The top of my panties peeked out, purple lace with a little pearl in the center of the bow. Killian caught the sight, and his nostrils flared. He lifted his stare back up to mine in time to make my heart skip at his quirked brow and wicked grin.

"Hmmm. Matching. Nice." He reached up, gliding hands

over my heated flesh until forming them over my nipples, now jutting through the purple lace of my bra. I let my head drop back between my shoulder blades, reveling in the warmth and nearness of the man I so desperately loved. His big hands covered each of my aching breasts, cupping me tenderly, keeping me safe yet taking me closer to the edge of naughty.

As I inhaled, he moved me closer in order to replace his right hand with his mouth. He nipped through the purple lace and caught my erect nipple with his teeth, I let out a high sigh. Hell, yes...naughty. And forbidden. Something about this man and this plane did this to me. Scratch that. It was the man, period. He loved roaming his fingers over all my illicit parts even though we were both still dressed—and I loved letting him do it, to the fullest, hottest extent. The best thing of all? He knew it made me wetter, and he torqued every ounce of pleasure he could from the knowledge.

I needed to feel more of him. But when I reached forward to twist my fingers in his hair, he pushed my arms back down. "No. Not yet."

I gave him a dirty glare.

He flashed back a dirtier grin. Though he was well aware that I hated not being able to touch him, he also knew it ramped me beyond measure. Sure enough, my panties were soaked and the tang of my arousal threaded the air. It all made Killian smile even wider. The man knew every single one of my buttons. Damn him. Thank God for him.

"Kil," I begged, "please!"

He chuckled while moving to my other breast, leaving the first tingly and wet from his rough attention. "Damn. The way you say my name, fairy...I fucking love it." He stressed the point by teething me harder. "Beg me some more, sweetheart. Say it again. Say *all* of it this time."

His tone hardened with solid steel authority. My pulse sped from the impact of it, because I immediately knew what he demanded and gave it to him without a speck of doubt.

"Killian Stone," I moaned. "Ohhh, Killian Stone..."

"Yessssss."

"Please, Mr. Stone. Let me touch you now. *Please.*"

I gasped as he growled and then sank his teeth deeper into my sensitive tip. He only backed off after my cry escalated to an aroused scream.

"Mmmm. Somebody likes that." Instead of waiting for me to agree, he did it again.

"Oh, God! Killian!" I lifted my hands a second time, but he easily captured them once more. With a couple of effortless twists, he used the hold to swing me around and leverage me under him onto the bed. When I giggled, he silenced me with a deep, searing kiss that had me completely breathless by the time he tore away. My lungs pumped hard and heavy as he moved down my neck in a trail of licks and bites. He rolled his hips into the V of my body, promising pleasure just moments away.

I reached down to tug at my jeans, desperate to get this barrier out from between us. I needed him. *Everywhere.* This very moment. If he wasn't going to do it, I'd take matters into my own hands. But again he grabbed them, raising both above my head this time, holding them easily in one of his own.

"Pushing for the tie-downs, Miss Montgomery?" His eyes blazed, making it clear he'd turn the tease into a promise if I tempted harder to wrest his control from him. I didn't dare look away, almost certain I'd imagined it...hoping that I hadn't. While the idea of playing master-and-servant on a daily basis wasn't appealing, it wasn't tough to make the psychological jump that some control would do him good right now—and some surrender would work miracles for me.

"Please," I repeated. And ohhhh yes, did it feel nice on my lips. "I want to feel you so bad, Kil. Please. *Please*."

His chest rumbled with satisfaction before he answered. "You will, sweet girl. You will."

"But—"

"Ssshhh, baby. I want to savor every single moment of this. When we get back home, all hell is going to break loose. God fucking knows when I'll have you all to myself again."

I nodded in reluctant spurts. "I don't want to think about that."

"So give me this time. Let me love you." He laid a trail of kisses from my mouth, down my neck, and back up to my ear, right in the spot that drove me most crazy. "Just let me love you, Claire."

"I can't ever say no to you."

"Thank fuck."

I pulled him down, kissing him with all the passion and emotions that had been building for the last few weeks, dammed behind the tension of all the weird fights we'd had. And I kissed him with all the support I yearned to give for the hell we were certainly flying home to. And yes, I kissed him with the hope I still held for our future beyond that. I hoped and prayed that he felt it all and knew that the depths of my soul still belonged to him...that they always would.

When he finally lifted his head from our kiss, his eyes glowed more magically than the stars we flew through. Apparently, I had done my job.

"I love you." We whispered it at the same time. Our

mouths met again, and even more heat sparked and flared, only this time, the flames were kindled solely by this moment. Killian slanted his mouth to claim me deeper, sweeping his tongue over mine in blatant carnal need. I bucked a little, trying to wrench free from his grip, but that only hardened his resolve—along with a lot of other things. He tightened the prison on my wrists with one hand while sliding the other into my hair, tugging hard to angle my mouth for his stabbing, searing invasion.

He finally tore from me with a lusty hiss and whipped his shirt over his head in the space of two seconds, letting me take a long drink of a gaze at his magnificent chest and sculpted abdomen. I scooted back on the bed to shimmy out of my jeans while he stood up and dropped his. He prowled back between my legs, erotic hunger filling his panther-black eyes.

I sighed at the sight of him. Even a blind woman wouldn't miss his erection, huge, full, and proud, ready for the action promised by his gaze. He yanked at the purple lace of my panties, shoving them down my thighs and onto the floor in an unceremonious swoop. By the time his eyes rose back up, I'd taken care of pulling off the bra. My areolae puckered beneath his scorching stare, betraying how much I still needed him to command me, despite my arms' newfound freedom.

As always, the man made all my fantasies come true.

He lined himself up and slid home in one full, hot lunge. I gasped in ecstasy, wrapping my arms and legs around him. We were both ravenous for this, needing the connection and closeness, right here and now. Reality peeled away, part of the planet that was still thousands of miles below burned back by the light and fire of our love. I looped my ankles around each other atop his ass as he buried his face in my neck. We were entwined, skin to skin, heartbeat to heartbeat, two beings as one.

"Killian, I love you so much. I need you so much."

"I'm right here, baby girl."

"I know. I know. I just love you. I don't ever want to be without you."

He moved at a perfect pace, something between nice-n-easy and ridden-n-hard, sliding in and out, letting his cock almost leave me before surging back in. It was exquisite and glorious. Beautiful and loving. Exactly the way we needed to love each other now.

"As long as I have anything to do with it, you will never be without me. Now feel me, love. Just feel me." He slid into me again, rotating his hips when he was pressed in to the hilt, rubbing my clit with his pelvic bone, taunting me until my heels pummeled the base of his spine and my fingernails scored the muscles of his shoulders. He made love like a god, every time better than the last. I wasn't amazed to hear myself begging him again.

"Killian, please. Please! I can't...I can't—"

He hummed against my neck and murmured with maddening control, "Can't...what? Keep being so beautiful? Keep turning my cock into solid lead with wanting you? Too late, sweetheart. I'm hard as all the damn diamonds in the world for you..."

"Oh!" I cried. "Oh, God, no. I...I can't stop it, Kil." I thrashed my head from side to side as I undulated my hips beneath him. "I can't...hold back—"

"And who says you should?" He squeezed both my hips and plunged in faster, deeper. "Come for me, Claire. Just let it go, baby."

My insides vibrated and my pussy clamped. I mentally rejoiced in how he stretched me, consumed me. I sank my teeth into my lower lip in an effort to stay quiet, knowing the crew moved about the plane throughout the flight, but was relieved when he sealed his mouth back over mine, absorbing my moans as he masterfully, tenderly coaxed my orgasm from me. The cataclysm overtook me, I knew the damn plane could've hit a meteor and I wouldn't have noticed.

When I opened my eyes again, Killian was still staring down at me. He looked supremely pleased with himself, a rogue's grin playing at his lips. "How was that for a warm-up?" he cracked.

I groaned. He chuckled.

"Damn, Chicago. I hit the jackpot with you, didn't I?"

Instead of a reply, he dipped his lips to mine again. As he did, he pulled out of me, taking little more than an instant to roll me to my belly. His mouth returned, this time on the back of my neck and across my shoulders. I arched like a cat in ecstasy, loving his weight pressing me into the bed like this. I was sheltered and protected but needed and desired.

Desired.

That definitely seemed to be the plan.

Killian guided his erection back to my core. With a blissful sigh, I raised my hips, helping his angle. Kil growled against my nape, picking up his cock's urgent pace.

"I love you." He uttered it while kissing his way to my ear.

"I love you too."

"And I need you. *Fuck*, Claire. Yes..."

"Take what you need." I ended it on a tight keen while he dug his teeth into my shoulder. "Take all of me," I rasped past the exquisite pain.

His rhythm grew frantic. The smacks of his body touching mine resounded off the walls. His cock surged and swelled, and his balls trembled against the outer lips of my sex. He bit me again, hard. Then climaxed even harder.

Many minutes later, he stilled and held me tightly to him, shuddering as sweat trickled between our bodies.

"Claire."

It wasn't a question, but a deep instinct dictated me to answer, "Hmmm?"

"Don't leave me."

"Huh?" I attempted to peer around. No-go. He dropped his head between my shoulder blades, smashing his forehead to the top of my back.

"Just say you won't."

The words were stunning, especially because he meant every syllable. I felt the gravity of them like positive ions on the air. Did he really think *I'd* leave *him* over the tensions we'd had in Europe? On top of that, how was that an unfixable matter by someone like him? Okay, so he'd proposed...in his strange, crazy way. But if things fell apart, he'd get over me. He'd fix it. That was simply what Killian Stone did.

Nevertheless, I turned back over, determined to look him in the eyes while I issued my response. "I will never leave you, Killian. Ever. Unless you tell me to. I will be by your side... always."

He nodded. Just once. But his kiss was a lingering, warm version of *thank you*...a gratitude I eagerly and openly accepted.

★ ★ ★ ★

We slept for a large portion of the flight after that, waking in time to shower and eat before landing in Chicago. Email updates informed us that three staff members had been injured in the fire—as well as Josiah. Killian attempted not to flip to caged-animal mode at that news, an effort mostly—but not wholly—successful. I was damn grateful when the wheels finally touched down at Midway.

Fred was already waiting for us on the tarmac, the town car idling and ready to whisk us to Loyola Hospital's Burn Center, where they'd taken Josiah—another piece of news that had turned Kil toward his leashed-wildcat side, pacing the length of the plane while we taxied.

"Mr. Stone, Miss Montgomery, welcome home." Fred's somber face greeted us as we stepped onto the blacktop. Killian gripped my waist tighter, though he extended his other hand to greet his valet, practically a family member himself after serving Killian for so many years. I could see the pain on Alfred's face when Killian quietly asked if there was any news from the hospital.

"No, sir. Nothing since the last email you were sent. I know they are anxious for your arrival."

We were speeding on the highway toward the hospital within ten minutes of landing. I had no idea how Killian had dealt with customs and wasn't about to ask. Killian stared straight ahead and gripped my hand so tightly I felt my knuckles protesting.

"Hey."

He grunted and replied distractedly, "Hmm?"

"It's going to be all right." I rubbed his back, but the gesture was useless. The muscles beneath my fingers tensed harder by the minute. I kept massaging anyway. Maybe it would soothe one of us.

Alfred knew exactly where to go when we pulled onto the hospital property. The car stopped, and Britta was waiting under the private-entrance awning. Killian flung the door open without waiting for Alfred to come around, something I'd only seen him do once before, on a night we'd been to dinner and he hadn't been able to wait to get me up to the condo to finish what we'd started in the car. This was a *very* different occasion, as illustrated by the bone-crushing hug he swept Britta into as soon as he reached her.

"He's been asking for you," Britta murmured.

Killian snapped into brisk-CEO mode, lowering a curt nod. "Okay. Let's get in there, then."

Britta hooked a hand into the crook of his elbow. "Killian." She ignored his impatient glare. "You—" Her lips pursed. "Well, I need to prepare you. He's in really bad shape."

"Shit," I sputtered.

"Okay." His walls were still up. Way up. I wasn't sure whether to count that as good or bad.

I glanced to Britta. "This is bizarre. None of the emails to our team stated anything about Josiah being badly—"

"Let's go," Killian interjected. "Now."

Britta led the way down the corridor of the first floor of the burn unit. I was about one pace behind, though Killian clutched my hand the entire time. The situation still felt strange, though Killian's tension on the plane now made more sense. Again, I wished he would be more open with me—though that train to Nowhereville got shut down real fast. Focusing on the wrong things wasn't wise or productive at a time like this.

"How long do they think he'll be in here?"

Killian's query roped Britta to a full stop in the middle of the hall. Kil and I nearly collided with her like the damn

Keystone Cops. She whirled and looked up at Killian with eyes that were shiny and wet. When she raised her hand and flattened it to Killian's cheek, the tenderness nearly brought me to my knees. He wrapped his hand around hers in return, looking into her face, seeming to finally understand some silent memo of gravity about the situation.

I felt my jaw plummeting. *What the hell?* Was Josiah in *that* bad shape?

"You okay?" Britta asked softly. Killian's nod wasn't so decisive now. "All right, then. Let's go see him."

As we continued walking, I tugged on Killian's elbow. "Kil? What's—" I didn't know what silenced me faster, the shadows in his eyes or the defeat in the shake of his head.

We rounded the corner and came up to a nurse's station. A kind-faced older woman in celestial-themed scrubs smiled when she saw us.

"Hello again, Carol," Britta said to her.

"Perfect. The gang's all here." The nurse smiled warmly at Killian. "You must be his son. You have his strong chin and thick hair." *Thick hair?* Wouldn't have been the term I would have selected for Josiah's well-styled comb-over, but I wasn't about to contradict the woman. "He's been waiting for you. And asking for you. Over and over." She took Killian's hand and patted it. "We've been making him as comfortable as possible."

I watched the heavy gulp go down Killian's throat. *As comfortable as possible.* Those weren't words one used for a patient who was feeling great—or going to recover, for that matter. "Thank you." He uttered the words in automaton mode, and I didn't blame him.

"You need to put this gown and mask on. We don't want extra bacteria in there, okay?" She started dressing Killian where he stood, seemingly shocked into stillness. "I'm sorry, but I can only let one family member in at a time. Since he's been going on and on about his son, I'm suiting you up first. Now, you cannot upset him, dear. Understood?"

"Of course."

I was even more bewildered now. The words were compliant murmurs on Killian's lips, instead of the sharp bites I'd expected him to fling back at Carol's bustling orders. Something was definitely strange about all of this. Not clicking at all...

Carol pulled open the glass door to the room and motioned Killian in. "Just five minutes." I figured she issued the mandate with the full knowledge that Killian would take ten.

As Killian walked through, Britta and I moved close to the glass, staring like voyeurs. At least that was what I felt like. Britta gave me an awkward smile, clearly agreeing. "Now that you're here, I think I'll go freshen up. I've been here for a while."

It was an understatement. The woman looked utterly exhausted. "Of course, Britta," I assured. "And thank you...for everything you've done... I truly can't say how much..."

"And if you do, I'll club you." She attempted a soft laugh while lifting one of my hands between both of hers. "We're an odd little family, Claire, but family *is* what we are." She dipped her head toward Killian's paper-gown-shrouded form. "You'll thank me by taking care of *him*."

After giving a grateful nod, I let Britta go and then slumped into a chair beside the glass. The hum of the monitors was strangely soothing to my nerves, allowing me a moment to peer around. The unit was shaped like a wheel with a hub in the middle, each of the spokes leading off to its own room. The nurses zipped in and out of the rooms, always coming back to the center to dash down notes on the computers located there and check on all their patients' monitors. It was a machine of mesmerizing efficiency.

There was movement off to my right. I turned to see a woman bustling down the hall and rose to greet her, still with the apples in her cheeks and sass in her step, even when her eyes were filled with such torment.

"Kitty."

She hurried faster at my hail, yanking me up into a robust hug and exclaiming, "Saints be praised—you two are finally here!"

I smiled, especially when she soundly kissed me on both cheeks. "We came as fast as we could."

She lowered into the chair next to mine and pulled me down too, giving my knee a sound squeeze. "Thank God, thank God." She pulled in a breath that wobbled with tears. "I was so bloody worried Kil wouldn't make it in time."

"In time? For what?"

She suddenly appeared like a parent just asked by their toddler about why God allowed Satan to exist. "Oh, darn it," she muttered. "If I knew you were about, I would have brought you some tea too. Here, have mine, dear. I can get some more."

"No, don't be silly," I chastised. "I just got here. I'm fine for now, and besides—"

An alarm, shrill and terrifying, blared from the center of the wheel. Kitty and I watched with wide eyes as a pair of nurses seemed to materialize from nowhere, racing toward Josiah's room. At the same moment, Killian bounded to the door.

"Nurse!" he bellowed. "Something's wrong. Damn it! Please!"

Carol stepped forward and clutched both his shoulders. "You need to wait out here."

"The hell I will. Damn it, I—"

"Wait," Carol decreed. "*Here*. Now!"

She pointed at Kitty and me. We lurched to our feet again. Kitty didn't waste time waiting for Kil's approach. She rushed up with the determination of a linebacker, sweeping Killian into a big, warm hug. He returned the embrace with fervent force, an event that finally wasn't so surprising to me.

"Kitty," he grated. "What am I going to do without him?"

Kitty shoved him back. "*Pssshhh*. Now, boy, I'll stand for none of that talk!" While her scolding was quiet, it was fierce. "He's going to pull through just fine. You'll see."

But like a heartless taunt from fate, the hospital PA system called out a Code Blue, asking for a crash cart in room 117B. Instinctively I looked to the door Killian had come out of: 117B. Killian registered the connection at the exact same moment.

"Shit," he spat. "No. God, no!"

"Kil. Baby. Maybe we should go down the—"

He twisted from my hand. "I'm not leaving him, damn it. I'm not going anywhere."

"Okay. But we need to stay out of the way."

Britta came hustling back when she heard the Code Blue and joined us along the corridor.

I took his hand again, refusing to let go, forcing him against the wall next to me. The gown Carol had tied him into started to loosen and slipped off one of his shoulders. The cloth twisted around his biceps, ripping as he dragged his free hand through his hair. We stood there with Kitty, pressed back and helpless while a legion of doctors, nurses, and technicians flooded into the room, *emergency* stamped across their faces. They were truly working as hard as they could to clear that damn Code Blue. I kept holding Kil's hand as tightly as I could while he stared with horror into the room where his—

Wait.

Something didn't make sense. *A lot* of somethings. Why the hell was Kitty here? And where was Willa? The man surrounded by the anxious medical team in the room... Why did his general size and bulk suddenly seem grossly different from Josiah's? And why hadn't I noticed before now? And if he wasn't Josiah...

I was really confused. Even worse, I didn't exactly know why. Britta had met us at the entrance, so I assumed the man in the bed to be Josiah—but here I stood, gaping at an openly terrified Kitty, who'd made it no secret that she had eyes for one man alone in her world. Banyan Klarke.

I whirled, battling to get a clear look into the room, but my view was blocked by a dozen bodies working together in orchestrated chaos. A clear shot to the bed was hopeless. I whipped my stare back to Killian. He was frozen, a statue with agony shimmering in his eyes, disbelief twisting his lips, and frustration coiling both his hands. I tried to form my lips around words to him. A question, just one—*who the hell is in there, Killian?*—but my larynx was a solid, stunned knot.

As if on cue, everything stopped. The small army inside the room sagged together, some shaking their heads. While we watched in mortified silence, the lead trauma nurse checked her watch and then wrote the time down on the chart she was holding.

They pulled the starched white sheet up...up...and over Josiah's face.

No. Not Josiah. I was so damn certain of it now.

Who? *Who?*

One by one, the team filed out of the room. During their somber shuffle, they gazed to the floor, their fingernails, their shoelaces—anywhere but our direction. Only Carol the moon-and-sun-wearing nurse stepped over, a sheen of tears in her eyes, her shaky rasp conveying what we already knew.

The team did everything they could. We are all so sorry for your loss...

"No. *No*, goddamnit!"

Killian's protest was shattered only by Kitty's mournful wail. I let Britta comfort her while I approached Kil.

"Baby—"

He crushed the air from my lungs when he turned and slammed into my arms. "I-I can't do this. Claire...I—"

"Sshhh." I stroked the back of his head, my heart collapsing for him. His big body trembled like a child's against mine. I held him tighter, as if my life depended on it. As if *his* did. Because that was quite possibly the truth...

"I need him. I can't do all this without him. I can't."

"It's going to be okay, baby. It's going to be fine, I promise."

He abruptly pulled back. Stared sharply at me but then wheeled his head around, his gaze glossing over as it had on the plane back here. "I need to see him. Need to say things to him."

I reached for his hand. "Do you want me to come with you?"

"Yeah," he replied absently. "Uhhh, yeah." Then, after shaking his head violently, "*Yes.* Please."

After getting the nod of approval from Carol, I let him lead the way into the room. I knew I'd always remember the poignant sorrow in Kitty's sobs as we stepped past her and

Britta.

Killian pulled the sheet back down.

It wasn't Josiah in the bed.

It was Ban.

He was burned so severely, he was barely recognizable. I almost wondered who had taken the modeling clay, striated it enough to look like flesh, and then reshaped his face into gruesome proportions. His hair was matted and caked with ash. Though I shuddered with grief, the sight of the man didn't break Killian's purpose at all. I pulled over a chair for him, but he barely seemed to notice. He fished beneath the sheet for one of the man's hands, dragging out a mottled extremity that shocked me more than Ban's face. If any part of Ban had ever expressed him in a better way than others, it was his hands. Big yet gentle, capable yet graceful...so very much like those of the man who gathered the lifeless fingers close to his chest.

After several long minutes of leaden silence, Kil's voice finally tremored in the air. "Hey." He wrapped his other hand around Ban's now limp one. "It's me. And...I know you already know this...but it needs to be said." A weak smile wobbled his lips. "I had to wait for the one opportunity when you could do nothing to stop me."

His voice clutched tighter on the last couple of words. His head fell between his hunched, clenching shoulders. I reached for him, fighting through the mist of my renewed tears to get my fingers on his nape. "It's only me here, baby. Just say it."

The muscles under my grip coiled with even more tension. Nevertheless, he faltered on, telling the man in the bed, "You... you taught me so much about life, even after everything... changed for us. After you made one of the world's hugest sacrifices for me."

I battled not to let bewilderment get the better of me. What sacrifice, let alone on such a massive scale, had Banyan made for Killian? Granted, he'd always been lenient about Killian giving table scraps to the kitchen cats and had never hesitated to give away the last piece of Kitty's pie to Kil, but I wasn't sure either of those measured as one of the world's hugest sacrifices.

Unless the inevitable, final piece to this puzzle was what my logic finally linked together...

"We'll rebuild Keystone." Killian's voice broke again, nearly surrendering to a sob. "I promise it to you. *I promise.* And you...will be honored in that home, Nolan Banyan Klarke. Just as you will be honored in my heart...for every minute of every day that I remain alive."

The force of his grief was so palpable, it felt like every air molecule in the room had turned to needles. His muscles convulsed and heaved beneath my touch, physical evidence of how hard he fought to control his agony. But sometimes, not even the Enigma of the Magnificent Mile was immune to the debilitation of heartache. I shifted forward, worried he'd explode or, even worse, implode. Yet when I clutched his shoulder tighter, he moved away, leaning over to kiss Ban's scorched, stilled face. His whispered words of goodbye, teamed with all the forces of shock and awe that fate could muster to throw at me, would be a revelation carved into my memory forever.

"I love you, Dad."

CHAPTER SIX

Killian

Shell-shocked.

It was how Claire looked, and how I felt.

Officially, I wasn't able to sign for any arrangements on Dad's body—odd, to call him that now when he'd been so strict against me using it my whole life—but the hospital, given only Josiah's name as a responsible party, made an exception to the rule.

Josiah.

Hearing the name of the man who *had* been my "father" jerked me around for a moment. After scribbling my name on a bunch of papers, I jabbed a hand through my hair and peered at the nurse—what the fuck was her name again?—who'd been the human keel in this surreal storm.

"Carol." Yes. That was it. Unbelievably, part of my mind still managed to function. "My fath—Mr. Stone... Did I hear someone say he's here?"

The nurse pressed my hand between her own. "He's downstairs. Because of his recent health concerns, they've admitted him for overnight observation as a precaution—but his damage from the fire was a few minor cuts and burns, thanks to Mr. Klarke's fast thinking."

I blinked, absorbing that information in what was likely

slow motion for her. Who the hell was I kidding? It was slow motion to *me*, the man with the office wallpapered in spreadsheets, topped by the bank of monitors with news feeds from across the globe. I was used to evaluating twenty pieces of information every minute of the day. That world seemed so far away now. So meaningless.

I looked around as if the button for normal life would appear again. Where the hell was it? When would I stop feeling as if every circuit in my body had been shorted out and blackened into a numb semblance of itself? If I'd been lost in a wilderness last night in Paris, I was in a fucking wasteland now. Nothing made sense, especially what Carol had just said.

"I don't understand." Claire said it as she stepped forward, one arm still around a quietly sobbing Kitty. "Mr. Klarke? Who's that?"

"That's...that's our Banyan, sweetie," Kitty supplied between sobs.

"And you're telling us...he saved Father?" I directed to Carol.

If the nurse was stunned that I'd just referred to a second man as my father, she showed no outward signs of it. Even if she had, I was damn sure I didn't care. The short circuit on my senses continued, convincing me this was all a freakish dream. Any moment now, I'd wake up back in Paris next to Claire, the city waiting for our exploration, my clusterfuck of a proposal just a bad, bitter nightmare.

But when Carol spoke again, the empathetic vibrations of her voice were all too real. "So, as I understand it, the fire was caused by a freak explosion in Keystone's boiler room?"

"Yes, and according to the preliminary accident report, that means half the manor's south wing was taken out, including the main hall, which is the exit route for damn near all the rooms in that wing." My childhood playground lay like a map in my mind's eye.

That area included Josiah's sprawling office, where the man spent nearly all his time if he was at home, damn any medical orders for his recuperation.

After confirming my statement with a small nod, Carol went on. "With the weakened condition of Mr. Stone's lungs, it wasn't likely he'd have survived the fumes and smoke for even another ten minutes. Though the service stairs were blocked by burning debris, Mr. Klarke somehow found a way up that route and brought Mr. Stone back to safety."

My lungs tightened. My imagination swam as the logistics of her recount took over. If the old boiler in the south basement had blown, it would have torn apart the kitchen floor. Since Banyan—*Dad*—had practically lived in the kitchen when he wasn't attending to Keystone's never-ending maintenance list, the blast would've likely blown right up his ass. Still, he'd found a way to make it to the service stairs, clear a path, and haul it up to the master study to retrieve Josiah.

My masquerade of a father, saved by the man who'd handed him the mask.

I had no idea how to react or feel. I was ripped apart, my two halves like the sides of a parchment contract, ragged and unmatchable, confused and raging.

I turned from the women. Stumbled toward walls that were painted in designer sterility and decorated with cheap art, all put together to impart a peace I couldn't be further from feeling. I glared at one of those prints, with its airbrushed words spouting bullshit about wisdom and hope, debating whether to pull the thing off the wall before I put my fist through it, when someone said my name. Someone sounding like strength—and the understanding that only came from growing up together.

"Kil."

I turned. Stared hard at the man standing there, appearing tan and strong in his rugged Southwest desert clothes, just as he yanked me into a firm embrace. I rebelled at once, shoving back at Lance. Like Carol and Kitty before him, he accepted my anger with a sympathetic look. I yearned to punch it right off his face. Why was everyone so goddamn understanding? Why wasn't anyone pissed off as hell about all this? Didn't anyone else see what I did? All the moments passed by. The time wasted. The feelings unexpressed. So many tomorrows taken for granted. A sham I was just as guilty of believing as all of them.

"I'm sorry," Lance uttered. "Damn it, Killian, I'm so sorry. It shouldn't have happened like this."

I locked my teeth, clenched my jaw, and twisted my psyche harder around the rage. At least that felt real. Tangible. Right.

"Yeah," I replied, lips barely moving. "Okay." I jabbed my hands into the back pockets of my jeans. "What the hell are you doing up here? Who's downstairs with—"

"Father?" He filled it into my awkward pause. "Mom's with him. Don't worry." With a steady lift of his gaze, he continued, "But he knows you cut your trip short, and he's asking for you."

"Why?"

The guy pulled back his head and grimaced. "What the hell do you mean, why?"

I let the thousands of things I could've answered to that slip into a thick silence. Inside my chest, the parchment tore a little wider, and I didn't even want to find glue for it. My sights found nothing but that lame point on the wall again, and

I sought comfort in indulging the fantasy of ripping it down, driving my fist through the glass, and strangling the watercolor dove taking flight beneath the empty words of solace.

When I'd made my silence excruciatingly clear, Lance finally jabbed a toe at the floor and offered, "Mason's already here too—so you can cross all the legal concerns off your list."

I wondered why his cryptic tone didn't make me feel like more of a cornered animal. For the last three weeks, I'd traipsed across Europe in a constant state of lashing out at Claire for making me feel the exact same way. Now I just tilted up a scowl and gritted, "'Legal concerns?' That's what we're calling them now?"

Lance's lips tightened beneath his beard, which seemed fuller than the last time I'd seen him, during his very quick stop home over the holidays. "I'm just here to help, smartass. I'm also happy to stand here however long it takes for you to ask nicely for it." He flashed a serene grin at a pair of older women who sat nearby, uncaring that they didn't understand how the *Fight Club* tone he'd wielded since high school was the exact kick of familiarity I needed right now.

"Don't you have a long walk to take off a short fucking pier?"

A soft smile took the place of his scowl. In the vernacular of the Stone brothers, family catastrophe or not, it was the closest to nice he was going to get. For at least a few bizarre seconds, things were back to normal.

"The staff on both floors have signed nondisclosure agreements," he stated. "And nowhere on Ban's paperwork is your direct relationship noted."

My head jerked up and down. The details should have been on *my* mind, but even acknowledging my mind existed was a torturous process. "Okay," I managed. "Yeah. Thanks, Lance."

"One more thing. Avoid the front of the building. We've corralled the press there. The doctors have already been out for a couple of press conferences, but they keep demanding an appearance by you and Claire."

"Of course." I made the crack with a mixture of dread and pride. Though Claire detested the public-persona part of being with me, she'd nevertheless captivated the press the same way she had me—with her humor, sass, and humility.

And open, direct honesty.

The only thing she'd ever wanted from me in return. The one thing I'd withheld...afraid of everything that had happened in the last twenty-four hours.

I stopped running, Killian. Now it's time for you to stop hiding.

I lifted my head. Extended my gaze across the waiting area to where Claire gently held Kitty, rubbing her hand up and down the woman's trembling back—utterly unaware that for the first time, I really heard her words.

Lance's boots made a couple of steady thumps on the tile as he stepped next to me again. His long pause indicated he followed the line of my sight. "You never told her," he finally queried, "did you?"

I let a rush of air explode off my lips. "Not exactly the stuff of light dinner conversation, brother."

"Not in the least." His tone was infused with compassion. "Though the air between you two is thick as three auras gone sideways."

I shook my head. "You seriously need to get out of Sedona more."

"Or maybe you just need to come visit." The jest eased things enough for him to yank me into a fierce hug. When he let me go, he murmured, "If you take the back stairs and keep a low profile, you two can probably make your way to the park across the street unnoticed. I'll sit with Kitty. Don't worry."

I nodded and pulled him into another clasp, this one tight with my gratitude. Lance might have shared plenty of culpability with Trey for making my life hell as a kid, but he'd grown up into a damn decent—if fake—brother. The recognition provided a connection I desperately needed right now, injecting much-needed steel into my spine as I crossed back to Claire. When I approached, she looked up and started. She scanned my face, likely wondering why I appeared to be the Killian Stone from sixty-seven floors over Michigan Avenue instead of the Killian Klarke who'd just wept out a final goodbye to my dad.

It was time she knew the answer to that.

It was time she knew everything.

I extended my hand down to her. "We need to talk."

The *holy shit* look on her face only intensified with every step we took across the grass in the park. Once we arrived at a little picnic table under some trees, the shade didn't diminish the anxiety in her eyes or soften the brackets of tension at her mouth. I tried to ease both once I sat her down, cupping her hands, brushing her mouth with a soft kiss. "I love you, Claire."

Her expression softened. She lifted the tips of her fingers to my face. "And I love you."

I cleared my throat. "But you're confused."

"You think?"

We attempted to laugh in tandem at her crack. Best we could do was a couple of soft huffs, a commiseration about the fact that this conversation was happening too fucking late.

Reluctantly, I let her hands fall. "You deserve better than this for an explanation, Claire. You always did. And I'm sorry."

"It's okay." Her soft utterance matched the brush of knuckles she lingered over mine. The moment was such a sweet contrast to how things had been for us lately, seeming like a ceasefire to a long skirmish. Now if my gut would only get the message.

"You really mean that," I murmured. "Don't you?"

"Of course I do." She frowned, her confusion apparent. "Killian, I've never wanted anything but your truth. I'm just sorry, not angry, it had to be like this."

"I'm sorry too." Repeating the words permeated them deeper into me. Though I leaned back from her a little, I sucked emotional sustenance from the brilliant amber strength in her eyes. So open. Giving. Caring. Would she feel like being so once I spilled the complete truth?

I didn't have a choice about that answer now. Hiding from her—from myself—was no longer a choice. If I'd come clean about all this sooner, perhaps fate wouldn't have stepped in to teach me the lesson in the shittiest way possible.

"You were scared." Compassion formed a thick underline to her declaration. "And now I understand why, at least a little better." She traced a figure eight over my wrist. "I'm just astounded I didn't see it sooner."

"See what?"

"The truth. About you—and Ban." She tilted her head to one side. "You're so much like him, you know."

I shot her a quizzical look—past a smile that began in the core of my chest. "Really?"

"Oh, yeah." While she nodded, she assessed my face as if

seeing it for the first time. "Talk about the truth hiding in plain sight." Her gaze intensified. "Only now, I'm just wondering why you never...well, why everyone hid it from—"

"The whole world?" I jammed my hands through my hair. "That's the thirty-million-dollar question, isn't it?"

She pulled her hands back into her lap and regarded me carefully. "In the case of the Stones, that's a pretty literal question."

"Damn straight." I turned on the bench, looking back across the park. "And in this case, you'd be right on the money—pardon the term—to think so."

I heard her scoot away from the table. Her words came as cautiously as her steps as she joined me on my side. "I'm listening."

Caution? No. It was more like suspicion...just as I'd expected. Claire Montgomery valued integrity like a nun prioritized chastity—which meant she hated where her logic progressed with my words.

Which meant this confession was going to be just as hard as I'd expected. *Damn it.*

I wasn't aware the words had spilled from my lips before Claire came closer. "Kil...it's me, remember?"

I let out a grunting laugh. "That's supposed to make this easier?"

"Generally speaking, yes." At the weighted silence I gave that, she took a long breath and then persisted, "Okay. How about we start at the very beginning? I know that you've lived at Keystone at least from the age of three."

The smile in her voice tempted one to my lips. The memory returned, as vivid as if it were yesterday, of the day I'd given her the grand tour of the manor, including the "portraits"

Trey and I had added in crayon to the corner of the grand gallery as toddlers. Mother had fallen so completely in love with our efforts, including my rendering of her as a queen atop a unicorn with flames for a mane, that she'd ordered a custom frame to surround the drawings.

As I turned back to Claire, grief snagged my heart—and a confession left my lips. "I was practically born there. And now—"

It's gone.

"I know." She reached up, grabbing the back of my head in order to pull me into her, cradling me through the wash of agony so deep I could only clutch her in return, digging my hands into her hips. The wind blew. The trees moaned. Leaves batted at our legs. The world went on, but I was stopped—and knew that getting this truth out to her had to be the first start at making things go again. She'd been right back in Paris. I'd started turning her into my enemy. More than ever, I needed her again as my ally.

I finally pulled away. Sat up once more. I needed the distance to find the memories—and the words.

"Everything was fine until a few months before my fifth birthday. That was about the time Stone Global jumped into the Fortune 500."

"And...that was a good thing, right?" Her tone was careful and slow. Like the observant woman she was, she already knew that when things were rosy for the Stones, that didn't mean a shitload of thorns weren't growing beneath the blooms.

"Yes...and no," I replied. I gave her a sideways glance. "You know a lot of the company history—and probably the fact that my father was able to grow it via funding from the traditional Chicago social circles in which *his* father first moved."

She nodded thoughtfully. "All the evidence does point to that, yes."

"Well, the expectations on that kind of debt run deeper than your standard country club membership and Assistance League fund raisers. To this day, there's a certain...code...about grooming the proper heir apparent for an empire like SGC. A successor who can produce perfect children who will in turn take *their* turn on the throne."

Her eyebrows lowered. "And....Josiah and Willa didn't see that heir in either Lance or Trey?"

I folded my arms and answered as gently as I could, "Well, not in Lance."

Her stare darkened to the shade of fire against a night sky. Angry fire. "Because he's—" Her jaw dropped. "Didn't you just say you were all *kids*? How could they even tell at that age?"

"Because at Trey's birthday party, they found him in the bathroom, charging each of the little girls a buck for a glam makeover."

She clearly tried—but failed—to hold back a giggle. "Well, at least he knew how good an artist he was even back then."

I gave in to a smile too. It felt damn nice. "And he actually was."

"Okay, that took care of Lance. But Trey—"

"Won't ever be able to have children." I paused to let her drop an expected gape. "They knew about it since he was a baby."

I could practically see the gears in Claire's mind working on all that information and arriving at a few crazy conclusions. The shitty thing was, likely all of them were right.

I decided to keep going. "By that time, I was pretty much a third musketeer to the two of them. The only time our parents couldn't find us running around together was when I wandered into Josiah's office. His spreadsheets were fascinating to me. I liked asking questions—and to my surprise, he liked answering them. Guess it didn't take anyone very long to figure that if I was challenged properly, I could go places with my life."

"So...Josiah and Willa just took you away from your dad?"

"Not exactly." The laugh I twisted into the last of it was sparked more by discomfort than amusement. "It was still my *mom* and dad, actually—and I even remember that they involved me in the decision a little too."

"*What?*"

"I was a kid, Claire. It all seemed like some big game to me. I was told I'd get to sleep in the big house with Lance and Trey and go to their school, where all the boys got to wear ties and ride ponies. In exchange, all I had to do was tell everyone my last name was Stone instead of Klarke and pretend that Josiah and Willa were my dad and mom when we went to school events. Life changed for me, but not that much. I saw my parents every day, even ate dinner with them in the service dining room. In my view, life was pretty fucking awesome."

A weighted breath left her. Now that I was on a roll, I wanted to simply push out all the rest. I clamped my jaw on another half minute of silence, knowing I'd just asked her to digest a whole bunch of *wow*.

Welcome to the rabbit hole, Alice.

"So...when did the veil fall from your eyes?" she finally murmured.

Well, that one was easy.

"A month before my eighth birthday." I leaned back against the picnic table. "Mother and Father—Willa and Josiah this time—gave me a skiing trip to Aspen as a gift. We were getting ready to leave...when we learned my mom had beat us at the game."

Claire scowled. "I...don't understand."

I crossed my leg and leaned my elbows on my knee. Didn't help the thud of pain in my gut—or the realization that I'd never had to speak this truth aloud to anyone before. "The ski trip...it was a tipping point, I guess, for Damrys Klarke, my biological mother." I stared down at the skin on top of my knuckles, stretched white from my painful squeezing. "She told Ban—Dad—that she couldn't bear watching my life from the sidelines anymore. Though Dad begged her to stay—told her he'd talk to Josiah and Willa and return things to the way they were—she forbade him to say anything." I unhinged one of my hands to brace my forehead against a curled fist. "So in the middle of the night...she disappeared."

Claire swung her stunned gape toward me. "Wait. She... she just left?"

I lifted my head. "One veil, officially removed."

"And she never came back?"

"Ban thought she might've gone back home, found a decent village to blend into," I said as the beginning of an answer. "She missed Ireland a lot."

When her lips finally came back together, she stammered, "And you never tried to look for her?"

"Constantly," I countered. "Sometimes obsessively, whenever Lance and Trey decided ganging up on the kitchen boy was a fun way to pass the time."

She snorted. "A game Trey never quite grew out of."

"They both got pretty good at knowing the limits our fathers would tolerate. And of course, their teasing only made me more determined to kick their combined asses scholastically." I rose to my feet, facing her with squared shoulders. "I'm not going to lie to you, Claire. I liked growing up as a Stone. Sometimes, the mantle was damn demanding, especially when Josiah tried to force the fit, but the man also taught me a lot—and Willa, in her beautiful way, tried to fill the maternal gap in my heart. And Ban"—I swallowed on a heavy sting behind my eyes—"*Dad* was there to remind me of how lucky I was to have it all."

Claire stood and approached me, not stopping until her arms were around me once more, her perfect embrace becoming my reality. "They were lucky too, baby. Damn lucky."

I dropped my head against the dip of her neck, breathing in the heady spring bouquet of her contrasting with the rain in the air and the storm in my heart, pulling in as much of her light and strength as she'd let me. In so many ways, weight flew off my shoulders—but where did those shoulders belong now? Life had once been about compartments. They'd been neat, sterile, clean—and painless. A few IEDs of fate later, the walls were in shreds and the blood flowed.

Could I rebuild things as perfectly as they had been before?

Not without Claire.

I drew her closer, harder, treasuring the pulse of her neck with mine, the warmth of her breath in my chest, the light of her love in my life. "Don't go," I grated. "Please don't go."

I felt her swallow deeply. "I'm not going anywhere. I promise. This changes nothing, Killian."

I couldn't help the snarl that erupted. "This changes *everything*, damn it." I set her far enough away that our stares could lock. "I'm asking you to lie for me, Claire. To everyone. That includes Andrea, Talia, your father—"

"I know." Despite the fervency of her words, conflict glittered in her eyes. "I *know*, Killian."

I was on the brink of letting her endure a long, skeptical silence from me when my damn phone chirped. A text message.

My heartbeat dove to my stomach.

"I've turned off alerts for anyone except Britta and Lance." I used it to explain why I reached for the thing, still vibrating, in my jacket pocket.

The message was from Lance.

Get back here right away. Meet me in Father's room.

CHAPTER SEVEN

Claire

If it were true about only being given what you can handle, then my cup was running over with the handleables. I needed a moment to digest all that had been thrown at me—about a hundred moments ago, back in the park. That was before the text message had blared from Lance, summoning Killian and me back to the hospital.

Josiah Stone—the man the world still knew as Killian's father—had taken a turn for the worse. The announcement turned a crazy, long day into an interminable, insane one. But we were going to get through it. I had to keep believing that. We were going to wade through this disaster and come out stronger on the other side.

Moaning about it all—even a whimper—wasn't an option either. This was exactly what I'd been pushing Killian for. He'd sure as hell given it to me. The truth, in all its untamed glory, was here. Now we would deal with it. Just as soon as he wrapped his head around mourning for his *real* dad. And walking the labyrinth of bullshit still surrounding Trey's troubles. And handling the nightmare of sifting through the remains of the home he'd grown up in.

He needed space. And patience. And time. I was confident I could help with the first two and would fight like hell to see he received as much of the third as possible.

We reentered the hospital the same way we'd left, via the back stairs Lance had turned us onto. Facing the press wasn't an option yet. We knew they needed their statements and money shots, but nobody was at their best right now, making the front lobby a disaster zone for us. Besides, I could use the downtime to whip out a press release and send it over to Andrea for approval and release, perhaps with a suggestion for a full press conference over the weekend, when more sympathetic B crews would be on duty.

As we rejoined Lance and Willa, tension rolled off Killian in waves. His stress was so seismic I wondered if they were picking him up on the local news station's Quake Cam. Wait—that was probably just a California thing. I still couldn't help feeling like the tectonic plates of his heart were about to collide. My own clenched from yearning to help him more than I was. I wrapped my grip tighter around his as we opened the door to Josiah's private room.

After Willa and Lance walked in behind us, the entire family was officially gathered. Trey leaned against the windowsill. Next to him was Lance's life partner, Zack, an attractive yet rugged man with a well-groomed beard and sandy hair that matched his sky-blue eyes. Britta, who, for all intents and purposes, was family to the Stones, was also there. She tugged at Zack, and they quickly excused themselves to fetch everyone coffee from the café on the corner. I wondered if I should go along, since the air in the room took on a somber, strictly family mood, but Killian had clearly turned on his mind-reading skills and shot me a glance that forbade me to even think it. I found the most inconspicuous corner in the room and tucked myself into it.

Against a backdrop of hushed whispers between Willa and her boys, I worked at sorting out the facts that had just been blasted at me.

Most immediately, from what I could piece together on the medical side of things, Josiah's lungs were resembling deflating party balloons. Translation? Things didn't look optimistic for their proud patriarch. That opened a forest of feelings for everyone to traverse, but in my mind, the emotions were boxed up, saved for another day when we wouldn't be in crisis mode. There was no room for feelings on this battlefield.

The situation called for some mental lists. It was the way I always sorted out whoppers like these, in order to best keep it all straight. I closed my eyes and pictured two columns. One was for essential information, the other for items that were important but not Earth-shattering at the moment.

Deep breath.

Fact one—Killian had been lying to me about his identity during our entire relationship. Which column? Believe it or not, I pushed it to the nonessential list. He'd been a child when put into the middle of the Stone family mess, likely unaware of the consequences *he'd* face, by a handful of adults who should've known better.

Fact two—Trey was likely blackmailing him because of the secret. Instant spot in the essential column. Killian's big bro would milk his power for everything it could get him, since he'd never organically produce *any* heir to the throne, let alone the perfect male boy everyone expected. Eventually, that might even include a bid to pull Kil and me apart in any way he could. There needed to be a game plan in place to deal with him. No, that was too kind. Dealing with him meant leashing him back up. Now that I knew the full backstory, I didn't trust

Trey as far as I could throw him.

A fierce jolt of protectiveness hit me on behalf of my man. And on behalf of me, a deep squirm of discomfort. I wasn't sure if I wanted to be in a canoe with this whole camp of liars right now. And sitting in the same room as witness to their boo-hoos over the man who'd orchestrated all these lies? To be honest, it pissed me off.

Refocusing on the list was a better idea.

Except for the fact that my day suddenly got worse.

If Killian's family wasn't a nuthouse in its own right to deal with, my head lifted at the unmistakable croon of Stepmommy Dearest. Sure enough, I watched Andrea practically float into the room on a cloud of Chanel No. 5, her St. John pantsuit as wrinkle-free as her face. But to the best of my knowledge, they didn't make Botox for wool yet.

"We got here as soon as we could," she told Killian as he crossed the room to her, "but honestly, Mr. Stone, I could have prepared something for you remotely. This should be a time for your family only." Her expression was tight. My senses were racing. *We got here as soon as we could?*

Sure enough, Margaux appeared the next moment, stunning in a to-the-minute Burberry trench. I noticed my two-day-old jeans and sweater combo and then rolled my eyes at myself for even taking stock of what she was wearing at a moment like this. Wait. That actually *was* easy to decipher. It was simpler to lust after her Burberry than try to fathom why she was here. The woman herself seemed to agree with me. Margaux appeared as comfortable as a nun on a nude beach.

Killian stood back, his own expression now puzzled. "I didn't call you," he told Andrea, his voice flat as—well, a stone.

A weak voice lifted into the air—from the bed in the center

of it. "I called you here, Ms. Asher." The gasps Josiah spurted between the words made the sentence more like a paragraph.

Uncomfortable had officially arrived at the party. In an instant, Andrea changed from sleek and cool to nervous and fuming. Everybody, even the sullen Trey, noticed the switch. The fact that Josiah even recognized her on sight seemed odd. Had they met before? And when? Andrea had never made one mention about having contact with the elder Stone in her life.

I stepped next to Killian out of habit, wrapping my arm around his waist and peering up into his shadowed eyes for any clue. Only confusion ruled those dark depths.

Willa hastened to her own man's side. She sat on the edge of the bed and pulled his paper-thin hand into hers. "Joe, please don't strain yourself. You need to rest." She stroked his arm and leaned in, the room's harsh lighting bringing out the hollows beneath her eyes. All of her usual twinkle was gone. I doubted she'd slept since the fire.

Josiah stared at her with an inscrutable scowl. "Rest is the last thing on my mind right now, my Willa-Wisp. I don't...have the luxury...of much more time."

A lump lodged in my throat at watching her chin wobble. "Oh, Joe."

"There now. There, there. Be strong, darling. I really... need you...to be strong for me now."

"Be strong?" Lance was the one to finally voice what the rest of us were thinking. "Why? What the hell's going on, Father?"

Josiah choked out a long cough before answering. "There are...affairs...I must get into order, my boy."

"Now?" Trey rose as he snapped it.

"Yes. Now. Before"—he hacked loudly again—"well,

before..."

"Joe!" Tears spilled down Willa's cheeks now. "No...*no!*"

Killian and Lance traded grave glances before rushing to the bed but backed away when their father swept his emaciated arm in foreboding command. As he fell back to the flat pillows, he seemed to age another ten years.

Miracle of miracles, Margaux hadn't uttered a single word. She seemed to have absorbed the tension in the room by osmosis, though her normal poise remained carefully intact. She remained by her mother's side, resigned to her chic silence.

There was still no explanation for why she was here.

Josiah finally found his voice again. He curled Willa's hand tighter. "I have...gathered you all here...for a reason. There are...certain things...I must tell you all. This is likely an overdue meeting, but the Almighty has...chosen His timing...for a reason." While Trey rolled his eyes, Kil and Lance exchanged another quizzical look. "There have been...so many secrets in this family. *Too* many."

Killian finally pressed forward again. I could feel the tension in him across all ten feet separating us. "Father, we don't have to—"

"Yes." It was a ferocious snarl. "We do, Killian." He coughed his face into the color of boiled beets before whispering, "Now bring Margaux over here."

Shockingly, Andrea cut first into the stunned silence. "Damn it!"

"Margaux?" Trey spat. "Why?"

Without a word, Kil beckoned a hand toward Margaux. She looked at his fingers like they'd turn to asps any second, though step by tiny step, she approached the bed. Even when weakened, Josiah Stone's authority couldn't be ignored.

"There is no easy way to say this," Josiah stated. "So I... shall simply...say it. This young woman you call Margaux...is, in reality, your sister."

Killian, Trey, and Lance practically laser-beamed their shock at one another. Not surprisingly, Trey pushed out the first verbalization of that sentiment. "Excuse the fuck out of me?"

"She is...my daughter," Josiah affirmed. "My own flesh and blood."

Killian's gaze had affixed to Willa with knowing steadiness. "But she's not *your* flesh and blood."

Willa winced. "Obviously not."

Josiah's stare softened as he turned to Margaux. "You were named Mary at birth," he explained. "You looked just like a little Madonna." He ignored Trey's scoffing snort. "And your mother here"—he directed a bony finger at Andrea—"adopted you from the woman I'd been having an affair with, a secretary of mine at the time. She was a good woman, Margaux—simply unable to care for you as she could have herself, because of her circumstances and mine." His long breath made his chest rattle. "For many reasons—among them to allow you a normal and happy life—we vowed to keep the secret for all these years. But now...I am a dying man. I will...keep secrets no more. I will...go to God with a clean conscience. All these truths...have been settled with my attorney. You shall...have it in writing. But I wanted...to say the words. For Mary. For all of you."

I should never have mused that the day couldn't get any stranger. Fate laughed in my face now, its morbid chuckles bouncing behind Willa's wordless rise before she went to stare out at the park where Killian had dropped his shockers on me only an hour ago.

Trey was the first to burst with actual words. "You *cannot* be serious. Honest to Christ, Father. Do you have a pet monkey waiting around to claim *its* stake in the family too?"

"Trey." Lance angled forward. "That's enough, damn it."

"Shut up," Trey retorted. "You've been out in the desert humping burros, cacti, and God knows what else. You know nothing about any of this. If you did, you'd be on my side right now." He glowered toward Margaux. "Her? Of all the fucking people? *Her?*"

"*Enough.*" Killian drove it at Trey in his boardroom voice. Quiet. Ominous. Unassailable. "It's time to take a breather, Trey."

Muttering a thousand more versions of the F-word during the trip, Trey stormed out. Just to make his point, he knocked over a small tray table on the way.

Andrea pressed against the countertop that housed the sink and door to the en suite bathroom—but her demeanor was far from defeated. "You had no right to do this, old man," she seethed. "None."

I shivered as she articulated her last words like a combination of Catwoman and Cruella de Ville. Both bitches had terrified me as a kid. I had no trouble recalling that sense of dread once more.

I stepped over and slipped my hand into Killian's again. He gripped me harder than he had through any of the other insane moments of the past two days. Other than that, his countenance was motionless. He stared at Josiah as if the man would suddenly spring up and shout "April Fools!" at everyone. Maybe follow it up with a little jig, make us all roar with laughter.

Josiah simply wheezed in another heavy breath. When he

let it out, he looked relieved of a huge burden. Off of his chest, onto ours. Six different versions of *The Scream* were now positioned around the room, like a high school art class had been assigned the famous work to copy and each student had put their own twist on it.

"Father, are you sure there isn't some sort of mistake?" Lance's question was respectful but firm. "Maybe the woman lied to you. Did she need money? Did you run a DNA test?"

During his little interview, Margaux had thrown her stare to the floor. Her shoulders had curled in, making her look like the self-conscious new girl for the first time since I'd known her. Talking about her as though she were a faceless science experiment seemed wrong and harsh, but no one could argue his point. Josiah's name was synonymous with wealth and power, meaning people were willing to do ruthless things for the commodities. Faking a pregnancy was child's play in that game.

Killian quietly kissed my fingers before untwining them from his. With as much care, he walked over to Willa. He gently turned her around, gathering her into his long, strong arms—and then held her while she silently fell to pieces. Yet another life flipped upside down by a carefully crafted lie. But how was this one any different than the charade she'd participated in with Killian at the center? Her heart might have been in the right place at one time, but continuing to go along with Josiah's deception to the world, convincing Killian to do the same... Karma really could be a clever little bitch.

My throat tightened and my stomach knotted. I hurt for Willa, but I hurt for all of them. Yes, even Trey's nastiness had its sympathetic side.

This train was derailing. Fast. The wreckage up ahead

was undoubtedly gruesome, and all I could do was stand by and watch. My heart hurt again. Everyone in this room faced a much different reality than the one they'd woken up to this morning. What a tangled fiasco.

With no preamble whatsoever, Margaux pivoted, strolled to the door, and left. No tirade, no explanation, no goodbye—utterly eerie.

The door closed behind her.

Whomp.

Horrible silence reigned once more.

Andrea had the good sense not to chase after her. Instead, in true Andrea Asher fashion, she smoothed her jacket, strutted to Josiah's bedside, and leaned in.

"You haven't heard the last of me, you bastard." The Cruella snarl was still in fine form. "You will regret this decision. I will personally see to it." Her shoulders bunched, leading me to believe she was actually considering strangling the man, before she went on, "I'm not the convenient little problem all you good ol' boys can stow away anymore. I did what I said I'd do, Josiah. I made something of my life and my daughter's too. I took your table scraps and turned them into a fucking feast. You have no damn idea what I'm capable of—but you can watch from hell as I give a glorious demonstration."

Catwoman made an appearance as she rose with smooth grace and swiped carefully at her hair. One perfect pivot later, she strode out of the same door her "daughter" had just used.

The beeps of the machines, along with the slight rise and fall of Josiah's chest, were the only indications he was still with us. His face was now bathed in peace. Andrea's threat meant nothing to him. He had accomplished what he'd set out to do, a selfish yet selfless act wrapped into a few catastrophic sentences.

Lance's murmur flowed out on the air. "Why don't we give Mom and Dad some time alone? Maybe we can find Zack and Britta downstairs. That espresso is sounding better by the minute."

I wanted to hug the man for his brilliance. I didn't give Killian any doubt about where I stood on his brother's suggestion, grabbing my bag and heading for the door. The walls were closing in. We all needed a break.

Kil and Lance took turns kissing Willa on the cheek and then patting their dad on the shoulder. Once we'd left the room and were about to enter the stairwell again, I turned to them both, overwhelmed by the need to embrace them. "Are you guys okay?"

They both blinked and stared like I'd spawned a second head. Clearly, it wasn't a question one asked a Stone male.

"Of course," Killian muttered. "We're fine."

Lance gave his brother a shoulder check before filling in, "What he means to say is that we'll figure out what the hell is really the truth, after Father stabilizes and we determine what shit was the drugs talking instead of him. Then we'll go from there."

Though I liked Lance more with every passing minute, I wondered about *his* sanity now—the same way I wondered when or if Josiah would ever stabilize.

"Andrea didn't seem surprised by anything your dad said," I replied, glancing to Killian to gauge if he agreed with my take. "She really just seemed pissed that she wasn't the one in control of the announcement."

Though Kil nodded carefully at my assertion, he didn't say anything. He looked more tired than I'd ever seen him, and the expression got worse as he watched Trey reappear down the hall, making his way back toward Josiah's room. "I swear to God, if he gets back in there and upsets Fath—Josia—" He dragged a hand through his hair. "Fuck."

"You need some fresh air, brother." Lance deliberately emphasized the last word, renewing my desire to kiss his big, booted toes. "Come on. Let's get out of here for a few minutes."

But just as we cleared the bottom of our private exit, Lance and Killian reached for their phones, suddenly vibrating in tandem with incoming texts.

"Trey," Lance said.

"Crap," Kil growled.

I peered over his shoulder at the message.

Old man stroking out. Get ur asses back here.

Trey wasn't a wordsmith, but we didn't need one. We took the stairs back up at a sprint, crashing through the doors at the top before wheeling around to witness an instant replay of what we'd experienced less than three hours prior—outside Ban's room.

A small army of doctors and nurses rushed in and out of the room. Willa and Trey were pressed against the wall outside, clinging to each other. The poor woman looked helpless and horrified at the same time.

What kind of nightmare was I waiting to wake up from?

Lance's and Killian's long strides had me running to keep up as we approached. Through her tears, Willa choked out that Josiah was apparently having a severe stroke. The medical team was doing everything they could do to keep him comfortable and safe—and alive.

Through the window, the man appeared to be sleeping

peacefully. The only new addition was an oxygen mask over his nose and mouth. But as additions went, it was significant.

I pulled Willa into a hug. The woman returned my embrace with fierce but trembling force. I whispered into her ear, "What can we do for you?"

She stepped back and shook her head. "You sweet girl. There's nothing we can do, Claire. It's all in God's hands now...a matter of time, I suppose. We just have to wait."

My gaze fell to the delicate gold cross hanging around her frail neck. The jewelry seemed a part of her, so natural that I'd never thought about it before now. That was probably because she was such an unstoppable force of nature. And today, though nature had turned the tables on the woman, Willa was definitely at an odd peace with everything.

That didn't stop me from wishing her husband hadn't dropped such a bomb on her, as what seemed to be his final act. What a despicable way to go out. But Josiah was an original, fully living up to the famous—*and* infamous—legacy of the Stone family name. This was how the man rolled. Always on his terms and always in a blaze of glory.

CHAPTER EIGHT

Killian

While Chicago bustled its way through another frantic lunch hour, I took the hand of the man who'd just dropped a bombshell in the middle of this hospital room. They'd finally let us back in with Father...and had urged us to say our goodbyes.

Father started wheezing again, to the point that a nurse rushed in to adjust the oxygen flow to his mask. The fix...wasn't one. Even with the extra air, he struggled for breath.

Lance grabbed Father's other hand. Mother was with him, tears coursing down her cheeks. Looking at her face, so beautiful yet wrecked, made it impossible for anyone to accept that the two of them had said vows forty-two years ago in a marriage that was more business merger than matrimony. Maybe that was why Mother had accepted the blow about Margaux with the peace of a fucking saint, though it was clear that somewhere along the way, she'd given her own heart completely to the man.

At last, his breathing evened.

Then slowed.

And shortly after one o'clock that day, the second man I'd called Father for most of my life slipped into the stars.

That night, the impending storm moved in fully over the city. Perfect. The sky shed the tears I refused to indulge anymore. At least that was the story I threw at myself. Deep—very deep—inside, my heart battered my soul with the truth. I was fucking terrified of those tears. They'd dissolve the last threads of the parchment inside, not an option no matter how appealing the idea seemed now. The strangest image kept appearing in my head, of a little framed plaque Britta kept on her desk in the office. It was an image of an ocean wave bashing a cliff, with the words *What you resist, persists.*

As usual, fate was getting the last laugh.

How long had I spent on the illusion that I'd get to take a pass on this day? That the great and mighty Killian Stone got to take a pass on this fucking pain?

Somehow, I had to keep putting the steps in front of each other. Keeping up this shell of a person so nobody saw the crumbling core beneath.

Fortunately, automaton status wasn't anything new to me. From MIT finals to all-night contract negotiations to putting on a face for the paparazzi, I was very adept at pretending I was somebody else—which was damn good now, since I wasn't sure who the fuck I really was anymore. The mask of the dutiful family representative fit better than ever as I followed Josiah Benjamin Stone's precise instructions for his postmortem fanfare. But making arrangements for Nolan Banyan Klarke that possessed the dignity and discretion the man deserved? The feat was finally managed but only with Claire's and Lance's help. Numerous times a day, God and his deity friends received an earful of my thanks for my woman and my brother.

The heavens continued to cry on the city. Which was just fucking fine by me.

By three the next morning, Claire stumbled into the bedroom at the condo and fell into bed. She was asleep before her head hit the pillow.

I felt like a caged animal.

I prowled the length of the condo. Attempted some work. Prowled again. Tried napping on the couch. Prowled more. Cued up one of my favorite movies, a classic James Bond. Connery didn't help. Neither did switching to Daniel Craig.

At eight thirty, I quietly changed into running gear. After scribbling a note to Claire, I was out the door.

Without a route in mind, I took off into the rain. The freezing lashes were the perfect pain against my face, collecting in my stubble, running down my neck and chest. I took a circuitous route before finding myself on the lakefront trail, the waves calling to me in the dark kinship of like spirits. My heavy steps splatted the pavement in strange syncopation with the freezing waters churning beneath the black clouds, an incarnation of my chaos-driven thoughts.

After a while, I stopped to recover and looked up. Oddly, or maybe not so, the logo on the side of Margaux's hotel beamed through the mist at me. Less than thirty minutes later, I found myself dripping in the hallway outside her suite door, rapping on the portal with soft but steady pressure.

A long minute passed. I heard rustling from inside and then noticed the peephole darkening before a soft "Oh, my God" punched the air. Margaux wasn't the source. It belonged to a man.

Correction. A boy. The door swung open to reveal a kid who looked about twelve. That meant I'd either aged a lot in the last two days or the pretty young thing was really barely through puberty. Logic dictated the truth was probably somewhere in between.

"Mr. Stone," he bade with chilly politeness. "Won't you

please come in?" After I stepped inside, he fingered the long bangs off his face and declared, "I'm Sorrelle, Margaux's Midwest assistant."

I schooled my features into neutrality. "Of course you are."

"Can I take your—uhhhhh—jacket? Looks like it's still a mess outside."

I unzipped my jacket and handed it over, if only for the brief amusement of watching the kid try to handle the soggy thing. "Thanks."

"Miss Asher will be out in a minute. She—ummm—wasn't expecting anyone."

"I know. I won't be long. I just—"

"Wanted to come and check on the fallout status from Josiah's blast?"

The accusation was hurled by the woman who pushed back the slider to the bedroom with a glare stamped on her face and tension defining every inch of her stance. Though the expression and the posture weren't anything new for Margaux, I was still compelled to give her a stunned once-over. It was the first time I'd seen her out of designer heels and three inches of makeup. Granted, her sweat outfit was some kind of name-brand thing, with rhinestones up one leg and a gold zipper pull, but it was her eyes that really stopped me. Normally alert and mischievous as a cat, they were now sunken and red-rimmed, indicating she'd had as little luck with sleep as I'd had last night.

"I was out for a run and found myself in the neighborhood," I finally said. "Thought I'd come see how you're doing."

"*Found yourself in the neighborhood?*" She spurted out a laugh. "Is that really what Josiah told you to say, brother dear?"

I almost boomeranged the laugh back. If she only knew

about the deception that canceled out the one she'd been hit with. The skeletons in the Stone family closet got more interesting by the day.

"You know I've never played messenger boy for my father, Margaux." I folded my arms and squared my jaw, emphasizing that I wouldn't take her lip even with shock and pain as its inspiration. "Besides...he's gone. You might have already heard. We prepped a statement for all the morning news feeds."

She popped out a hip and folded her arms too. "In case it's not evident, I'm not feeling Miss Mary Sunshine about dealing with the world right now. But I'm sorry for your loss." Her tone was taut but sincere. "Well...*our* loss, I guess."

"Thanks."

"I hope you don't expect me to attend the service or anything."

I leveled my head and studied her. Really looked. I took in the depths of her green eyes with a strange new understanding. From the start, I'd written Margaux off as a desperate clone of her mother, engaged in a daily competition with Andrea by fighting to be a bolder, bitchier version of the woman. But now that I knew the ice floes in Andrea's veins were literally not the same stuff as in Margaux's, I saw things differently. Margaux's stockpile of selfishness was learned, not inherited. Her life had been a series of expectations in strict black and white, good and bad, with love itself withheld if she made the wrong choice. A person's world became a narrow place with programming like that. A miserable place.

Now I *really* had to hold back from hugging her.

"Chill, sister." I injected half a grin to attempt setting her at ease. "Nobody's expecting a thing from you right now."

"Except a request for a check." She added her own

sarcastic snort, until new comprehension seemed to slam her face. "Wait a second. *That's* your angle, isn't it? That's why you're here...to start the ball rolling on buying off my silence."

I wished I could've admitted her statement shocked me. But the words were classic, caustic Margaux. "I'm going to allow you credit for the reasoning behind that," I answered tightly. "But I'm also going to tell you that it's wrong. Margaux... listen..."

"I don't need your damn money, Killian, okay? I won't let you control me just because Josiah Stone didn't know the right hole for his dick twenty-seven years ago. I have my own money and my own life and have done just fine with both. I won't dance on the Stones' puppet strings simply for a few extra zeroes in my bank account."

That did it. I cut loose with an incensed growl and advanced on her. "Damn it, Margaux! Lower your safety shields for one minute." She skittered backward by a few steps. Good. She'd come out of that bedroom thinking she could keep her cool-girl center intact, but she'd never listen to me that way. "Sometimes, it's about more than money." I grunted. "Fuck. *A lot* of times, it's about more than money. For the record, I don't care if you keep your life and your bank account and all five hundred pairs of your shoes, but what you *may* need, at some point, is a brother. Perhaps even three."

Brother.

The word weighted the air between us—right after it punched a hard breath out of her. It was impossible not to notice the unsteady sheen in her gaze now or the way her fingers shook as she refolded her arms.

"Right," she returned. "Because I haven't survived twenty-seven years without the loving torment of a few siblings, right?"

Her awkward laugh betrayed how she'd likely fantasized about exactly that.

"It's not all that bad." I feigned a wince. "Except when the asshats turn off your alarm so they can get the last two bowlfuls of Count Chocula in the pantry *and* make you late for school."

That garnered a genuine smile, perhaps the first I'd ever seen on the woman's face. Damn. Margaux was actually stunning when she was sincere. "So...you going to start beating up on my boyfriends now or something?"

Sorrelle looked up from where he'd been nursing a cappuccino at the work desk. "If he doesn't, goddess, I will."

I rolled my eyes for Margaux's benefit only, inciting a silent snicker from her. The moment lasted for two seconds. She cut herself off with a sharp gasp and a horrified gape. "Ohmigod!"

"What?" I asked.

"Shit. Killian, I seduced you last year! We almost slept together. Ew!"

I didn't bother with the amendment that her "almost" was my "not-if-we-were-the-last-two-people-on-Earth." I also decided it better to let her keep thinking her seduction had been a near miss interrupted by Claire's arrival at the condo than inform her that even if things had developed between us, she wouldn't have really slept with her brother. One messy secret at a time.

"Well, we didn't." It felt like a sufficient icebreaker. Before she could protest, I stepped over and yanked her into a hug. As I expected, she stiffened. As I *didn't* expect, she finally relaxed enough to sheepishly pat my back. "So maybe now, we can be friends." As I pulled away, I gave her the sincerity of my own gaze. "Believe it or not, I might understand a thing or two about this maze called the Stone clan."

For a second, Margaux let herself smile back. All too quickly, she returned to her comfort zone of sarcastic and snotty, despite the affectionate jab she delivered to my shoulder. "Yeah. Whatever. And, for the record, I hate Count Chocula."

I grinned, enjoying this repartee. Maybe, just maybe, it would be semicool to have a little sister around. "You've clearly never had it my way."

"Oh?"

"On top of ice cream."

"For *breakfast*?"

"I had special pull with the kitchen staff."

My chest tightened. *Dad...I miss you.*

Another knock on the door rescued me from wallowing in any more of that shit.

"Hell," Margaux muttered. "Two wrong room service deliveries and one soaked brother later, my room has become Grand Central Station."

Sorrelle peeked through the peephole and then backed from the door with both hands cupping his mouth. "Cheese and rice, M. It's your mother!"

I was unsurprised that the announcement pressed the rewind button on Margaux. Her laughter faded and the haughty angle to her chin returned as if our conversation hadn't happened. She dipped a determined nod at Sorrelle. "Let's just get it over with. She'll only come back if we don't."

Andrea hardly acknowledged the assistant on her way into the room. Unlike Margaux and me, the woman was already coifed to the eyelashes. Her tailored navy-blue pantsuit was layered over a white turtleneck with flecks of silver woven through it. Her stilt-level ankle boots matched the suit. Ah, my world was right again. I'd journeyed to the land of the Ashers and could brag at least one moment of will-she-die-from-the-next-step-or-not thrills for the effort.

"Margaux, darling, did you lose your cell? I've been trying to—" Andrea halted in her tracks. Damn, even that move didn't topple the woman. "Oh. Killian. Hello there. I...well, I barely recognized you. You're a bit soggy."

"It would seem so." I looked down but lifted my gaze back up with clear confusion. Was this the same woman I'd hauled off Father yesterday as she'd spat her vow for revenge on him during his last breaths of life? The same person who'd watched her daughter run from her because of a heart-stabbing truth revealed? It seemed like she'd strolled in from a week at a spa retreat.

Andrea smoothed the front of her pants, realigned her features into a poised smile, and offered, "Well, I did hear the press release about Josiah this morning. It received excellent coverage. All the local affiliates, of course, and many of the major networks." She stared me directly in the eyes when adding smoothly, "It was beautifully written."

I planted my feet a little wider and folded my arms. "Yes, it was."

"Claire's handiwork?" Her fishing expedition for information was charming but unsettling. Was she really worried more about her company's place in the new lay of the land at SGC than the hundred painful questions flashing through her daughter's eyes?

"No," I answered, adopting the cold tone I was famous for. "Father had it prewritten."

Only a spark of amusement crossed the woman's lips,

amply coated in whatever the hell color was trendy right now. "A fact that's surprised no one, I'm sure." She strolled slowly to the window, gazing out at the point where the mist swallowed the lake. "Joe Stone...in control to the end."

"The father I'll never know."

Though every word of it was accusation, there wasn't a drop of Margaux's normal venom. There was only soft sadness, matched even deeper across her face. Thank fuck I turned to watch Andrea's reaction, because I was just in time to watch a sole second of remorse flash across her features.

"Margaux." It was a strange combination of reprimand and entreaty. "You *know* that all I've ever wanted is to see you succeed and be happy. And you are both, am I right? Look at you, darling. Young, beautiful, at the very top of your game, held to nobody's rules but your own"—she swept a hand toward the expansive view beyond the windows—"the world literally at your feet."

I couldn't help my derisive interjection to that. "Hmmm. The perfect glass tower."

Andrea's perturbed glare was swift and silent. If I wasn't the client throwing the biggest checks into Asher and Associates' bank account, there'd likely have been some choice words along with it. She kept the comments in by flattening her lips to a terse line. "Margaux, your life has not lacked for anything. I have provided everything you could ever ask for—"

"Except the truth." Margaux approached Andrea with stiff steps and coiled hands. "The *truth*, Mother—you know, despite everything else, that little tie we've *always* shared?" A lightning flare from the skies illuminated the sharp green sheen in her eyes. "The dirty little secrets I've always kept for you? The things I've forgiven you for? The loyalty I've shown, thinking to myself that even if everybody else in the world deceived me, my *mother* never would. She'd always give me the truth, no matter how ugly or painful it was. She'd always care enough to be brutally honest with me. There'd never be any shocks or surprises or walls between us, and—"

"Stop it." Andrea's comeback couldn't have been more vicious had she spun on Margaux and physically slapped her. "You pitiful, ungrateful girl! You will stop—"

She clutched into silence when I caught the hand she jabbed out, my palm smacking hard against her wrist. "No," I growled. "*You'll* stop. Now."

Andrea ripped her hand away. She glowered so hard at Margaux I wondered if her nostrils would spew flames too. "You want the truth, girl? Fine, then here it is. Your real mother was a whore who slept her way into Josiah Stone's boardroom. I watched it happen because I was engaged to be married to his best friend and business partner."

I felt my eyes narrowing and my chest imploding. Somehow I bypassed the shock to stammer, "Harry Furwell?" To my knowledge, the man had been Father's closest friend until passing away last year. I remembered Father discussing the adventures of their early business deals as well. "But Daisy was his wife. They had four children."

"Correct." Andrea's smile was all cruel lines and bitterness. "Daisy was the bitch who moved in after Harry broke our engagement. After I left college for him before I graduated, breaking the terms of my scholarship. After I planned our wedding to the last detail and was even sending invitations to the printer. And after he wanted to sample a little 'cake' before the wedding and then panicked like a child when the condom broke—forcing me to confess that he had nothing to worry about."

Margaux frowned. "I don't understand."

But I did. "You're infertile," I ventured.

"Barren," she spat. "Yes. The cosmos correcting a blessing with a curse, I suppose. I mean, a woman with a one-sixty-one IQ can't possibly expect to be blessed with a bountiful womb as well...right?" She gathered her hands together at her waist, the pose I liked calling Warped Mother Superior, while pacing across the suite as if it were a boardroom. "Regrettably, that logic wasn't shared by the majority of Chicago's social elite twenty-seven years ago. Daddy Furwell called me into his study to quietly inform me that I'd sign a nondisclosure agreement and accept their outrageous payoff for it and then get as far away from their son as I could."

Margaux's lips trembled. "And you accepted it? Just like that?"

"Of course I didn't." The woman rocked back on one heel. "And I paid handsomely for that stupidity as well. Within a week, the gossip mill circulated about Harry's supreme dissatisfaction with my 'cake' and how he was having severe second thoughts about our compatibility." She sniffed. "The bastard was desperate. He'd waited too long to get married and get started on his heirs. Joe and Willa already had the three of you, and Harry was feeling the pressure from his parents. Marrying me would've meant waiting for years for a proper adoption, if that would even fly as an acceptable alternative."

I parked my ass on the couch's arm before supplying, "So the Furwells played dirty."

I almost knew the answer already. I'd liked Harry Furwell, but the man had possessed a ten-mile-long devious streak.

Andrea confirmed it by elaborating, "Within a few days,

the men scoffed at me. The women simply didn't pay attention anymore. Half my bridesmaids backed out of the wedding via answering machine message. And when I went back to Furwell to finally accept the payoff, the amount on the check was cut in half."

I nodded in a moment of sympathy. Growing up at Keystone Manor had given me special insight into the cruelties of the social elite gossip machine. It was Smaug the Dragon in high form, fire and death to anyone who dared piss it off enough. "So how did my father's indiscretion play into all this?"

The only thing missing to Andrea's cat-in-the-cream look was a smug lick of her lips. "Obviously, you boys don't linger in the country club bathroom like we girls do. I'd just stopped in to clean out my locker and was primping a bit in the salon when little Violet came running in and donated the contents of her tum-tum to the porcelain goddess. When she broke open every tear duct right after, sobbing Josiah's name between the blubbering, it was simple to string together all the pearls of their interesting—and unwanted—secret."

"And you saw a way to help them out—for a price," I filled in. "Making back the money the Furwells welched on and gaining a special weapon to hold over Josiah as an emergency backup."

I longed to retract the words as soon as they spilled out. The corporate strategist in me had simply taken over to arrive at the conclusion. I didn't think about the look Margaux would flash at me, her breath catching as if I'd hurled a dagger at Andrea and really missed the target—or the way Andrea would react either. The victorious smirk on her face turned my gut to lead.

"Yes, well..." she crooned, "nothing like a few million dollars and a gorgeous new baby girl to turn your ex-fiancé apoplectic. Seeing me in full mother mode made the man harder for me than a Jolly Rancher. And believe me, he was just as delicious—down to the last drop I sucked out of him, the night before his oh-so-proper nuptials to Daisy Harper."

Damn.

So, this was what it was like to stand beside a nuclear core that had melted down. The disbelief and inability to accept what had just happened, followed by sickness that wouldn't stop. I traded enough of a look with Sorrelle to know he felt exactly the same way. And Margaux? To be honest, I wasn't sure if her silence impressed or alarmed me.

Studying her profile, now dipped toward the floor, didn't clarify anything. Her face, lined in sorrow, tore at my heart. All the woman's efforts to objectify herself suddenly made sense. She'd been seen as nothing more from the day she was born. But the knowledge of it and the words, spoken aloud, confirming it?

Yeah. Nuclear reactor core breach. Big-time.

"Andrea." Margaux's lips barely moved with the syllables. "I'd like you to leave now."

For the first time since I'd known her, Andrea Asher's face flushed deep red. "Margaux. *Darling.* Come now. You know that I didn't—"

"Let me rephrase." Margaux snapped her head up. Her shoulders ratcheted back. "Get. The. Hell. Out."

Sorrelle had already crossed to the door and flung it open. He grimaced at Andrea like she was a used makeup wipe as she strode past him. As soon as she was clear of the portal, he let the door click shut while smoothing both his eyebrows and muttering something about how the room needed a thorough karmic cleansing. After bustling back to the desk, he produced some incense cones and instantly lit them up in a ceremony that sounded like a Latin-Klingon fusion.

Margaux hadn't moved.

I carefully approached. "Hey. You okay?"

She didn't say anything. I tugged at her shoulder, wondering if I'd shatter her with the move. But maybe a good shatter was exactly what she needed.

Feeling her head slam into my chest was one of the best and worst sensations I'd ever experienced. As her tears spilled out and blended with the rain on my shirt, the storm obliged the moment by breaking into a torrent outside the window. I cradled her head against me, eschewing the normal platitudes in favor of what Margaux needed the most—an anchor in her tempest.

Fuck. I knew that feeling well.

"Killian?"

"Yeah?"

"When does this get easier? When does everything go back to normal?"

I pulled in a long breath and pierced my gaze into the fathomless gray chaos, which seemed to take over the world around us. "I wish I knew, Miss Mary Stone. I wish I knew."

CHAPTER NINE

Claire

I stretched and rolled over in Killian's mammoth bed. Regardless of how far I reached in any direction though, I came up empty. The sheets on his side were undisturbed and cool... but I didn't let that stop me from running my arms across them in need of feeling him near.

The past week came thundering back like a stampede of stallions. Ban, Josiah. Dad, Father. Margaux.

My God. Margaux.

Sister.

Not just my stepsister. Killian's real sister. No—that wasn't right either. Trey and Lance's real sister. Because Killian had separate blood in *his* veins. Hell, maybe Lance was half something else, too. Sure would explain why he and Kil hadn't grown up into half-lunatic asses.

No matter what, it was all a mess. In every tangled, fucked-up sense of the word.

My head started pounding again. Same rhythm, different day—for the seventh day in a row. It had been a nonstop week, working with everyone on the team, including Andrea and Margaux, who were definitely on an as-necessary basis for their communications. Despite that new jolt of weird to the team, we'd coordinated a memorial service for Josiah that likely made some people in Chicago wonder if his canonization was next.

Two hundred people attended. Nobody wept, except Willa.

My second project was accompanying Killian to Ban's service. With Willa's blessing, we buried his ashes in a small clearing in Keystone's forest, one of his favorite places on the estate.

Fifty people attended. Everyone wept, except Killian.

At three the next morning I'd found him in the office at the condo, staring out at the rain...his face more wet and streaked than the window.

Project number three was the source of all the headaches. A press conference in the lobby of Stone Global's headquarters, scheduled for this afternoon right before the evening news cycle went hot, had to flow without a hitch. It was the first public announcement from the Stones since the fire and would set the tone so Killian could guide the company forward with the same support always thrown behind Josiah's name.

With a normal client, our team would have urged waiting at least a week longer for this kind of event, but the stock market had already reacted to the drama surrounding the fire, as well as the rumors abounding about Josiah's less-than-peaceful passing. SGC's stock values had taken a fearful drop. As soon as that had happened, Killian had ordered the press conference bumped forward. It was never far from his mind that the SGC name was responsible for employees making their mortgage payments, buying their groceries, and putting braces on their kids' teeth. If that meant he had to shove aside his grief and, in his own words, "Put on the lampshade and dance on the table" for investors, then he would.

Though none of the market's behavior seemed odd to Kil, I'd been floored by confusion. It didn't seem to matter to anyone that he'd already logged years in his "father's" seat, having stepped to the company's helm when Josiah had been ill, Trey had been drunk, and Lance had been six states away. The critics apparently had the memories of fleas, leading to the significance of today's event. Kil's most important opportunity to silence the doubters lay in sixty simple minutes this afternoon.

I needed to take something for the headache. Regrettably, that meant moving—the first time I had since collapsing to the mattress last night. After quickly snatching my hoodie off the chaise at the end of the bed, I dashed across the room and hustled some socks out of Kil's drawer. While his bare floors were gorgeous, even with radiant heat built below them, his California girl roomie was constantly cold in here.

Get your ass in gear, San Diego. The blood circulation will help.

I let a smile tilt my lips. In my head, the decree was issued in Killian's beautiful baritone. I wondered where he was as I trudged to the kitchen for coffee and ibuprofen. He'd been full of restlessness since we'd gotten back, a few clicks higher than his usual on-the-go speed. In light of the enormous impact of today, I hadn't blamed him for it last night. I'd wanted to stay up with him, but sheer exhaustion had finally taken its toll and I'd passed out.

I expected to find him sacked on a couch in the office or living room, but a look through both didn't turn him up. I felt a frown replacing my smirk as I started the coffee brewing and then grabbed my phone. It was still ungodly early, but if he'd gone to the office, he would've messaged me.

That was when I saw his note on the counter. I ran a finger over his elegant handwriting.

Went to clear my head with a run. Be back soon.

Love you, Fairy Queen.

—K

I took my coffee and phone and headed back toward the bedroom. As I crossed the living room, thunder boomed overhead. Thick clouds billowed over the lake. The rain pelted harder at the floor-to-ceiling windows.

"A run? Seriously?" Irritation underlined my mumble, brought on by a wave of concern. Why the hell was he exposing himself to a storm worthy of the Wicked Witch and all her cousins—today of all days? On the other hand, how had anything about the last week made any sense? If the man needed to get lost in a squall to feel clear, who was I to stop him?

I decided to be grateful he hadn't asked me to join him. To celebrate that fact, it was time for a nice, scalding shower. The bathroom steamed up while I grabbed my robe from the closet to lounge in afterward.

I sighed in bliss while stepping under the spray, allowing my limbs to go limp as the hot water cleaned off some of the difficult memories from the last seven days. None of it had been easy, but Killian and I had hung on to each other through it all, despite running in our operations mode for far too long now. My discomfort with that was hard to define. We weren't as broken as we'd been in Europe. We just weren't connected again either. The rigors of life had drained us both...and I was badly in need of a recharge, Mr. Stone-style.

While towel-drying my hair at the vanity, I heard the condo's alarm system chirp. Two seconds later, the front door *whumped* shut. I smiled. Carl Lewis had returned from his session. Deciding to let him find me instead of crowding him the moment he walked in, I sat on the bed to start combing through my hair. It was getting long and thick and difficult lately. When I got back to San Diego, a trip to the salon would be on the priority list.

I felt his presence before turning to behold him in the doorway. He'd shucked his running shoes, but that barely mattered. The rest of him, from the ink-black waves on his head to the socks that squished when he stepped, was soaked straight through. And was sexy as hell.

"Hey," he greeted. "Here you are."

I didn't fight my appreciative smile. Or the warmth in my wide eyes, undoubtedly telling him how utterly hot he was in his chilled clothes. Tiny drops ran down his angled cheeks and then dripped from his chin to his chest. His windbreaker clung to the ridges of his pecs, biceps, and abs like an obscene second layer of skin.

"Yep. Here I am." *Now getting* very *hot and bothered, thank you, Mr. Stone.*

"Miss Montgomery?"

"Hmmm?"

"You're staring." The bastard had the nerve to laugh a little.

"And you're...wet."

"It's raining outside."

All that was missing was the "duh." It raised his fuck-me-please factor by about a gazillion. The man's sideways smirk told me he grew more aware of that by the second. Had he turned up the thermostat on his way in too?

"So where all did you run? Though I guess a trip to the corner would've turned you into just as much of a human sponge. Guess it's good that I didn't cancel the stylist for you this afternoon." I'd gone for conversational, but it all came out like an accusation, the last effect I ever intended. Fortunately, the heat we'd just exchanged still lingered in his gaze. If he'd noticed, he didn't say.

"Had to muck out the stalls," he said softly. I replied with an understanding nod. Though he played water polo now, he'd grown up on the real horses-and-divots version, meaning the equestrian terms came out as metaphors for the state of his gray matter. That didn't explain the strange quirk to his lips after that. "And I also..."

The hesitant drop-off to his voice was like a button blaring *push me*. "You also...what?" I set aside my comb and stared harder at him. "Kil?"

His lips quirked again, this time with awkwardness. "I actually ended up at Margaux's—Mary's, whatever—hotel." He looked up and tilted his head. "I went up and saw her."

"Tell me you're joking."

"Nope. I started running, and kept running, and before I knew it, I was in front of the place. It felt like a sign, I guess—so I went in to speak with her. I figured she could probably use a friend."

He shrugged—*shrugged*—like it was no big deal. On the other hand, my mouth still hung open.

"I'll bet she did," I responded, words clipped. "And I bet she was more than pleased to let you into her hotel room."

Hell. The snark was alive and well this morning. Then I realized what I'd just said and almost laughed. The next moment—unbelievably—I almost pitied the woman. To Margaux's mind, her case of Killian fever was now all about her *brother*. The poor woman was probably ready to check out of the Knickerbocker and into the Hotel De Freak-Out.

Luckily, Kil seemed to read all that in the chagrined twist of my lips. He raised an eyebrow, hit me again with that damn grin, and then packed the final punch of oh-my-God goodness by whipping his windbreaker and T-shirt off in a couple of tugs.

"Whoa." I leaned back on both my hands. "Are you *trying* to steal the apology off my lips?"

His eyebrows lowered. The words genuinely confused him. "Apology? Why?"

I forced myself into a dismissive grunt. "My snark-a-palooza? Just now? I really *am* sorry. It was out of line. I'm overtired."

He walked over as if to kiss me but stopped short. Conflict pulled at his features. Now *I* could read *his* thoughts. If he came much closer, the PG-13 part of our conversation would be over—and the R-appropriate section wouldn't last too long either. "We're both tired, fairy," he stated. "It's okay."

"Stop saying such sweet things when you're wearing such a sinful grin."

His eyebrows arced. "Sinful?"

I nodded. "And sexy, for that matter."

"In that case..." He covered the last three steps between us, reaching out for me this time. "My forgiveness has a condition."

I let out a little squeal. "Dear lord, Chicago. Your skin is freezing."

He chuckled while pulling me off the bed and up against him. "Good observation." Nuzzled his chilled lips to my neck. "Now you can help me get warm."

I gasped as his cold fingers sneaked beneath my robe, cupping my ass. "That's your condition?"

"Mmmm-hmmm." He pulled the ties of my robe free. His soaked sweats pressed against my crotch, awakening it in a dozen delicious new ways. "My body needs yours, fairy...in all the biggest ways possible."

He sure as hell wasn't kidding. The pulsing ridge of his erection made me sigh and soften beneath his exploring hands. It was so damn impossible to tell this man no. But I really wanted to talk about what had happened in Margaux's hotel room. Maybe a stall tactic would work.

"Wh-What about a bath first...to warm up? Want me to run one, my love? Then maybe I can climb in with you?" He dipped his mouth to the base of my throat. Then the valley between my breasts. Oh *God*, that felt good. "I can...umm—" What the hell was I talking about again? A bath. And him. Right. "I can wash your back," I finally forced out. "You always like that."

"Not right now." He murmured it while teasing his lips up to the rigid peak of my right breast.

"Oh. Okay." I swallowed hard as he rolled his tongue along the needy nub. *Focus, damn it. He went to Margaux's room. And they talked. And—*

And holy shit, it was hard to think when he nibbled on my nipple.

"Well, do you...want to talk...about what happened with—" What the hell was her name again?

"No." He shifted his mouth to my other breast. "I don't

want to talk right now." In one fluid movement, he kicked his sweats off. In another, he lowered me back to the mattress. Within seconds, he pushed aside the halves of my robe so we finally lay skin to skin. "I want to fuck you, Claire. Hard and deep. Probably several times. *That's* what I want."

"Oh."

"Yeah. Oh."

He rolled us both over in order to get me completely out of the robe. As I yanked the thick cotton off, he gazed up with a devilish version of his grin that managed to exude innocence as well. The effect was intoxicating. I gave in to the temptation to run my fingers over his broad, bronze chest—that still felt like ice.

"No more running in ice soup, Mr. Stone." My admonishment was gentle but stern. "You're going to catch pneumonia."

"*Psshhh.*"

"Killian!"

"I grew up in the ice soup, baby. I'm not going to catch—"

"I can't live without you." I didn't try to hide the hoarse crack in my voice. "Okay? Happy now?"

For a long moment, all he did was continue to stare. After that pause, he raised a hand to the space directly over my heart—and pressed it there. "You always make me happy."

Slowly, he drew that hand down the center of my torso. Though the action brought a thousand shivers, his face still captivated me the most. I couldn't stop picturing what he must have been like at five years old, so young and innocent, brought into the middle of a complicated mess by adults wrapped up in their warped and convoluted sense of "doing right."

The heart he'd just warmed with his fingers now swelled

from the power of his honesty. If he asked me again to marry him, I'd shout my acceptance at the top of my lungs. As odd as it was, the pain of the last week had finally brought me the Killian I'd been searching for.

Unable to hold back anymore, I leaned over and kissed him. The pillows puffed up around us with the force of my passion—and his in return. His powerful body, especially the part pressing most intimately against me, grew. He circled both arms around my waist and clutched me tighter, inviting my mouth to stay right where it was as he opened his lips for me.

Warmth. Invitation. Safety. Solace. Home. He was my home.

I lost myself in that kiss. Drowned in the luxury of his taste, the perfect feel of his tongue. Moaned as he stroked his tongue with mine with increasing urgency and growing desire.

There was so much more to our connection than the physical need of man and woman—and never more than in that moment. The force of his need filled me, pushed me, consumed me.

When we tore back by a few inches, Killian dug a hand to my scalp. "My queen. My Claire. You're my anchor in this ocean. My compass in this storm."

Peering into his eyes was looking to the depths of that uncharted sea. Fathoms of darkness lived there...gray and black and pewter, liquid and shadows as mysterious as the bottom of the Pacific or Atlantic themselves. When I gazed at him like this, the origins of the world's labels for him were so easy to understand. *Cryptic. Enigmatic. Secluded. Guarded.* He was unknown to so many, only allowing the most worthy into his sanctum—and now, all the reasons for that made such sense.

Currently, he'd made me the most worthy person on the planet. The way he held me in his embrace, touched my skin, kissed my lips...I'd never felt closer to him. I yearned to press him for more. Damn it, why did I always want more? I needed to thank the universe for what it had already given me this week. At the moment, this connection was enough. More than enough.

It was perfect.

"Killian," I whispered. "When we're together like this, when it feels like we are the only two people on the planet, I feel like I can take on the world." I emitted a little growl as he reacted to that by slowly wrapping my hair around his fingers. "I know it sounds corny..."

"It sounds wonderful." He rasped it, seating my hips more firmly against his, letting his engorged cock slide softly between the moist lips of my sex. "Don't stop," he encouraged.

Denying him wasn't an option. "We can do anything we set our minds to," I told him, "as long as we're together. We're a force, Killian—you and me. I'm not sure the world's prepared for it yet. They have no idea what they're messing with."

He growled again, harder and louder. "Hmmm. My fairy has tiger claws too. Always ready to fight for what's right."

"Damn straight, especially when it comes to the man I'm madly in love with." I bent and kissed him again.

"And what about the Killian Stone you're not so fond of?" He wasn't playing at the question this time. "Answer me. I've seen the look on your face when that bastard comes out to play."

"You're right. He *is* a bastard. But I love you, Killian. *All* of you." I seized the chance to splay my hand to the center of his chest now—to the heart inside that beat so strong and sure. "You're just one man. And when you are this open and real with me, I love you more than my own life. I want our lives to be one. As sure as I breathe, that's what I want."

We kissed again, but I let my lips linger on his for a very long time, simply tasting him, savoring him. I fitted my body deeper to his, eliciting a groan from him, matched by my own aroused sigh. It was no longer time for talk. Nonverbal communication could speak our remaining words—a skill my man knew just as well as fancy boardroom speeches. Thank God.

As I slid forward and then down, capturing his body inside mine, Killian braced his hands on my hips, establishing a rhythm of fire, light, and love that blazed through the room despite the dark clouds swirling outside. Our bodies moved together as our hearts already did, affirming exactly what we'd just promised each other. From now on, we'd handle whatever the world threw in our path—hand-in-hand, side by side— exactly how we should be.

I wasn't afraid anymore.

CHAPTER TEN

Killian

"It's official. We're at standing room only down there."

Britta issued the news upon reentering one of the second-floor conference rooms at SGC headquarters. The rooms were normally reserved by the HR department for functions like employee training sessions and job fairs. No training was happening today, unless one counted dealing with a media frenzy. Backing up the accuracy of the course title were a little over one hundred media reps and reporters—a.k.a. the best-dressed pack of blood-sucking parasites in the city—jammed into the lobby below, waiting for me and the two most visible members of the board of directors to appear and make the corporation's first public statement since the disasters of last week.

Fletcher Ford and Drake Newland, the two board members who'd accompany me to the podium, rose from the table as I did. Clearly, they were both reluctant to do so. The two men were also on the club's water polo team with me and were in the middle of regaling Claire with details of the asses they'd handed to the Diamond Club's team on the morning after we'd buried Josiah...and Dad.

"Well, damn," I drawled, tugging Claire tight to my side. "Did you hear that? Lobby's full. Guess Claire won't have time to judge the final outcome of your pissing match, boys."

Fletch tugged at both his sleeves, aligning his Brioni suit perfectly on his lanky frame. "She doesn't need to. I threw the winning point. Case settled."

"As opposed to the twelve shots I blocked?" countered Drake. "*Pssssh*. Back of the line with you, cretin."

Claire's shoulders shook beneath my grip, betraying her sweet giggle—and lending some much-needed light to this ordeal for me. Despite the circumstances that had made it necessary, I'd loved the excuse to keep her in the city for this extended time. Between the two weeks in Europe and the long days since we'd returned, it was the longest time we'd been able to spend with each other since the project that had originally brought her to the city, nearly a year ago. This time, her presence counted for more. A vast amount of more. Waking up each day with her in my arms and then having her by my side every night... I was living the best dream possible and never wanted to wake up. As soon as the chaos was over and life returned to normal—whatever that would be like now—I fully planned on pulling out that ring box again and putting that jewelry on her finger in the *right* way.

"Boys!" she called, breaking up what looked to become a real Fletch-versus-Drake pissing match. "Peace accord time, okay? I hereby declare you *both* king of the pool...at least until Killian gets back in the water."

Fletcher shot a mocking chuff. "Hate to be the bearer of bad news, Claire, but our swim suits aren't forgiving." He gave me a soft fist in the stomach. "Not sure flab boy here is going to like rocking a muffin top during the next game."

I flung him a snort. "Fuck you." But finished with a smile.

Britta stepped forward. "Mr. Stone? Speaking of news

and bearing it..."

My respite was over. Britta grimaced as her way of apologizing for being the messenger, but I returned it with a reassuring nod. "You're right. Thanks, Britta." Before I reluctantly stepped away from Claire, I gave her a tender kiss on her forehead. Because Fletch and Drake were watching, I lingered.

"Bastard," Fletcher groused.

Drake grunted. "I had something more colorful in mind, but bastard works too."

I curled a gloating grin. "We ready to get this dog-and-pony on the road, boys?"

Their composures sobered in tandem. Fletcher grabbed my hand and leaned in to give my shoulder a gruff bump. "We're with you, Kil."

Drake nodded his agreement. "Let's do this shit."

He finished by yanking open the door, allowing the din from the throng to flood into the conference room. Though the noise didn't faze me, as I knew about the hell storm of media phone calls Claire had once again helped Britta to field over the last couple of days, I hadn't done a very good job of prepping my friends for the cacophony.

"Holy fuck," Drake gritted. "And I thought Afghanistan was the loudest fire balling I'd ever have to endure."

"What the hell else did you tell them was going on today, Stone?" Fletch added. "You giving away free TVs off the back loading dock and not filling us in?"

I snorted again, if only to mask the sudden urge I had to yank both of them into something more than dumbshit shoulder bumps. Since there was no way we could risk Trey at the podium with me, thereby nixing the possibility of having

Lance either, I was grateful that my wingmen were the two best proxies for brothers that I could think of.

And right before me...was the best incentive to keep trudging through this shit.

Claire exited the room steps ahead of me, looking as regal as a princess in her cream skirt suit topping a light-pink cashmere turtleneck. As soon as the reporters noticed she'd emerged, they directed their photographers to start shooting. Flashbulbs ignited, indeed making the lobby look like one of the battlefields Drake had served on in the marines. But despite the chaos, I was calm. She was my anchor. She turned and reached for my hand, taking my breath away with a soft smile meant for me alone but shareable with the whole world—which I suddenly, really, did not want to do. Gazing at her from head to toe in that outfit, with her legs enhanced by her heels and her makeup all dewy and prim, made me want to hoist her over my shoulder, march her back into the room, and fuck every pin out of her perfect chignon, right in the middle of the conference table. If I remembered right, this was one of the tables in the building we *hadn't* christened in that way yet.

"Ready?" she asked, gripping my hand tighter.

I tilted my head so our eyes would directly meet before I responded. "With you by my side, baby, I'm ready to slay fucking dragons."

She answered by lifting her lips to mine. She tasted like breath mints and rain and the simple, sweet perfection of Claire. I wanted so much more, and dared just a tiny slide of my tongue against hers, resulting in a spatter of applause from the reporters.

"Awww, shit," Fletch grumbled. "Kil, you seriously need to keep it PG, man."

"Yo, Prince Charming." Drake smacked me on the back. "That's enough slobbering on the fairy queen for now."

As I pulled away, Claire giggled. "Dragons, baby," she prompted. "Go get 'em."

I grinned and winked. "Dragon stew for dinner, then?"

"I'll be waiting right here with the wine to match it."

I squared my shoulders and then moved ahead of Drake and Fletch, leading the way toward the staircase that consumed one wall of the lobby in a dramatic sweep. The piece had been designed by Olafur Eliasson in crackled glass and wood, making it nearly a crime to cover the bottom six steps with a small riser and platform, put there to give us space to address the throng. But the effect, conceived by Claire, was brilliant—all the images from this event would show the SGC logos everywhere, from the modernistic globes etched into the lobby's glass to the dozen custom banners that had been mounted just for today's announcements. The messaging would be crystal clear. It was business as usual at the Stone Global Companies—in short, we were still the corporate powerhouse we always had been and always would be.

Both my fathers expected no less of me.

With every step I took down the stairs to the podium and microphone, I vowed they'd receive what they expected. And I knew, without a doubt, it was their pride warming my chest as I approached the plexiglass pedestal. I also knew they'd found ways to infuse themselves into the encouraging dual shoulder claps delivered by my friends as I spread my grip to both sides of the thing. In Drake's forceful grasp, I felt the fortitude of Josiah Stone. In Fletcher's firm squeeze, I felt the moral and spiritual compass that Nolan Banyan Klarke had always lent to my life.

One last shot of strength came from another glance at the landing I'd just descended from. True to her word, Claire was there, even more breathtaking and beautiful from this distance. Stepping out to appear on either side of her were Willa and Lance, also smiling in support—then one more figure appearing on the family support bench, face tucked beneath a navy-blue fedora.

For a moment, my chest throbbed in a weird mix of dread and joy. Even after everything, Trey had really shown up.

No. Not Trey.

The fedora was pulled off to reveal a mane of blonde hair pulled into a side braid.

My sister was here.

I kicked up one side of my mouth in a fast smile at Margaux. Then swung my head back into the glare of a hundred camera lights.

"Good afternoon," I began. "Thank you all for coming today. I'll attempt to make my words brief in order to keep the session open for as many of your questions as possible. My name is Killian Stone. I am the Chief Executive Officer of the Stone Global Corporation, a multicompany entity based here in Chicago. I am joined today by two of SGC's board members, Mr. Fletcher Ford and Mr. Drake Newland. They also happen to be close friends, and I am grateful for their support during this emotional week for our family."

I gave the presentation a pause, letting some of the print reporters catch up on their smart pads—and resettling my composure.

"As many of you are aware, our family estate, Keystone Manor, suffered a near-catastrophic fire last Tuesday night. Though there is an ongoing investigation into the event, the fire authority is allowing me to relay that the cause was a boiler explosion based beneath the estate's south wing. The blast immediately destroyed the kitchen and service-staff quarters. Five of our loyal employees were injured at the time but discharged after emergency care. Two remain in intensive care and are expected to fully recover. One staff member, Nolan Banyan—"

In spite of all the times I'd rehearsed this part and made it through, my voice clutched into a long, hard pause. A thousand lights glared at me, but my senses tumbled into a tunnel. Pulled by instinct, I looked up again at Claire.

Who smiled and banished the tunnel.

"Nolan Banyan Klarke," I repeated, "our estate's lead engineer and groundsman, perished due to injuries sustained in the accident. Our family is grateful to Mr. Klarke, who served us for over thirty-five years."

I let another silence pass, this time because it was expected. The news everyone had truly come to receive was at hand. "As all of you know, there was one other casualty of the fire. My father, Josiah Benjamin Stone, died last Wednesday afternoon due to complications from smoke inhalation and cardiac stress. He passed peacefully, with the whole family by his side." This time, my practice paid off. My determination to maintain eye contact with the crowd was a success. Nobody outside that hospital room could learn that Father had departed life due to the emotional debris from the mortar shell announcement he'd just made. To get technical, the term family was a loose connotation too. "To all of you who sent condolences and flowers for the memorial service, your thoughtful gestures were appreciated. The Stones are also grateful that you've respected our privacy during this difficult time. We are now prepared to repay the favor and address any questions you have—especially about the exciting plans for the Stone Global Companies as we move into the future."

A perfectly coifed blonde edged in front of everyone else. I recognized her from one of the television gossip shows. "The future," she echoed. "That's a great subject."

I sent a cordial smile. "Thank you, Merrilee. I happen to agree."

"And are you ready to give us a little insight about what that's looking like for you, Killian? Perhaps something involving diamonds, white lace, and reservations for a large party at a destination hotel?"

A buzz of chuckles danced over the crowd. Everyone's eyes, including mine, rose to where Claire stood, blushing so bright that even I could see the stain on her cheeks. We exchanged subtle smiles before I looked back to the blonde, shaking my head. "Cutting to the chase, hmmm, Merrilee? Wanting to get back to Beau?" I deliberately brought up the hot boy-toy model she'd been dating for a few months. "Maybe he's waiting at the Fairmont with that diamond you're craving."

The reporter flashed her signature grin and good-naturedly endured the next round of laughter. "All right, all right," she conceded. "Touché, Mr. Stone."

From the middle of the throng, a younger reporter raised his hand. The motion had aggression written all over it, so I decided to save him for later, when there would be a greater chance of him tiring of the need to be probing and relevant. But while I pointed to the seasoned business correspondent from CNN, the puppy shouted his question anyway.

"Mr. Stone! My sources tell me that your father's passing wasn't 'peaceful' at all. That there was tension so thick they needed a buzz saw to get through it, and—"

"I'd be interested to know who those sources are." The decree came from Drake, who stomped forward with such force, I wondered if he was wearing his old Marine Corp. marching boots disguised as Ferragamo loafers. "Because you certainly didn't ask me, and I was at the Loyola Burn Center that day. Let me tell you that after the ambulances started arriving from Keystone, the entire place was ready for a few buzz saws on the air." He took another step, angling one shoulder out in a pose of deliberate challenge. "I don't have to be as nice about this as my buddy Killian, so let me be clear. We're here to take questions about the future plans for Stone Global Corporation, not Mr. Stone's personal life. He just buried his father. Show some respect, grasshopper."

I reined Drake back with a tug of his elbow—and a quick nod of thanks. With the pup finally silenced, the CNN reporter was able to ask his question.

"So, can you give us an overview of how the leadership of the company will shake out from this point? We understand that *some* plans were afoot before the tragedy at Keystone..."

I leveled a respectful stare toward the man. He had his shit together, saying enough without pushing too much, though deliberately leading everyone's mind toward the obvious. Trey was already conspicuous in his absence. The truth behind it just needed to be corroborated.

"Good question, Jim," I replied. "And you can be reassured that upper-level management will remain largely the same. We plan on a few shifts, of course, but the company has represented the blood, sweat, and tears of the Stone family for nearly fifty years—and will continue to do so."

"Bullshit."

The shout bounced off the walls like a crack of lighting and reverberated in the air. Heads turned and cameras followed suit, their bright lights colliding and then ricocheting off the glass walls of the big space. The heckler caught everyone off guard, clearly his intention—

Or so I hoped.

A party crasher was easily handled—and then controlled. It was likely just that. The occasion was ripe for some asshole to chug a shot of crazy and show up spouting shit like this. It was best to react exactly how I did, by leaning one elbow on the podium and trading a brief eye roll with Fletch. As building security scrambled toward the source of the bellow, I schooled my features into something between irritation and patience.

I sincerely hoped to fuck this wasn't Trey's way of making a grand entrance.

But hope wasn't going to be my buddy today.

I knew it by simply looking over at Claire, Lance, Mother, and Margaux. Their tense stares were fixed on the figure who was moving through the crowd now, the cloth of humanity opening as he approached and then zippering behind him, everyone clamoring for better vantage points.

Hell.

Inside a couple of minutes, Trey Rainier Stone stood directly in front of me, smiling like the tom cat who'd just made the day of all the pussies in the neighborhood. He wore a bespoke black suit that fit him to the millimeter and had indulged in a shower, shave, and haircut straight from a damn fashion spread in *Esquire*.

In short, I barely recognized my own brother.

Who clearly wasn't feeling the whole fraternal connection, either. His eyes were as dark as jade, his mouth a straight line of flint, his posture as rigid as granite.

"Well, hello there." I leveled my voice to a plane of marble. *Dark* marble.

"Good afternoon, Killian." He did the exact same.

"How kind of you to show up. And to be so punctual about it, as always." The sheen of sarcasm lay perfectly atop my marble.

"I'm pretty certain everyone will forgive me in a short time."

The annoying gossip blonde pushed forward once more. "Why do you say that, Trey?"

"You called bullshit when you first got here." Somehow, eager-puppy reporter had finagled his way to the front as well. "Why the beatdown on your brother, man?"

Trey whirled on the kid. "*Don't* call him my brother."

I think the pup responded to that. I wasn't certain because the blood thrummed too hard and loud in my ears. Thank fuck I still had an elbow braced on the podium, because I gripped the stand now in order to keep my spine straight. "What the hell are you doing?"

He joined his pivot back to the stage with a leap up to it. "What I should have done a long time ago, Mr. Klarke." Using measured steps, he approached the podium. From inside his jacket, he pulled out a small sheaf of papers and set them down like a preacher about to deliver a sermon personally handed down to him by the Angel Gabriel. Only it wasn't Sunday. And Trey clearly cared about only one kind of biblical value right now. Retribution. "I'm taking it all back."

"What on earth is going on?" Another reporter, the woman who covered exclusive pieces for the *Wall Street Journal*, threw her stare between Trey and me. "What did you just call him?" she pressed. "And what do you mean by taking it all back?"

Trey turned a serene stare toward her. The woman actually flashed back with a smile. Had a three-thousand-dollar suit and a bleached grin made everyone forget that the man had almost gone to jail on drug-possession charges ten days ago?

"There are no hidden meanings here, Nancy. For the first time in a long time, the Stone family means exactly what it says." His shoulders straightened. My throat constricted. "I called Killian Mr. Klarke because that's his real name. Though you all know him as our brother, raised with us as a Stone, he is, in truth, about as much a blood relative of mine as the Kardashians." He brandished the sheaf in the air. "I have all the proof here, easily sent to any of you upon request. As for the rest of my assertion"—he soared his gaze over the throng, confidence and authority now welded to his features—"that was also the truth. I promise all of you, as well as our valued stockholders, that *my* father's legacy shall be honored in *every* way—including a true Stone family member at the helm of the company."

He didn't have to say more than that. He didn't have to. The implication was crystal clear.

After the ten seconds it took for the point to sink in, the crowd exploded with questions.

"Mr. St—errr, Mr. Klarke—were you aware this announcement would be made?"

"Mr. Ford! Mr. Newland! Is the SGC board aware of all this?"

"How and when is this going to happen?"

"What about your personal legal troubles, Mr. Stone?"

As the queries lobbed in like relentless mortar fire, I turned and locked glares with the man who'd just exposed me. Trey was on top of the world. His eyes glinted with triumph. He smirked like he'd just eaten out half a cheerleading team.

"No need to stick around, Killian." He threw in a gloating snort. "I can get it from here."

While my head pounded harder with every flashbulb in my face, I kept my features neutral—except for the rage searing through my eyes, churning from the pit of my gut. "Well, stepping into shit has always been a specialty of yours, Trey."

"And humiliating me has always been one of yours." His features stepped on the edge of ugly with his own fury. "Did you really think I'd let them simply boot me off the board? Me, one of the rightful heirs to this empire?"

"I'm surprised you noticed what was happening." If he wanted a go at dueling smugness, I'd be happy to oblige. "The last time we spoke, you were *celebrating* in a bath of tits, booze, and oblivion."

"Perfect timing for you to move in for the kill."

"Timing created by *you*, asshole." I leaned close to him, near enough to smell the expensive cologne he'd sprung for along with the fancy sow's ear of a suit. "The blood may truly run in your veins, Trey, but if you want to sit in the big boy chair, keep it pumping to your brain and not your cock."

Trey swung his eyes toward Claire and grunted. "Like you did?"

I planted both my feet and cocked an eyebrow. "Do you remember the name of the last woman you fucked, brother?"

His face mottled. His shoulders shook. "I'm *not* your brother."

"I think you've made the fucking point." The gravel beneath my reply was unplanned—and definitely unwise. But there was nothing I could do to bottle it back up.

The smile he lifted at me was slow, savoring...and chilling. "Oh, Killian...I haven't even gotten started."

★ ★ ★ ★

He wasn't lying.

Every day that passed over the next two months, I learned that the hard way.

It wasn't like I hadn't envisioned this happening—at least a thousand times—before. But even the simpler events turned out to be shittier than I'd thought.

I didn't even try going into the office, knowing Trey would move into the CEO suite before Britta phoned with the news—through her tears. I was just dandy about letting him have the damn office, but I did care that he'd upset Britta by denying her request to leave early for her son's soccer playoff game. I also let him have the SGC town car, VIP sports club membership, and preferred table reservations at most Michigan Avenue restaurants. All of that crap was simply window dressing, and it wasn't like the douche could officially imprison me or bankrupt me. Until the SGC board met and voted on the issue, the company still needed my sign-off on its high-level decisions. In every legal and financial sense, I was still Killian fucking Stone.

But in every other sense of the word, I wasn't so certain anymore.

Like a brat peeling bark off a tree, Trey picked away at a handful of little things each day. Innocuous shit that ended up carrying deeper importance, despite my staunchest efforts at sloughing it off. He was the sole person on the planet who knew all my weakest spots and exactly how to exploit them if he so chose—and now, damn it, he chose. The way the polo team suddenly "forgot" to inform me about changes in the practice schedule, along with the obligatory bonding-over-beer afterward. A load of dry cleaning that was inexplicably lost, including the sweater Claire had had custom-made in Ireland for me as a Christmas gift. Even Alfred seemed distracted and irritable, not that I blamed him. I couldn't even send the man to the market without knowing he'd have to stare at my face on the gossip magazines and overhear whispers about how he worked for "the enigma who'd fooled the world."

That was the kinder version of the story. Most resorted to simply labeling me a fraud and a liar who hadn't possessed the balls to come forward with the truth before this. Not that it was my business to care about what the world thought anymore. The circus had a different ringmaster now, and God only knew what his show would look like. As long as Claire was willing to hang on with me in order to find out, I could face anything.

Even having to watch my girlfriend pay cash for our Chinese takeout.

Which, at the moment, had me seeing ten different shades of red.

On the grand scheme of challenges, my irritation was pathetic. This barely bumped the needle on the scale of first-world problems. I'd have written off my ire as ridiculous— except for the fact that I'd been a loyal customer of the Happy Panda since moving here three years ago. I knew Ming and Shan personally, even brought their kids red envelopes for Chinese New Year every February. They'd never had problems running my credit card for orders, except now they didn't know if Killian Stone's credit card would be good for the money—and they clearly assumed Killian Klarke would skip out on his bill.

I didn't realize I'd grumbled the sentiment aloud until Claire shot back a loud huff. "Stop it," she added to it. "I kind of liked getting to buy you dinner for a change, okay?"

I watched her load up my plate with noodles, broccoli, beef, and tofu, tempted to tell her I was good for all of three bites of it. To say the least, my appetite was soured. Didn't stop me from relishing the chance to smash open one of the fortune cookies with one pound of a fist and then pulling the slip of paper from the wreckage and reading it. "Hmmm. Your panda will fall off his rainbow of bliss—and bust every bone in his happy little body. Sounds damn good to me."

Claire rolled her eyes and broke apart her chopsticks. "Grab the wine, Confucius. Let's eat. I'm starving." As she grabbed both our plates and headed for the living room, she called, "I'm even going to be a good girl panda and let you pick the movie tonight."

"No way. It's your turn—and you bought fucking dinner." I sounded as moody as a fishwife—and was just as disgusted with myself too. I watched Claire bite the inside of her cheek to keep from snapping at me, a little thing she did that normally tempted me to try to soothe her laceration with my tongue— which was normally an excuse to slide my tongue into other places on her body. But common sense stepped in, warding me away from the move tonight. Or maybe it wasn't common sense at all. Maybe I just hated the goddamn possibility of being shunned by her as well.

My mind force-fed me the logic behind all this. By indulging all these gothic thoughts, I was letting Trey win.

And the shit-fest of a follow-up? I'd never wanted the fucking competition to begin with. The only thing I'd wanted for either of my brothers—who, in the deepest truths of my soul, would always be my brothers—was their happiness. The only thing I'd refused to sacrifice for that goal was the company Josiah Stone had put into my hands. There'd never been middle ground with either of them about that. While Lance respected the integrity of the family business and made his way off into the world to grab his own truth, Trey had let some strange chip on his shoulder, perhaps a compensation for the biological grandchildren he'd never give Father, grow into a blister on his spirit—feeling fine about making me the target when he poked the thing and let the poison seep out.

I took a drag on the wine in lieu of decking myself in disgust. When the hell had I become a gold medalist for self-pity? The weight wasn't right around my neck. It was time to get my shit together. Maybe I could convince Claire to assist in that department after all. The food and the movie could wait until after we'd loved each other into sexual oblivion...at least a few times.

But several nuzzles at her neck later, it was clear she wanted her money's worth out of the thirty bucks she'd just given to Happy Panda. "Kil." She had to make that point with a cock-hardening pout to her voice as well. "Come on. You haven't eaten all day. Coffee and a protein bar don't count."

I hadn't had the chance to be a persistent bastard all week. The thrill of her challenge spiked my blood, giving me the resolve to try one more time. I went for the bold approach, lowering my head to her thigh and biting gently. "I can think of better things to do with my mouth right now..."

She gasped. A hopeful sign. Then grunted. Damn. "Killian.

The food's getting cold."

A snort rose in me as response. By the time it erupted, it was a full growl. Not a nice one either. After grabbing my wine, I rose and stomped toward the patio.

The snow had all melted, but winter clung to the air, turning the night wind into a harsh bite as I walked outside. Ideal. Despite the picture-perfect view, I wasn't in the fucking mood for balmy and picturesque.

I heard Claire rise as well. Her steps weren't dainty or gentle, either. Great. Thanks to the arrival of my inner asshole to the party, she was in the mood for a dirty dustup too. I only hoped that after we fought the sex would be as filthy—though knowing my luck, a night in the guest bedroom felt like the more logical conclusion for things now.

A cell phone ring joined the howl of the wind. It was thick with Irish whistles and folk guitars, the Fenians tune that served as Claire's ID for her dad.

Thank fuck for you, Colin.

She managed to pull the device out of her pocket while maintaining her we're-not-done-yet glare at me. "Hey, Dad. What's up?" Within seconds, her gaze fell and her eyebrows knitted. "And...what's wrong?"

I left my wine behind on the terrace and went to her. Protective instincts instantly eclipsed my gloom. I lowered to the couch along with her, gathering her hand into mine as she persisted with her father. "Dad, listen to me. I love that your tomatoes are growing and the mayor loves his new yard, but neither tidbit is getting you off the hot seat, mister. What am I talking about? Seriously? Colin Montgomery, you fake cheerfulness worse than I do—and that's pretty damn badly." Her fingers tensed inside mine. "Spill it. Now." She let a meaningful pause go by. "Is it...things with Andrea?"

Her long exhalation told me that she'd gotten to the right nail with that one. She didn't look one inch surprised, and nor was I. While Andrea Asher was a corporate beast, an anomaly formed by the natural ambition in her blood combined with the freak circumstances of her life, it was surreal to imagine her even possessing an intimate side, much less being adept with it. I'd already given tons of secret props to Colin for handling the woman as well as he had until now—though the cracks in the couple's castle were clearly starting to form.

Claire confirmed the conclusion once she disconnected the call. Her grip was tight, her features the same. In the golden centers of her eyes, I saw the shimmer of love—and pain.

"What is it?" My tone was gentle. It was actually therapeutic. It felt good to be really taking care of her again. "Trouble in paradise?"

"I don't know." It was a sparse murmur. "He won't talk to me. Not over the phone like this. Just generalities and his way of making excuses for Andrea."

"Excuses?" I repeated. "In what way?"

"Things have been strained with Margaux since last week's fun little turn of events."

I nodded, now understanding. "Which has likely given her an excuse to take it all out on him."

She set the phone down and wrapped both of her hands around mine. I didn't want to admit that her heartache was helping my tension, but it felt damn nice to be needed, if only for a few seconds. "But that's only what he's saying on the surface, Kil." A grimace tore across her face. "The things he'll say over the phone. There are deeper fissures going on there. I can feel them, damn it, and—" She stopped herself, clearly yearning to say more. I pulled a hand free and lifted her chin, knowing exactly what those words were.

"And you want to be nearer to him."

The sheen in her gaze turned a molten gold. "My place is by your side, Killian."

"Which can now be in San Diego just as easily as here." I filled in the blank in her question with a cocky grin. "My big brother has decided he wants the penthouse office, remember? The rest of the city's decided to write me off too. Maybe what I need is a change of scenery."

Just saying the words was like opening a new window of perspective. Claire's quivering smile made me feel even better. "Really?" she rasped. "You'll come back with me?"

I tugged her face up and kissed her softly but deeply. "I think it's what we both need."

Conviction lined every syllable of it. For very good reason.

★ ★ ★ ★

I had to admit, living the beach-bum life was a nice change.

For about three days.

By the fourth day, even the goddamn sunshine gave me a headache. I needed the fog rolling in off Lake Michigan in the morning. The clamor of the L over the streets. The taxis honking, trying to take over the millions of sidewalk conversations happening at once.

The nonstop email pings from my laptop.

After a long morning run beside the beach, I sat down at Claire's office desk and opened the computer.

I had three pings total.

The first was from Britta, who'd been sending me updates

three times a day. On many occasions, answering the email might take up to a few hours, depending on the follow-up messages or calls that needed to be made. And though the recipients of my messages clearly felt weirder by the day about the process, I really loved those goddamn emails.

Until today.

Britta's note consisted of less than ten words spread over two sentences. If she'd written the note out, I was sure the paper would be warped with tears.

I'm sorry, Killian. So sorry.

I was suddenly, painfully, aware of every pound of my heart. And every drop of bile in my stomach. And every letter in the name of the next sender on the Inbox list.

Trey Stone. CEO. The Stone Global Companies.

I opened the email with a furious stab at the mouse.

The letter was shockingly well-written. I almost wondered if he'd made Britta write it, until recognizing Trey would never pass up the opportunity to deliver the final stab into my gut and twist the blade several times. And, oh, he definitely went in with the intention of carnage. Lots of it. Branded specifically with my name.

I read over it once silently but re-recited parts out loud, if only for the opportunity to dilute the words' impact with my scoffing laughter. "Mr. Klarke...emergency meeting of the board, due to your extended and notable absence...regret to inform you...effective immediately..."

The remaining details were redundant and pointless. I'd be bought out of my contract for the ungodly sum arranged by the lawyers years ago, only partially assuaging the agony. With a grimace, I remembered what I'd told those stuffed shirts when they'd sneaked the clause into my contract. I'd rocked back in my chair and told them that if the Stone Global board ever felt the need to boot my ass before the contract terminated, then I certainly wouldn't deserve the millions that walked out of the door with me.

I didn't do the cocky rock now. After I opened the third email, time-stamped right after Trey's and sent from Drake's phone, I let my lips curl into a grimace as the acid in my stomach mixed with the fury in my heart. The venom erupted into the air as the underline to my slow growl.

"Make sure you deposit every last penny, assholes."

Drake's email contained a screen capture of the official, final vote from the emergency board meeting.

He and Fletcher were the only members who'd voted in my favor.

I'd always had this half-stupid motto in life about trying to see the lessons in everything, even my adversities. Though I was fairly certain this morning's shit dump had made adversity its bitch from the moment I'd opened Britta's email, it was cool to discover a silver lining of a lesson in the day anyway.

A bottle of wine and a binge-fest of *Deadliest Warrior* were damn good medicine for gut-deep rage.

By the time I'd cheered everyone from the Comanche to the SEALs to Joan of Arc on to victory, I swung off the couch in a woozy haze, stumbling for my phone. When I found the damn thing, the Italian opera that belonged solely to Claire had flipped into voicemail. Once I checked the screen, I could see she'd opted for a text instead. Would I be interested in attending a VIP opening for a hot new bar in town, over by the university tonight?

I tapped back a fast reply.

*Hold on. Lemme ck packed sched. Think I can
squeeze u in, baby. Or maybe u can squeeze me
in too…*

"Hmmph." I chuckled while pushing Send. "You're not
the only one with the mad sexting skills, Mr. CEO Trey fucking
Stone."

Seemed like it took Claire forever to respond. On the other
hand, she had a job to attend to. After she finally answered that
she'd pick me up by seven, I tossed the phone aside and got
ready for the Crazy Horse versus Pancho Villa showdown.

By seven thirty that night, we walked into the party Claire
had been invited to. The bar, located in former industrial space
in a newly gentrified area of town, was called Fins Up—and
officially proclaimed itself as San Diego's hottest and wettest.
It featured a modernistic mesh of décor and lighting that
highlighted dolphin and shark imagery. Oddly, the blue and gray
color theme worked well—though I still had my doubts about
the sculpture atop the backlit bar. The shark and dolphin had
been morphed into sexless humanoids which were positioned
in a way that left little to the imagination about *their* plans for
late-night fun. After a few rounds from the complimentary bar,
I wasn't sure I cared.

My expression must have spoken differently, because
Claire peered up from her wine with an open curiosity. "A shot
for your thoughts, Mr. Stone?"

I returned the look with hooded eyes and a derogatory
smirk. The room tilted a little—maybe more than a little—but
I didn't mind. She was in focus. That was all that mattered.
"Don't you mean Mr. Klarke?"

She thrashed her head back and forth. "Nope. Uh-uh. Shit like that is banned for tonight. We're here to have fun. Now tell me what you were really thinking about."

I blinked a couple of times. Grinned wider and swung my head toward the couple above. "That."

Her eyebrows rose. "That?"

I nodded. The room spun harder. It wasn't a wholly unpleasant sensation. "Not sure whether that makes me want to reach for the eye bleach, order another of these, or take you out back for some illicit alley sex."

She bit into her bottom lip, turning it an even juicier shade of red. "Mmmm. I think I pick door number three."

"Oh yeah?"

Though I ended with a growl, she cut it short by dragging my face to hers in a long mush of a kiss. "Why don't you finish that while I take a fast trip to the little girls' room?" she purred. "Then we can find that alley."

"Your wish is my command, fairy queen." I brushed my lips across hers again. The feel of her fingers through my stubble was more intoxicating than the Scotch. She'd encouraged me to let the scruff go unchecked back in Chicago, and I liked what my compliance did for her libido level tonight.

She licked her lips while commencing her backward trek to the restrooms. Her stare, silken with sensuality, held mine. "Behave, knave."

My lips held the curve of my chuckle as I circled my finger, ordering her to turn around before she killed herself or anyone else with that loopy gait and those high fuck-me heels. Besides, the new view of her ass and thighs started giving me creative ideas about justifying the nickname for the blood-red booties. Damn, I couldn't wait to hit the alley.

My vision veered for just a second. Correction. It was hijacked—by a guy who leaned from the wall and eyed Claire's body with intent that left no room for imagination. Luckily, the Scotch soothed my nerves enough to let logic speak some sense to me. I was here with the most stunning woman in the building. That was the case no matter where we went or ever would go. I'd better get used to the feeling of watching assholes slobber all over Claire—even if they were ripped college boys with *Staying Power* practically stamped on their foreheads.

I maintained my cool even when the kid turned his cocky puppy stare at me, his slow grin letting me know that *he* knew just who I was—and what he planned on doing with that knowledge.

Goddamnit.

Sure enough, when Claire emerged from the hallway leading to the restrooms, he stepped into the doorway, spreading his long arms across the opening and bracing his legs wide. Claire stopped, rolled her eyes at the X he'd made of his linebacker's physique, and then giggled as she tried to pass.

The puppy really wanted to play with her.

I polished off my Scotch and slid off the barstool.

My ears buzzed, muting the throb of the Pitbull song from the dance floor and turning the night into a pleasant careen of numbness with every stomp I took toward Claire and the dog. I approached in time to watch her attempt another pass by him. When the kid hooked a hand around the bottom of her elbow, Claire resisted. He was about to attempt another grab when I stepped up.

"Baby, is there a problem?"

Alarm flared in her eyes. "No. None." She whipped her glare, accusatory now, back at the boy. "Isn't that right?"

Junior leered at me as if she hadn't spoken. "Awwww. 'Baby, is there a problem?' Isn't that cute?"

Claire's nostrils dilated. Her eyes turned the color of a volcano's core. "Look, Scooby Doo, this just isn't going to happen. I'm sure there are other girls in here who'd prefer to be your snack tonight—"

"But I'm hungry for you...baby."

The booze in my blood hit the frustration in my chest, combusting into the vicious yank I gave his wrist. "The lady has asked nicely, damn it. Now leave her alone."

"Killian—"

"Claire." My tone left no room for pushback. "Stay out of this."

The puppy snorted. "She *is* this, dude. But maybe you don't get that." He threw a scoffing glance down the front of my black Henley and black jeans. "Maybe you still don't comprehend you're not the fancy billionaire in the pretty glass tower anymore. Welcome to the land on the other side of the disguise, Superman—only you twisted it backwards, didn't you?"

I got in my own turn at the eye roll. It didn't do a damn thing to dampen my rage. "Wow," I snarled. "You are so fucking brilliant. That is so goddamn original. Don't think I've heard that one in about the last ten minutes, Scooby. Good on you."

The pup tossed his head, settling his surfer haircut back enough to stare at Claire clearly again. "So you want to go get another drink?"

Claire burst out in laughter that was pitched with disbelief. That was a good thing, distracting her enough not to notice my reaction was very different. Before she could stop me, I'd twisted one hand into the front of his MMA souvenir

T-shirt hard enough to tear the seams at the arms. "Let me be clear about this. She's. With. Me."

The boy's eyes narrowed. One side of his mouth yanked up. "She *was* with Killian Stone, man. Now?" He blew a mocking sound out through his teeth and glanced at Claire. "If you're happy with the Enema of the Magnificent Mile, then have at it, beautiful."

A couple of onlookers chortled at that. Scooby Doo wasn't lucky enough to join them. Could've had something to do with my fist smashing into his jaw. To his credit, the kid recovered nicely, only falling against the wall instead of toppling to the floor. He shook his head, laughed, and instantly came back at me—but the years of dodging Trey's bullying had never left me. It all came back as easily as riding a bike, a gritty blend of dodging and ducking that served me well until the kid swept around to my flank and landed a breath-stealing blow to my ribs.

My vision went total Chinese New Year. Fireworks. Dragons. And a shit ton of red.

One glance at Scooby told me his did too. Screams and cheers roared around me as we toppled to the floor, grappling and grunting, sliding down the hall toward the bathrooms. The crowd jammed into the narrow passage following us, their shouts pinballing everywhere, finally revealing that the pup's name was Jeff. Or maybe Jess. Not that it mattered. Before long, he wore Trey's face—and it felt damn good to be pummeling the shit out of him.

The walls spun. The floor became the ceiling and then vice versa and over again. I sucked in my own blood and then spat it out. My head whirled as my fists kept flying, and my senses sped into an oblivion that was—

Good.

So damn good.

Through the violence, I finally found escape. With every punch, I finally knew retribution. I didn't care that it was only a few seconds' worth. I'd take it. The relief from my mind, letting the logic go and the fury set in, was like being given a clean cancer scan. I was free. I no longer had to be the better man or pretend the gossip headlines weren't degrading. I didn't have to let logic, patience, or forbearance have a seat at my fucking table anymore. I was done with sucking up my pride, swallowing down my humiliation, and pretending I hadn't hated every goddamn minute of every day since Trey had walked into that lobby and unmasked me before the world.

He'd betrayed me.

And now I'd show him just how deep the pain from that went.

"Killian! For God's sake! What are you—?"

"Stay out of this, Claire."

"No! Damn it, you're going to—"

"I said stay the *fuck* out of this!"

The burn behind my eyes matched the fire in my chest as I swung my glare around at her. Though I still had both hands coiled in the tattered collar of Scooby's shirt, she tumbled back against the wall as if I'd physically lashed out too. Pain, shock, and disbelief crashed across her features. Her beautiful, incredible face—now gaping like I was a goddamn stranger.

"What the hell are you doing?" Her lips spilled the words, but her eyes betrayed how she'd edited the question. In those scorched gold depths, I beheld her truth.

Who the hell are you?

I swallowed hard. I had no answer for her. I had no answer

for *myself*. Killian Stone...was gone. He'd been murdered. And Killian Klarke was—

Nobody.

The word echoed a hundred times through the shadows of my mind.

And suddenly...it had a damn nice sound.

Nobody. Yeah. I could do that. *Nobody* was exactly the person I wanted to be. And *nowhere* my perfect destination. No more probing stares from the world. No more questions to answer or strange looks to endure. No more places to be. No more decisions to make. No secrets to keep.

No more fear.

Or pain.

I let the puppy fall out of my grip. He choked and rolled away, blustering every expression in his limited vocabulary about my general state of asshole-ness. I laughed for a second because the kid was right. Without a word, I helped him up. As I did, I slipped a C-note into his hand. After slapping down a couple more hundreds for the bartender, I motioned him to hand over a full bottle of the Scotch I'd been chugging—though refused the glass. If I was going down Trey-style, I'd at least do it like a real goddamn man. After peeling the wrapper, yanking the cork, and then tossing both, I swigged a mouthful of the shit straight from the bottle. It went down like fire. Fucking perfect.

"Killian. Where are you—?"

I cut Claire off with a violent sweep of my arm as I trudged back down the hall, slipping a little on the sweat the junior Scoob and I had left behind on the floor.

"Killian!"

"Leave me alone."

"Excuse me?"

"Leave. Me. Alone."

I shoved out of the building's back door, grateful for the cool night air on my face.

"You're wasted."

I laughed. Hard. Slammed my head back against the wall and let the sky spin in my vision. "Among other things."

Claire let out a little huff. It was tinted with confusion. "Other...things?"

I chuckled again. "Wasted," I repeated. "And ousted. And nameless. I guess that means jobless too."

Her hands pressed on my chest. I moaned. I think. Her touch felt nice. So fucking nice. Her nails were painted so pretty, a light-mint color. I gazed at them, trying to get one into my mouth. Her fingernails were never boring. My adventurous little fairy...

Killian Stone's fairy. Not yours anymore, phony. Liar. Pretender.

"Okay. I think we need to talk, Kil."

I grabbed her wrist and pushed her away. "No talking." Right. Like *that* was a conversation I looked forward to.

She exhaled again, sounding determined about the subject. I couldn't confirm the conclusion since her face had doubled in my vision. "Damn it. You can't walk, can you?"

"Hrrrm. Not so sure." In the air, it sounded more like *nah so shurr*, but I was beyond caring.

"I'm going to get my car. Can you stay put for ten minutes?"

I nodded, probably too eagerly, at that. But if she caught on to my plan, she didn't show it. Ten minutes? Only if she got lucky enough to make it through the throng and back out to the valet stand, which would already be busy by now.

I had at least fifteen.

And that gave me more than enough time to slip down the alley and then the one after that, followed by a dozen more, before she came back. The night swallowed me up, and I embraced its numbing shadows in return. With the amber magic in my bottle to help, I wandered deeper into oblivion, only one goal consuming my mind now.

Stay here for as long as you can.

CHAPTER ELEVEN

Claire

I was curled in my old recliner in the living room, gawking like an idiot at the screen saver on my phone.

The picture was one of my favorites. In it, he was laughing, his head thrown back and his eyes closed. His hair, thick and inky and oh-so-touchable, was a little too long. I'd teased him about it right before I'd taken the shot, saying that if it got much longer, Lance would start calling him Jenny instead of his shortened middle name turned nickname Jamie. My joke had been the instigation for his laughter. I loved it when he let his guard down like that, especially when I had the treat of being the source, so I'd quickly captured the moment. One of so many...all so treasured.

Why hadn't I taken pictures of all of them?

I gripped the phone harder. Hated the tear that spilled onto the screen, frantically wiping it away in fear it would ruin one of the only things I had left of him.

Is this really it? Damn it, Killian, is it?

The words tumbled off my lips after they consumed my heart, bleak rasps that matched the screen saver on my spirit. Tomorrow, they'd likely be screams again. If the sadness wasn't tearing at me, then the outrage was—until I begged Cupid to just rip the arrow out of my ass and let me bleed out into unconsciousness. But the little brat wasn't listening, likely because he was laughing too hard in my face.

The conclusion swung me all the way back to anger. A lot of it.

He'd left me.

"How dare you," I sobbed at his gorgeous, laughing face. "How *dare* you, Killian."

I surged to my feet, struggling to root my thoughts in reality again. But the reality he'd left behind was fucked up and tangled, a bizarre mess made worse by the Stone family, version 2.0—capricious, confused, selfish.

Trey had instantly fired everyone at SGC's executive level. Though the company was contractually obligated to retain Asher and Associates for another year and a half, we were told to stay away due to conflict of interest—that interest undoubtedly focused on Andrea and me. Lance, temporarily relocated to Chicago to help shore up the cracks left behind by Trey's siege, looked miserable in every picture I saw of him. Willa was doing what she did best—playing the Stone queen mum by attending every last social function she'd been scheduled for—outfitted to regal perfection, of course.

Shockingly, Margaux was the only one who managed to completely avoid the spotlight. She'd gone underground with impressive hermit skills, disappearing almost as thoroughly as Killian had.

Almost...but not quite.

He was gone. Despite all the tears I'd shed, calls I'd tried, dishes I'd shattered, and small electronics I'd ruined, he was gone. And I was here, clinging to my phone, mooning at his picture, turning into a lame sixteen-year-old.

And still beyond desperate to find him.

What if he hadn't left on purpose? What if he was hurt—or even captured? What if Trey actually had something done to him?

I shook my head, realizing it all took my lameness to another level, as if I'd been reading too many spy novels. But when I'd run the concept past Talia, Michael, and Chad, they hadn't thought it too crazy. I just didn't know what to do after that. I was certain Lance would take me seriously, but he was clearly in the camp of the rest of the family in accepting Killian's disappearance as something nearly normal. Everyone kept writing it all off, turning the phrase Typical Kil damn near into a T-shirt slogan.

Their attitude—and yeah, I included Lance in this one—had led to the touchdown pass of my toaster across the kitchen one morning. The Killian I knew was responsible to a fault. He'd been the glue of that family and company since before I'd met him. This wasn't typical of him in the least. But none of them could be swayed. Hell, they barely accepted my calls anymore. Willa was too busy defending her dead husband. Lance was too busy trying to rein back Trey. And Trey was too busy snapping those tethers.

The days began to blend too seamlessly. They all ended the same way. I went home and opened a bottle of wine. At two glasses in I dialed his cell, listened to his voice, and then hung up after sobbing at him, swearing at him, or both. Usually both.

After seven days of that, I gave up the futile ritual, except the wine part. I got greedy about needing his voice. I'd replay the last few messages he'd left on my cell. Three were from the days just before we'd left for Europe. There was a time gap, represented by the weeks we'd seen each other every day, and then three more calls, filled only with his desperate breathing—

time-stamped from the days just after he'd disappeared. I'd physically force myself to listen to those, thinking that some noise in the background might give me a clue where he was, but that trick worked much better on TV shows than real life.

Needing more, I'd move on to my next hit—the two messages I'd saved from him on the home answering machine and the five still left on my work line. I'd committed every single message to memory now. Every inflection of his voice, all the spots where he inhaled or exhaled, the adorable moments he chuckled at his own ridiculous humor, and those heart-halting times where he dropped an octave in seductive suggestion. The string of his voice, rambling and resonant, was the perfect memento of the days when everything had been normal—and my nightly lullaby. Wine in one hand and phone in the other, I'd finally tumble into sleep before waking up with puffy eyes, papery skin, basket-case hair—and the realization that the nightmare was still real, depressing and endless.

I was going nowhere. Fast.

Enough was enough.

Though rage drove the decision, hiring a private investigator was an instant balm for my spirit. At last I was *doing* something. Being with Killian had allowed me to save tons of money. Besides the man's medieval insistence on paying for everything when we'd been together, he'd negotiated a ridiculous retainer for me as the Asher and Associates advisor to SGC. In short, nearly every paycheck was going into my savings account. Finally, I could put the money to good use. I never dreamed it would be to finance the quest of finding the man I loved.

I pulled my Audi into the parking structure of Horton Plaza, figuring a quick trip to the mall after meeting with the investigator would cure a little of the Where In the World Is Killian Stone blues. I arrived at his office at six o'clock on the dot. His name was Ian Charles, and he had an impressive office filled with art deco furniture, capped by a distinct air of commanding professionalism. I immediately felt as if he'd get results. I wanted my other half back, and if all the framed parchment on the man's wall meant he could make that happen, then damn it, he was my guy.

We agreed to a fee, followed at once by a string of questions from the man. He pulled out a smart pad, tapping steadily while he listened carefully to my answers. I was stunned to realize it had been three weeks, nearly four, since I'd last locked gazes with Kil, in the pale light of that alley behind the bar. No wonder my friends had looked at me with pity and concern and mumbled crap about interventions when they'd thought I hadn't been listening. No wonder my clothing was starting to hang on me like a bad Olsen twin design. And it definitely wasn't any wonder that I felt like a cast member of *Dawn of the Dead.*

My introspection was interrupted by Charles again. "Can I see your cell phone?"

"Sorry?" Did I not just explain I hadn't heard from Kil in almost a month?

"Well, if you don't mind, it's actually the sim chip I'm after. If you haven't already started there, I'd like to see if we can use it to trace the last place Mr. Stone called you from."

"But that was over three weeks ago."

"And he's also trying to stay off the grid." Charles finished my thought with quiet efficiency. "Yes, I've heard everything you've said, Miss Montgomery. This won't lead us to him. But with any luck, it'll supply a jumping-off point."

"Okay." For the first time in weeks, hope lifted my voice. It felt wonderful. "That's good. I'll take that."

I opened my bag and fumbled frantically through it for my phone. Naturally, it had sunk to the bottom, and I had more trouble finding it through the tears blocking my vision. All too easily, memories sprang of Killian teasing me about the size of my handbags—exactly for this reason. My feverish diggings through the luggage had always made him chuckle, crinkling the corners of his eyes, sometimes even making some of his hair fall against his forehead in all the best and sexiest ways...

"Damn it," I mumbled. "Sorry."

Why did *everything* remind me of him? I was about to lose my shit in a big way, in front of a complete stranger, even more so when my fingers finally closed around the device. *Just freaking perfect.* I swiped at the tears that had escaped down my cheeks as I all but threw the phone at Charles. In return, he shoved a box of tissues at me, though the rest of his mien had gone completely "guy," making him look everywhere other than at the whimpering female in front of him. Could the man be blamed? I was a jittery mess. Maybe the double shot in my morning latte order, even after three hours of sleep, hadn't been a great idea after all.

After a few minutes of foreplay between my cell phone and Mr. Charles's computer, the man leaned back in his plush office chair with a satisfied grunt.

"Did you get something?" I tried not to surge out of my seat.

"Well, something more than we had before," he confirmed. He punched another couple of buttons and then swung the monitor so I could view it too. The screen was filled with a map of California from San Luis Obispo to the Mexican border.

"Here is where I presume you live. Looks like Mission Hills?" I nodded, and he moved on to the next red dot. "The next call from Stone's phone to yours came from about sixty miles up the coast. Looks like he was just around San Clemente. Let me zoom in. Yep. Looks like a rest stop just past the border check point."

I nodded, all the way into the game on my focus level. I even would've been fascinated by the technology if my stomach didn't turn while watching the red dots move farther from me. Now that I knew what they represented, I quickly followed the path, which continued north—until stopping in the middle of Los Angeles.

"So he's in Los Angeles?" I queried.

"He was three weeks ago."

Elation turned my heart into a happy-face balloon. Hell, a whole bouquet of them. *A jumping-off point.* Well, now I wanted to go skydiving. "I have a work cell too," I blurted. "There are some calls from him on that too. Maybe I missed a message that came in after these, or—"

"I think this is a good place to start." He smiled diplomatically while pointing at the last red dot, near LA's downtown hub. "I have a man in this general area on another assignment. I'll send him to this location and have him sniff around today, see if he turns anything up. We can go from there. My hunch is that we *will* find Mr. Stone's cell...discarded or destroyed." He took a second as I leaned back, the balloon bouquet deflating. "I know this is difficult," he offered, folding his hands in his lap, "but I wouldn't be worth the money you're paying if I were blowing unproven sunshine at you. Miss Montgomery, I'm going to be honest. There's a damn good chance your guy doesn't want to be found."

I lowered my head, refusing to let him see the fresh crop of tears now splattering into my lap. "Nothing I haven't told myself before," I muttered. Though it was usually at midnight, drenched by gulps of a good cabernet.

"I'm sorry. He's an idiot, if you ask me. No guy should've left a lady like you."

After making a follow-up appointment, I left the office and headed for the parking structure. The last two hours had drained me so much even shopping sounded like a trip to the dentist.

"Sister mine."

My head snapped up from where I still leaned against my car, scrolling through my incoming emails. My she-devil stepsister stood there, a multitude of bags hanging off each arm. Margaux had clearly contributed enough to San Diego's commerce today for both of us.

The thought wasn't comforting. In the least.

Why did it seem that some days just rolled like a giant shit snowball?

"Margaux." I was too exhausted to even trade insults with her at this point.

"You look like shit."

I didn't look up from my phone. "Nice to see you too."

"No. I'm serious. I think I may actually be worried about you."

I nodded back toward the mall. "Go tell the guys at the little kiosk with the crystal thingies. Maybe they can engrave it on a bunny's butt for you."

A weird sound emanated from her. If I wasn't so sleep-deprived, I'd have thought it a soft snicker. But the woman didn't dole out props like that. "Have you heard from Killian?"

It was official. My brain really *was* shedding cells. Now I could've sworn there was real concern in her voice. Just a trace, but...*whoa.*

"No." I decided to ignore my hallucinations. I wanted to get started on tonight's bottle of wine, and that plan didn't include a sparring match with her.

"I'm not the enemy, Claire."

She kept up the soft tone, though she seemed uncomfortable with it. My own disquiet thickened the air. Tears burned my vision as all too clearly, I remembered the same words spilling from me, not so long ago. *Kil, I'm not the enemy.*

Paris. Him. Me. The City of Lights. The stage for such darkness. We'd fought so hard, when we should have been treasuring our love. Gone now. We'd wasted it...

My shoulders sagged. I looked up at her, daring to give her a glimpse of my grief, certain I'd regret it. "Of course you're not," I muttered. "I'm sorry." Hell. I'd regret that too. "It's been shitty lately."

I expected the tigress any second, pouncing on my weakness like a gutted gazelle. Instead, she tugged her bottom lip between her teeth and mumbled, "Do you want to grab a drink?" Then blatantly blanched. "Or something?"

I flipped a once-around for the camera crew. Had Margaux Asher—Mary Stone—just asked me to go for a cocktail?

"Actually, I was just heading back to my place for a bottle of wine. The paparazzi have been more ravenous than usual. Public and stationary aren't pretty for me right now."

"Then can I be gauche and invite myself over? All the sidewalks are cracked in my frontal lobe too. Things with Moth—err, Andrea—have been pure shit lately."

I was shocked to feel a sympathetic grin at my lips. "So I've heard."

She swallowed hard. "Home is definitely *not* where the heart is."

I sensed she had more snark to release on that subject. The idea made me smile. It was a moment of insanity I'd surely live to condemn myself for, but I answered, "Sure...why not?" And yes, I'd really just done that. How long would it take the woman to use my act of kindness against me? At the moment, I didn't care. It actually felt nice to be looking forward to some company.

"Are you still at the same house in Mission Hills?"

I just nodded while pressing the key fob to the car and then climbed in as the A8's lights came on. At my place, Margaux parked her BMW right behind me and then followed me up the walk. Hal and his buddies were there, recording the start of our girl's night for posterity, though both of us barely waved in greeting. The guys knew I'd give a few words when I was good and ready. Right now, I *wasn't* ready.

First thing to go for both of us were our heels. Our purses quickly followed, dumped on my entryway table, though I still gripped my cell phone. It was always in my hand now, in case—well, just in case. I excused myself to go change into pajamas and, when emerging back into the living room, found Margaux sitting on my sofa, both feet tucked under her. Two of my biggest wineglasses were already filled, with the bottle standing between them like a very brave soldier, ready to take on a night of girl talk. After tossing out an appreciative groan, I picked up a glass, handed Margaux the other, and pulled the throw blanket off the back of the sofa. Margaux reached for the blanket's other end, tucking it in before raising her glass.

"Wait," I interjected. "We need a toast."

She tossed a perplexed glare. "Huh?"

"We always need a toast."

"Oh, hell."

"My house, my rules. And my rules say there's always a toast."

She abandoned the glare for a full eye roll. "You're weird, Montgomery."

"Thank you." I extended my glass toward hers. "To Killian coming home."

Delivering about her twelfth shocker of the day, my stepsister nodded and softened her features into a smile. "Okay," she said softly. "That's actually a good one. To my—" Her lips trembled a little. "To my brother coming home," she finally murmured.

After we both took a hearty swallow, I closed my eyes and let my head fall back. "Oh, that's good," I groaned, letting the warmth permeate my bones.

"So. He's really gone, huh?" Her voice carried the same quiet concern she'd hinted at in the parking structure, only more of it. I opened my eyes just to make sure it was still the same woman sitting there. I'd never heard that voice out of Margaux. Ever.

My head felt made of lead as I sat up and nodded. "I...don't know what happened. We were at that grand-opening party for the new club over by the university."

"Was he drinking?"

"You mean donating his liver to Glenlivet distillery's bottom line?" I stared at the waning sunset outside the window. "Yeah. You could say that."

While Margaux showed her appreciation for my snark

with a little smirk, she stated, "That still doesn't seem like him, though. Killian's always held himself to a limit."

"You mean Killian *Stone* held himself."

"Ahhh." As she took another sip, sadness glimmered through her eyes. "The holy-crap-who-am-I thing. I actually relate."

"Well, he was definitely getting in touch with the turmoil. After he turned one of the kids there into his personal primal-aggression toy, I hauled his gorgeous-but-wasted ass out to the alley while I went back for my car. When I pulled around to pick him up, he was gone. Literally here one minute and gone the next." My voice cracked. Maybe the wine and girl-bonding thing hadn't been such a great idea. Of all the people to show weakness in front of, Margaux was the very last person on my list. Still, I babbled on. "I don't know if he even wants me to try to find him. I don't know if he's in danger, or if he just needs time, or—*shit.*" A lone tear slid down my cheek, and I was pretty damn sure it was the last one I had left. I was so drained and angry—

And now frustrated as hell. Margaux's giant green eyes were enough to get used to in their bitter and bitchy mode. But this wave of soft and understanding from her...

Damn it.

"Oh, for the love of God," I snarled.

"What?"

"Don't you pity me too, Margaux. I just can't take it."

"Pity you?" She blew out a dainty snort. "I don't pity you, Claire. I envy you. You're so caught up in your own shit you can't recognize the difference." Though the words were sarcastic, her tone was gentle.

For a moment, I only blinked. Then laughed. "Okay. You

can be serious now."

"I *am* serious."

"Margaux, at what point in your life have you ever felt envy...for anything?"

"Do *not* make me call you a brainless bitch for real." She paused to take another long sip. "For nearly a year, the entire world has been watching that man trip over himself in love with you. Tell me this is not fresh news, little girl. Tell me you know that he's become a fucking fool for love, all in the name of Claire Allyn Montgomery. You have the most delectable, eligible bachelor in just about the entire free world eating out of the palm of your hand, and everyone sees it but you. How is that?"

Looking proud of herself for the mini speech, she threw back the rest of her wine and then leaned forward to refill our glasses. Well, hers. Remarkably, the craving for the stuff just wasn't in me tonight.

"So is that part of your girlish charm?" she went on. "Just...be innocent in it all? Hmmm. I haven't tried that bit yet. Maybe I need to. Mother always taught me to be confident and independent, that men loved a woman like that. Look where that got the fucked-up bitch. Look where it's getting *me*." She frowned like her wine had gone sour and then flopped back against the sofa. I was stunned when she pulled my legs across her lap like we were really girlfriends hanging out at a sleepover.

"Margaux—"

"Hmmm?"

Shit. What to say now? *I'm really sorry your mom lied to you about your real dad your whole life and that your birth wound up as the by-product of spite, regret, and a secret psycho power play?*

Rewind.

"I...just know things must really be turned upside down for you right now too."

"You think?"

Her bitterness was actually comforting. A commiseration of sorts. "This isn't a fun situation for any of us to be in. The Stones have certainly lived up to their damn name. They've dropped a few five-ton bombs lately."

She propped her glass in the crevice between my calves. "Amen, sister."

"It had to have been catastrophic for you and Andrea. I know that, and I really am sorry. Please believe me when I say that."

She cocked me half a smile. "Yeah, you dork. I do."

I wriggled my legs, threatening to topple her wine. After she replaced "dork" with "bitch" and we laughed, I continued, "I know we don't have the best history. I also don't expect to be in your Top Five on your new phone plan or some crazy thing like that, but I get how devastating that day must've been for you."

She accepted that part in silence. An easy pause extended between us, probably as we both struggled to process all the shit that had gone down in the last three weeks, which felt like three decades by now. I supposed the adage was true. Misery did love company. Hell, all we were missing was a cat. And maybe a Duraflame log in my little fireplace.

She finally broke the quiet with a wistful murmur. "Okay... this is going to sound strange..."

I cocked both eyebrows. "You know all about the last month of my life, and you dare to say that?"

"I actually like being Mary Stone now. Well, the name itself still sucks balls, but the bigger point of it...learning there was more to my life than what I knew about...it makes sense somehow, though I can't explain why." She slowly shook her head. "It probably sounds stupid or like the wine is talking. And, by the way, this is damn good wine."

As she leaned to look at the label, I cracked, "You're never going to believe this, but I wasn't raised in a barn."

"Well, hell," she volleyed. "There go my summer vacation plans. A week in the country was *just* what I dreamed of..."

"I'll hook you up with Michael, then. *He* was raised on a farm. I'm sure there was a barn involved in there somewhere..."

Before I could figure out why her face quirked so weirdly at that, she went on. "Most of my life was spent being molded into Andrea Asher's mini-me—but the whole time, I was being forced into something that *wasn't* me. It turned me into a really bitter person. I always felt like I never really fit or was good enough and didn't know who to be pissed at for that...except maybe myself." She looked out the window just as I had a few minutes before. Her forehead furrowed and her lips twisted. "But after a while, even self-hatred gets old. So I fought back at the whole world, pissed at everyone that I was being forced into being something I never chose."

"Wow," I murmured. "That explains...a lot." And also lifted her a few notches out of the bitch pit, in my mind. It had taken courage to confront all that about herself. Guess I hadn't been the only one staring at the stars in one-woman therapy sessions lately.

Margaux shrugged. "I guess it does," she replied. "All I know is that this feels like a second chance. A big one."

She glanced at me then, and I caught the glint of

desperation in her gaze. Or perhaps confusion. Or simply commiseration.

"But your mom—" I halted for a second, taken aback by how fast the glimmers in her eyes turned to razor blades. "Come on, Margaux. Do you think you'll be able to take it all away from her now?" I explained. "She spent her life raising you. Even if it was messed-up and weird, maybe she really thought she was doing all the right stuff for all the right reasons. But maybe it's too early to see it all that way."

She slanted her gaze into her wineglass. "Yeah. I'm pretty sure it is. And maybe I'll just never understand." She shrugged again. "But Killian had to deal with no better, right? How does anyone take a kid and deliberately turn him into someone else completely, no matter what damn empire is at stake? I mean, this isn't the Middle Ages, where a shiny crown has to be passed down in a straight line and kids are dying right and left from plague and shit. What the hell were they all thinking, expecting him—and Trey and Lance, for that matter—to grow up keeping a secret like that?" She wasn't so ladylike about her snort this time. "Seems like child abuse to me. At the least, it sure as hell wasn't right—just like what my mother did. Lives being moved around like pawns on a board. And now the world has two more fucked-up adults because of it."

I battled between yearning to hug her and grabbing a second bottle of wine for her. "There's no doubt that it wasn't right," I conceded instead, "but I also think the world they all moved in was a different place than what we know. When people are used to getting what they want, especially if they think it's the right thing, they'll do anything to make it happen— even manipulate birthrights and outcomes of pregnancies. I know it sounds weird, but everyone, in their own way, really thought they were choosing the best course—in your case *and* in Killian's."

My "sister" had sat eerily still while I'd given the explanation. In the tense set of her mouth, I could see the inner war she still waged about all this. She was so hurt by the things Andrea had withheld from her that healing wouldn't occur in the space of this conversation. She and Andrea would have to rebuild their relationship damn near from scratch—if that was even what they wanted anymore.

She nudged my knee with hers, a blasé attempt at affection. "You know this is part of it, right?"

Now I was lost. "Part of what?"

"What he loves so much about you."

"Huh?"

"Killian. And his love for you. And why. You have an amazing ability to see the good in just about anyone."

"Oh, I don't know—"

"*I* know. You're fair to a fault, Claire, and I would bet my favorite pair of Zanottis that this is one of his favorite things about you."

I took my second sip of wine of the night as a way to deflect the comment. It was difficult to take a compliment from anyone, let alone Margaux. Despite this little "Kumbaya," it was still hard as hell to trust her. I was happy about the effect Mary Stone had on her, but would it stick? There had been times, *plenty* of them, when she'd inflicted some deep pain on my life—and had done it with glee. It was best to keep up the battle shields, at least at half strength, for a while longer.

Still, she'd been doing most of the drinking tonight. I wasn't at the point of asking for her keys but concluded a more subtle approach might be effective. "Hey, why don't you just stay in the guest room tonight? I know it's still early, but they graduated a load of marines today, and there's that huge boat show starting tomorrow, so I don't want you out on the road with those crazies."

It was the right thing to do, even if it sounded beyond odd to my own ears. Margaux looked as surprised at the offer as I was, making me feel strangely guilty.

"That's...pretty cool," she stammered, as awkward as a twelve-year-old. My heart clutched. She'd probably never gotten the chance to make friends the normal way. "Are you sure you wouldn't mind? I'll stay out of your hair. I've had a lot of this wine—and I really want more."

"It's no trouble at all. There are towels in the bathroom under the sink, and I have about fifty pods stocked for the brewer."

A timid smile curled her lips. "Okay, then. Thanks."

I looked up, realizing it was later than I thought—almost midnight. I was actually tired for once. After leaving Margaux in front of the TV, taking advantage of the ten thousand pay cable channels my over-the-top boyfriend had paid for a year in advance, I headed down the hall to my bedroom.

I picked his old MIT shirt as my pillowcase tonight. He'd left behind eight T-shirts, and I rotated them as my sleeping surface, using the remnants of his Armani Code as part of my relaxation technique every night.

I was about to start the next phase of that routine, listening to all of his voice messages, when my phone rang instead. Though the screen displayed a San Diego area phone number, I gave serious thought to letting it go to voicemail. More tenacious members of the press had been hacking records and getting my number, but they normally wanted to catch me in a good mood, instead of my crabby and tired side. Still, something urged me to pick up the call.

"Hello?"

"Yes. Hello. Is this Claire Montgomery?"

"It is."

"I'm sorry to bother you so late. My name is Karin Nelson. I'm an ER admissions nurse at Mercy Hospital in San Diego."

"How can I help you?" I forced calm to my voice. Panic set in that something had happened to Dad. I knew the drama with Andrea was bleeding over into his life too.

"Well...this is so unusual for us to do, but..."

"What? It's okay, Ms. Nelson. I'm awake."

"We're holding a man here, brought in through the emergency department about two hours ago. He was carrying no identification and was rather incoherent at the time. Looks like public intoxication, but the police didn't want to handle him because it appears as if other factors are at work."

I sat up straighter, mind racing. The behavior was so far removed from anything Dad would do that I truly had no idea why she was calling me. But the same instinct that had nagged me to pick up the line now urged me to echo, "Other factors? Like what?"

"Well, he was extremely agitated. And strong. Most of the homeless or mentally ill that we receive have distinctly atrophied muscles." She let a pause go by before laughing nervously. "This guy...well, his muscles are *not* atrophied."

My heart raced up my throat and then back down again. I knew that tone. Flustered. Embarrassed. A little aroused. It was what Killian did to any woman with a pulse.

I shook my head hard—and beat back my imagination. He was somewhere up near Los Angeles. Wasn't that what Ian

Charles had told me, just five hours ago?

No. He'd said Kil had been there *three weeks ago*.

"Wh-What's his name?" I had to focus to force the words out.

"That's just it. We don't know. He won't tell us. All he says is *your* name, over and over again. One of our case workers finally calmed him a bit, enough to get your phone number from him. Are you by chance missing a relative or a loved one? A tall man with dark hair and a beard—"

"A *what*?"

"Well, he's rather dirty. The beard might be recent. But he has really striking dark eyes. And a cute smile, when he uses it."

The voice again. That pull *every* woman had to him, even when he was filthy and incoherent and—

Alive.

He was alive.

And just fifteen minutes away.

Tears welled and spilled. My heart leaped back to my throat and then did several laps of joy around my chest. Possibilities pinged through my head like a ricocheting bullet while I threw on clothes like a madwoman. None of them matched—Hal and the gang would have a blast ribbing me with cracks about resembling Bozo the Clown, but I didn't care. The crazy on the outside matched the crazy on the inside right now, and they could all write about it until *next* year's Oscars for all the shits I gave.

"Thank God." The sob in my voice was evident. Karin laughed a little, and I joined her. It was the best damn laugh I'd had in a long, long time. "And thank *you*," I blubbered to her. "Thank you so much for calling. I live very close. I'll be there in fifteen minutes or less."

"That's great, honey."

"*Karin!*"

"Yes?"

"Do *not* let him out of your sight. Please...*please.* If he's the man I think he is, he's been missing for three weeks."

Her gasp was audible. "Oh, my goodness."

"He's also my fiancé—and I can't live without him, Karin. Okay?"

"Yes. Okay. But, hon, you need to do something for me in return." She breathed deep, a wordless decree for me to do the same. "Calm down. Got that? I'll make sure they don't let him leave, but you have to make sure to get here in one piece. I'll let him know you're coming—"

"No!" I forced in the deep breath despite my panic. "Please. If it's possible—"

"I understand," the nurse assured. "We won't spook him any more than he already is."

"Thank you so much. My God, thank you."

"Be *careful*, Claire," she stressed one more time. "We're already very busy tonight. We don't want to be admitting you to the bed beside him."

I hung up, mentally promising to ensure the woman was given a medal of honor and a raise by the next morning.

A rustle from the doorway snapped my head back up. Margaux stood there, obviously having overheard everything that had just happened. "You want me to go with you?"

Who was this woman, and what had she done with my wicked stepsister? No time for contemplating the answer. "Thank you, Margaux, but no. I'm terrified he's going to bolt again, so I've got to go solitary and stealth on this one." I dragged my hair into a ponytail and ran a cold cloth across my face, stripping off the makeup I hadn't bawled away already. "Let's just hope I return with Killian by my side."

Margaux dragged me into a fast hug. The woman seemed determined to unleash every shocker in the book on me tonight. "Call if I can help. You have the digits."

I gave her a watery smile. "I do. And thanks."

"Do you mind if I still crash here?"

"Well, you're sure as hell not driving in that condition." I had no idea where my teasing tone came from. Sobering, I added, "Of course. Make yourself at home. I'll—*we'll*—try not to wake you when we get back."

I grabbed my purse and was out the front door in a flurry. Behind me, Margaux slid the dead bolt in. The sound cracked through the night, hard and brittle, an aural embodiment of every nerve ending in my body. Could the night get any more bizarre?

I regretted the question as soon as it entered my senses. Every time I'd asked it, fate hadn't been good to me with the answer. As I ran to the car, I prayed things would be different this time.

CHAPTER TWELVE

Killian

I woke up in a blinding crash of pain. And consciousness. Neither had been remotely familiar for—

How long?

Not fucking long enough.

I groaned. It hurt. A lot. "Fuck. Gaaahhh." After managing to connect the heels of my palms to the sockets of my eyes, I tried to sit up. The world spun. I fell back.

Oh, this was going to hurt, too. But I was used to that. It was a fast lesson when the floorboards of train cars and the cement of alleys were a guy's bed pillows. Not that I hadn't been tempted to indulge in a motel from time to time—or hell, a suite at the fucking Ritz, given the billions that were sitting in my bank account courtesy of the Stone Global board of directors and their emergency-session decision—but that all required becoming a somebody again. And figuring out what that name meant. What *I* meant.

"No." The denial sputtered out of me just as my head hit a pillow.

Goddamnit.

Pillows meant I had to be somebody. And face all the disgusting ramifications of that.

"No." I repeated it with more force. "Uh-uh. Not now. No

way."

Fast footsteps approached. As they got nearer, the shadows around me were killed by blinding light. "Well, hello there. You're awake again."

Again?

"Uhhh. Yeah." I forced my eyes open. A field of bright pink parrots made me yearn to lose whatever shit lingered in my stomach. The Jimmy Buffett tribute was joined by the smell of roses and mint. Feminine scents. Nice, but not Claire—so it didn't agonize me to smell them.

"Welcome back." The woman had a pleasant, comforting voice as well. "Did you sleep well?"

I sucked in a hard breath. The roses and mint disappeared. "Shit," I spat. "Something smells."

"That would be you."

She touched my chest. I jumped a little. Cold fingers. No. A stethoscope.

A stethoscope?

Battling the Tilt-a-Whirl of the room—*don't fucking go there, do* not *think about Tilt-a-Whirls*—I peered around, forcing myself to focus on my surroundings. I was in a bed, with rails caging me in from both sides. The room was so clean I wondered why it didn't squeak. There were monitors and other medical shit on carts in the corners. Glass jars lined the counters, filled with white things in various shapes.

"Where the hell am I?" I only muttered it but sounded like the biggest dick on the planet anyway. At this point, it was probably a good thing.

"Mercy Hospital. Emergency Room." The woman, with a name badge identifying her as Karin, punched fingers at a screen displaying what looked like my chart. I lurched forward, heart beating at my ribs, until I observed the writing under Patient Name.

John Doe.

Thank fuck.

"Got it," I returned, ignoring how good it felt to play CEO again for a second. "But *where*?"

Nurse Karin cocked a curious look back at me. "San Diego," she filled in. "But you knew that, right?"

I dropped my gaze. She was peering too hard now. Trying to match the filthy homeless guy in front of her to the educated clip of my voice. I'd said too much. Less than ten words, and it had all been too much. I needed to get the fuck out of here before she connected the dots.

"Why the hell would I know that?" I mumbled. That much was the truth. The last city I'd been coherent enough to look at city signs in was Malibu. I'd liked it there. The TV and film crews had always left food behind when they had been done shooting for the day.

Somehow, I'd made it back to San Diego. Wasn't a damn bit surprising. Though my mind hadn't been along for the trip, my body and my soul were, guiding me back to where I'd be nearest to Claire. The cognizance of it was comforting. And terrifying.

I didn't want to be comforted. Or terrified. Or anything. It was time for another drink. *A lot* of other drinks. And another nameless alley. Another big city where I'd be just another face in the crowd.

"Are you from around here?"

Her question had *that* lilt to it. The I'm-trying-not-to-act-too-interested pitch. I glanced at her from behind the curtain of my eyelashes. She hadn't broken stride in her tasks while issuing it. Yeah, she was after something. But what? Damn it, how long had I been here? And what had I said without knowing? My chest tightened. My nerves spiked.

Again, so much feeling. *Too much.* There were a few too many steps between this and the other feelings now. The betrayal. The humiliation. The dark-gold eyes of the gorgeous redhead, glaring like I'd turned into a beast as she'd watched. One of the dragons we'd always fought together...

"No." I gave it as much as an order to the thoughts as an answer to the nurse. Restlessness clawed my veins. I jerked at the bed rail on the right. "Listen, I feel fine now. I'm going to get out of—"

"Now, sweetie. What's your rush?"

The lilt again. She'd changed it up a little this time, infusing the nonchalance with enough concern to sound genuine to an untrained ear. The poor woman had no idea she was talking to someone who'd once made a damn good living out of reading deception in people.

I channeled that inner CEO while bracing both hands to the bed rails. Though I kept my head down against my bare chest, I knew the exact angles of my arms and set of my shoulders that would convey enough command for my purpose. "So many questions, Nurse Karin. Maybe it's my turn to ask *you* one."

That got her to stop tapping at the smart pad. Though she'd settled on a swiveling stool, she hadn't felt the need to rotate the thing—until now. "If you think it'll help," she offered. "You seem confused, Mr...?"

"Nice try." I jabbed my head toward the door. "Why don't you just tell me how many people are out in your waiting room."

She stopped swiveling. "Pardon me?"

"How many?" I persisted. "It's noisy out there. I can hear it from in here. You're busy tonight, right? It's probably Friday or Saturday..."

"Friday," she confirmed. "Technically, Saturday morning. The bars just closed, and they graduated a fresh crop of marines today, so—" She audibly clamped her jaw shut. "You shouldn't be concerned with any of this. You need to simply rest."

"And you need my bed." I made the logic easy for her. I might not have been a CEO anymore, but I sure as hell hadn't forgotten how to win a client. "And I don't. So I'm—"

"Karin." Another nurse appeared in the doorway. She wore parrots too. They must have all gotten drunk one night and dared each other to hit the wild-n-crazy bin on the Smocks-R-Us website. "Phone call came in while you were doing intake on bed three."

"Oh?" Karin's cheeks flushed as pink as her shirt. "Was it Billy? Was he able to get the Comic-Con tickets?"

"Sorry, no. It was a woman. Claire something? Says she's parking right now and—"

"*Shit.*"

Karin hissed it as I jolted my head up. And yanked the monitor leads off my chest. And flung every stitch of the sheet off my legs with one sweep. She repeated her curse as I grabbed the left bed rail and catapulted myself over it.

"Shit is a damn good way to put it, Nurse Karin." I crashed against the wall but by the grace of fucking God kept my footing. Okay, I was a little dizzy. *A lot* dizzy. And probably dehydrated. And hungry. Make that starving.

But all of that was manageable. I liked it that way, damn it. Thirst, hunger, equilibrium—the basics, right? The easy stuff to handle.

Claire in the parking lot was *not* the easy stuff.

The pain she'd infuse in the air. The questions she'd sear from her eyes. The accusation. The anger.

And the love.

Ah, fuck...the love.

The stuff Killian Stone had known how to handle.

The stuff Killian Klarke had no idea what to do with.

My body reacted to the recognition exactly as I'd expected. Fear and loss, consuming and icy, balled in my chest and raged out to my extremities. I forced my body to crash past the icicles, my steps jerky and desperate as I raced into the hall. Directional signs were everywhere, pointing toward the main exit, all but announcing where she'd be coming from. It made my decision all the easier. I lurched and lumbered the opposite way, scrabbling down the hallway toward my escape.

"No!" Karin's cry was as urgent as the chase she gave, though she skidded to a stop as I did when reaching the back exit door. "Please," she cried. "Please—don't!"

With one hand on the knob, I swung to glare at her over my shoulder. There'd been no time to grab my shirt, not that I cared. I was drenched in sweat, breathing hard and beyond happy I'd be out in the night air instead of standing here, dealing with the searching pity in her eyes—and the silent questions beyond that. The ones I watched forming now, as the light of recognition began to finally hit her. As she looked at the man beneath the beard and the dirt—and snapped it into a name. Then let all the questions in. The same queries, silent and bewildered, I'd seen all over SGC's lobby after Trey's fireworks show. The same wordless wonderings pelted at me from the crowd at the bar after the skirmish with Scooby Doo.

Isn't that the dude who used to be the hotshot billionaire?

What's his name now?

How'd he deal with that lie for so long? And why?

Didn't he love his real parents? Didn't they love him?

Did his girlfriend know? Did he even tell her?

I clenched my teeth against the craving to scream at them all. *Shut up. Shut the* fuck *up.*

I really needed to get out of here.

I *really* needed a goddamn drink. Then three dozen after that.

I needed to be alone with my ugliness. Quasimodo in the solace of my bell tower.

"Killian." Karin visibly shook when I flinched at her invocation. I hadn't heard the word in weeks, and it hit me like acid now.

"Don't," I spat back. My voice was as harsh as sand on glass and felt the same way, but the command was there, fueled by my desperation. "Don't say it again."

"Fine. I won't. But that doesn't change what she needs— and that's you. I only spoke to her for a few moments, but even then, I could hear such desperation in her voice, such pain—"

"*Enough.*"

It caused the woman to back off by a step. I almost smiled. It should have been vindicating, knowing I could still physically affect people with the power of one word. But one compassionate nurse in a hospital hall was a huge difference from boardrooms filled with captains of empires. And the beast I'd become was a much different creature than the mask I'd worn.

Karin didn't move from her new location. But she did tuck her hands together in front and gently offer, "She loves you, you know. Deeply."

I raised my head again. Drove all the burning pain of my glower into the woman. "No, Nurse. She loves a lie. A man who doesn't exist anymore."

"I know what I heard over that phone line, Mr. Klarke."

"Good night, Karin."

★ ★ ★ ★

For a few hours, I let the city simply swallow me. After buying a T-shirt and a bottle of vodka from the nearby CVS, I wandered through the quiet streets, letting my thoughts settle on a new plan. Returning to LA was the logical choice. The city swallowed people every day. I was faceless and free—and it was comforting, in a strange way, to know I could see Claire's beloved ocean every day. Mexico also wasn't off the board. I knew about colonies of ex-pats who lived there. They'd let me blend in without the damn questions first.

Before long, I ended up in Balboa Park, my soul guiding me toward a path near the zoo. I sat on a bench shrouded by shadows from banana palms, listening to the restless growls of the nocturnal animals...my kindred spirits tonight.

I opened the booze but didn't drink it. As my senses cleared even more, I was able to hear the giant paws of those animals in the dirt, pacing back and forth in their "habitats." I grunted in commiseration. *Life in the zoo. Not always free food and lounging in the sun. I understand, guys.*

My chest tightened again. A comprehension struck.

The cage had been my world for so long—but in many ways, wasn't I still living in it? The view was different, the bars painted a new color, but I was still trapped. Still trying to break free, to disappear.

But it sure as hell didn't mean I could pick up where I'd left off either.

I was still lost. But maybe it was time to root the bell tower in one place for a while.

A couple of hours later, I watched the sun turn the sky pink over the waters of Mission Bay before tromping down the dock at Marina Village. At the end of the walkway, I turned right, hopping onto the forty-foot vessel moored in the slip there. I opened the cabin and climbed down inside, flipping on switches and nodding when observing all was in place...just the way I'd specified when having the yacht built six months ago. I had originally intended the boat to be a wedding present for Claire, so just stepping onboard was like tearing off another scab.

After tossing the unconsumed vodka into the trash chute, I climbed back out onto the deck. Then climbed higher. As the sun started glowing across the water, I yanked out the burner phone I'd stopped for after leaving the park. Punching in the digits felt odd yet comforting, like turning up the volume on a song I hadn't heard in a while.

"Hello?" I smiled when the familiar voice filled the line, already bolstering my spirit and strengthening my resolve.

"Alfred." I sucked in a deep breath. "It's me."

The man exhaled hard. "Thank God."

"I have to ask a couple of huge favors."

"Favors are what people request from strangers, Killian." Holy shit. The man actually growled at me. "You have but to ask me. You know it will be done."

"Even denying you ever had this conversation with me? To anyone?" My push on the last word implied exactly who I meant by it. As far as Claire Montgomery was concerned, I was still a ghost.

"Done," he replied without hesitation. "And the rest?"

I deliberately paused. There would be no turning back after this. But if I was going to try a version of this shit called life again, especially if I insisted on doing it *here* for a while, I was going to need help—and had to shove aside my fucking pride to ask for it.

"How'd you like to live in San Diego for a little while?"

CHAPTER THIRTEEN

Claire

Four months.

Sixteen weeks.

An entire season of Mother Earth's biological clock.

That was how long he had been missing from my days. And nights.

I didn't say his name out loud anymore. It hurt too much to hear it, let alone form the sounds on my tongue. I trudged through life in a fog that made San Francisco winter mornings look like clear San Diego summer nights. Fate was kicking me in the ass, taking its excruciating revenge for all those years I'd breezed along as a teen, arrogant about avoiding the soul-crushing heartbreaks all my girlfriends had been sobbing their way through. And the disaster with Nick? Hell. Even disaster felt like a glorification. It certainly hadn't been a relationship. Maybe a convenience that had turned into a mistake.

Killian hadn't been a mistake.

He was the love of my life. The one who helped the rest of life make sense. The one who made it all better with the power of his smile alone, who'd seen all of my idiosyncrasies and found me more perfect because of them. The one who sent texts that made my toe hairs curl and doodles that made my heart turn over.

He was the one, period.

Which meant the chasm in my soul wasn't closing up anytime soon. *Just flipping fantastic.*

Through every agonizing second of every bleak day, the emptiness dragged on. The minutes and hours as vacant as the room I'd stumbled into at the hospital that night, with Nurse Karin Nelson's apologies ringing in my ears. I'd grabbed the pillow that still carried his warmth and clutched it despite the nostril-numbing street stink, willing him to reappear—but he was gone.

Again.

"Claire. Did you hear me?"

Poor Michael. He was trying so hard to be a great friend. He and Chad had been taking turns babysitting me on the weekends. They even let Margaux pitch in here and there, which had been shockingly fun times. We'd discovered a mutual love for pairing strong Italian wine with stinky French cheese and then watching bad romantic comedies with the sound turned down so we could fill in our own dialogue.

But tonight, it was Michael's turn to rein in my wandering brain. And I wasn't making it easy.

"No." I went for the truth rather than try to fake my way through a fib. "I'm sorry. What were you saying?"

"Never mind." He sighed and pushed through the crowd, leading me along. He'd dragged me to a summer art festival along Mission Bay. Local artists were invited to display their talent, and proceeds from the sales were being donated to charity. As soon as we hit a little spot of open space, he gently hooked my elbow. "Come on, sweetie. At least try to have a good time."

I sipped my complimentary flute of half-flat champagne.

"Because it's for my own good, right? Time to get back on the horse?"

"Getting back on the horse is Chad's thing. Mine is learning to ride the bike again."

"Horse, bike, back in the saddle, back in the game—" I waved a dismissive hand. "Whatever. Save me the speech, okay?" I nodded farther up the boardwalk, to where the top of the Asher and Associates tent was visible. The firm was sponsoring petit fours for dessert. Michael and I were due to start our shift in a little over a half an hour "Besides, this a pure mission of mercy."

Michael held up both hands. "Okay, you have me there."

After good-naturedly socking him in the shoulder, I wandered off to visit an artisan displaying her custom-created jewelry. Fantastic hammered sterling silver dangling charms caught the orangey beams of the setting sun. I fingered the sparkling trinkets and instantly remembered the Harry Winston box sitting on the couch in our suite that night in Paris...

What would have happened if I'd simply accepted his proposal? Would it have been the difference in making him stay? Would we be planning our wedding right now? Maybe we'd even have decided to do it quick and dirty in Vegas and would be dealing with Trey's shit as a married couple, instead of living this nightmare.

I shook my head, shoving aside the ache—or at least trying to. Not that I helped myself at all, when the next moment, my gaze fell on a stunning man's leather bracelet...with a *K* embossed in the middle.

My fingers wobbled in front of my suddenly blurred vision.

When Michael's warm, solid hand lowered to my shoulder, I let the bracelet slip through my fingers, back to its velvet display pad—before I turned into Michael's chest and completely fell apart. He yanked me closer, fierce with the comfort of his embrace.

Busted.

Again.

When was this going to stop? It seemed like never. I would spend the rest of my life regretting every single mistake I'd made with Killian and never having the chance to atone for them. My moods still couldn't decide who to dance with anymore, circling from sad to miserable to furious and then back again. But I kept begging for the dance to stop. For the music to cease. For the silence to reign. I never wanted to take another step.

Michael patted my back. "Claire—"

I cut him off with a tearful growl. "Do *not* tell me this will get better, damn it."

"But it will. I swear. And I also swear I'm going to punch that motherfucker in the face when we find him. He has it coming, so don't deny me."

I smacked him even as I soaked his shirt even more. I kept thinking it impossible to have tears left at this point, yet they still came at the shittiest moments—like this. Disgustingly timed reminders of the wretched mess I had become.

I finally pulled back and looked up into Michael's face. *Way* up. The sunset's glow strawberried the edges of his hair, tugged high by the breeze off the water. Given a doublet and a scabbard, he'd look like a noble prince from another time—and I was so grateful for his chivalry. Only he, Chad, and Margaux had gotten me through these past few months. They were the only ones who knew my whole, disgusting truth. To the rest of the world, even Dad—maybe *especially* Dad, still mired in his own hell with trying to keep his marriage to the alien bitch intact—I was being strong, smiling through the survival, faking it till making it. If it wasn't for the three of them, I'd have likely faked myself into adopting all the neighborhood strays and chatting them up all day in my old robe and ladybug slippers.

"So...I don't get it," I finally said to him.

His eyebrows lowered. "Don't get what?"

"Why the hell aren't you sweeping some lucky woman off her feet? You shouldn't be here holding my hair while I emotionally puke every day." I shook my head as a harsh truth dawned on me. I'd become so damn selfish. Held my friends in this tight orbit while I pined for Kil in self-pity, refusing to move on with my life.

Maybe it was time to suck it up and slam back into the big-girl panties. Move upward, onward. A gulp thudded down my throat with the repercussions of the thought. It wasn't the easiest choice—but the right ones sometimes weren't.

I pushed back from Michael and straightened my shoulders. "Let's get our asses to the booth and get this ordeal over with, shall we?" As we started walking again, I found some tissues in my bag and used them to mop up my face as best as possible. It seemed red-rimmed eyes and a swollen nose were my new black. They went with everything I wore these days.

We strolled at a leisurely pace, the heavy crowd making quick progress impossible. It was great to see the event doing so well. Though I was aware San Diego fostered an artistic vibe, I'd still had no idea so many of them lived here.

Michael stopped cold in the middle of the walkway. As in, practically froze. I stared hard, wondering what the hell had seized him up like that. And imprinted a look of such deep shock on his face.

"Michael. What the—"

"Damn." The force in his tone assured me everything was working okay with him physically. But mentally, he'd been yanked into some strange tractor beam by a sight across the grass.

"What is it?" I tried following his gaze, but my line of vision was a good eight inches shorter than his. Michael said nothing. The next second, I found myself yanked by him through the throng, headed toward the area of grass he'd just been gaping at. "Michael, what the hell are you—?"

My breath caught as we stumbled out of the crowd, in front of an artist's expansive display. In the center of the display, in soft shades of lavender and gray, was a watercolor portrait of a woman. Her head was slightly turned down, a smile hinting on her lips, the light captivating on her features. She was stunning.

And she looked exactly like me.

Exactly.

"Oh, my God."

Michael blew out a vindicated huff. "So, I'm not dreaming this."

"Not unless I am too."

The proprietor of the booth strolled forward. He wore a beachy artist's smile framed by sun-bleached hair in typical surfer's waves. I damn near assaulted him, seeming to stun him for a moment. Life at anything other than cruiser bicycle speed was clearly not his thing. "Whoa. Hey. Easy, girlfriend. Can I help you?"

"Who painted this?" I demanded.

"Awesome work, isn't it?" He threw his whole upper body

into his nod. "Are you wanting to buy something?" But then he stopped short too. "Whoa...chica...that totally looks like you. I mean, totally. Trip-py." His amazement pulled the single word into two.

"Who painted this?" I repeated myself with slower emphasis, hoping he could focus long enough to answer me.

"Dunno the dude's whole name. He's righteous, though. Lives on one of the boats down in the marina there. He paints like a god, right? I see it now. You must be his muse or something." He laughed and added a flip of his bangs, seeming to congratulate himself on using the word muse in a complete sentence.

Thank God Michael stepped in, because I was getting ready to strangle the crap out of Surfer Bob's long-lost cousin. "Why doesn't the guy sell his own stuff?"

"He's not into socializing, man. At all. I've only met him once. Another guy usually brings the work over to the gallery. I sell other shit for them too. Cityscapes, mostly Europe, I think...and some exotic animals."

"But you've only met the artist himself once?"

"He's a head trip, dude. Says he's not about the man anymore, you know?" He made air quotes around "the man," punctuating it with a weird grimace.

I exchanged a similar look with Michael. This was starting to feel a little creepy—especially when we observed the watercolor wasn't the only "Claire" piece here. There were at least a dozen works in all, each featuring a different pose. They were rendered in various media—oils, pastels, pencil sketches. I bought them all, asking Hang Ten Fred to stow them off to the side until I could think straight.

Michael pulled me over by the elbow again. "This is some

heeb-worthy shit, right?"

I nodded, peering around, not feeling watched but not feeling safe. Why did I think Stephen King was about to pop out and start taking notes? *The sun shone so pleasantly on the water that day. The charity art event seemed to be going so well, everyone sipping wine and having a grand time in the early balm of summer...*

"You have any strange exes who've boiled bunnies in your name lately?"

"My God, no. You know about Nick the Dick—who, according to Margaux, is gone for good. He found God and settled down with a little wife in Idaho."

I didn't offer the rest of the story, about Margaux sharing that as a way of reassuring me that she was over being spiteful about the secret she carried regarding Nick and me. We'd been young and stupid and just trying to get through college. Nick had simply chosen a dangerous way to make that happen, and I'd been the infatuated fool who'd helped him. Neither Michael nor Chad knew that part of the story and never would.

"Okay," he replied while helping me stack the paintings, "so now we have to look at—" His voice trailed off and that possessed-by-someone-else expression washed his face again.

"Look at what?" I prompted.

"The signature on the paintings." Bewilderment doused his slow tone. "Doesn't that look like the name—?"

"Klarke."

It spilled off my lips just before the world went completely dark.

★ ★ ★ ★

"Claire? *Claire?*"

Michael's voice sounded strange. Hollow. Weren't we just walking together on Mission Bay? When the hell had we made our way to the La Jolla Coves?

"Christ. How long has she been out?"

"Not long." Not Michael, but somebody official. "It's all right. She's coming around."

I blinked. Michael exhaled, appearing relieved. The sky was peach and purple behind his head. Wait. Why was I lying on the ground? And who was that other guy? *San Diego Fire & Rescue. Paramedic.* Okay, that answered that. But who were all these people around us?

"Oh, shit," I muttered. It all rushed back. The art festival. The crowds. Michael yanking me through them. The booth with the paintings.

The paintings of me.

Klarke.

"Killian!" I surged up and smacked a hand into the grass to steady myself. Somebody needed to turn off the horizon. It was on the fast spin cycle.

"Okay, easy," Michael ordered. "You're going to end up right back where you started, girl."

I shoved up from the cradle of his arm. "I'm fine, damn it." My breath echoed in my ears as it shot in and out of my lungs. "We have to find him. Michael, we have to."

"I know. I know. But you were just passed out for a minute solid, sweetie. You need some air in your lungs and some blood in your brain, and then we can worry about that bastard."

"Stop it," I retorted. "Only I get to call him that. And I want to do it to his face, damn it. So let me get up, and—"

"*Damn it*, Claire." He pulled me back by a shoulder, exasperation twisting his features. "You *will* listen to me this time." A heavy, almost apologetic, huff escaped him. "Listen. We've all been watching you torture yourself for months over this guy. Ten more minutes isn't going to hurt anyone. If he's even around here, he has no idea *you're* here, so it's not like he'll bolt. Sit back, have some water, and tell me I'm right."

I grumbled but sipped the water. "Fine. You're right." But just the thought of Killian slipping through my fingers again was enough to make me shake harder. I blinked as the horizon tilted again. When it balanced out, fear slammed in an icy sluice. What if Killian didn't want to see me? What if he really didn't want to be found? Was he really here, in San Diego—and if so, for how long? Had he been here since the night of our near miss at the hospital ER? Longer?

He'd never reached out to me—and no one was making him stay away from me.

Conflict assaulted, twice as agonizing as the fear.

Maybe I needed to just walk away. All of the vessels in the marina were huge. If he *was* on one of them, he wasn't suffering, that much was clear. That part wasn't so much surprising as agitating.

I grew increasingly restless.

After about ten minutes, the small crowd dispersed, assured—or more likely bored—that I was really okay. Michael finally let me stand up. As my embarrassed flush subsided, I righted my maxi-dress and then walked back over to the art dealer, determined to learn exactly what boat Mr. Righteous-God-Painter lived on. The guy was hesitant. Make that completely close-mouthed. I actually found that admirable, pleased Killian had at last found someone he could trust. It was going to make my job a lot harder, though.

Or maybe not.

After a fast phone call to Ian Charles, supplying him with the name Killian Klarke for the search, the investigator had a hit in less than a minute. Sure enough, there was a yacht registered in Marina Village, slip B16, under the name K. Klarke. In a rush, I thanked him, disconnected, and pocketed my phone.

"What now?" Michael asked.

I dipped my head, wondering if I looked like I felt—the she-bull who'd just had the red flag wiggled in front of her face. "Was that a rhetorical question, Mr. Pearson?"

Michael quirked one side of his mouth and emulated my nod, his version of an atta-girl. He quickly phoned Talia, who was already at the booth, and apprised her of the situation. She relayed the verdict from Andrea—our shift was covered at the booth as long as we promised to report back if we found Killian. I hated getting everyone involved in my personal life, but after my moping around for over four months, I pretty much owed all of them. Yeah, even Andrea.

The walk over to the marina was tense and quiet. I battled to equalize my feelings between hope and heartache, though the latter gained the edge. If we found Killian aboard the boat, there was a hefty chance he'd order me away. Now that this moment was finally here, was finally real, I didn't know if my heart could stand the anticipation. I almost hoped the lead was another false alarm, rather than face the possibility that this showdown might blow up in my face.

With the crowds so huge, it was easy to sneak past the guard shack and start down the dock as if we belonged there. With every step, my heart climbed higher into my windpipe and my knees threatened to slosh like the water against the pilings. Thank God I'd worn comfortable kitten heels in anticipation of being on my feet at the booth. My stomach clenched. My head throbbed.

And then everything stopped.

I turned and stared at the most magnificent yacht I had ever seen. It was huge, modern, sleek, seemingly built for speed *and* luxury. The decks shone. The upholstery of the seats was a rich Caribbean blue.

The matching lettering across the transom read *Fairy Queen*.

"He's here." I rasped it as every nerve ending of my body and every chamber of my soul seemed to pop back open, alive and free—and terrified. My legs shook harder. My fingers trembled.

Despite that, Michael guided me toward the gangway before giving me another hug of encouragement. "I'm not going to be far," he affirmed and then let me go and turned me back toward the yacht.

Part of me yearned to run all the way up, but I held on to my dignity, walking to the top and then knocking on the door there. Then waiting. Then waiting.

Then knocking again.

Just walking aboard was the nautical equivalent of entering someone's house uninvited. Not cool. So I knocked again. The third time would either be a charm or a kiss-off. I breathed deep, telling myself I quite possibly would have to face the latter—along with the thousands of questions that would remain unanswered with it.

That was when I heard the rustling of someone approaching. I fidgeted with the strap of my purse. Everything below my waist froze. I couldn't breathe. I wanted to throw up. I wanted to pass out again. There was still time to leave.

You don't want to leave.

Yes, I do.

And there he was.

Now I really couldn't breathe. He filled the portal, looking rugged and as wild as the sea itself. His hair cascaded past his nape, tempting to hit his collar bones. And he had a beard. It was shaggy and messy yet oddly hot, an ideal match for the clothes that appeared straight out of an ad for the Bahamas. His barely buttoned white shirt hung over baggy khaki shorts. He was dark and barefoot and glorious—and all he did was stare. I stared right back.

I had no idea how much time passed. I was aware of everything and nothing at once. He looked *so* damn good. He smelled even better, natural and salty and windy.

"It— It *is* you." I finally croaked.

"Yeah."

"I...can't believe it."

"How did you find me?"

The question whacked me like a sack of bricks. I stumbled back, shaking my head. "How did I—?" A choke fell out. "That's *it*, Killian? Not hello? Not I've missed you? My name is Claire. Do you remember that part?" I stepped back again, throwing up my hands against the vexation, anger, disappointment, and pain. "This was a mistake, wasn't it? A big one. You"—I fluctuated between wanting to punch his balls and kiss his rugged lips—"you *ass*! How long have you been here, gazing out across that water and—" The words clutched in my throat, wrenched as tight as the ropes tethering this monstrosity to the pier. One half of me gave the order to slice the lines free and simply let his sorry ass float away forever. The other zinged and pounded and saw the world once more in the Technicolor only he could bring. "Damn it!" I finally sputtered. "I should go. I really should have left well enough—"

His sudden lunge caught me off guard. In less than a heartbeat, he covered the space between us and hauled me into his beautiful arms. For a moment, I thought he'd grabbed me so hard that we'd fallen over and were drowning together. No. It was the consuming perfection of his eyes instead, dragging me under as he gazed long and hard at me.

"Oh, God." My heavy sob spilled out. I'd dreamed of this for so long and had just as easily dismissed it as a fantasy that would never come true again. The reality was even better— especially when I saw the tears that shimmered in Kil's own eyes.

His jaw clenched. I could see it even beneath his beard. He dragged a hand up to my face, bracing my jaw in the broad L of his finger and thumb, before slamming his lips to mine.

Yes. *Yes.*

Sweet reunion.

Perfect bliss.

The answer to so many questions. The start of so many more.

But all of that could wait. It had to. Right now, I had the answer to my dilemma.

I needed this. Just this.

Just him.

I wrapped my arms around his neck and held on for dear life. My mind still worked at comprehending that he was actually here, wrapped around me, groaning against me, twining his mouth deeper with mine. I kissed him with so much emotion I wasn't sure I would ever resurface—or ever want to. The ache in my soul was so deep, forged from these months of loneliness and grief, turning me into a thirsty, needy creature for as much of him as I could get. Not knowing if he was safe had been the worst of it all, so the reality of holding him in my arms was the nirvana I craved the most. And, oh yes, it was better than anything I'd fabricated on those endless nights. *So much better.*

We separated, but I couldn't let him go. To be honest...I lost my shit. There was no pretty sidestep for the description. I fell apart with gobby, sloppy thoroughness that felt like heaven and hell in one incredible, horrible moment. I'd sworn that if I ever saw him again, I'd be strong, noble, and resilient. I'd never cave to weepy, weak, and—and I went there without passing *Go* or collecting my two hundred bucks. I sobbed until I couldn't speak. I wept tears that somehow kept regenerating, replenished by four months' worth of pain and worry and darkness. All the moments of imagining him sick in some ditch without medical treatment, wondering if I'd given up on him. The wide-awake midnights, wondering if he was simply naked with another woman. The times I'd thought he might have died and was lying on a slab in some morgue, an unclaimed John Doe.

I cried and cried and then cried some more. He held me until his shirt was soaked and I was exhausted. I was embarrassed by the time I hiccupped to a finish, but the anger kicked in with perfect timing, refueling my engines to chew his ass to ribbons about where he'd been for the past sixteen weeks. But some things hadn't changed—like the man's ability to read every nuance of my moods, even just seconds in.

"God. Claire." I had no idea how he turned the coarse rasp into a command and a plea at once. It possessed me as magically as he slid his hands into my hair and gripped the sides of my head. "I'm fucked up, okay?"

"No shit." I copied his move until practically twisting his hair in my grip. "And I don't care."

His eyes squeezed shut. His face contorted. "*Damn it*. Claire."

Before he tumbled any further down into his mental sludge pit, I pulled away one of my hands to grab one of his. Pushed it into the space between my breasts. Pressed it there hard. "Do you feel that, Killian? It's truly beating for the first time in four months."

I had much more to say. So much more to demand. A million questions that needed answers. But nothing else surfaced beyond that...and I didn't want it to. Not right now, standing here in the intensity of his presence, the power of his hold, and the dark magic in his eyes...

A moan, high and urgent, tumbled out of me. I'd missed him so badly. My body hadn't stopped being perfectly tuned to his. It was a basic, primal truth. I needed him. Every flame in my blood, beat of my pulse, and throb between my legs confirmed it.

Yes. *Yes*.

I clutched the back of his head, curling my fingers into his hair and urging his mouth tighter onto mine.

Killian didn't need another hint. He groaned and slipped his tongue into my mouth with deep plunges of passion. "Fuck," he finally uttered, his lips still on mine. "I've missed you. So damn much."

The strain in his voice twisted at my heart. "I'm right here," I whispered. "Right here, baby. Needing you...so badly. Oh, Killian...please..." I was past the bridge of needy and now at the shore of begging, but it didn't matter. I had no idea what lay ahead, but I sure as hell knew about the path behind, and I couldn't return to it.

As we kissed again, more urgently and desperately, I scrambled a hand into the few buttons keeping his shirt together. They all came free except one, which I finally ignored in my quest to savor every beautiful muscle of his torso again. The moment my hand glided along his waistline, he groaned and fully mashed our mouths, filling my senses with the force of his hungry desire.

The world spun and dipped and turned as if my senses had taken a ride on one of the seagulls on the wind above. Everything was upended again when he swept his hands beneath both my knees and hiked my legs around his waist. Still claiming my lips in constant kisses, he turned back onto the yacht and carried me down a small set of stairs. We continued through the teakwood passage inside, passing several doors before he kicked one open, revealing a large master suite. The plush bed remained undisturbed, as if he hadn't ever used the space before this moment.

We tumbled together into the center of the bed, where he quickly covered my body with his. I reveled in his weight on me, surrounding me with the same panther-perfect heat as his touch, his smell, his kisses, his presence. He was familiar yet new, a mystery yet my home, the lover who electrified just as much of me now as he had when we'd first discovered each other in this way.

For a few moments, he seemed to return to that time too. His mouth brushed me softly, as if it were the start of our first kiss all over again. He was chaste and warm and worshipping, roaming his gaze across my face, stroking my hair back from my cheeks and tucking the strands behind my ears.

"You cut your hair. It's much shorter than it was."

His observation sped my pulse with an adolescent thrill. He'd noticed my new haircut.

"You haven't." I pouted and tugged on his long strands. "You look like surfer Jesus."

A chuckle shook his whole body. "Oh, I'm *not* Jesus."

"Thank God, because it's awful."

He laughed a little harder. Dipped his head and kissed me with the same intent. I answered him with lust and longing. We twisted our mouths more frantically into each other as our hands searched for buttons, zippers, or any mooring that could be undone, baring more skin to each other by the second.

I pulled the last button of his shirt free. He helped me shove it away, finally ditching the thing on the floor. Next I went for his khaki shorts, thankfully secured with simple ties and Velcro. I was a little stunned that the fastenings had held all of him in. As his cock surged into my grip, there was no denying how much certain parts of him had *really* missed me. We smiled together when he swelled against my fingers, the strong veins standing out under the stiff skin, leading to a head already wet with silken drops of desire.

His smirk vanished the moment I started stroking him. His eyes flared as he bent his head to watch while I serviced him with greedy hands. "Damn," he gritted, just before sinking his mouth to my neck. He bit and kissed and suckled my heated skin while pumping his hips in and out of my fist.

Before long, he set his own hands to work. I arched back, tingling all over, his long, powerful fingers dragged beneath my dress, finding my panties soaked and definitely in the way. With a deep grunt, he yanked them down, letting me kick them off after they bunched at my calves. I started to close my leg back in, but he caught it by the ankle, kissing it and then spreading it back out.

"Keep it there," he commanded. "This one, too." He pushed my other leg wide. The motions lured my dress toward my waist, helping his effort to drag the whole thing up and off.

Only my bra was left. He didn't bother opening it. With illicit urgency, he just pushed the cups off my breasts, serving to push up my flesh into his hungry mouth. He feasted on me like a starved man, abrading my nipples and areolae with the scratchy whiskers of that awful, delicious beard. Hmmm. I instantly started rethinking the merits of the new look while sinking my fingers into his hair, tugging as hard on his strands as he did with his teeth on my nipple. We wrestled and clawed, bit and hissed, touched and tasted...and needed. God, the need. *The need...*

"Killian!"

"I know, baby." It was a gorgeous combination of a growl and groan.

"Don't stop. Don't stop."

They weren't the words that should've been on my lips— we needed to be sitting on this bed and talking, not writhing— but perhaps this passion was the perfect door into that difficult room. Opening the door to the mud room before dealing with the full tempest.

Being in a mud room had never turned me on more.

I sawed my legs back and forth on the outside of his hips, working at instilling some ideas about a new focus for his mouth, but he kept up the torture on my breasts, shifting so he got that godforsaken beard along the sensitive underside of both mounds. I'd be red and sore when this was over, and every scuff would be well worth the pain.

I finally summoned the strength to speak again. "Need... you," I told him. "Please!"

He slid up to scrape my ear with his teeth. "Need me where?" he demanded. "Tell me. You know how I like to hear it. Every detail, baby."

"Mmmm." I ran my hands along the coiled muscles of his shoulders. The man hadn't lost an ounce of his definition. He even felt a little bulkier. I suspected ocean swims and heartily approved. "I need you...inside me. With your cock. Make love to me, Killian. Please."

After what seemed like an eternity—who was I kidding? It *had* been an eternity—he lined up his erect length at my entrance. After his first nudge, we both moaned. I was tight, but I was also wet, open, and more than ready.

With one lunge, he slid into my body.

Our mouths fused, the connection absorbing his groans and my pleas for more, *more*. When he tore away to get air, I verbalized the need.

"Faster. Please, Killian! Harder!"

I should have known my begging would be useless. He took his damn time about plunging his cock every inch inside me, twisting and rolling his hips in the way that drove me batshit with need all over again. Our bodies greeted each other with shivers and shudders as timeless as the sea outside, moving together in a synchronicity that bordered on magic. Considering how badly I'd been craving him, I was stunned I lasted even a dozen strokes before coming apart beneath him.

He barely gave me any time for recovery and then ramped me back up with wickedly wonderful bites, licks, and teases. As I sighed and gasped with need, his rhythm intensified. He pulled my legs higher, cupping my ass as he pounded harder into me. His face, etched in lines of pain and passion I hadn't seen outside the frescoes of Italian chapels, locked against my neck as his orgasm thundered through his body...and into mine.

Everything turned shockingly quiet as he gave the last of his hot release to me, his body slackening...and his voice descending to a bare, almost frightened, whisper.

"I love you, my fairy queen. Nothing will ever change that."

I didn't respond. It was the most ridiculous impression to gather, but I wasn't certain he intended for me to hear the confession. But of course he had...right? Every cell of my spirit recognized it as the truth. Despite everything that had happened, I'd never doubted he loved me—and he sure as hell knew how much *I* still meant it. But a belly-deep instinct held me back from voicing the words. *Not now. Not now.*

Perhaps I already sensed what he'd do next.

With his body barely free from mine, Kil flipped to his back, whooshed out a heavy breath, and threw an elbow across his face. Two long beats like that were all he needed before surging from the bed entirely and clearing the three steps into the bathroom. As awkward silence and I kept each other company, he thumped the door shut and then locked it. I heard water running, but it wasn't a shower, so I didn't get the impression he'd be in there for long. Suddenly feeling like an intruder, I righted my bra and scrambled to the end of the bed, pawing through the sheets and blankets for my clothes. Pulling up my stretched panties felt weird and tawdry—and I couldn't shake the feeling that in spite of everything feeling so right for the last hour, it was about to go all wrong again.

"Breathe, girlfriend," I whispered. "You're jumping to conclusions."

Just because he's been right here, in the same damn city as you for months, and has never once tried to reach out? Just because you pulled a surprise party on his deck and the two of you decided to let animal attraction talk before reason and logic? Just because you decided an hour with your body could magically fix all the shit in his head—and now you're getting the vibe otherwise?

Shit.

Shit.

Shit.

He reappeared, water still dripping from parts of his beard. I felt awful for noticing his cock was still at half mast, ready and willing to be talked into more of the "fun" we'd just had. But his face dampened the desire right out of me. Fun seemed exactly the category he'd just filed this into—something in the same range as eating a supersize ice cream and then taking three rides on the roller coaster. He looked wholly satisfied—and supremely ill.

"What?" I asked, not diluting the shiver in my voice. If he didn't have an idea of what this had meant to me before, he did now. "What is it, Killian?"

"Claire." He made no move to leave the doorway. Despite the tender threads in his voice, he braced his elbows to both sides of the portal at shoulder height. "Look, this was...great. But—"

"Stop." I let my dress fall to the bed. "And just save the buts for a few minutes, okay? I know we did this backwards, that we need to talk. But at least we're both here now, and we can—"

"You need to leave." It had to be a world record. From postcoital poet to naked dictator ass inside of three seconds. "I'm sorry, but you must."

I blinked. "Okay...since you got to the point, I will too. What. The. Hell?"

His jaw hardened. A tic pushed at the plane between his lips and cheek. "You remember what I said, right? Up on deck?"

"Of course I remember," I snapped. "Fucked-up. You. Bosom buddies. Got it. Guess that asshole's been really good to you, since you've been in the same damn city as me since... when was that again...?"

"Long enough," he muttered.

"'Long enough,'" I taunted. "Great. That's just great. Hope you and Fucked-up have been having a blast down here for long enough, catching some waves, creating my image in every artistic medium except M&Ms collages, and *not* thinking how much a simple phone call would've meant to me!"

His stare turned the texture of cracked black glass. "And if I *had* called?" he retaliated. "Don't bother answering. I can give you this one, Claire. You're brilliant enough that the call would've been traced, even if I used three burner phones for it. Then you'd be knocking on my door—and we eventually would've been doing this. Exactly this. Three months ago or three days ago, *this* would have ended up...like this."

I sprinted my gaze across the cabin, willing to trade my favorite shoes for something substantial to hurl at him. Everything worth anything was secured to the damn walls except the bed pillows. I had to be happy with clawing my hand through my hair. "Well, I hate this."

"I'm sorry."

"Oh, yeah? Well, guess what? I don't accept it. Or any of this bullshit. Damn it, Kil—" I stopped short at his sudden pounce across the cabin. When he twisted the handle and rammed the door out into the narrow hall, I instinctively stepped back. "You're completely serious about this, aren't you?"

He kept his gaze fixed down the hall. "Yeah. I am."

Damn him. He looked so tall and perfect and glorious, standing there with the cabin's gold light glinting on his long hair and rippled nakedness, that my heart actually ached. My chest squeezed on the damn thing as I stepped outside the situation for a moment—and saw myself as the service whore he was dismissing me as.

"I can't believe this," I rasped. "I can't believe you actually thought a toss in the sack is going to send me peacefully on my way." I stepped closer to him, hating that the motions carried me closer to the door as well. "Do you know me, Killian? At all?"

"I know you too damn well," he finally said. His tone was crisp—and forced. "That's exactly the problem."

I tore my dress off the bed. Put it on in furious jerks and stabs. "The problem, huh? Thanks for clearing that up. I'm now the problem. I *was* wondering exactly where I fit into your new, artistic, fucked-up life."

He grunted. "Nothing's a fit in my life anymore, Claire." He sent a reluctant swallow down his tense throat. "So, needless to say, I won't be here the next time you look. Don't bother coming back."

Every ounce of joy he'd just defrosted from the winter in my heart was frozen again, blasted by an ice storm as vast as it was devastating. Part of me still tried to be stunned while the other part tore off one of the ice daggers hanging from my soul and then jabbed it into my stupid, hopeless heart. "This is truly how you want it to be now?"

"No. This is how it *has* to be now. I get no choice in the matter. All of my choices were made *for* me, remember?"

I was damn near grateful for the rage that fired back at the ice. "Whoa. You're...you're kidding, right? *That's* how you're playing this?"

The glass in his gaze turned into ruthless lead. "Believe me, baby, I *want* to be kidding. I want to be playing even more."

Now that I stood just inches from him, I jabbed up my chin and braced my feet. "Oh, boo hoo hoo for you, *baby*." I stabbed a finger into the middle of his chest. "*You* are Killian *fucking* Stone. No one does anything for you! The pity-me trip is for losers and wastes of DNA like Trey. Even when you disappeared, I never thought you capable of this bullshit, Kil. Ever."

He clamped a hand around my wrist and pushed it away. "I'm not Killian *fucking* Stone anymore, Miss Montgomery—and you may be the only person deranged enough not to remember." Inexplicably, the backs of his eyes gained bemused little lights. "But hey, I *am* glad you wanted to take a little trip down Memory Lane, baby. Four months is a hell of a dry spell, right?"

Behind my own eyes, an all-too-familiar heat began to surge. Shit. Not now. Not again. "Fuck you, Killian."

He left the door open and moved into the bedroom, giving me room to leave. "Alfred can show you back to the parking lot."

"Just...yeah...fuck you."

I was so angry my knees shook with each step up to the yacht's deck. I wanted to punch Alfred when he appeared out of nowhere. He was a smart man, instantly sensing it and wisely stepping out of my way.

The air on the dock was so refreshing it took my breath away. Oh wait, that was the rush from finally setting all my emotions free. Not that it felt great. Not that it would ever feel great again.

The moment my feet hit land again, I jogged toward the parking lot. Even in my kitten heels, even with tears blinding my vision. I needed to get as far away from that damn boat as I could. I stopped beneath a huge palm tree, catching my breath and shoving away my tears before getting back to the parking lot. I had to pull myself together or Michael would go after Killian now like a damn Claire-Bear vigilante.

Before that happened, I had another gallon of tears to shed.

The dream that had kept me going for months...was done. As in *done*. As in one of the most devastating experiences of my life. I almost wished it was yesterday again and I still wallowed in the emptiness and the aching.

At least then, I'd still have hope.

CHAPTER FOURTEEN

Killian

I'd never believed in Reset buttons.

Even during the years when I'd hated Killian Stone with my whole being, yearning to bail on his life like the identity refugee I had been, I'd never edged an inch toward the button. I'd sucked up, dug in, and dealt with the path life had laid before me. Made it the best I could.

And then it had gotten *really* good—those months of showering Claire with all the milk and honey that *Stone* could bring, actually earning every beautiful drop of her love—before it had all gotten ripped apart.

I shook my head while leaning back against the door of my truck. I'd slammed it a minute ago after parking a few houses up from Claire's, along with the vow that I was done with falling back on victim statements like that which had driven Claire from the yacht in confusion and rage.

Which was the goal...right? Devastate her once or keep destroying her. Those were the choices, man. You stuck with the former instead of leading her on with hopes of having her Killian back—dreams as pointless as even trying to find that man anymore. God only knows how hard you've been looking for him.

You did the right thing, ace. Amputated the limb of yourself from her life before you paralyzed her.

Which is exactly why you're hanging out in the dark near her house, fumbling with the words you came here to say.

Loser.

I swore and kicked at the ground. Wasn't the first time the rebuke had grabbed me by the nuts and squeezed during the last seventy-two hours. I accepted and bore the pain, admitting I'd royally fucked up on the delivery if not the message—and acknowledging she deserved a better truth than the bullshit sidesteps I'd pulled on her. The *whole* truth. That though I'd love her until my dying breath, I couldn't ever be with her again. That despite what the sappy songs said, sometimes love wasn't enough. Not for me. Not *with* me. Whoever the hell "me" was anymore.

Did I wish I was like one of the guys up on the boardwalk, happy with life as it came, willing to push the damn Reset button every time the sun rose? Only every minute of every day. But I was the schlep who'd been allowed a free pass into the castle for only a few glorious years and, during that visit, had managed to snag the most beautiful princess in the land. Trouble was, she still deserved a prince—not just the one in pinstripes but the one with the noblest heart. The one who wouldn't be mocked, whispered about, and laughed at everywhere they went.

The man who could love her with everything he still was, not a shadow of what he had been.

She didn't—and wouldn't—see that. Because she was Claire. Because she saw the best in the world, in everyone. She still brought out coffee for the paparazzi in the morning. Fed the neighborhood's three stray cats. Hell, from what I could gather from the gossip-magazine pictures, she'd even started up a friendship with Margaux. She had no concept that though her world had been bleak without me, it would be pure hell with me. The press would turn. The whispers would start. The daggers would be unsheathed.

And every day I subjected her to that would be another reminder of what was impossible to give her anymore.

All of me.

Well. Now that I was clear about that cheery news...it was time to share it with her too.

With determined steps, I approached her house. During the trip, I lowered the top of my hoodie and attempted to finger-comb my Jesus look into submission. Like that helped. The shit felt like Bigfoot's pelt beneath my hand. That was likely for the better anyhow. I'd played with the idea of having Alfred trim the shit up for me, but Claire would have a better time accepting the finality of all this if I came in with the hippie style she hated.

I was so preoccupied with the self-style session I didn't see the pile of dog crap on the sidewalk. As I wiped my shoe across her next-door neighbor's lawn, the irony didn't escape me. *Tonight on* America's Got Talent: *Killian Klarke will step in shit yet again! Cue applause!*

I really had to get off the boat more at night.

I turned to make the cut across Claire's lawn—but was jolted to a total stop by a sound I'd hoped never to hear again. Her sobs. Wrenching. Hard. And nonstop. To any passerby on the street, they likely would have blended with the normal noises on the hill, but I was ten feet closer and a thousand times more sensitive to the sound.

Because I'd desperately prayed not to hear it tonight.

Her outrage? Her snarls? Her adorable gift for creative

profanity? Fine, I'd take that. Any of it. All of it. But damn it, not her tears.

I gritted the F-word at the feces clinging to my foot before treading closer to the fence on ninja steps. As I approached, I swore I could hear fate's laughter on the wind along with her sobs. Arrogant fucker.

I arrived just in time to hear her blow her nose and mutter a soft thanks to someone.

"No problem." The source of the encouragement was easy to recognize. Michael Pearson, her teammate—or so I'd assumed until tonight. What the hell was he doing here? Had he done this lean-on-me routine with her before? The guy's good looks were the kind of shit that turned heads, female *and* male. On top of that, he and Claire had great rapport and a solid base of friendship.

He was exactly the kind of prince she needed.

The kind I'd all but told her to go and find.

I suddenly hated every bone in his body.

She blew her nose again and sniffed loudly. "I can't stand this part. Oh, God, Michael, I really can't stand it."

"I know, sweetie. I know."

Yep, it was official. I hated him. And coiled my hands into fists as I eyed the fence, wondering how hard it would be to tear the thing out of the ground on my way back to hauling her out of his arms and ordering his hands off her.

Because you're suddenly willing to take over the job again? Because what you're prepared to provide for her, emotionally and spiritually, has changed so damn much over the last thirty seconds?

I swore at the dog shit on my foot again.

"Sister mine. Come here."

My head snapped up at the new voice in the conversation. New to me, anyway. I'd never heard Margaux sound like that before. All the hallmarks of her inflection were still there, the sarcastic blend of world-weary woman and insecure girl, though a fresh element made her seem an entirely new person, at least through the fence.

Affection.

I listened to the scrapes of chairs and the rustle of bodies— and fought to get a better look at things through the fence slats. Was Margaux actually hugging Claire? For support? Just because?

"Thank you," Claire rasped through her tears. "Thank you both so much...for coming over so fast."

"All you had to do was send the bat signal up." Michael borrowed a little of Margaux's wryness. "Besides, we were just sitting around—err, *I* was just sitting around—bingeing on the new *Walking Dead*."

"Is it any good?" Margaux's query reminded me of Nurse Karin Nelson's fake charm. A question asked when the answer was already known.

"You can finish it here if you like," Claire offered. "Or just watch your friend Claire Montgomery, the zombie who craves the one human being she can't have."

Michael grunted. "You sure he's still human?"

"Hey." The reproach came from Margaux. The pattern of shadows across the patio indicated something had been tossed at him too. "No chopping the balls off a girl's boo when she's still got it bad for him."

"So I can chop his balls off next week?"

"I'll still be in love with him next week."

Her voice crumbled on the last word. Sobs took over her

body again. I snarled softly, realizing I'd picked the wrong fucking night at the wrong fucking time to come here and do this—whatever the hell *this* was.

The answer to that made me take a step back, scattering stones out of the side path as I did. I glowered at the results, a demonstration of my conclusion if there ever was one.

Stones. Flung apart. In the dark. Because of haste and subterfuge—and selfishness.

I'd come here for the wrong reasons. For my benefit, not hers. To assuage the garbage pile of guilt in my gut, ignoring what it would do to her to see me on her front porch before I turned and left her again. The Reset button hadn't been pushed, nor could it be.

She needed to move on.

And I needed to let her.

No matter how deeply it eviscerated me...I needed to let her.

Every muscle in my body screaming as if it had been torn off its bone, I backed farther away. The concrete of the sidewalk couldn't have come any sooner beneath my feet, bringing the hard, cold smack of reality with it. That was it. My castle days were behind me. I fought to silence the sound of the drawbridge chains, clanking through my head with morbid finality.

"Well, damn. Came out here to retrieve my phone and look what I found instead."

Margaux's quip, though soft, halted me faster than a whip around my ankles. I jammed both hands into my jacket pockets and turned, locking my teeth around a smile. "We never run into each other under dull circumstances, do we?"

"No." A genuine chuckle left her lips. They weren't

plastered down in her normal berry lip stain. I liked the new shade. The lighter pink was flattering on her. "Think the world would explode if we tried a normal brother-sister chat over coffee sometime?"

I looked toward the sea of city lights spread below us, letting her watch the smile fade off my own mouth. "I'm not your brother, Margaux."

"Well. A girl can dream."

I slanted a quizzical glance. "Didn't you say that when you wanted me in the biblical sense? And, let's face it, you were a little relieved to know you didn't make a half-naked pass at your real brother."

"No," she answered with a definitive nod. "I'm still *ew*'ed out." She tilted her head too. "Probably because I keep hoping the karma wheel hears my prayer and turns you back into my biological brother again."

I let my eyebrows drop before replying, "You're after a specific reaction to that, aren't you? I just can't tell what it is."

Margaux did one of those female huffy things, a double stomp disguising a shift of weight. "By all that's holy, Killian. You really don't get it, do you?" She folded her arms when I gave her nothing but a searching stare. "Okay, I'm going to assume, by the stench of that dog crap on your shoe, that you just tromped through the grass to spy on us over Claire's back fence—so the issue of you shattering her heart has been covered by the conversation you overheard. With that done, I'll move along to the subject of your company—or should I say, what's left of it."

I whipped up my head. "SGC?"

"You have any other company these days?"

"What's *left* of it?" I echoed. "What the hell do you mean?"

"Really?" She teeter-tottered her head. "Okay, when was the last time you picked up a copy of the *Journal?*"

She didn't need to explain the verbal shorthand. There was only one *Journal* in the world of business, and it emanated from Wall Street. I winced, privately admitting to a slight hard-on from simply hearing the word again.

No.

I whirled and paced, staring hard at each step I made. There were scuffed deck shoes on my feet now, not polished Cole Haans. And one of them still reeked of dog shit. "That's not my reading material anymore, and you know it, Margaux."

"And I call bullshit on your ass. You crave the *Journal* like a thirteen-year-old lusts for the Hot Topic catalogue. It's your crack, Mr. Maverick of the Magnificent Mile."

I was grateful she could see only my back now. God only knew what the woman would do if she witnessed the shit-eating grin flowing across my lips. *Maverick of the Magnificent Mile.* That sounded a hell of a lot better than Enigma.

No.

It was the second time I'd had to tell myself off in this futile exchange. Margaux had made her point with shameless transparency—and part of me actually wanted to hug her for the effort—but in my life now, cool was defined by a strong offshore breeze and a round of crab legs at Miguel's before an afternoon in front of my easel or sketchpad. Nothing else. *Nothing else.*

But ignoring what she'd just said would be like denying I had blood in my veins. Or that it suddenly felt like somebody sliced open my carotid and was letting the stuff form a puddle beneath me. Floating in the muck would be giant chunks of my incredulity—and dread. Fearing Trey would drive Stone

Global to ruin was a hell of a lot easier than hearing he actually was.

Despite the insight, I pivoted back around and ordered, "All right, tell me."

She rocked back on one of her booted heels like a model pausing on a runway, complete with the too-cool-for-the-rest-of-you gaze. "Well, you know I'm not good at the actual numbers and shit. That's Claire's and Chad's department. I only handle the part about making the messes look pretty—which means I'll have job security for years after the Trey-ster gets done calling every shot at SGC from the wisdom of his ass."

I barely held back a tight growl. Make that a hard roar. "You're exaggerating. He has a degree from MIT too. He's not a complete idiot." Though if I'd banked a dollar for every time I'd called him one, there'd be ten grand more in my account. "And before he fell back off the wagon, he had his nose to the grindstone at the office. Some of it must've sunk in. It really can't be all that—"

"Killian." She shifted her weight—actually shifted it this time—before tapping an impatient rhythm with her toe. "He let Sunbreak go."

Shock crushed my lungs like a pair of aluminum cans. "What?" It was a lame rasp, and I didn't care. "How? We were ready to sign. There was an addendum on the contract, but I looked at every fucking letter of it myself. I sent it over on the morning of Father's funeral—"

"And Trey took it back the day *he* started. Then changed it."

"Why?"

"Said he felt the marketing burden was shouldered too

much by SGC. He also deleted the product-training portion."

"But they're all about training! Half the board knows that too. Did any of them step in to reach out and try to save the deal?" I clamped my teeth so hard a few crickets fell silent from the *whomp*. "Christ. Maybe somebody better change that *Stone* on his office door to *Moron*." I brandished a glare when Margaux answered that with a distinct giggle. "What?"

"And you think nobody will welcome you back just because the name on *your* door says *Klarke*?"

A soft snarl escaped me. "My situation is different, and you know it."

"Oh?" The smirk clung to one side of her mouth. "So enlighten the blonde here. Different how?"

I squared my stance. "I lied about being a Stone."

"And Trey lied about having a brain."

I saw the validity of her point more clearly by the minute. And didn't like where it took my mind—or my blood pressure. I grew itchy. Restless. I'd nurtured SGC into a magnificent giant of commerce with my sweat and blood—often literally. Now Trey was throwing shackles around the beast and leading it to slaughter.

I had to do something.

I couldn't do a fucking thing.

Frustration rumbled up my chest. "My hands are still tied, damn it. I'm nothing but the kitchen boy now. I'm not one of them anymore."

"And they don't *care* anymore." The wind caught Margaux's hair as she stomped toward me. Or maybe that was the force of her sudden wrath. "I swear to God, I'm going to add *your* name to the moron list next."

Two seconds after she knocked me on the side of my head,

I recovered enough to retaliate. "Hey!"

"Shut up. With any luck, I knocked something important back into place." Her hands jammed to her hips. "You sure there's not a drop of Stone blood in those stubborn-as-shit veins of yours?"

"Margaux. *Damn it.*"

"No. Uh-uh. I'm not done yet. I haven't gotten to the good part, where I get to say that I expected better than this from you, Killian. Yes, *you. Killian.* Not the kitchen boy or the pretender or whatever the hell you think you are, based on standards of a world that existed nearly thirty years ago. Standards that have changed, in case you haven't noticed." She dropped her head to one side, hitting me with her worst evil eye. "I wasn't just being cute, Killian. You *are* a maverick. That means busting barriers, even when they're hard. Nobody gives a shit what the name on your door says." She paused, as if debating her next words, before stating, "They simply don't care—and neither does the woman who just sobbed a river in my arms either."

Here it was. The real shoe she'd been waiting to drop. I narrowed my eyes and growled, "She's clinging to a man who doesn't exist anymore. Don't *you* get *that*?"

Margaux barely flinched besides a prissy huff. "Not one damn bit, dude."

I shook my head again. "She fell in love with a mask, Margaux. With Killian Stone. A dream that doesn't exist anym— *Ow!*"

The cuff she gave the side of my head was twice as hard as the first.

"She fell in love with a *man*," she snarled, "not a name. When the hell are you going to crack open that boulder you call a brain and accept that?" Just as fast as her blow came a whole new look across her face. If I didn't know any better—and maybe I didn't—I could have sworn she was getting a little mushy, especially when she placed her hand on the center of my chest. "Killian...she fell in love with *this* good man."

She gave me one more press, as if wishing the words straight into my heart, before flashing one more soft smile and then turning to retrieve her phone from her car. She didn't look back during her walk to Claire's house, and I was glad about that. I wasn't sure I wanted anyone to see the scowl forcing its way across my face—or the insane rush of thoughts behind it.

Forcing his way into SGC hadn't magically made Trey a great leader. Nor had being booted from the building changed the depth of how I cared for every single person in the place. It hadn't brought either of my fathers back from the grave or provided the biological heir to the kingdom as had been the plan all along. In the end, all we had were a bunch of meaningless labels on a lot of miserable people.

Had Claire seen that truth all along? As dazzling as all my labels had been as Killian Stone, had she simply not cared about any of them from the very beginning? Had she truly, simply, just fallen in love with the person I was and not the flash of my masquerade?

I stumbled back, dizzy from the impact of it. Awash in the joy of it. But still unable to receive the enormity of it. This was likely an elephant I'd have to eat in tinier bites.

But as I walked back to my truck, I made a promise to myself.

I'd start eating fast.

CHAPTER FIFTEEN

Claire

Michael owed me big-time. Margaux too, for that matter. Not that they noticed, past the lingering stares they kept throwing at each other.

It wasn't that the guy—shit, what was his name? Jonathan, yes, that was it—wasn't attractive, sweet and energetic. He was trying. Hard. But my heart was so obviously not into this double date, it was torture for both of us.

Okay, it was torture for me.

Jonathan? I wasn't exactly sure. The poor guy scrambled so valiantly for his A material it blocked him from seeing that that I couldn't focus on anything longer than a hamster on crack could. Even at dinner, when Margaux attempted to trip him up by changing the topic to the most uncomfortable of all, feminine discomfort at *that* time of the month, he was right there on the field, ready to go for the touchdown drive with some home remedies his mother and sister swore by. I would've smacked my head on the table if I didn't risk spilling a full glass of a great Andrew Murray Syrah all over the place.

When we arrived at the theater, we all got a break from his nonstop story telling. By that time, I was convinced the guy had a story for *every* occasion. It was ladies' choice on the movie, thank God, and we shamelessly went for the most popular chick flick on the marquee. At least two *Saturday Night Live* vets were in it, along with the newest hunk out of Hollywood with the ability to roll his eyes with the best of them. Though the movie was sticky, sweet, and predictable, at least Jonathan's tales were silenced for two hours.

We wound the evening up back at my place. Exhaustion dragged at me, as it often did these days, so I didn't invite anyone in. That seemed to be fine by Margaux and Michael, who left as they'd arrived—in Michael's car. The observation didn't surprise me as much as I thought it would, but I made a definite mental note to explore the situation with Michael the next time we chatted.

For the time being, I had a bigger challenge on hand. The man on my front porch, staring at me with such earnestness that I wondered if he'd forgotten how to blink. I winced at the ground, thinking I'd never bitch about my waxing appointments being uncomfortable again. Jonathan didn't get the hint. He stepped closer. I moved away. The night was really chilly, and I couldn't wait to get back inside. Alone.

"Well, I had a nice time. Thank you for everything."

He pressed close again. Anxiety rose in my throat. And incredulity. Could he really not have picked up on the signals I'd sent all night long?

"I had a really nice time too, Claire. You're a lovely woman, you know."

He reached to brush at my hair. I ducked away from the gesture. "Listen...Jonathan...I hope I didn't give you the wrong idea tonight."

"It's okay. I know you just got out of something." He waved the same hand out, an attempt at casual that came across more as epilepsy. It made me squirm again. The thing he dismissed as "something" had been my everything.

"I'm just not looking for anything right now," I stated through tight lips. "At all."

"I understand. Maybe we can just be friends, see where that goes."

"That's just it. I don't want to go anywhere. With anyone. Ever again."

He emitted a soft *pssshh*. "It's just the breakup talking." He reached for my hand, ignoring my blatant flinch. "I know it's too soon."

"I don't want to talk about it, okay?" I battled for the diplomacy. He was a friend of Michael's from the gym, and I knew they'd see each other again soon. Forcing Michael into the role of buddy therapist, especially when a power workout was at stake, wasn't my goal or intention. "Perhaps you'd just better go now. Good night."

The clueless ass didn't move. "Maybe we could just try a little see-you-soon kiss."

I let him talk to my hand. "*Not* going to happen."

"Claire—"

"Good *night*."

I stabbed my key into the lock and got into the house as soon as possible. After closing the door, I turned and peeked out of the front window. Jonathan had started down the front steps toward his car. I exhaled in relief. I almost wondered if turning the garden hose on him would've been my next move.

I watched him drive off, just to be sure he'd really left—but that was when I noticed an unfamiliar vehicle across the street. An old white pickup truck was parked in the darkest area of my block, just beyond the glow of the street lamp. It was strange, by more than a little. I'd lived here since Andrea had hired me, at least a few years now. Everybody knew and looked out for everyone else in the neighborhood, including the working knowledge we had of everyone else's car. That truck definitely didn't belong here.

I kicked off my heels, pushed into my flats, and then grabbed my hoodie off the chair by the front door. After stashing my pepper spray into one of the pockets, I headed across the street to investigate. If some creepy jackass had decided to camp out on our street, I was ready for him.

With cautious, quiet steps, I approached the car. There was no way to sneak up on the jerk since he'd parked in a direct sightline to my front door. I wrapped tight fingers around my spray can when observing "he" really was a he and he sat nearly motionless in the driver's seat. He was hunched down, sort of like a cop on stakeout, though nothing about the sight of him said cop to me. Nope, he simply looked like a pervy assmunch who was trying and failing at being inconspicuous.

But then I realized who he really was.

"Damn it," I whispered.

My comprehension was even more disturbing than Jonathan's working knowledge of douche products. My traitorous body worsened the ordeal. The hair on my arms stood on end. My heart trampled my ribs on its ten-second trip from normal to hypercardiac. I welcomed all of it with the same bitterness I threw at the bastard in the truck, banging on the window and then gesturing at him to roll down the window of his piece of shit—if the hand cranks still worked.

His gentle, sexy-as-hell smile—the same one I'd been battling to forget all damn night—didn't make this one inch easier. "Well...hi."

"Hi?"

"Errrr...hello?"

"What the hell are you doing here, Killian?"

"Zip up your jacket. It's really chilly tonight, fairy."

"It's almost August. And you don't get to tell me what to do anymore, remember? And do not ever call me that again. Ever."

A breeze kicked up the street. Crickets began their night songs. An awful silence stretched between us, a wordless throwdown on who'd be the next to say something.

I hated myself for being the first to crack. "Well?"

"Well what?"

I leaned an elbow on the side of the truck in order to brace my shaking head and borrow one of Dad's favorite Irish oaths. "I'm going to get feckin' sick on this pish." When Kil went to open the truck door—I swung up a hand. "*No*. Stop. You don't get to come any closer either. You *do* have to tell me what the damn hell you're doing here."

The corners of his dark eyes tightened. Then the creases beside his mouth too. Though his confusion seemed real, I couldn't help but feel manipulated. He was unsheathing every little mannerism that dampened me the most for him.

"I've been concerned about you."

His tender tone flipped my heart over. But before it had finished the first rotation, it was frozen in place—by fear. Letting myself feel *anything* from his words, his gaze, his presence...it gave me that awful, peeled-grape sensation I'd had when we'd first fallen in love. And now that I knew how well all *that* had turned out...

"Well, stop it," I snapped.

"Claire—"

"No!" Hell. I should have checked my horoscope before

leaving the house tonight. If I'd known beating back the assholes was part of my cosmic duty for the evening, I would've stayed home with popcorn and a good J.R. Ward novel. "You don't get to be concerned anymore. I don't need you to watch over me either. Don't do this again. I'll call the police next time."

He respected my request, still not rising from the truck, but as he hitched up one knee and rested his elbow on it, I turned into a puddle. There, in his grungy truck, faded T-shirt, scruffy hair and beard, he was just as commanding as the day I'd first met him in that imposing conference room at Stone Global's headquarters, a D&G ad come to life in his tailored suit and impeccable hair. "All right, then. I'll just get to my point now."

"You don't get to have a point, either."

He hoisted the knee like I hadn't spoken. "Things...the other night, on the boat...got strange."

I bit out a laugh. "Outstanding observation, buddy. Did you come all this way to share the tidbit with me?"

"Maybe we should have...talked."

"Well, that's not happening now." Yeah, I really should have hooked up with the horoscope. Jonathan had wanted a kiss. Now Killian wanted to talk. And all I wanted was any creature with a Y chromosome to leave me the hell alone. "Just get out of here, okay? Go back to your reclusive hideaway, wherever the hell that is now, and stop spying on me."

"Wait a second. That's not what—"

"I. Don't. Care!" My shout caused Mrs. Binkley's three beagles to start barking. I threw up my hands and brought them back down to my thighs with cracking smacks. "Don't you get it, Killian? This...talk...isn't happening. You don't get to roll out of bed on me and dismiss me from your realm like some call girl and then come back lurking in the shadows at my house like you're my protecting knight. You know what? I get it now. I *believe* it now. You don't want to be Prince Charming. You don't want to be anyone or anything. So I'm cutting the tethers. You're free. I won't bother you anymore as long as you don't bother me. Just get out of here."

I flung a hand at him. To my horror, he smirked—smirked!—while rising out of the truck and catching me by the wrist. "You're so damn cute when you're pissed."

"You think I'm pissed? I'm not pissed, Killian. I'm enraged."

"Hey. *Hey.* Easy, baby. Don't do something you'll regret."

"If you think slapping you is something I'd regret, you've truly have gone insane, Mr. Stone." I wrenched away from him, not holding back on the violence in my jerk. "Oh, wait. It's Mr. Klarke now. How on fucking earth could I have forgotten?"

The silence he answered me with was palpable. He didn't move from where he stood. He didn't break our eye contact, either. And God help me, I didn't want him to. We were still connected yet so torn apart. It was all right. It was all wrong.

"Don't come back here. Please." My throat constricted, almost strangling the words from getting out. "I can't take it again. I just...can't."

I managed to spit out the rest without sobbing. Barely. As the tears tore up from my gut, I spun from him and sprinted toward my front door. The distance seemed to have doubled. Maybe that had something to do with the lead bars taking the place of my legs.

I slammed the door and rammed the dead bolt in before turning and sagging to the floor in a pitiful heap. Feeling the pieces of myself, of my life, crumbling around me again.

Maybe we should have talked.

Too little. So late.

"No," I rasped. "No!"

Don't fall farther down the rabbit hole, Alice. In the end, the Cheshire Cat disappears—and all the cards tumble down before they try to kill you.

Less than five minutes. That was how long it had taken him to bring every awful feeling back to the surface...to undo every triumph I'd gained in trying to forget him. For some reason, it hit even worse now. I could easily determine why. The jeans, the scruff, the truck...he was human now. Accessible. Touchable.

All mine.

Never to be.

The inexhaustible tank of my tears went into overdrive. They rolled down, fat and heavy, over my cheeks and even into my ears. How were there any tears left for this man? And why did the answer matter?

I stumbled into my kitchen, pulled out the vodka I kept in the freezer, and dumped it into a tumbler along with some OJ. *One triple screwdriver, heavy on the screw.* The popcorn only took another three minutes, and then I was wrapped up in my favorite throw blanket on the sofa.

There were no illusions about getting any sleep after tonight's disasters. Maybe I'd find a good movie on TV. When that didn't happen, despite having every goddamn pay channel available courtesy of the unmentionable ex-mega-bastard-boyfriend, I grabbed my laptop and decided to catch up on some work.

The first thing I typed was a note to myself, at the top of

my to-do list for tomorrow.

Cancel all the pay cable channels

I spent the rest of the night with nice, cold facts and figures for a new case we were starting. At last, the screwdriver—and the two I made after it—kicked in. Around three a.m., I hauled my sorry ass to bed and prayed Sin Squared had done something spectacular to woo the paparazzi away for the day tomorrow.

Spreadsheets. Screwdrivers. Popcorn. Bad TV.

This was what I could expect of my new life. On a good night.

Yay, me.

★ ★ ★ ★

"Claire! What gives? We know Killian's still in San Diego. So have you seen him?"

"When's the big day? Or are you planning to do it secretly?"

"Come on, Claire. Where are you hiding him, darling?"

"Awww, Claire. You never smile for us anymore."

The world was still a sea of flashbulbs. And no, even after all this time, I still wasn't used to it.

It was actually a little endearing. The photographers came up with new one-liners when they popped out of the bushes in their desperate bids to coax a smile from me. At Target, they advised me about toilet paper brands and even recited my favorite order at Starbucks. My own father tripped over the sugar-free hazelnut part.

It made my announcement all the tougher to issue.

"Okay, you guys. For the thousandth time, we aren't together anymore. And I really don't know where he is. You probably know more about him than I do at this point. And I don't smile because I'm miserable. So I'm going to ask nicely. Please step aside so I can get inside and shuck these sweaty gym clothes. I'm sure you all smelled me before I even pulled up."

They all chuckled and complied, though their laughs had lilts of empathy. They could see how much I meant the *I'm miserable* part and, with sympathetic smiles, gave me room to walk up the path.

When I was halfway to the house, a car's toot turned us all back around. I almost didn't recognize Christina from Mystic Maids inside the clean but older-model car. I hadn't recognized her at first, since she normally drove the company's wrapped Prius.

I made a fast mental note—*cancel the housekeeping service.*

She hopped out, making her way past the photographers with her buckets and mop in tow, and smiled as we climbed to the porch together. "So sorry I'm late. The company car had some trouble. I had to bring my own, but I'll stay as long as it takes."

"Oh, honey, don't apologize," I assured, letting her into the house. As I turned to close the door, I studied her cute little Honda. Something about the car looked so familiar, but I had trouble placing it. I chalked up the confusion to needing some protein, having hit it pretty hard at yoga today. As I made myself some eggs in the kitchen, Christina moved happily around the rest of the house.

I bit my lip, reconsidering my mental to-do item. I

didn't really want to give her up, but the issue was a matter of principle. I wasn't speaking to Killian, let alone accepting his extravagances in my life.

I *wasn't* speaking to him.

The resolve echoed through my head for the hundredth time today. But who on earth was I kidding with it? I'd been mentally drop-kicking myself since last week's meltdown on Kil, when he'd come with his figurative hat in hand, plainly asking to finally talk. What the hell had I turned down by letting my temper get the best of me? A fresh start with him? Even a chance just to get clear with him?

No. He'd been more than clear back on the yacht, when ordering you to leave like nothing more than his newest fuck buddy.

I hadn't been ready for him then. But maybe I was ready now.

Too late.

Even if I was clearer about seeing him now, I wouldn't know where to find him.

I pushed the rumination aside and focused on my dilemma with Christina. Perhaps I could just turn around and hire her back myself. Not a bad idea at all, one I congratulated myself for while sliding the eggs onto a plate and sitting down to scroll through my emails. There wasn't anything urgent, which was a good thing—because something about her car kept nagging at me. Something that turned my stomach into nervous mush and my chest into a spawning ground for wild butterflies.

What was it about her little car...?

After I finished eating, I went to the front window and peeked out again at the Honda. Ironically, the sun off the neighbor's roof glinted directly in my eyes, just as it had the first day Christina had arrived. I had to step out to the porch to see the whole car.

As soon as I obtained a good angle at the front windshield, I instantly realized what had hitched in my brain. There was a San Diego city parking permit sticker on the driver's side. The bright-yellow square measured about five inches on each side, displaying a bold white *A* in the center. Parking stickers like that abounded across the city, necessary for a place with lots of apartment buildings, dorm dwellings, beach houses, and public recreation venues. In many neighborhoods, lack of the right permit meant being towed.

My chest began to ache as I stared at Christina's neon *A*.

I closed my eyes, envisioning the exact same sticker in the windshield of a beat-up white truck while I chewed a whole new ass into its owner. And conceding that every night since, I'd peeked restlessly through the blinds, half hoping Killian would choose to ignore my tirade and come back. But out of all the times to take me seriously, he chose this one.

So what now?

The matching stickers meant Killian's land-based home was in the same neighborhood as Christina's. But I couldn't just straight-up ask her where she lived. *One cuckoo-creepy employer, coming right up.* Nope, nope, nope.

I had to be clever about it. And maybe a bit sneaky. Maybe a lot sneaky.

I wasn't very good at sneaky.

Hell. Where was Margaux when I needed her? She'd already have three or four schemes for us to pick from on how I'd perform a flawless mental extraction on Christina. Better yet, she'd just do it herself, having Christina all but eating out of her hand, disclosing address, social-security number, and even blood type if that was what we needed.

So all I had to do was...think like Margaux.

"Well, shit," I muttered as the concept strutted across my mind in a pair of five-inch, take-no-shit Louboutins. Blood-red, of course. Okay, it was strange but true. The woman had actually mellowed since the events around Josiah's death. And yes, she really had got fucked over royally by her own mother—but I wondered if what we had could even be qualified as friendship yet, let alone stepsisterhood.

But the channeling worked. Once I came up with a cover tale, which actually took longer than I thought it would, I wandered back into the kitchen, where Christina was finishing with the countertops.

"Hey, do you have a second to talk?" The girlfriends approach seemed the easiest way in. It wasn't a complete sham, at least. I'd grown really fond of Christina.

"Sure. What's going on?"

"You know that Mr. Stone and I really broke up, right?"

She blushed but laughed. "Sorry, Claire, but I'd have to be living under a rock not to. Is that why the photographers won't leave you alone?"

"Yeah. Pretty much." I returned her humor but infused it with a rueful glint, hoping to play on her sympathy.

"If it means anything, it's his loss. I'm sorry you're hurting."

Damn. She truly was the sweetest person. I felt about one inch tall, but it didn't stop me. "Well, this means I'll have to cancel Mystic Maids."

She frowned. "Why? I think he prepaid you for a year."

I winced. "It's the principle of the thing."

"Ah." Disappointment tinged her tone. "Okay, I understand."

"Well, hear me out fully," I protested. "The thing is, I really like what you do around here." Her blush was unmistakable even through her light-olive skin, so I moved in for the kill before losing my nerve. "So I was wondering if you ever do any work, you know...on the side? I mean, I'm not sure if you even live nearby or not, but if it's not a logistical hardship for you to come on your off time from the service, maybe I could hire you myself, on a cash-pay basis?"

Her bow-shaped mouth burst into a full grin. "Oh, wow. That would be great. And it's not a tough thing at all. I live down in Mission Beach, right off Grand. It's not far. I actually have a few clients I clean for on the side, mostly friends...but I really like you too, Claire. I hope we can be good friends."

At least my answering smile wasn't feigned. And I didn't feel like the world's *hugest* ass for the ploy. Maybe just second or third on the list. "Me too, sweetie." A slight pause fell, edging toward uncomfortable, so I went on, "Well, look at your schedule and decide where you can fit me in. We can work out the rest, okay?"

It felt like I'd crossed into some dark territory of unapologetic subterfuge, especially because all of that had been easier to accomplish than I'd expected—in both execution and aftermath.

It was only after Christina left, when I was sitting at my laptop and downloading a map of the eight-block square area covered by the yellow parking stickers, that the enormity of my plan struck once more.

I was going on a Killian hunt. Again. But this time, I refused to fail at reaching him—in every sense of the word. It still sounded a little crazy, but I wasn't ready to give up. The look on his face from last week, just before he'd gotten back into his truck, had clung relentlessly to my mind's eye. The sincerity. The need. The empty months *he'd* known too. Somehow I knew that if I hadn't lost my shit on him, maybe we'd have talked. And maybe he'd have been really honest. I knew he was afraid. Hell, *I* was afraid. Everything in our relationship was different now—and *would* be different—but different didn't have to mean bad. We'd renew. We'd rebuild. We'd recreate. If we could get past this.

We had to get past this.

My intention crystallized. Strengthened. Became resolve. I was going to find him in Mission Beach and bring him home—for good. And together, we'd fight for the love we shared, the life we'd started building together. We'd made promises. Shared our dreams. Committed to things that didn't get abandoned just because life aimed its shit missile at the front door. Killian had spent his entire life rising above the rest, a truth he'd clearly forgotten. I'd remind him, damn it— and didn't plan on leaving until he left with me. It was time to stand with each other again. *For* each other. Hiding was simply no longer an option on his table.

Sheez. Maybe my stepsister *was* rubbing off on me. And maybe that wasn't such a bad thing.

The rest of the day dragged on. I ate thirteen unnecessary meals consisting of carbohydrates only. I took two naps I didn't need but slept better than I had all week. It felt damn good to finally have a plan in place—and the box of Count Chocula I'd consumed at lunch probably added to the relaxation mix. Yes, even the cereal that filled my pantry reminded me of him now. I needed him back before I developed a serious case of Chocula ass.

After another shower, I slipped into serious prowling

clothes. Black stretch jeans and a long cowl-necked sweater were completed by my favorite pair of black Doc Martens. I was ready to rock and roll.

I rechecked the route I'd planned to take through Mission Beach, focusing on each quadrant like a laser. Killian didn't stand a chance if I found his truck tonight. Or, better yet, crossed his path.

The first block was well-lit, so I could easily see all the vehicles parked on the street as I slowly drove up and down. In this part of town, apartment complexes outnumbered homes, due to the proximity to the Pacific. Since the residency turnover was also high due to the military and university, everything was faded and worn. Many complexes had parking spaces under the buildings themselves, making it harder to check out those cars.

Wait.

There.

I stomped on the brakes, making the driver behind me lay on his horn in disgust. As his bellows and the newest Nicki Minaj jam faded into the night, I confirmed the sighting.

The tailgate of a beat-up white truck jutted from an overhang near one of the apartment buildings.

I parked my car and walked into the shadows of the lot. Make that *Shadows*, capital *S*, as in *Shitty* and *Scary*. When a cat ran out in front of me, yellow eyes glowing against its ginger fur, I nearly met its hiss with my scream.

Perhaps I hadn't properly thought through *every* detail of this quest.

I wished I'd brought Michael or Chad with me but just as quickly dismissed the idea. Neither would have agreed to the stunt. Most of the gang at Asher was completely fed up with anyone bearing the last name Stone. Trey was a nightmare to deal with in any form. He was like an eight-year-old, with SGC as his shiny new toy—but nobody had ever taught that child good playground manners. Willa only wanted to get her hands around Andrea's neck, and Lance had cashed out on *all* of it several weeks ago. I didn't count Margaux on the list, mostly because she didn't. Not yet, at least.

The truck in the shadows turned out to be a bust. Two hours later, I'd covered five more sections of the grid with nothing but exhaustion to show for it—unless I counted the three skunks, five homeless guys, and two more feral cats in the tally. I craved a shower. And a Dove Bar. And at least two more screwdrivers.

While easing down an alley between a strip of night clubs and a bunch of apartment buildings, I slowed to let some partiers walk in front of my car. When they cleared away, I could have sworn angels sang as my neck hairs prickled, my pulse accelerated, and my throat wadded shut with emotion.

At the end of the block, tucked against the building, was Killian's truck. I didn't know how I knew it with such clarity, but I did. The feeling was identical to what I'd experienced at the art show, the tingling that told me—*told me*—he was near.

I stepped on the gas, startling one of the pedestrians with my rev. I gave a quick wave as I passed but didn't let up my speed. Anticipation soared through my senses as I swung into an empty spot about fifty feet in front of Kil's truck.

I stepped out, locked the car door, and then turned to determine which building would be the logical choice to go looking for him first.

That was when I saw the group of guys that I'd passed on the way in.

Coming back the way they'd come.

Toward me.

"Unwanted attention" had never had a clearer definition. Obviously, they'd just left one of the clubs and didn't want the party to end. From about twenty feet away, their trash talk began about my car—thank God I'd taken my old car and not the Audi—my driving, my clothes, my figure...my aloneness.

They were big. And young. And cocky. And very, very drunk.

Shit.

A large part of me screamed to get back in the car and speed away. But I zeroed in on the beater pickup. Killian's truck. He was so damn close. I hadn't spent my entire night trudging through every alley in this neighborhood to turn back now—except for the small fact that I was currently circled by four large, tanked college cruisers.

"Hey, guys. Nice night. Uh...excuse me?"

"Whazz da big hurry, honey? You know...you almost hit me with your cah."

"Her *car*, you moron. But yeah, she did almost hitch—hip—*hit* you with it. Vroom, vroom!"

"You should at least say you're sorry."

Wonderful. It was the stupid, sloshed, and rambling show. And the plot was *not* going my way. Fortunately, I still gripped my keys. I angled the biggest one out between my fingers. It wasn't much of a weapon, but other than my wits, it was all I had.

"Okay. You're right, gentleman. I am very sorry. I was distracted. My apologies."

New strategy. Appease them, hurry back into the car, circle the block, and then repark after they were on their merry way. But when I whirled around, the biggest of the bunch stepped into my path. Another of them scooped up my wrist and twisted it so hard, I was forced to drop my keys. They splatted into a puddle as he pushed me back, pinning me against the backseat window.

"Where you goin' so fast, little bang-bang?"

The big brute chuckled. "She looks like she's got nowhere to be, bro."

"Ohhh, yeah. I'm pretty sure her Iditarod is totally free."

"You mean itinerary? Holy Christ, you *are* a moron."

"Whatever. She's hot. I want her to stay with us."

"I agree with Aaron." One of the guys slipped behind his friend, helping him out by spreading my other arm to the window. "Come on, honey. You're hot, we're hot, let's have a good time."

He emphasized by thrusting his sad erection against my thigh. I would have giggled had I not been so mortified—and terrified. "Let go of me. Now!"

This was bad. Really bad. My sobriety had nothing on their strength. As the other guys closed in tighter, turning my personal space into a zone ripe for violation, panic set into my veins. True, deep fear.

Fleetingly, I thought of my pepper spray—still in the pocket of my hoodie, from last week's confrontation with Killian. Not that it would've helped now. Somebody suggested that they take me back to the house so they could tie me up, sending me into scratching, kicking wildcat mode. If I was stuffed into a vehicle with this many horny puppies, I was so screwed—with the humor in that pun as drenched and useless as my keys.

"I'm meeting someone." As I snarled it, I forced my glare

to confront each of their sweaty leers. "*He'll* be looking for me. If you let me go now, we can just forget this and you can still have a great night—with someone else." I was babbling. The words swayed all over the board with my fear. But all of the things I'd learned in self-defense class? All the little tricks I'd read about online? Gone. Out of the window. I couldn't think of a single logical thing to save my skin. Another utterly useless pun.

"Shut up." The moron cocked a finger at one of his friends, who pushed forward with a neck tie in hand. The thing looked and smelled like the receptacle for a dozen spilled cocktails and half a dance floor of sweat. Moron Boy stretched it out and then jammed it between my lips. He let one of his friends tie the knot at the back of my head while he unclasped his belt. "Screw the house. I want some of this sweet pussy now. Right now."

Vomit rose in my throat while he disengaged his zipper. A wave of laughter took over the others. They pressed in tighter, chuckling at Moron as he apparently struggled to find his dick.

"Come on, man! Flip it out! What're you waiting for?"

"Fuck her, dude. Fuck her good. She should've never pulled out in front of you like that. Like she owns the goddamn street or something."

"Yeah, Bri, teach her a lesson."

"Hey, asshole! Shut up! Don't say his name. Don't you know shit?"

The stench of the tie invaded my senses, sending even more bile up from my stomach. My muscles turned to noodles from terror, though that didn't stop me from attempting to struggle. But while two of them kept me pinned, more of them moved in and helped with yanking at the button and fly of my jeans. Thank God I hadn't worn yoga pants, or that son of a bitch would've already been inside me. I kicked and squirmed and bucked, determined not to be their easy little victim. If this was happening, I wasn't going down without a fight.

"Gentlemen."

The word boomed up the narrow passage. Consumed it. Commanded it.

In a baritone that replaced the bile in my throat with a scream of joy.

A voice that had spoken that exact word when it had taken over other gritty, impossible situations—like boardrooms filled with looming sharks and press conferences with circling piranhas.

Was it him? Really him?

My senses careened. I barely knew where the sky was anymore, let along what was real and not. I sobbed as logic dragged me toward the doorway of despair. Surely I'd only imagined him. It had to be my mind's way of dealing with the trauma of a gang rape. It had simply manifested my deepest fantasy to life.

One of the guys wheeled around. "Who the fuck said that?"

His answer came, as dark as the shadows themselves. "You don't want to know, asshole."

My heart set off fireworks.

Killian. Oh, God, it *was* him. Though I'd never heard his voice in that kind of snarl before. It was horror-movie dark, filled with the sinister intent that accompanied action plans like buzz-sawing people to pieces or going rogue ninja on all the enemy's penises.

"Oh yeah, *asshole*?" the biggest of the brutes slung back.

"Well, what the fuck do you want?"

"I want what's mine." Every word was low, lethal, measured. "And right now, you're groping her in ways that make me very, very pissed."

He dotted that sentence with a distinct *chi-chuck* that made even my jaw go slack.

Where the hell had Killian gotten a damn shotgun?

"Shiiiiit." Two of the guys whimpered it in tandem. They took off running. That left the ones who were actually still pawing me, their hands frozen and their eyes looking like deer in Mack truck headlights.

"He don't mean it," one of them whispered.

"No shit," concurred Moron Boy. "I mean, like a dude's going to fault us for—"

"What the *hell* are you not comprehending, motherfuckers?" Finally the shadows gave him up. Like my breathtaking avenging angel, Killian stalked across the pavement, his renegade hair and leather trench flying from the midnight wind. And, no kidding, there was a shotgun in his hand. "Let. Her. Go. If you care to test me, I'd consult your balls first. I promise I'm an amazing shot."

The assholes gave that two seconds of thought. Then turned tail—whatever they had left—and ran.

For a long moment, I was too stunned to move. With the tie still in my mouth and my hands still slammed to the window, I gaped at my CEO-turned-Terminator ex, handling that weapon like he'd trained Schwarzenegger himself. The moon highlighted the fury in his jaw. His jacket rose and fell with each of his heavy breaths. He was bad-ass and beautiful—

And here.

For me.

"Oh, my God." I wrenched the tie free and crumpled to my knees. It was impossible to stay on my feet because everything shook too badly.

The periphery of my senses picked up on the thunder of his approaching steps. But when he reached me and kneeled beside me, his touch was like the softest rain. "Claire," he breathed against my hair. "Oh, damn. Claire."

I didn't talk myself into expecting anything more than the comfort of this moment, but I greedily took it, scrambling into the shelter of his embrace. "Thank you. *Thank you*. I don't know what would've happened if—well duh, I *do* know what would've happened, but—how did you? And where the *hell* did you get that gun? And where did you come from—?"

He cut me short with a quick kiss. But right after, a longer one. Ohhh, it was so much harder not to read any meaning into the way his tongue coaxed mine, into how his mouth slanted and moved, truly seeming to echo the word he'd just used to designate me to those asshats.

Mine.

The effort moved into the realm of impossible when he pulled away his mouth but tightened his hold, shifting his arms beneath me and scooping me into the air. The entire time, his gaze didn't leave me. And in a murmur filled with equally dark determination, he said aloud...

"Mine."

CHAPTER SIXTEEN

Killian

As little as a week ago, I could've never imagined this scenario being added to the memory book of my life.

Shotgun slung across my back. The woman of my dreams in my arms. Lungs still throbbing at the nightmare I'd just nearly witnessed her endure.

My horror that I almost hadn't gotten here in time.

My vow that it would never happen again.

"Killian?"

She'd queried me like that so many times before—yet none of them meant as much as the word did now. She'd asked a thousand questions with it. At that same time, she demanded no answers. And why would she? I'd given her no reason to expect them. No trust in anything I could offer anymore.

And yet...here she was, wrapping her arms around my neck like I'd become her savior once more. Selflessly giving me her sweet, open tears. Gazing at me in these tattered jeans, this faded T-shirt, this scruffy beard, and this secondhand coat as if I still wore Tom Ford and smelled like Armani.

All she asked for in return was my belief that she meant it.

My belief in myself.

My belief in us.

"Kil?" she prompted again. "It's all right. I'm okay now, I

think I can st—"

"No." I growled it. Backed it up with a stare I didn't allow even a blink to interrupt.

"No?"

"It's not all right. Not yet."

Her eyebrows knitted like I was the homeless lunatic I resembled, spouting about the world's end in three days. That was okay. Better than okay. It made turning back toward my building—I used the term loosely—a much easier journey.

"Where are we going?"

"Someplace those dickwads won't come back for you."

"*Or* you," she pointed out.

The undertone in her voice, so silken with her soft concern, almost caused me to falter. I'd blocked out so much of how this felt—to have her care for me, even in subtle little ways like that line. But I'd been so lost and hadn't wanted to find my way back, so I'd burned the whole damn forest behind me. Cauterized the good memories along with the shitty ones. Like that had worked out so well. I'd ended up back here anyway. My soul had guided my body back, even when I'd been too drunk and stupid to figure it out on my own.

I'd returned to her.

I always would.

The elevator was broken, so I walked up the stairs to the third floor, still refusing to let her go. When we got to my apartment at the end of the hall and I easily opened the door, Claire's soft stare sharpened with alarm. "Your door's not locked."

"Not right now."

"Is that a habit of the new Killian?"

"It is when he looks out of his window and spots his

woman being mauled by half a dozen douche bags."

I pulled off my coat and the gun. Though I'd locked down the safety on the weapon before slinging it across my back the first time, I double-checked the lever before setting it in the corner, next to the new leather couch I'd bought after moving off the yacht. To the outside world, I was an incognito eccentric artist bum. That didn't mean my living space had to keep up the act too.

Claire barely looked at anything. Though her gaze definitely skated over the easels in my work space and the massive bed in the studio-bedroom corner, her *eyes* held the glimmer of another meaning. She was somewhere else altogether. Locked in a thought. That musing finally pushed up the edges of her mouth and made her lift a hand to stroke the opposite forearm.

"His...woman." She echoed my words in a wistful murmur. The sweet longing beneath it was all it took to make me clear the two steps back to her side. I pulled her hand off her arm and pressed it between both of mine.

"Yeah." I drew her fingers up to my lips. Curled them against my greedy mouth and nose. Goddamn, she smelled so good. Not the way I remembered. Better. Her lavender and wildflowers were mixed with wind and night and woman, a mixture that drove me to my knees before her.

"Claire." It wasn't just her scent that took me here. It was relief. And agony. And awe. And gratitude. She was here. I finally had her.

But did I *have* her?

"Damn it." It came out in a thousand pieces of meaning. And supplication. "My Claire."

Without a word of response, she uncurled her grip from

mine.

My head dipped beneath the weight of despair.

Too late. You're too fucking late.

With just as much silence, she tangled her hands into my hair. Then pulled my face back against her body. Hard. Urgently. So ferociously, I now heard every wild thump of her galloping heartbeat.

I growled. Then moaned. The sounds welled from places inside that I'd forgotten about, the deep, animal places only she could reach and understand. They resonated with my raw joy, my pure jubilance. As I wrapped my hands around her, hands feeling more like paws and senses enslaved by instinct, I also knew I didn't care. Primal cravings burst loose, prowling higher up the walls of my composure, ascending into a perfect spiritual realm that only she could take me to.

I needed her. I belonged with her. We were moon and tide. Twilight and daybreak. Thunder and rain. Nature that never should have been denied—or run from.

"Killian." Her voice shook, and so did her hands. "Oh, Killian."

I dared to look up. She gazed at me with eyes that reminded me of dawn, sparkling and brilliant and bright. "I sure as hell hope those are happy tears, fairy."

She spilled a watery laugh. "Me too." Her lips wobbled. "Please tell me they are, Kil."

I drew her tighter to me. Craved her so much that I began seeking her skin through the thickness of her sweater, taking soft nips with my teeth. "I've been such a goddamn idiot," I finally grated.

Above me, she let out another quiet laugh. Her fingertips dug into my scalp, as if my gray matter had turned into a balloon and she'd watch it float away if she let go. I didn't blame her for that perception either. Lately, it had been closer to the truth than not. "Well...yeah," she replied in a teasing murmur.

"I've also been so damn...lost."

"I know, Killian." Her hands flowed to the back of my head. "I know."

She did. Her conviction flowed into me like the stardust her eyes evoked. I took some deep breaths. Held her tighter. "My pride and my confusion collided. Before we came back from Europe, when we were in Venice, I'd said goodbye to Klarke. I loved how you looked at Stone. For the first time in my life, I liked being him."

"But you still *are* him." Her vehemence yanked her down to my level. On her knees with me, in the middle of the shag rug in the center of my *Les Miz* apartment, this beautiful, adamant woman lowered herself to become equal with me once more. "I don't care if your last name is Klarke or Stone or Smith or Beetlejuice. I love you, Killian." She brought her hands forward, delving her fingers into my beard now. "I love *you*, Killian."

I ran my hands up either side of her spine, gripping her shoulders from behind, clutching her as close as I could. Still not close enough. I yearned to make her a part of me again. Drag her strength and goodness inside me and never forget how good that felt, *ever* again. "And I never stopped loving you."

A tentative smile flitted across her lips. "I know that too."

"But you don't trust it." The cautious smile on her lips, in lieu of her full and perfect one, proved that much. "It's all right," I assured. "If I were you, I'd be keeping me on the end of the yardstick as well."

"I get it." Her mouth twisted and her chin wobbled. It looked like she was going for an encouraging one now but hit the fail switch. "You're scared."

"I'm terrified." The confession was easier than I'd expected—yet the hardest thing I'd ever said. I swept one hand to her nape in order to steady her face as I stared the intensity of my meaning into her. "But I want to be terrified with you." I took her lips in an urgent but closed-mouthed kiss. "Tell me we can. Tell me you'll be there even when I don't get it right— because believe me, I *won't* get it right." I couldn't prevent myself from kissing her again. Longer. Deeper. Tentatively opening to her again. "Tell me it's not too late, Claire. I'd rather face the world again with you as Killian Klarke than escape it as Killian Stone."

She tucked away from me a little. I couldn't get a bead on what that meant, since her eyes, welling with tears, never left me. Another anvil of dread pounded the center of my gut.

Until her whole body convulsed with a harsh sob.

Before she launched it all at me in a searing kiss.

I groaned from the perfect impact of her open, beautiful passion—and held nothing back on what I gave her in return. I let her pull at me, fill herself with me, wrap herself around me. I adored her for it. Clawed at her for it. Needed her more for it. I loved how she dug her nails into my skin, not leaving an inch between my neck and shoulders unmarked. I loved the pain that etched its way down my body in response, awakening my skin and my blood in all the best, hottest ways. I loved the roll of her tongue against mine and the darling mewl of her pleasure at my taste. I loved savoring her in return, even sucking her tongue deeper into my mouth, delighting in the startled catch of her breath in response.

And I loved how she couldn't seem to get enough.

Because I sure as hell couldn't.

We all but stripped each other there on the floor, with her hitching my T-shirt higher and me roaming beneath her sweater, snapping her bra free and groaning when I was able to toy with her sensitive nipples again. In a frantic fever, I finally ripped my shirt free. A grin plastered itself to my lips as she eagerly did the same with her sweater.

I pushed off her bra myself, using the movement as an excuse to dip my mouth to each of her taut, needy breasts. "Fuck," I growled between licking and biting at her sweet flesh, "you taste so good, baby. So damn good."

After I turned her into a writhing, panting mess, I hitched up, forcing myself to look at her. *Really* look at her. We'd done this just ten days ago, and I'd turned the after-party into an emotional bloodbath for her. If she needed to talk, go slower, or put this locomotive on full brakes, I needed to know now. I wasn't sure my cock would be onboard with any new track changes after this point.

"Talk to me," I urged. "What do you need? What do you want? Say the word, and it's yours."

Say the word, and I'm *yours.*

I loved being the witness when a deeper point connected for her. The glint of golden triumph in her eyes. The impish delight that sneaked into her dimples. Yet, as she gathered the full impact of my words now, her beauty was tripled—because it was magnified by her love.

"You really want to know what I want?" When I only nodded slowly in acquiescence, she went on, "What I want, Mr. Killian What's-Your-Face, is for you to make me forget everything in this room exists except that bed. And us in it."

Goddamn. Nobody but her could rev me so fast from desire to lust. A handful of words, and I really was hers. A long, fire-infused stare later, and I was ready to grant her wish in all the ways she dreamed—and maybe a few she hadn't.

"I meant it, you know." I stated it to her as I sat back on my haunches and brought her knees forward, giving me the chance to untie her boots and slide them off her feet. "I'm your genie, baby. Your wish is my desire..." I paused, biting my lower lip for emphasis. "Right after you feed mine."

Her eyes flared. Then darkened. "Of course, genie," she breathed. "Command me. Use me in any way you need to stoke your...magic ways."

I unfurled back up to my feet and brought her along with me. Keeping our bodies nearly entwined, I claimed her mouth in a deep, sweeping kiss that left out the coy and cautious this time. I spread her lips as far as she'd let me, stabbing my tongue at hers in blatant caveman possession. Claire, her blood already spiked from fighting off the asses in the alley, moved her cat scratch fever to my chest. I broke our connection to reward her with hisses as she tore her way down my pecs, barely giving my nipples a bye on the slashes. When she was done, I pinned her face with a stare that gave her no choice of reaction. She was going to obey me. Period. She licked her lips for a fast second, conveying how she already agreed.

"Walk over there," I instructed. "To the bed. Strip for me. Then stand and wait for me."

She lifted a sultry smile that turned my heart into mush and my cock into stone. "As my genie wishes."

Thank fuck I still knew a lot of self-control. It took every ounce of the shit that I had to stand in place and watch her, a miracle of grace and color and movement, as she slid down her jeans and panties, revealing every curve of her incredible body. Dear God, how I longed to take her picture. At no other time did I yearn more to capture a moment with her, perhaps even to paint the image soon. She was perfect and bare, bathed in the silver moonlight and peach streetlight filtering in past the dingy shades, turning her creamy skin into a pastel palette that hypnotized me.

And allured me.

Unable to tolerate the distance between us anymore, I followed the path she'd just taken. Along the way, I got rid of my boots and set free the top button on my jeans, though I left my fly up. I had a few shreds of common sense remaining, and one of them decreed that if the zipper came down, all bets were off on how fast my dick would demand to be inside her. Tonight would *not* be like the mindless, pointless fuck we'd had on the yacht.

This one was for keeps.

I intended to show her that...no matter how thoroughly it killed me.

Or how much this felt like the first time I'd made love to her.

The impression wasn't as meaningless-pop-lyric as it sounded. In so many ways, this *was* the first time we'd be together—without my masks, without the illusions I'd given her because of them, even without the cavalier cad I'd pretended to be last week on the boat. Playing another role because I'd had no idea who to be otherwise.

Now, there was just me. And only inches away from the most perfectly created woman since Eve, standing so still that she seemed my sacred gift, waiting...for my worship alone. I hadn't lied—the concept of this was fucking scary. At least on paper. My body hadn't gotten one word of that memo, especially the blood engorging every inch of the flesh between my thighs. Christ. Did *every* part of me have to feel fifteen again?

I took another soft step toward her. As the floorboard creaked, she visibly shivered. The movement shifted the light that glinted in her hair, making her strawberry strands glow. I reached to touch them first, sliding fingers reverently over her trendy, slightly asymmetrical style. The shorter cut made it easier to get to her neck, the slender column all but begging for my kiss, my licks, my sucks.

But not yet.

I flowed the tips of my fingers across her shoulders, back again toward her spine, down into the hollow at its base, over the sexy ass below that. Her breath hitched sharply as I applied deeper pressure there, pulling her silky cheeks apart with the force of my thumbs. I smiled when she arched for me, unknowingly begging for more of my illicit exploration in that warm, tight crack.

I sneaked my thumbs deeper in.

Claire pushed and moaned in deeper arousal.

"You look like a fairy princess, baby...but you're begging for sin like a naughty little sex demon." I lowered to my knees behind her, taking the chance to bite at her firm flesh as I did. "Be careful what you wish for. I'm not an uptight Stone anymore. God only knows what I'm capable of."

"Ohhhh." She finished it off with a lusty grunt, turning me on in about twenty new ways. "Oh, please show me what you're capable of."

I didn't answer her in words. Instead, I dipped my head lower, breathing in the salty, heady scent beckoning from her sex. I slid my hands from her ass to silently order her into a new position. After she'd bent her torso to the bed and parted her legs more for me, I pressed my thumbs into the exact same position.

Claire trembled when I teased that delicate little hole, brushing just the edges, pulling her apart by excruciating degrees. I relished every second of her fast little gasps as I stretched my index fingers forward, sliding them into the slick folds of her pouting pussy. When I joined my mouth to the effort, she abandoned the gasps for a full outcry.

"Killian! Jesus!"

I chuckled. My girl had the most creative talent for the English language sometimes.

And the most intoxicating taste on the planet.

Her folds really were like juicy peaches, bathing my tongue in her delicious fruit, infused with the tang of her creamy lust. I explored every inch of her in my ravenous need, sucking when licking simply wasn't enough. Her moans and profanity, now turning into pleas to the saints themselves to help her, were like the most sensual rendering of *Bolero* to my ears. Her body was my orchestra, and I relished every new, carnal note that I conducted from it.

Before long, my fingers were drenched. I dragged that extra moisture to the little aperture I'd been exploring with my thumbs, giving them extra lubricant to penetrate her ass deeper. My new investigation was answered by a high keen and an invocation of saints I'd never heard of. Her ass clamped on my thumbs, and her pussy captured my tongue. I matched the rhythm of my attention in both places, fucking her with my fingers and my mouth, ramping the speed to correspond with every shudder and thrust she gave me in return.

"Killian," she pleaded. "Oh, Killian...I'm going to...so good...so good..."

She bucked and screamed. Then stiffened.

And came.

And came.

And came.

They were the most perfect minutes of my life. And when they were over, my cock was harder than I ever remembered.

Lowering my zipper was agony. Getting my jeans and briefs pulled off, a lesson in restrained torment. I hissed from the pain, giving my shaft a cursory glance just to make sure it had made it out in one piece, before feverishly kicking the clothes from my legs and mounting the bed, sliding up behind her.

It was my intent to kiss my way down her body and steadily warm her up again, but apparently, I had one more idiot card left in my deck. The moment I felt her beneath me, so warm and moist and compliant, my head swam from the effort of fighting my cock. The damn thing had been switched to Claire-seeking-missile mode and wasn't about to be deterred. Even the woman herself didn't help, lifting herself toward me at the most sexy angle of her delectable ass. The position gave me such a tantalizing view of the juicy pink flesh I'd just sampled, I was stunned my eyes didn't roll back in my damn head from the bliss.

I tempted fate by seating my hips behind hers but managed to keep my erection nestled between her labia, rubbing us both into greater need, as I tucked my mouth against her neck.

"You're the most incredible sex demon fairy princess I've ever known."

Her soft laugh, finished by an aroused gasp, was just the

right amount of distraction from my craving to fuck her raw this second. "I bet you say that to all the sex demon fairy princesses that you give mind-blowing orgasms to."

"Only you." I scraped at her neck, in the sensitive spot between her ear and nape, as punctuation. "There's *only* you, Claire. There only ever will be."

She sighed but not for very long. A long moan took over, flushing her in heat that permeated me as well, as she curled both fists into the comforter and shuttled her body back against mine. The effect on my cock was instant heaven—and hell. Her pussy knew all the right ways to taunt my stiff dick. I told her so with an ominous growl of my own, sinking my teeth into the top of her shoulder and relishing her provoked keen in response.

"Oh, my God, Killian!" Something in her breathy emission stirred me to roll my head to the other shoulder. And bite her just as hard. "Ahhhh!" she screamed—and then laughed.

"I can't help it," I snarled. "I have a craving for fairy tonight."

"Shit! Mmmmmm. Shit. *Shit.*" She kept up the little whimpers, shooting new blood into my cock with each one, until finally blurting, "Goddamnit, Beetlejuice. Fuck me now, or I'm putting on the Docs and marching out of here!"

My mind took that visual suggestion and ran with it. Only in my fantasy, she stomped around in nothing *but* the trendy combat boots, sashaying her naked curves, tossing back her cute little haircut, flashing her adorable golden eyes—until I grabbed her in all that fiery beauty, shoved her back down on the bed, and—

"Fuck."

I rammed myself into her in one dominating stab. She

was already drenched and ready for me, and every inch of her tunnel throbbed around me to confirm it. Her little burst of sass had flipped the switch on a thousand possessive instincts, making me stretch my hands out over her wrists and pin them to the bed while I rocked deep and hard into her, claiming her as thoroughly as I could.

As my balls constricted around their impending release, I scored her neck with my teeth again, drawn by the need to reinforce what I'd told her during those dark moments in the alley.

"Mine," I grated.

"Yes," Claire whispered in return.

"Yes what?" I needed to do this. To push her—and me. To lay my claim over her mind and her heart as well as her body and soul. To hear it from her lips and know it was really true once more. "Yes *what*, Claire?"

"Yes, Killian. I'm yours. Always. *Always.*"

Her surrender opened the floodgates of mine. Like *Bolero*'s final timpani roll, my release pounded through my cock and exploded into her. As my climax burst into her core, Claire shouted my name. Her walls clenched my cock, squeezing every last drop of my heat out.

The world was a bizarre blend of real and surreal. While the bliss of my body was pretty damn great, it was also a secondary pleasure, almost a pleasant side detail to the glory and beauty of really fusing with Claire again. Molding our spirits again.

Joining our lives again.

A long time later, I finally drew myself out of her and then rolled to my back, falling to the pillows with the first perfect exhaustion I'd had in months. It was one of those rare nights in San Diego that the weather reminded me more of Chicago, sticky and hot, so I lay bare atop the comforter while the ocean breeze cooled my skin. Claire snuggled against me, one leg curling around one of mine, and we both fell asleep fast.

I was roused—make that awakened by the equivalent of a heart attack—by her shrill scream.

"Claire? Claire!"

What the hell? Where was she? Not in bed with me anymore, that was for damn sure. A frantic scan of the apartment's main room didn't turn her up either.

A thousand awful thoughts slammed me, topped by the sickest of them all—that one of the bastards from the alley had followed us last night and now they were all here to dish out payback.

"Killian! Oh, my God! Aaahhhh!"

I bolted out of bed and ran to the bathroom. Thank fuck she hadn't locked the door. I wrenched the knob and slammed back the portal, looking up to see her braced on the narrow ledges of the shower, brandishing my shave gel in one hand and a haphazardly rolled hand towel in the other. Even in the awkward position, she was sexy as hell.

"Fairy, what the hell?"

"Behind the door!" she shrieked. "You've trapped it, I think. Oh, God, no you didn't! It's coming back out!"

I peeked behind the door. The only thing back there was—

"It's Felix." I gave her a quizzical look. "Baby, come on. It's only Felix."

"It's a rat, Killian. A *rat*!"

"Okay. Technically, yeah. But he's a good guy. Aren't you, dude? He's probably hungry too. I haven't seen him in a few days."

"So...he's your pet?"

"Not really. I just found him here. He's kept me company."

"He's...kept you—" Her face twisted into a bunch of different expressions, so gauging her reaction was impossible. I didn't move though. She was fascinating as hell to watch. And sexy? Standing there with her naked legs spread and her frantic breaths making her breasts jiggle like that? My twitching cock filled in the answer to *that* equation—until she noticed. And followed up with a censuring glower. "Get me out of here," she dictated. "Right. Now."

Once I swung her into my arms, carried her into the main room, and then set her down, the woman pounded directly over to her Doc Martens. I had to chomp the inside of my cheek to prevent a wide smirk from taking over my face as she brought my fairy-in-combat-boots dream to beautiful life. And yes, the reality was *much* better than the fantasy, made even better when the woman turned, planted hands on her hips, and glared me down like a misbehaving grunt in her sex platoon.

"Well, that was the straw on the very thin camel's back," she stated.

I shook my head, glad for something to do other than fight back my grin. "Not sure...I follow?"

"The apartment." She clarified by swooping out an angry hand. "*This* apartment. It goes, Killian. I love you, but I am *not* coming back here." When she pulled the hand back in, she folded her arms, pushing her nipples straight out. *Thank fuck for you, Felix.* "The bed...can come with you. And the easels. But the rest of the apartment goes. The rat goes. And—"

"I know, I know." As I interrupted, I could no longer contain my shit-eating smile. "The beard goes too."

She released a relieved breath and tacked on an adorable

little giggle. As she stepped over, fitting her nakedness to mine once again, she whispered, "We're going to get along just fine, mister."

I growled against her lips. "I've no doubt of it, Miss Montgomery. Though perhaps I can talk you into letting Jesus fuck you one more time...?"

CHAPTER SEVENTEEN

Claire

"Breakfast is ready!"

I called it out toward the beehive of construction workers in the backyard. They were already hard at work, hammering and sawing in the morning sun, trying to beat the worst of the heat by getting an early start.

Killian appeared through the haze of sawdust, grinning from ear to ear. I eagerly soaked up the beauty of his tight T-shirt hugging the V of his torso, pulled on over a pair of blue and white Hurley board shorts, with Vans on his feet. The shoes likely would have been flip flops, but closed toes were required for the construction zone, so Vans it was today. Praise to all the heavens, he'd shaved the beard off. His hair, though shorter, could've stood for another trim. I'd force that issue when he owed me a good favor.

For the time being, I'd settle for that body, that swagger, and that smirk.

"You look like a boy on Christmas morning," I remarked when he entered the kitchen. He kissed my cheek as I handed him a cup of coffee. He'd been so excited about watching the crew transform the detached garage into his new art studio, filling me in on the progress every night over dinner. He'd sold a few more paintings since the Mission Bay show, of tigers instead of me this time, and was entertaining the idea of opening a small gallery on Ray Street. I didn't think I'd ever see him in a suit and tie again. That was *really* okay by me.

"I can't believe how fast it's shaping up," he supplied. "The foreman thinks they should be ready to paint next week, and the windows should be delivered this afternoon. I think everything's right on schedule."

"You *think*?" I raised my eyebrows at the clipboard he slid onto the counter. "To the tune of knowing how long this project has taken, down to the second?"

He laughed. "I don't think I'm driving them *too* crazy with the micromanaging yet."

"You? Micromanaging? I don't believe it." I giggled, but he gained retribution on me in the form of a long, tongue-tangling, balance-stealing kiss.

"All right, watch yourself."

His growl stole more of my equilibrium. Thank goodness he still held me so tight. "Or what?" I challenged playfully.

"I'll think of something. I can be very creative when motivated. And you, Miss Montgomery, are most motivating."

I let him have the satisfaction of my girlish sigh. He took my breath away, and there was no use hiding it. I stared up into his onyx eyes, now so alive and passionate again. So many times, I'd been certain that look was gone forever. Just to confirm this all wasn't just a dream, I tugged him closer, inhaling his rich scent, now infused with ocean wind and his own perfect musk. Okay. This was real. I could trust that I hadn't tricked myself into thinking it was all better now, and I wouldn't open my eyes to find out I was still alone and desperate—and without him.

Killian's grip suddenly tightened. "Stop," he softly ordered.

"Okay." I ducked my head and blinked quickly, banishing the bad memories. "I know, I know."

He pressed his lips into my hairline. "I will spend the rest of my days making it up to you, fairy. I swear."

"You shouldn't have to."

"But I will anyway."

I put a couple of fingers over his lips and beamed him a smile. And meant it. "Let's eat. Breakfast is getting cold. And I'm starving."

"I'm not." His tone was ripe with suggestion, making me blush to the bottom of my feet—including the sensitive inches between my thighs *he'd* used for a morning appetizer a few hours ago.

We took our seats in the breakfast nook of my kitchen, where I'd already dished up a couple of spinach omelets. Mine had mushrooms, his did not. How did a person not like mushrooms? I would never understand it. On the other hand, he didn't rib me for grimacing at his side of bacon either.

He'd just mowed down one of those slices in three bites— no appetite, my ass—when he looked up at me to murmur, "Surf's great today, fairy. You want to head down to the beach for a few hours?"

My face split into such a wide grin it hurt. And yeah, the sensation that I'd stepped into an alternate reality sneaked back in, fast and unexpected. It was just taking some time to get used to all the changes. Although I loved every single one of them, they were a cosmic one-eighty from anything I'd ever known with the man. After his first few bites, Kil sat back and ate at a more leisurely pace, flipping through the pages of this week's *Reader* with his coffee on one side and wheat grass juice on the other. Gone were the Gucci loafers, *Wall Street Journal*, and espresso shots.

Finally, he seemed at peace.

Finally, we'd found where we belonged.

"I would love that," I answered softly. "Let me check my email and voicemail to avoid any fires, and then I'll be good to go."

In less than an hour, we climbed into his beater pickup and headed north to La Jolla Shores. The truck was great for the beach because Kil could just throw his boards in the back. With my Audi, we had the hassle of a rack on the roof and sand in every interior crevice. We arrived in less than thirty minutes, and I grabbed the small cooler into which we'd packed some sandwiches, fruit, and water. Across my other arm was our sturdy beach blanket, purchased from a vendor in Old Town during one of our recent date nights. My surfer god took care of hauling his boards down to the sand, though the second he got there, he had one under his arm while he jogged into the water. I laughed indulgently when he saw a few beach buddies and high-fived them while they all paddled out. The surfers didn't know who he'd been in his other life, nor did they care. It was a comforting balm to my thoughts as I dozed in the lazy summer breeze.

Life couldn't be more perfect.

We had lunch late, agreeing to stop for dinner somewhere on the way home. After we repacked the truck, Kil scooped up my hand and beckoned back toward the sand with a swing of his head. We took our time strolling along the shoreline, daydreaming about buying a home on the waterfront, watching all the families with little ones running about. Killian even stopped to show a pair of young girls how to scoop up the sand and let it run out between their fingers, letting the tiny crabs beneath scurry over their palms. They squeed in delight, and I threw him grossed-out grimaces. Along the berm, I found a few new seashells for my collection. After waving goodbye to the two newest members of his fan club, Kil stashed the shells in his pocket for safekeeping.

The tide was coming in, making froth that chased our footprints away almost as quickly as we left them in the sand. As the sun starting dipping beyond the waves, we paused to watch a couple exchange wedding vows beneath a tulle-swathed arch up on the cliff. Even from where we stood on the sand, I saw the tears glistening in the bride's eyes as she stared into the face of the man who took vows to share his life with her forever. When the minister announced that they were husband and wife, doves were released and their family and friends applauded and cheered.

I wasn't surprised to feel tears trickle down my own face... happy ones now. It was a magical moment, the love of the couple surrounded by the majesty of the ocean...and it took my breath away. I also wasn't that surprised when a glance at Kil showed his own wonderment at it all. But he didn't say a word, just meshed our fingers together again, pulling me back toward the truck.

Our silence wasn't uncomfortable. But it was a little apprehensive. Watching that couple on the cliff...had altered the air between us. But how? What was this new alchemy all about?

The questions weren't sad ones. I knew that without a doubt. I was happier now than I'd ever been in my life. Kil and I had made it through the darkest days and found our way back to each other, stronger and more secure because of the trial. We were more right than ever, knowing now that we could weather any storm. No more running. No more hiding. I'd never be totally grateful for all those months of hell, but the heaven we'd made it to on the other side was a place I gave thanks for every day. I was pretty certain he felt the same way.

I sat on the tailgate of the beater while he loaded his surfboards and the rest of our gear. I wasn't ready to say goodbye to the Pacific yet.

He hopped down from the truck bed and leaned up against the tailgate beside me. "You've been quiet," he murmured. "What's going through that beautiful mind of yours?"

"Everything. Nothing."

"Uh-oh."

I lightly smacked his shoulder. "Now *you* stop. I was mostly thinking about how much I love you."

"Just that, huh?" He flashed his Lucifer's grin. The panty-melter version. *Damn.*

"We're lucky we found our way back, Killian. I don't ever want to lose sight of that."

"I don't think we ever will." He pulled both my hands up to his lips, smashing fervent kisses to my knuckles before grating, "It was too dark without you, baby. Way too dark."

I extended my fingers, stroking both sides of his jaw. "I couldn't agree more."

He swallowed hard. "You know, seeing that couple on the cliff today, looking so happy..."

"Yeah," I whispered.

He leaned closer, his face set with a deep, strange intent that made my stomach flip and my heart thud at the base of my throat. "I want that, Claire. For us. I want to make you the happiest woman on the planet. I want to be the person who makes you smile the biggest. The reason you look at your phone when it rings, hoping it's me. The hope you have when you go to the window to see if it's me pulling up in the driveway. I want to be the one you think of when you see something at the store, knowing it's my favorite. Because, baby, you are all of those things for me...and so much more. I don't know where I stop and you start, and I don't even want to."

"Killian." I think there was some volume in my spurt. Maybe a little. Tears strangled me in all the best, happiest ways.

"Claire Allyn Montgomery, I don't ever want to spend another minute without you."

He finished that part off by lowering to one knee before my tear-flooded eyes. And there, in the public parking lot at La Jolla Shores Park, he asked me to be his wife.

And this time, you can bet your sweet ass...I said yes.

CHAPTER EIGHTEEN

Killian

"That's the last of it. I think."

As Claire proclaimed it, she stood back with hands on hips, gazing with bewilderment across my nearly empty condo. Sunlight flashed on a boat out on the lake, catching on her left hand and turning her marquis-cut diamond into a temporary prism projector. Until the day I died, I wouldn't tire of seeing that ring on her finger. Of knowing she was all mine.

I taped up the last box and stacked it atop the others. "Moving crew will be here at nine sharp tomorrow." Then I tossed the tape gun and approached her on steady steps. "Until then, I want to concentrate only on ordering a pizza from the hotel room and then licking parts of it off your body."

After we'd savored each other in a long, lingering kiss, she turned, though she kept my arms locked around her waist. "I know this sounds weird, but I may miss this place a little. We've had some wonderful times here."

I buried my nose against her neck. She smelled different in Chicago than she did in San Diego. Spicier. Darker. More milk chocolate than creamy vanilla. It had been months since I'd smelled it, and the effect on my body was more than apparent. "You can come back and visit it as much as you want. I'm pretty sure Talia won't slam the door on you."

"You're so sweet for subletting to her, Kil. She's had nowhere to go since the blow-out with Gavin. I think getting out of California may be the ticket to get her head straight."

I snorted hard. "That asshole's parents should be shot for letting him think it's all right to slap a woman. She was right to leave him. And she can stay here as long as she wants."

"I'm not going to repeat that," she asserted. "In fifty years, you may find a dotty old lady and her six cats still living here."

I smiled and kissed her temple. "Good. There'll be a kitty for each of our kids to play with when she babysits during our visits."

She groaned and smacked my forearm. I grinned and nuzzled her deeper. It was time to mention the pizza again. And the part about eating it naked in bed together...

With piss-perfect timing, my cell rang.

I growled. Claire giggled. She glanced around the condo as a backup to her jibe. "Just like the old days, hmmm?"

"Bite your tongue." I picked up the intruder from the kitchen counter and studied the Incoming Call window. *Pssshh.* It was only Fletch. He could wait another second. "On second thought"—I threw back a look full of intentional seduction at Claire—"come over here and let *me* bite it for you."

While congratulating myself for the dark-pink flush I could still bring to her face, I opened the line. "What's up, wingman?" Though it had been forever since we'd been in the pool together, it was wickedly fun to use the nickname we'd loved flinging at each other before polo games, borrowed from the movie *Top Gun.*

You can be my wingman anytime.

No. You can be mine.

"Fucker," Fletch flung back. I'd barely gotten done

chuckling when he continued, "So, is Casa de Killian almost ready for its big move to California?"

"Just about. Boxes are done. We were just headed back to the hotel for a little pre-moving-day celebration." Translation: *I'm not meeting you and Drake for happy hour, so don't even ask.*

"Cool. That's cool."

Okay, it had been months since I'd talked any longer than a minute with the man, but I knew weirdness in a voice when I heard it. There wasn't a remote hint of happy hour in Fletch's tone. "Cool isn't what you're tossing out there." As I spoke it, I caught Claire's eyes once more. As always, her expression lent the compassion I needed to offer my next words. "You need to meet up and talk or something?"

Fletch's reply came after a strange pause. "Uh, yeah. Okay. Talking. Yeah, I think that's what I need right now. Thanks, Kil."

I pushed aside thoughts of nibbling cheese and tomato sauce off Claire's thigh and stated, "You bet, man. So call your turf. Is this about work, women, family, or all of the above? I've already shipped the Aston Martin to the West Coast, so I'll have to catch a cab, but I can be anywhere in—"

"Not necessary."

"Huh?"

"The car's pulling in front of your building now. Oh, and bring Claire too. I think she can lend some insight."

"Wait. Car? *What* car? And insight about what?"

"I owe you, Kil." It was like my questions had been muted. I actually checked the window to see if one of my fingers had accidentally strayed over the button. "Thanks. See you in a bit."

"Fletch?" I spoke it into the distinct silence of a line gone dead. And, like an idiot, repeated myself. As I held the phone out and peered in perplexity at my home screen, Claire approached.

"I'd offer a buck for your thoughts, but they're written all over your face," she said. "What's up?"

"I'm not sure. But there's a car waiting for us downstairs."

Not just *a* car. It was *the* car. Even after a couple of stunned blinks, the sight remained the same. Parked in the Lincoln Park 2550's porte-cochère was the Stone Global Corporation's town car. Same sleek black finish. Same black-and-silver incarnation of the company's logo on the doors. And goddamn, even Walter jumping out from the driver's seat and beaming an eager grin as he sprinted around to open the door.

"Mr. Stone! How good it is to see you again!"

"Uhhh, yeah, Walter. And the same."

The words were lip service, and I was pretty damn certain the guy knew it. Nevertheless, Walter bravely stood at attention next to the open door, giving me a peek at the black leather upholstery that had been like my second home for so many years.

My gut clenched. My veins decided between the texture of icebergs or a lava flow. Either wasn't acceptable. *This* wasn't acceptable.

"Miss Montgomery, you look stunning, as always."

"Thank you, Walter." Her reply was cordial, but the glance she threw to me was filled with the same case of *what-the-fuck?* I endured. We stood there in box-packing attire—jeans, T-shirts, work boots—a fact that Fletch could not have been so blind as to overlook. But even if we'd emerged from the building in designer trends, the thought of getting in *that* car made my body feel wrapped in custom suits of everything from rage to resentment to disdain.

I finally turned and faced the driver again. "Hey, Walter. It's been great to see you again, but Miss Montgomery and I will find our own way to meet up with Mr. Ford." I held up my phone. "Can I just sync up to your device with the name and address of the bar where he wants to—"

As I looked at my phone, it rang again.

Though I really wished it was Fletch, it wasn't.

Willa Stone's face, smiling from a shot I'd taken during her big birthday party last year at Keystone, flashed over the screen.

"Mother." There were many habits I'd broken myself of over the last few months. Calling her that would never be one of them. "Hello. Are you all right?"

I asked the question because I'd had lunch with her yesterday. The experience had been more pleasant than I'd expected, and she'd seemed as spry as a nymph in both spirits and health.

"Killian," she greeted warmly. "But of course I'm fine." She let a long, deliberate pause stretch by. "I'm phoning because I understand that Fletcher's invited you out for a bit."

I felt my eyebrows bunch down and my gaze narrow. Just like Fletch's, her tone had an underline of cryptic to it. Was there a secret decoder ring I needed to understand everyone in this city all of a sudden? "Yes." I'd never know the answer to that unless I played along. "He has. How do you know about that?"

"And he sent the SGC car for you?"

"How did you know about *that*?"

"And I'm wagering you're not fond of that whole concept."

I pivoted toward one of the porch's pillars and rammed the heel of my free palm onto its concrete. "Do you even want my contribution to this conversation, Mother?" Which was turning even more bizarre than the exchange with Fletch...

"Get in the car, Killian."

I pivoted again. And, for a moment, expected the air to vibrate with portentous Hitchcock film music. Or the theme to *The Twilight Zone*. "Excuse me?"

"Killian, I need you. *We* need you."

"What the hell? We who?"

Her long-suffering sigh rustled across the line. "Please. Just get in the car."

She disconnected the line before me. That left the silence of the device in my ear—and the chaos of my conflicted thoughts. Secretive phone calls. A meeting that now felt like a showdown. The damn company car at my doorstep. My gut in a ball of tension and my mind racing in a thousand directions.

And the world wondered why I'd turned my back on all this?

The light in my shadows appeared once more at my side. Claire's stare was as clear as morning sun, her smile as edifying as the dawn behind that sun. "What's the plan, hot stuff?" she asked.

Wordlessly, I shrugged.

Then turned and pulled her into the car with me.

★ ★ ★ ★

"Damn." I muttered it as Walter swung the car up to the rear entrance of the Stone Global building. The doors were just as imposing and polished as the building's front portal, only without the wind tunnel of an entrance plaza to accompany them. I'd often preferred this entrance in the days when I'd ruled the building. Tonight, it felt like a not-so-subtle slap in the face. "I hate it when I'm right."

Claire picked up the hand I'd been using for a drum solo against my right knee and sandwiched it between both her own. "Okay, this *is* weird," she said. "But I'm right here. We'll do this together."

"Guess there's the certainty that Trey doesn't plan to publicly humiliate me again." I spoke the words in a controlled murmur while we crossed the lobby. The lights were dimmed, half the flowers in the arrangements were withered, the leather furniture was worn. Even the security guard—from an outsourced company now, not wearing the SGC logo—didn't glance up from his newspaper when we walked in. If this had been my first time in the building, I'd have labeled the look "corporate creepy."

"The whole place feels really different." Claire said it in just as hushed a tone, hooking her arm through mine just like an ingénue from a horror movie walking through the graveyard with her boyfriend. Which boded so well for the fate awaiting us.

Shit. I was really nailing the tone on the metaphors tonight, wasn't I?

I got in a nod of agreement to her assertion before we rounded the corner toward the elevators and found Fletcher already waiting for us. He stood in front of a lift that was open and waiting.

"Kil." He paced over and grabbed my hand to shake it. A second later, he shook his head and just went in for the full embrace. "Thank fuck you came." He pulled away and smiled at Claire. "If you had anything to do with the choice, then I thank you."

Claire pushed out a little laugh. "It was actually all Willa. Instinct tells me she's around here somewhere, so just thank her."

"No," I interjected, clutching her hand. "If you weren't by my side, I'd have told these fuckers to go drown themselves in the river." I nodded Fletch in Claire's direction. "So yeah, you can thank her too."

The elevator had started its smooth ascent. I assumed we were bound all the way to the penthouse. Fletcher followed up my declaration by giving Claire a lopsided smile. "You know, you've been damn good for this big sack of serious." He jerked a thumb at me. "I think I like Killian two-point-oh."

"Yeah, yeah." I also couldn't prevent a grin from breaking through. "Flattery will get you nowhere, wingman."

"Oh, yeah? Hop on my wing and we'll see."

"Choad bucket."

"Nut squeezer."

We weathered Claire's disgusted eye rolls with barely suppressed snickers. The only thing missing from the moment was Drake, who'd undoubtedly have a few golden nuggets of derision to add, former US Marine-style.

The next moment, my wish was granted. And my worst nightmare realized.

The elevator doors opened, revealing a smiling Drake on the welcome landing. Behind him, lining the path to the main conference room, was every member of the Stone Global Board of Directors.

"Holy shit," Claire rasped.

"Can I double down on that?" I added.

"Stow your tomahawk, Tonto," Drake asserted. "They all come in peace."

"Tomahawk?" Claire volleyed. "Oh, he's moved on from that. *Way* on. A few boys back home can attest to that one."

I quirked an eyebrow at the gaze Drake threw to me in question. "It's a pretty piece of heat. Blaser F3. Gold inlays on the sights. Custom-carved stock. Hand-engraved barrel base."

He threw up a hand. "Okay, okay. You *trying* to give me a hard-on here? Now?"

I smirked. "Why not?"

Drake snorted. "If this show wasn't so much about getting your ass back here, I'd tackle it here and now."

It took a full ten seconds, maybe twenty, for his words to throw me back like the ton of bricks they felt. "Excuse the fuck out of me?"

I knew I'd heard him right by the tremble of Claire's fingers against mine. I instantly squeezed them, becoming *her* calm in the storm for once. *Don't worry, baby. This place, even all these people, have no sway over me anymore.*

"Great." Fletch spat it, moving forward to fling the full force of his glare at Drake. "Way to jump the cow over the moon, shit nozzle."

"Like he couldn't figure it out on his own?" Drake retorted.

"Figure what out?" I stammered—though his bricks seemed to have been a good thing. They jarred me into noticing a crapload of details about this whole situation, besides the fact that the lobby wasn't the only place in the building that had received a makeover in corporate creepy. The after-hours meeting time. The entire board of directors present. The way they all stood as I approached.

And no sign of Trey anywhere.

The observations should have had me turning every other step into a strut by now. The outcast prince, returning to the kingdom in ruins under the rule of his evil brother...

But I didn't feel like gloating. I didn't even feel like ranting. I felt like grieving.

In spite of everything, I couldn't call Trey a monster. He was just a loser, supersize on the order. An idiot numb nuts who'd never grasped that losing was often the best way of learning how to win and kindness wasn't something you showed a whore when her jaw was sore. It wasn't like anyone had taken the time to teach him. He'd been tolerated by Josiah. And loved, though fearfully, by Willa. Then betrayed by his own body, letting its sterile state define how he looked at the whole world—enough that he'd sure as hell burned all his bridges with me.

"Figure *what* out?" Drake echoed, popping both eyebrows up and then looking to Fletch. "Damn. Maybe he *has* been baking in the sun too long."

"The sun's actually a good thing, Newland." I flicked two fingers back against his chest as I passed him on my way in to the boardroom. "You should try it sometime."

Drake growled. "Already had the Afghanistan tan, thank you very much."

I dipped my lips to Claire's ear. "He needs to be invited out for a visit. We can take him to the house of mouse and loosen him up with a pair of plastic ears. Then I'll teach him how to surf."

"Deal." She whispered the word, but I heard every thankful note embedded in it. She'd needed that little piece of reconnection—and the truth be known, I needed it too. God only knew what was in store for us now.

By the time Fletcher waved us into the boardroom with the flourish of a maître d', the energy in the room intensified.

Well, as intense as a room full of corporate notables would allow themselves to be.

"Killian." It didn't surprise me when the daisy-bright greeting came, accompanied by the woman I'd called Mother since the age of five, emerging from the sea of faces with a walk to match her impeccable Chanel suit. "Darling, I'm so glad you came." She clasped one hand around mine and then extended the other to Claire. "And look! Your beautiful fiancée is here too. Ladies and gentlemen, have you all met Miss Montgomery? Hmmm, but don't get used to calling her that for long. She'll be a Stone soon enough, and we'll be planning quite the celebration to honor the occasion."

Claire flashed me a puzzled glance, a perfect fit with the single word she mouthed. *Stone?*

"Mother...Willa—" Hell, I'd gone through this yesterday. She'd insisted I continue to call her Mother, which had been fine at the lunch table with just the two of us but felt odd in this setting. "What the hell is this all about?"

Another familiar face pushed back from the table toward the other end of the room. Well, more familiar than the rest. I'd made it a point to connect with every board member beyond the surface demands of our business, and seeing them all in one place did remind me how I'd missed them. But Mason Donner and I had logged a lot of miles together over the last few years. Part was due to the diversification I'd forged into the company. The other part was due to Trey's nonstop legal adventures.

"Killian." He too shook my hand, his grip twelve times tighter than Willa's. Though he was a burly guy, I also beheld the fires of desperate emotion in his eyes. I had the feeling that to him, this handshake wasn't just a handshake. "Damn, it's good to see you back in here."

"Even if I look like a stinkin' roadie?" I lifted my head and sniffed. "Shit. Probably smell like one too."

Some of the older board members shifted uncomfortably at my humor. A lot more of them chuckled. My language had always been as impeccable as my suits, my hair, my shoes, and likely my tight little sphincter too. Then I'd learned to surf. The world was a different place.

"Well, that makes two of us, baby," Claire murmured in support.

Mason squared his stance. "I don't care if you smell like a rabid monkey who hasn't cleaned his ass in three weeks, Stone." He jabbed up his chin at my furrowed eyebrows. "Yes, that's right. I said *Stone*. It's still legally your name, Killian. It has been since you were five. The only thing left to change about it is how *you* feel."

I impaled him with a glare. Circled the look out to the rest of the room. "Don't you mean how *you* all feel?" A chuff escaped. "With all due respect, I was just fine with everything until my dear 'brother' stirred everyone's pot."

Daphne Ravine, a former model originally from France who now helped with SGC's foray into vitamins and organics, stepped out. "And zee stew, it sucks."

"Yep." Larry McGraw, the hugest Texan I'd ever known, nodded. "Suckage, Kil. Big-time."

The room erupted into a buzz of agreement ranging from quiet nods to more dramatic gesticulations. I watched in amazement as people I'd known for years, normally possessing the most genteel manners on earth, all but staged a rally behind a message I'd already heard a dozen times but hadn't truly seen or understood until I'd walked into the dingy lobby tonight. A lobby I'd once personally inspected each week.

To my shock, Mother was the one who eased everyone into silence again before serving as the mouthpiece for their final point.

"We've rendered a unanimous vote of No Confidence in Trey's ability to run the company." She shook her head. "If you think the building looks awful, you won't believe the P and L ledger." Her huge eyes lifted to mine, thick with entreaty. "We want to reinstate you as the CEO of Stone Global Corporation."

I didn't move. I was pretty damn sure that if I did, I'd wake up from what was turning out to be a crazy dream. On the other hand, waking up meant I'd be back with Claire in the real world, not having to deal with this mental overload of *holy shit* and *you've got to be kidding me.*

"I—" Well, that was eloquent. "Whoa." Yeah, even better.

"It's in trouble, Killian. The company *you* built. The company nobody cares about more than you."

I wanted to laugh, and I think she knew it. "Cares" was a funny word all of a sudden. My care had consumed years of my life, twenty-four hours a day, seven days a week. That same care had been booted out of the door when they'd all bowed to Josiah's old-school bullshit and let Trey start playing house up here.

But the reasoning, once capable of twisting my gut with such rage, just...didn't. To borrow a phrase from Woody, one of the regulars in the waves at La Jolla, I was over it.

Didn't stop me from being damn confused when the board members broke out in applause following Willa's words.

Applause?

Was the situation here that desperate?

As if fate read my mind, a herd of footsteps sounded from the doorway behind us. I turned to find a sea of faces too. Identifying every one of them broadened the smile on my face. One of them was Britta. Another was Brett from the mail room. And there was Terryn from the lobby coffee cart, whom I'd befriended when getting Claire's afternoon caffeine hits when she'd been in town. There were receptionists and janitors, sales managers and their assistants—even Walter had come up, joining the throng with a huge grin on his face. They were all shapes and sizes, genders and colors, ethnicities and lifestyles.

They were the people who'd cared as much as I. Who'd logged in a lot of off-the-clock hours, just like I had. Who'd mixed their sweat and blood with mine to raise SGC into a symbol of commerce and success but also fairness and diversity.

They were all family. All Stones.

Just as much as I was.

Turning my back on them would be like ripping my soul out. Again.

I turned to the woman who'd soon bear that last name as well. I had no idea what I'd see on her face. To my shock—well, not *that* much—Claire was already crying. The tears were clearly happy ones, aglow in a stare that matched her proud, huge smile. She squeezed my hand tighter, bouncing it in support that needed no words.

She floored me. Not for the first time today but perhaps with the biggest wallop. Supporting me in this choice meant our California dream could at best be only part-time.

Or did it?

I pulled free of Mother and Claire in order to lift both hands, hushing the room once more. "I'd be honored to return—on two conditions."

Larry McGraw gave an encouraging fist pump. "Name your figure, Stone. It'll be some of the best dough I've rolled all year."

"Nope," I countered. "I don't draw a damn penny in salary until this place is on its feet again. And we get something living back in the lobby—including the body at the security desk." After everyone chuckled, I moved to the head of the long conference table and spread my arms to its corners. "Since I assume nobody has any objections to condition one, I'll move on to two." I set my shoulders and steeled my jaw. Big bombs required tough purpose. "I'm only running this business if I can do it from California."

I gripped the table, preparing for the backlash.

Instead, I received Claire's stunned gasp—followed by another burst of applause.

As the impact of the reaction swelled over me, I pivoted back, reaching for Claire again. Everyone clapped louder when I yanked her close and smashed my mouth over hers. It was the connection of reality I needed in this surreal moment and I took full advantage of it, savoring her until we both couldn't get any more air.

"Killian," she finally rasped, "are you sure?"

I gazed into her breathtaking bronze eyes with a soft smirk and a steady nod. "Best business decision I've made all year."

Fresh tears welled in her gaze. "I can't believe it."

"Why? You're the fairy queen who rescued me from hell, remember?"

"Yeah, but look at what the hairy beast turned into." She raised gentle fingers to my face, caressing them back into my hair. "My fantasy king."

Her touch sent desire through my body, light through my heart...and love through my soul. As I did so many times each day, I thanked the heavens for this brave, beautiful woman who'd believed in me when no one else did, loved me even when I couldn't do it for myself. I would wake each day vowing to be the man she'd believed in...the king she deserved.

The resolve inspired me to kiss her again. My lips lingered over hers after. "Hey, queen of mine?"

"Yes, king of mine?"

"Why don't we go build a kingdom?"

It was a damn good plan.

At least for starters.

Continue Secrets of Stone with Book Three

No Perfect Princess

Available Now
Keep reading for an excerpt!

EXCERPT FROM
NO PERFECT PRINCESS

BOOK THREE IN THE
SECRETS OF STONE SERIES

CHAPTER ONE

Margaux

Fashion icon. It was a dirty job, but someone had to do it.

Even if all I saw outside the window of San Diego's most exclusive couture bridal shop was a parade of last year's jeans and ugly Christmas sweaters.

Ugh. The humanity.

I turned away from the horror show, sighing as I stopped in front of a mirror to readjust my beanie. It was a bold choice of accessory, running the risk of tumbling from damn-she's-fabulous to oh-no-she-didn't inside five seconds. The trick was the backside dangle. If that fell right, you were golden.

Perfect.

I sat on a couch and thumbed impatiently through a magazine. China patterns, honeymoon locales, reception favors, more china patterns...

I threw the thing down, pretty damn sure I felt a migraine

coming on.

"Claire!"

For the love of Louboutin, how long did putting on one wedding dress take? Okay, so she was my sister. Sort of. Technically, my soon-to-be sister-in-law—even if only a handful of people on the planet knew that. I wasn't sure I wanted the news expanded past those boundaries either. It had been sheer hell working out the bullshit surrounding the family everyone did know about.

No. Today wasn't a day for moping about Mother. Or the way she'd used my birth like a bargaining chip. Or the fact that she'd kept that truth from me for twenty-six years—and not felt a moment of remorse once I did find out.

Christ almighty. What was Claire doing in there? Sewing the damn thing by herself? Since there were three attendants with her, that was the *mystère du jour*.

"Claire!" I repeated. "Honestly, I'm growing roots from standing in the same—"

My derision died as my doe-eyed stepsister stepped out of the small room, silk and lace trailing behind her in a wave of tulle and princess-bride splendor. If I were a weaker woman, which I most certainly was not, I would cop to a lump in my throat at the vision standing before me, eyes aglow, dimples bracketing a shy smile, red hair tumbling into the gown's regal neckline.

Holy hell. Wait until Killian saw this. He thought he was head over heels before? Brother of mine, prepare your gut for a real train collision.

"Claire Bear. Wow."

It was all I could manage. And no, the tightness at the base of my throat had nothing to do with it.

The sales bitches beamed like they'd just birthed the fucking Baby New Year. They had this one in the bag and knew it—the exact reason why I pulled a full ice princess, glaring just enough to let them know the real bitch would come next. In an instant, they rushed forward to fuss around Claire once more.

"This dress was made for you, Miss Montgomery."

"Mr. Stone's eyes are going to fall out of his head."

"Amazing. Simply amazing."

It went on for fifteen minutes, one blah blah blah after another. I tuned out, my stomach turning on the latte I'd subbed for breakfast this morning.

This would never be me.

Never.

I would never walk down the aisle into the controlling clutches of a man. Ha—I didn't even have a father to walk me down the aisle. Like it was even a big deal anymore. Until ten months ago, I'd written off the dad angle from my life, with no reason to disbelieve what Mother always asserted—that my father had run out on us and didn't deserve a moment more of my attention. That all changed in a Chicago hospital room, where Josiah Stone had confessed to something much different—before taking his last breath.

Never knowing that his death had also killed off one of the most enduring fantasies of my life.

That somehow, my father would realize what a huge mistake he'd made in running from me—and return to embrace me with tears of grateful reunion. He'd tell me he didn't care about my makeup or clothes, that he only wanted to know what I was really like, on the inside, before sweeping me off to his mountain cabin, where—

Like going any further down that road was going to help right now.

Thank you, Mommy Dearest.

I officially hated that woman.

No, you don't.

Hmmm. I was pretty sure I did. Though I was too damn afraid of her to ever say it to her face, which was...unnerving. At really deep levels.

"Margaux? Are you okay?"

Claire's enormous brown eyes were fixed on me through the mirror. This chick didn't miss a beat with her attention or her concern, which pounded the unnerving right down into disturbed.

Christ, I was a mess lately. And the kicker? I was actually aware of it. Puke. Life had been much simpler when all I thought about in the morning was digging into someone else's dirt—and how fabulous I'd look while helping them with it.

"Have you seen the back of this one, Claire?" I flashed more daggers at the bitches. "Did any of you think to show her the back? It's stunning, Bear. Truly."

My diversion tactic worked, at least on the sales flock. They flurried again, turning Claire so she could see, erupting into more gibberish about the gown and its perfect fit, flare, and hemline. But damn it if my sister didn't keep her eyes fixed on me, silently—and unashamedly—trying to probe. I finally rolled my eyes and gave her the Margaux salute, jabbing my middle finger when the attendants weren't looking. She suppressed a giggle, but that didn't fool me. She'd be all over me the minute we were alone—because that was simply the kind of girl she was. Observant. Intuitive. And caring to the point where it was her damn superpower.

Lucky, lucky me.

The morning from hell transitioned into afternoon. Dress after dress. Perfection upon perfection. Okay, some not so much. The lavender one had to go. Who the hell wore a lavender wedding dress? I suspected Claire tried that one on to see if I was still paying attention. Thank God I'd paused between emails, which had become my new obsession lately. Now that I was on the full-time roster with Stone Global, I needed to be serious about shining there.

The idea of continuing on with Mother—with Andrea— had seemed impossible when we returned from Chicago. After all her secrets had been unveiled, I couldn't even stand being in the same room with her. Even a simple explanation might have helped, though I never gave in to the illusion of receiving a full apology. That kind of thing happened in worlds where unicorns descended from heaven to save humanity from the zombie apocalypse.

She'd never come. Never called. Never said another word. And with her silence had wrecked whatever connection we'd had, however dysfunctional. I sent a formal letter declaring a leave of absence, but she and I both knew I was never coming back. Too many lies, too much deception. I was tired of Andrea Asher's games and refused to be a pawn in them anymore. Or so I told myself on the good days.

I'd barely had a chance to realize that woman of leisure wasn't a role I enjoyed playing, when Killian approached with the opportunity to stay on permanently with Stone Global's expanded PR department. It made perfect sense from a couple of angles. The Asher and Associates team had already been working exclusively with SGC, so everything already felt like my home turf. And as they say, blood is thicker than water. Or did it form the ties that bind? Or coagulate if you used hot honey? Whatever. It was irony at its best, however you phrased it. Killian, only a Stone by adoption, hired me, the real Stone, for the family business. To add a ha atop of that ha, Killian's lineage was now full public knowledge—and mine still a carefully guarded secret.

Because I demanded it that way.

***This story continues in*
No Perfect Princess: *Secrets of Stone Book Three!***

ALSO BY ANGEL PAYNE

Secrets of Stone Series:
No Prince Charming
No More Masquerade
No Perfect Princess
No Magic Moment
No Lucky Number
No Simple Sacrifice
No Broken Bond
No White Knight

Honor Bound:
Saved
Cuffed
Seduced
Wild
Wet
Hot
Masked
Mastered (Coming Soon)
Conquered (Coming Soon)
Ruled (Coming Soon)

The Misadventures Series:
Misadventures with a Super Hero

For a full list of Angel's other titles,
visit her at angelpayne.com

ABOUT ANGEL PAYNE

USA Today bestselling romance author Angel Payne loves to focus on high-heat romance starring memorable alpha men and the women who love them. She has numerous book series to her credit, including the Suited for Sin series, the Cimarron Saga, the Temptation Court series, the Secrets of Stone series, the Lords of Sin historicals, and the popular Honor Bound series, as well as several standalone titles.

Angel is a native Southern Californian, leading to her love of being in the outdoors, where she often reads and writes. She still lives in Southern California with her soul-mate husband and beautiful daughter, to whom she is a proud cosplay/culture con mom. Her passions also include whisky tasting, shoe shopping, and travel.

Visit her here:
angelpayne.com

ABOUT VICTORIA BLUE

International bestselling author Victoria Blue lives in her own portion of the galaxy known as Southern California. There, she finds the love and life–sustaining power of one amazing sun, two unique and awe-inspiring planets, and four indifferent yet comforting moons. Life is fantastic and challenging and every day brings new adventures to be discovered. She looks forward to seeing what's next!

Visit her here:
victoriablue.com